CAPTIVE AUDIENCE

William Hatfield

Published by William Hatfield

Second printing

ISBN: 978-1461066477
PUBLISHED BY William Hatfield
Printed in the United States of America

Dedicated to my parents, Howard and Louise Hatfield, whom I can thank for the strengths that allowed me to find the will and way to write and get published.

Thank you to the Crawford County Library in Grayling, Michigan for having such a fine selection of science fiction when I was growing up in a small town without a bookstore, and Michael Toman, a roommate in college that gave me an example of what it takes to try and be a writer. Persist in writing, submit manuscripts, get rejection slips, and then do it again. And again.

My thanks to the many writers that have at one time or another been a part of the writing group that was at first, five women needing a male point of view, then the Novel Ideas writing group, and finally RAW. What that stands for, I leave to your imagination.

I would also like to thank Joe and Gay Haldeman and the other writers, friends, and supporters that have encouraged me over the years. They gave good advice, some of which I even took.

I received a wonderful birthday present from my good friend, J.W. Baker, and it is the front cover art for this book. He is an extraordinary artist, but you can see that for yourself. Thank you, Jim.

And most of all, I thank my wife Karen for putting up with me and this whole writing thing over the years.

PROLOGUE

Deep in space...aboard the Ananab Merchant Ship P'Tassum

Captain Storhesh glared at the figures on the computer screen. Of course, the data was nothing new. He'd known from the voyage's beginning that unless some new source of wealth was discovered, he would lose his ship upon returning to Station Chaq. There had been too many unprofitable trips, too many expensive equipment upgrades, and he and his brothers had no choice but to put the ship up as collateral for supplies for one last venture.

Storhesh had no illusions. The Commander of Station Chaq was a fellow Ananab, but he wouldn't hesitate to seize the ship, even though it had been in Storhesh's brood since the day it had been commissioned, countless cycles ago.

He and his brothers had argued long and hard before agreeing to strike out into unclaimed territory, looking for new worlds, untapped wealth.

It appeared their gamble had failed. Fuel and supplies were getting low and soon P'Tassum would have to return to port. Even now their circular route was winding back towards Ananab space and almost certain failure with nearly empty storage tanks.

Captain Storhesh used one of his delicate feelers to turn the screen off, then his rage took hold and he smashed the console with his right claw. Sparks flew in all directions. He lifted his eye stalks to stare at the ceiling in resignation, then pivoted on his left legs to go to the bridge.

He was running out of time and options. He would spend time looking for something, anything, to keep his ship. Without it, he was just one of the swarm.

The computer of the P'tassum.

> *Diagnostic complete. All systems fully functional.*
> *This terminates fourth complete diagnostic check*
> *this cycle. Scanning nearest star systems for anomalies.*
> *Negative findings. Beginning full diagnostic of life-support*
> *back-up emergency systems. Findings...FLAG!*
> *Receiving transmissions via electromagnetic waves.*
> *Unknown origin and language. Recording phonetics and*
> *initiating accummulative sorting and attempting translation. Transmission*
> *starts: "...and it is out of here! The Babe has just hit his sixtieth..."*

Thirty years ago...Cedar Key, Florida

"Hyah!"

Jimmy sent a smashing karate chop to the kneecap of his giant opponent. He leaped back and went into the stance he'd seen his hero on television use. He held his arms extended in front of him, his right hand straight up, his left sideways, almost touching his right elbow.

"Hyah!"

He let out another cry as he leaped as high as he could, kicking out with his left foot. The giant didn't block the attack and gave a muffled grunt of surprise as the small foot hit him in the stomach.

Jimmy landed hard on the floor, the air knocked out of him. He gasped for a moment as his lungs slowly began to work again. Large hands helped him to his feet.

"What kind of stance is that supposed to be?" The giant, Sergeant McCoy, held Jimmy by the shoulder as he was inspected for damage.

"That's the way Jim West does it!" Jimmy couldn't believe that McCoy didn't recognize a good karate stance when he saw one. "That's the way Captain Kirk kicks."

Jimmy heard his father laugh from the comfort of his recliner.

"Ah, syndicated television. That silly cowboy show, you know, the wild west one. And of course, his namesake on the trekkie show can do no wrong."

McCoy snorted and shook his head ruefully. "Tell me about it. If I get called 'Bones' again, I'm going to start breaking some." He turned back to Jimmy. "You don't want to fight like those guys, kiddo."

Jimmy frowned. "Why not?"

"It's a television show, Jimmy." For such a large man, Sergeant McCoy had a surprisingly gentle voice. "Those fighting styles don't work in real life. And you shouldn't be so eager to leave your feet. You don't have any control until you come back down. Here, turn your shoulder so you offer a smaller target." McCoy picked him up and set him sideways, pulling his arms into an unfamiliar position.

"And, if you are going to leap, you need to learn how to fall." McCoy collapsed backwards, using one arm to slap the floor, breaking his fall. Jimmy tried the same.

"Very good!" The sergeant sounded surprised. "Now try to roll over your right shoulder, using the same move."

Jimmy tried the roll, falling awkwardly to one side. He frowned, trying to picture the action. Then he did it again, using his arms to direct the motion. The forward momentum carried him back to his feet.

"Very good!" McCoy grinned at him. "You've skipped ahead. That was my next lesson."

Jimmy's mother came into the room, took one glance and pursed her lips. "John, have you seen my briefcase?" She gave the two men a look of disapproval, then took Jimmy by the arm.

"Take it outside, young man." She gave him a gentle shove towards the door. "Don't leave the yard. And I don't want you getting dirty again, either. It's almost bedtime."

"Ah, Mom." But Jimmy did as his mother said. As he got outside, he stepped quietly over to where he could hear their voices through the screened windows.

"Don't you think four is a little young to be teaching him martial arts, Henry?" Even from here, Jimmy could hear the disapproval in his mother's voice.

"He's going to try it anyway, Margaret." His father John Morris laughed. "He might as well do it right. And who better to teach him than the Special Forces."

"He shows a lot of potential." Jimmy grinned to himself at Sergeant

McCoy's words. "For his age, he can really jump. He also has excellent hand/ eye coordination."

"Still, on a full stomach..." Jimmy backed away from the window, trying not to make a sound. He wasn't interested in listening to his mother list the numerous reasons he shouldn't have fun.

He dove over his right shoulder, rolling back to his feet. He had too much momentum and pitched forward. He caught himself with his hands and fell sideways, using one arm the way McCoy showed him.

Hrumph, Jimmy thought as he climbed back to his feet. *That was sloppy.*

Thirty minutes later, he lay sprawled on his back, exhausted. He had tried the rolls from every angle, time after time, until he could either break his fall or continue the motion back to his feet. The grass beneath him was cool to his skin and he sighed with satisfaction.

This trip to Florida was great. There were so many things to do. Today they'd seen mermaids swimming and dancing underwater. Dinner had been at a restaurant that extended out over a river that had real fish in it! He'd watched several people catch some as he ate.

And the names were really funny, too. Steinhatchoo, hatchee, or something like that was where they'd had dinner. And yesterday they'd looked at bunches of old stuff at some place called "My can o' peas."

Jimmy became aware of an approaching sound. It seemed to be coming from the left and, as he watched, something flew overhead.

It was moving so fast, he didn't get much of a look at it, but it was long and dark, flying just above the trees. He could see its exhaust glow a bright red for a moment before it disappeared over the horizon.

Before he could move, two more came into view. These two were much higher, with visible lights. They came from the same direction and steadily moved across the sky, following the path of the first.

After a few moments, they also flew out of sight.

Jimmy jumped up and ran into the cabin.

"I saw a flying saucer!" he shouted, startling the three adults sitting around the room. "Maybe three!"

"Flying saucers?" His father laughed and raised one hand to halt the excited boy's words. "Okay. Slowly now, tell me what you saw."

Jimmy managed to calm down enough to recount what had happened. He watched the adults look at each other thoughtfully, and realized they believed him.

"Navy?" His father looked at Sergeant McCoy questioningly.

"Probably." The man shrugged. "Could be a cruise missile test with fighter escort."

"Jimmy, come here." John Morris sat upright in his chair and smiled reassuringly. "Those were Navy jets, doing test runs out of Jacksonville or Pensacola. There's no such thing as flying saucers."

"James Morris, you are filthy!" His mother took him by the arm and eyed the grass stains on his clothes with disdain. "Let's get you cleaned up and ready for bed. UFOs, indeed. You can get that thought right out of your head. There's no such thing."

"Yes, there are!" Jimmy was stubborn. "I'll bet there's lots of aliens out there, just waiting for a chance to meet us!"

The two men laughed.

"What would you say, if you met one, Jimmy?" McCoy grinned at him.

"I'd say, 'Hi, my name is Jimmy. Let's be friends.'" He watched the adults exchange amused looks. "And if they were bad aliens, I'd kick 'em, just like you taught me!"

McCoy winced, and carefully avoided Margaret Morris' frown.

"See what you've done, 'Sergeant'." She pulled Jimmy along as she headed to the bathroom. "Putting these ideas in impressionable young minds…"

Jimmy's mother hummed under her breath as she ran hot water for another bath and began pulling his clothes off.

"You just forget about these 'UFO' ideas, young man. There's no such thing."

That's what you think, Jimmy thought to himself. *There are flying saucers, and I just saw one. And someday I'll meet an alien, too.*

Someday.

CHAPTER ONE

He knew something was wrong because he could see himself. Not in a mirror, just standing in front of him, in a loose defensive stance. He faced a woman well over six feet tall, rangy with broad, heavily muscled shoulders. She had short-cropped blond hair, bright blue eyes, and chiseled features that were dominated by a large boney nose. Somehow he knew she was German.

He watched as he circled to the left, keeping his hands casually out in front of him, left hand and foot slightly forward. The woman moved towards his other self and led with a sidekick. The block with the left hand was automatic, as was the counter kick. It fell short and he realized he wasn't taking the opponent seriously. After all, she was a woman, and he was...the undefeated young warrior.

He knew he could take her any time he wanted to. But he tried to shout a warning to himself. He'd already lived through this horrifying scene many times, and knew what the cost of being over-confident would be. But he couldn't seem to help himself!

She came at him with a constant barrage of punches and kicks, trying to keep him off balance. His other self decided to let her know she was outclassed and did a sweep, knocking her off her feet. He was lying on his back as he gave her the coup-de-gras heel kick to the chest.

But he could see he was pulling his kicks and punches. After all, she was a woman, and he didn't want to hurt her, even though they were in a battle that wouldn't stop until one of them could fight no more. His heel snapped down, intended to stun and disable her. She flopped backward with the force of the blow.

He was careless as he began rolling to his feet, and was unprepared for her counterattack. Her foot caught him right between the legs and he felt his own pain as he watched himself stumble backward, trying not to fall to the floor. She was back on her feet, the sheer ferocity of her assault threatened to overwhelm him.

He shouted to warn himself not to use that counter combination, but again he didn't hear.

Then it happened.

He blocked her barrage of punches and spun around her side and finished with a sharp kick to the back of her head. She plunged face first to the floor and didn't move.

He wanted to feel something. But he couldn't. He could only watch as he went to her side and knelt, shaking her shoulder. But he could tell from her position that she would never rise again.

A roaring began to grow in his ears, and he looked around at the sea of screaming faces in the crowd around the arena. Many were yelling approval, others swore vengeance. The sound grew painful, and he couldn't stand it anymore. But it continued, and the spotlights grew brighter, and brighter...until the faces disappeared and all that remained was the glaring light.

Jim's eyes popped open. And closed immediately, recognizing his mistake.

He pressed fingertips against his forehead, groaning. He didn't know which was worse, his hangover or the bright sunlight in his eyes.

He tried to orient himself. A rocking sensation gradually sank in.

Cautiously, he opened his eyes, slower this time.

Directly in front of him was a round window with bright, irritating light shining right into his eyes.

Round window?

Memories slowly seeped into his consciousness.

A ship. He was on a ship at sea. The Jade Viking, with its 3,500 plus passengers and crew members could not be hoisted aboard another ship. Thus, by definition, Jade Viking was a ship, not a boat.

Jim tried to see what time it was.

I can't do this without moving my head, he conceded. Hmm, shouldn't the window be behind, not in front of him?

14

Ah, of course. Tonight I am sleeping with my head at the head, and my feet at the foot of my bed. Reachable goals are good, he decided.

Okay. Enough, already. He swung his feet to the deck and pushed himself upright, letting out a little groan. He held that position for what seemed many minutes, but was probably more like ten seconds.

Focusing on his watch, he saw it was 6:30 a.m.

At least I didn't sleep through anything. Filming doesn't start this morning until ten.

Jim stood, gathering his strength. He hadn't had that dream in months. It was from a part of his life that he'd just as soon forget, but knew he never would. Just when he thought enough time had passed, it crept back into the early morning hours to haunt him. He shuddered, put the dream away for the moment and looked around.

The room was luxurious by ship standards. His cabin opened both directly onto the upper deck and to an inner corridor, with separate bathrooms, and even such amenities as a wet bar, microwave, refrigerator, and a small desk. With all this, there were still several square yards of open space in the center of the room.

Jim looked in the large mirror over the dresser, and saw a man with haunted eyes. And deep inside those eyes he could see ghosts. He stared until the phantoms receded, and a curtain closed, leaving his expression unreadable.

Enough self-pity for one day, he decided.

Jim pulled a pair of gym shorts out of a drawer and donned them. Opening the refrigerator, he got a bottle of seltzer and took a long swig. He began stretching and turned the portable CD player on. Rock music ground out a beat as he set the now empty bottle down and began to work out in earnest.

Kimberly Martin sank into her seat with a sigh. She nodded to the three men already well into their breakfast. Two of them returned her greeting with welcoming smiles. They both wore captain uniforms which, at first glance, was about the only thing they had in common.

To her immediate right, at the head of the table was the current master of the cruise ship Jade Viking, Captain Jason Lang. Kimberly knew from reading his file that he was a widower and 63 years old, but the only clear sign of his age was his white hair, with just its hint of blond. Lang was a shade under six and a half feet tall, broad shouldered but lean, with little body fat, a square jaw, and a manner that radiated assurance and competence. With a beard, he could have passed for one of the original Norsemen of his ship's namesake.

Kimberly had spent a lot of time with Lang during the previous six months and liked him, appreciating his professional attitude in what had to be a difficult situation. For this was to be his last voyage as captain.

It wasn't by his choice. She knew he dreaded early retirement.

The finish of every meal, every watch, every social function brought him that much closer to the end of his job. In four days, this ship would dock in San Francisco, and he would relinquish his command.

A steward appeared at her side with a pot of coffee, and she nodded her thanks. *Ah caffeine, nectar of the gods,* she thought, immediately raising the cup to her lips and taking a healthy swig.

It took every ounce of her resolve not to spit it across the table. The boiling hot coffee scorched her lips, then her mouth and throat, as it tore its way to her stomach. She could feel instant tears trying to spring to her eyes, and fought them.

Kimberly carefully set the cup down and tried to look casual as she drained her glass of ice water. *You handled that pretty well, Martin. Good to know all those years of learning to maintain a poker face in the courtroom were useful for something.*

Then she looked at Captain Jason Lang and found him eyeing her with concern. "Are you all right, Ms. Martin? I like my coffee very hot, and they bring it to the table at a near boil. I should have warned you." He gestured, and the steward immediately refilled her water glass.

"No, no, I'm fine, thank you. I like it hot, just like that, really!"

Captain Lang nodded with a straight face and Kimberly knew she hadn't fooled him a bit. But at least the other two men had gone on with their meals, oblivious to her discomfort.

No weakness, Martin. Show no weakness.

To Lang's immediate right, across the table from Kimberly, sat the future lord and master of Jade Viking, Captain Hiroaki Tachibana. The two captains were as different as night and day, yet alike as two waves breaking beneath the ship's bow.

Captain Tachibana was a decade younger, a foot shorter, slight of build, with jet black hair, rounded chin, but shared that same manner of assurance and competence. Lang was jovial and a little self-conscious about his size, as if afraid he would trample smaller folk. The diminutive Japanese captain seemed to flow when he moved, and yet still be stiffly formal.

Kimberly had only spoken with Captain Tachibana twice, but found hiim to be a pleasant surprise. Until meeting him, her contacts with Sukuru, the corporation buying the ship, had been nothing but irritating.

Actually, Martin, that sounds a lot like the "gentleman" seated on the other side of Captain Tachibana.

Yoshi Toshida was a senior vice-president of Sukuru Corporation in direct line for future rule of the firm. The Toshida clan had dominated Sukuru, among other corporate giants, for decades, and he reflected their control of power perfectly. Ruthless, shrewd and, if rumors were true, quite deadly.

Kimberly detested him.

The sale of Jade Viking to Sukuru by her own employer, Spencer Corp., was just a small portion of the biggest deal either company had ever been involved in. And it was Kimberly's baby, the whole thing. It had taken every bit of her lawyer training and persuasive skills to convince her boss, Will Spencer, to let her have this project.

Difficulties had begun surfacing immediately. The Toshida clan was very traditional, and having to deal with a woman infuriated them. But Kimberly stuck with it, through the snubs, the not-so-subtle insults, and the clever attempts to circumvent her authority.

And you did it, Martin, she thought smugly. Four days to dock, then we close the deal and I get the biggest bonus anyone's ever gouged out of Will. Of course, then I also have to deal with closing the door on his romantic advances. She was enjoying her career too much to risk everything by dating the boss.

And I thought this was a challenge, she mused. Will Spencer was not a man that accepted "no" as an answer. Not that he wouldn't be considered a great catch to most women, she conceded. He's young, good-looking, personable when he wants to be, and incredibly rich.

Those qualifications would do for most, she knew. But Kimberly had been burned once, and was in no hurry to chance heartbreak again.

Kimberly also swore she would never again get involved with a man she had the slightest suspicion would be anything less than honest with her. And she'd worked too long with Will to have any illusions about his ability and willingness to lie, or to justify the means with the end.

Kimberly wistfully looked at the basket of muffins in the center of the table. They would have all the flavor of cardboard with her taste buds in the condition they were in.

"It looks like our Hollywood friends are late risers," Captain Lang said, startling her out of her thoughts. He smiled at her and nodded at the four empty seats to her left.

"It doesn't surprise me at all," she said, making a face. "I could hear them partying down at the far end of the corridor late into the night."

"I hope they didn't keep you awake." The Captain frowned, then continued in a hesitant tone. "I could speak to them about..."

"No, no." Kimberly hastened to interrupt. "Please don't bother, it really wasn't a problem." The last thing she wanted was to give the impression she was a complainer. Anyway, she was used to fighting her own battles. "If it gets to be too much, I'll go down there and handle it myself."

"Just so," Captain Lang said with an infectious grin. "If you can't beat them, join them, right?"

"Or get a bigger stick to beat them with," Kimberly muttered under her breath.

Lang picked up the words and his smile broadened. "Well, here's your chance." She saw a late arrival was being seated next to her.

Kimberly recognized Jim Morris from his movies and had seen him the night before from a distance, but hadn't actually met him yet. She was disgusted as she felt her pulse quicken at the prospect of finally meeting the actor up close and personal.

Martin, you're pathetic.

But he was impressive.

At about 5'10," and around 200 lbs, he had a solid, but not heavy build. Broad shoulders tapered down to slim hips, with muscular thighs giving him the look of a large cat, she decided. Powerful, but with more than a suggestion of agility. His close-cropped beard and shaggy, longish hair completed her wild beast analogy.

He looked relaxed in a casual golf shirt and white slacks, sharply contrasting the formal, dark business suit that Toshida wore. Of course, both captains were in uniform, and she was wearing her usual suit for the professional woman that hadn't seemed uncomfortable until a moment ago.

Three months earlier, when she was approached about having the final scenes to an action movie shot during this voyage, she'd had her doubts. But Corporate had been adamant, and she'd reluctantly given in.

What a zoo, she thought, the memory of the apparent bedlam and confusion leading up to departure yesterday still clear in her mind. The film production company had truckload after truckload of gear, and it all needed to be stowed just so.

"Good Morning," Jim Morris said, giving a slight bow of his head to Kimberly as introductions were made. He glanced at the remaining empty seats. "It looks as though my people are still recovering from that fine reception last night. Or the party after."

"I would have thought you'd be doing the same," Captain Lang chuckled. Kimberly was relieved when he made no mention of her earlier complaint. "I've never seen anyone mix champagne and sake like that before. At least not in those quantities."

"It would seem the stereotyped excesses of Hollywood are based in fact." Toshida made no attempt to conceal the sneer in both his voice and expression as he stared across the table at the actor.

Morris gave him a level gaze, then raised one eyebrow pointedly. "Well, I'm absolutely certain I've never seen anyone from Japan drink too much sake. No siree."

Toshida stiffened and Kimberly bit her lip to keep from laughing out loud. Toshida was not used to anyone challenging him at anything. After a moment, he relaxed.

"There are weak people everywhere," he conceded.

"Oh really now, Toshida-san" Kimberly decided to play devil's advocate. "Surely the first night on a voyage such as this warrants a little celebration. Transferring command from the American crew to the Japanese. Filming a movie on board. A 'Jim Morris' action movie at that!"

Kimberly Martin ignored the speculative look Lang gave her and continued, addressing the actor. "Actually, I didn't expect to see any of your people at breakfast. When do you start shooting?"

Morris smiled at her. And it was a nice smile, too, she noticed. And was that a glimmer of warmth creeping into his eyes?

Oh no, wipe that train of thought away, Martin. No actors. You're not some silly airhead he can smile at and seduce over drinks. You've worked hard to get where you are. Anyway, God only knows where he's been. And with whom.

"I think they're starting at nine on the forward deck with some of the action sequences. Kiri and I have a scene scheduled for around ten."

"Ah, yes. The beautiful Kiri Oshiba. The fantasy of every Japanese schoolboy and one of our most revered actresses." Toshida gave a haughty laugh and Kimberly winced. Did he practice sounding so condescending? "You aren't in these 'action scenes' yourself because you have someone else do them for you, am I right? A double, I believe they are called, Morris-san."

"Actually, I do all my own stunts and action scenes. I think you have me confused with someone else, Toshida-san." Morris smiled, but a steely look had replaced the warmth in his eyes. "This scene has only innocent bystanders being ambushed by villains. Ninjas, as it happens. I'm sure you've heard of those."

"Oh, come now!" Toshida pressed on, and Kimberly wondered that he couldn't feel the tension around the table. Or maybe he did, but didn't care. "I've heard there is much doubt about your actual martial skills. That you have no trophies, medals, belts, won no championships. I have also heard stories about the drug excesses and alcohol abuse, Jim Morris-san!"

"Now I know you have me confused with someone else." Jim Morris met his gaze for a moment, then glanced past him towards the entrance. Kimberly kept her face straight at the pun Toshida had unwittingly made. She glanced at Lang and thought he'd also caught it.

"Ah, don't you...love her madly?" Jim said, his face back to its usual expressionless mask.

As one, they all turned to see a young, stunningly beautiful Japanese woman enter the dining room. It was Kiri Oshiba.

Kimberly made a muffled sound as she quickly covered her mouth with a napkin. Across the table, Captain Tachibana looked at her, and then at Jim. He cleared his throat delicately.

"Are you a Doors fan, Mr. Morris?" he asked with a straight face.

Kimberly looked back and forth between the three, and then at the confused Toshida.

He hasn't a clue. I shouldn't, but...

"People are strange," she said in a mild tone as she picked up her coffee and took a cautious sip.

Silence reigned, during which both Morris and the Japanese captain attacked their breakfast. Lang met Kimberly's eyes. She felt the corner of her mouth twitch. Lang leaned back and smiled broadly. The other two men continued eating, but a glimmer of humour came to Tachibana's face. Jim Morris looked up with such an innocent expression that Kimberly almost lost her composure.

Toshida looked around the table baffled, as if he knew there was a joke, but had no idea what it was. His face reddened and he set his napkin down. Rising, he nodded curtly to Captain Lang and shot a glare at his own captain, who gave a courteous bow of his head, but made no move to join him.

"Thank you for your hospitality, Captain." Toshida maintained his dignity as he strode out of the dining room.

No one said anything for a moment, then Captain Tachibana looked serious.

"This may have been a tactical error," he admitted.

"Probably not a great career move," Kimberly agreed. "What do you think...Jim Morris-san?"

Jim looked at Kimberly Martin, bemused. *How did I not notice her last night at the reception*, he asked himself. *Beautiful blond hair, hazel eyes to die for, and even disguised by her business suit, what appeared to a body to kill for.*

All that, and brains, too?

He gave an inward sigh and shrugged. "Some people have no sense of humor."

Kiri Oshiba sat down next to Jim.

"Sorry I'm so late. Did I miss anything?"

Jim looked at her gravely. "No, not really. We're just stuck in the revolving Doors routine."

A groan sounded around the table, and Kiri gestured at him menacingly with her butter knife, then shook her head in mock despair.

"Surely not that old 'Morris-san' joke again?" She smiled mischievously. "You people don't know how to have pun at all!"

Jim shook his head and leaned a little closer to Kimberly Martin. "You know, there's never a cream pie around when you really need one," he said in a stage whisper.

Kiri sniffed. "Well, what do you expect before my first cup of coffee? Thank you," she said to the steward as he poured. She raised it to her lips and Kimberly and Captain Lang both began to speak at once, trying to warn her.

They were too late, and were rewarded with what Jim suspected was their first experience of vehement swearing in Japanese.

CHAPTER TWO

"Cut!"

Frederick Farmer stood in satisfaction. With his right hand, he touched his thumb to his forefinger, signaling the camera crew.

"Alright, that's a take! Start setting up for the midnight tryst scene." Farmer reached out without looking, and his go-fer, Tim Spear, handed him his clipboard. He glanced at the remaining scheduled shoots and sighed in contentment. "This is looking good, Timothy. We're going to finish on time and under budget."

The young man grinned. "That's what happens when you work with professionals, sir."

Farmer smiled and turned back to watch the crew prepare for the next scene. He had directed dozens of low budget films, and even one or two high-budget projects. This film landed somewhere in the middle, but it had huge profit potential. He had a high-profile cast including Jim Morris, arguably the most popular action movie star in America, who also had a very strong following in Asia. Combine this with young superstarlet Kiri Oshiba, sweetheart of Japan, and you had a box office winner, regardless of script.

And then there was the home video market...

"We're going to do well with this movie."

With a start, Farmer realized he'd spoken out loud. His go-fer just looked off into space, whistling cheerfully.

"I know, I know." Farmer raised a hand in surrender. "Professionals."

It was true though. He know only too well.

Farmer hated prima donnas. They always had to have their favorite hairdresser, irreplaceable make-up artist, camera men who could film their gift horse far better than anyone else, supporting starlets that looked great, but had marginal acting skills. Farmer had worked with Jim and Kiri many times, and knew that this cast didn't fall into that category.

Kiri kept it simple with her agent, make-up artist, and costume specialist. Farmer knew from experience that her people were actually competent. And she, of course, was a delight to work with.

Jim Morris brought a larger number of people, and all had contributions to make. Hakim Riahi was his personal cameraman. They had worked together for over fifteen years, dating back to when Jim and Hakim were in college, working with a variety of producers in Ann Arbor. Hakim was the consummate professional.

Another longtime comrade was Yvette Stephanian. She and her "significant other," Janice Wooley, worked as his personal assistants. Whether it was stock options, investments, costumes, make-up, or travel plans, the two women handled it quietly and efficiently.

Morris also had a list of extras he used as often as he could arrange it. Many of the same faces had appeared in most of his movies, sometimes dying at his side, other times by his hand.

Farmer glanced back at Jim and Kiri standing inside the walkway that ran most of the length of the Jade Viking at this level. He held up his open hand, signifying five minutes before they were needed, and turned back to the set.

The powerful wind coming over the bow was strong enough to play havoc with the equipment, not to mention people. So, they built a portable barricade to put up during filming. Then they put in several large fans to simulate the breeze. Special directional microphones focused on the actors' mouths caught most of the dialogue. Any touch-ups needed would be dubbed in later on.

Some of the actors from the scene were just trooping into the walkway as Jim and Kiri turned away from the window.

"Ah, Oshiba-sama," they bowed to her and then to Jim. One flashed a big grin. "Morris-san. As always, I am honored to work with you again."

"Kabu-san! You've worked my last four movies," Jim frowned in mock frustration. "You'll work my next four. And more! But only if you quit calling me Morris-san!"

Kiri giggled and pushed him gently.

"You love it and you know it."

Jim smiled ruefully and shook his head. "Maybe the first thousand times. Sometimes it gets a little old," he admitted. "Like this morning. What a pompous twit."

Kiri grinned mischievously at him. "Yeah, and I could tell that you felt the same way about that yuppie lawyer from New York, too.

Jim felt his face redden and shook his head. "Forget it. You're not playing matchmaker this time. She and I have nothing in common. She's so...New York, and Wall Street."

"And cute," Kiri continued, leaning against him. "I saw you two talking this morning, don't forget. You know you can never fool me, Jim. We go back too far." She gave him an elbow to the ribs. "No secrets, right?"

"No secrets," Jim agreed. He thought back to the breakfast and tried to remember when he'd enjoyed a meal quite so much. He shook his head. "Okay, she's cute, pretty even. But what I said still stands, too little in common. Even if she is beautiful."

Kiri laughed out loud. "Did you just hear how fast you went from kinda cute to beautiful? You're hooked, little fishie...you just don't know it, yet. Anyway, you already have one thing in common, you both dislike Toshida."

"I'll give you that." Jim remembered Toshida's comments and forced himself to control his breathing. Sometimes...no, he swore never to be that kind of person again. "He's just a big mouth on a little man." Maybe if he said it enough, he would believe it.

Kiri bit her lower lip. "Don't underestimate Toshida." She frowned. "I've heard rumors about his family, and Sukuru. And your comment about ninjas may have hit closer to home than you realize…even we aren't totally immune to that kind of power."

She fell silent as two men strolled up behind them. They were both Japanese and in suits that would have been more appropriate in a corporate boardroom.

Jim had already noticed an inordinate number of Japanese businessmen on this cruise. Usually, on a cruise ship, they would be accompanied by their families. Real business trips would be via air. Time was money, and the Japanese were too efficient to waste this kind of time when business called.

These men were obviously corporate efficiency experts and snoops, watching the crew and probably everything else, filing regular reports back to Sukuru headquarters. It was also obvious that both the outgoing American and the incoming Japanese crews recognized this, and didn't care much for the spies.

Jim shivered, and turned to find Kiri gazing at him intently. He rolled his eyes back in an exaggerated fashion and said, "I think that was Frederick calling us for the next scene."

Kiri smiled, but it didn't quite reach her eyes. He winked and offered her his arm.

"It's showtime!"

"Mariko, you should not be out here alone!" Jim Morris stood beside Kiri, facing out over the rail, his hand next to hers. He gently touched her fingers with his own; touching, but not holding. "The Yakuza have control of this ship," he reminded her.

"Nothing matters anymore, Clint Barkley-san," Kiri/Mariko murmured. "Tomorrow we land in Japan. Our life together will end. I must honor my father's wishes."

"The hell with your father," Jim/Clint bit back his anger. "You love me, and I love you. We both know it. And so does he!"

She bowed her head, brushing back a single tear. "Ah Clint-san. Love is a luxury, a fantasy for books and movies. This is the real world. I am Japanese, you are Gai-jin. You cannot understand."

"I understand that we are two human beings that love each other." Clint was gentle as he pulled her around. "Please look at me. Tell me to my face that you don't love me!"

Mariko shuddered, and then straightened her shoulders. Taking a deep breath, she raised her head to face him.

"Clint Barkley-san. There can never be a 'we.'" Tears now cascaded down her face. "There is more than an ocean between us. We may as well be from two different species. We are certainly separate cultures. And you will never understand or be a part of mine."

"You take the easy way out, my love." Clint's voice was hoarse. "We will defeat these obstacles!"

"I think not." As one, they turned to face the mocking voice from behind them.

An older Japanese man in a tuxedo stood there, four henchmen behind him, tensed for action.

"You are a fool, gai-jin. Twice, we have warned you." His eyes went from mocking to cold in an instant. "You meddle in our business, and you try to steal the woman who will be my wife." The eyes flickered to Mariko and then fastened on Clint.

"I will deal with her poor judgement later. Training her will be a pleasure, exciting even."

He raised a hand. "No more warnings."

One of the men brandished a knife. Rushing Clint, he raised it to strike. Stepping away from Mariko, the American shifted to avoid the blade, then had a firm grip on the Japanese thug.

Using the momentum, Clint swept the man across his hip, flinging him over the rail.

Whirling, he faced the remaining attackers.

"Cut!"

The director bounded forward.

"Yes! That was perfect!" Frederick Farmer gloated. "That was the one, right there!"

Jim gave Kiri a nudge.

"That a take, Frederick?" he asked in an innocent voice.

The director back-pedaled and cleared his throat, reasserting his self-control.

"Well, I would like to see it a few more times, perhaps with a little variety in intensity..."

Jim and Kiri leaned back on the rail. Jim gazed at Frederick fondly.

Some people never change.

"Yo! Kabu!" he called out. "Two or three more takes?"

They turned and peered down at the young Japanese "thug" he had tossed over the rail. Kabu was laying spreadeagled, face up, on an inflatable raft on the deck below. He looked up at them.

"Ah, honored sirs and madam. I think that scene passed with flying colors!"

Kabu paused. "However, if certain females with 'specialized' massage techniques were available later tonight, to sooth my aching body, I could do this any number of times."

Farmer rolled his eyes, without ever lifting them from the monitor screen replaying the scene.

"Okay, okay. That's a take." He looked up sternly. "But don't plan on getting this next fight scene right the first time. I'm going to make you guys work for those favors."

Jim sighed and began stretching. It had been a long time since his early morning workout.

Kimberly Martin was fascinated, watching Jim and the other actors run through a complex fight sequence and was fascinated. One person would rush Jim, but in slow motion. Jim would guide his opponent through the action, exaggerating each movement, the blow stopping mere fractions of an inch away from contact.

After several rehearsals, the scene would be shot at full speed. Then shot again, and yet again. Finally, Morris and Farmer would look at each other and nod. Then they would move the camera crews around and redo the same sequence. After two, three, sometimes four angles had been shot, they would go on to the next tiny segment of the scene, and start all over.

Kimberly shook her head, impressed in spite of herself. "Amazing."

"Isn't it though?"

Belatedly, Kimberly noticed she wasn't alone on the deck. The young girl who had spoken was very pale, her milky white skin contrasting sharply with her glossy, black hair. Large, startlingly blue eyes almost captured attention away from the rest of her, which was also spectacular.

At a glance, the girl was thin, nearly emaciated looking, barely five feet tall. Her weight on almost anyone else would have seemed unhealthy. Upon second take, it became apparent that she was more lean than gaunt. Hard muscles moved smoothly under semi-translucent skin.

All this was accented by the tiny, black bikini she wore. Kimberly blinked and did a double take. That wasn't all that was accented by the swimsuit. Her breasts weren't unnaturally large, but for someone with her build, they certainly...stood out. And with a firmness that only the very young or the surgically enhanced could attain.

Kimberly realized she was staring. The young girl watched her with an amused expression. This obviously wasn't the first time she had encountered this reaction.

In fact, Kimberly noticed that two Japanese businessmen at the other end of the deck were making no attempt to conceal their interest in both Kimberly and the young girl.

She turned back to the girl and couldn't help grinning as they both rolled their eyes in unison. The men saw their reaction and pretended to be engrossed in the scene below.

"It's probably just as well they aren't wearing swimsuits," the girl whispered conspiratorially. "They don't have much control over their, uh...feelings."

Kimberly was puzzled for a moment, then got it. She smiled despite herself, then looked frankly at the other.

"You're not exactly shy, are you?" Their eyes met and Kimberly liked what she saw. She held out her hand. "Kimberly Martin."

"Afsaneh Riahi. I know who you are. A lot of the crew are talking about you."

Kimberly didn't like the sound of that. "About me?"

Afsaneh laughed again. "The Japanese are furious that your company sent a woman to close this deal. They think it was an intentional insult." She impulsively took Kimberly's hand and pulled her farther down the deck, where it was difficult for the men to hear.

"The Americans think it's pretty funny." Afsaneh leaned close to her and whispered dramatically, "I don't think there is much love lost between the two crews."

"It didn't take me long to figure that out." Kimberly nodded in disgust. "This was an experimental concept that seemed like a good idea at the time, though."

Afsaneh nodded and looked down at the actors. "You like this?"

Kimberly laughed. "I don't know if I like it so much as I'm intrigued by it. It's karate and yet, it's almost ballet."

Afsaneh nodded, knowingly.

"Martial arts and dance have a lot in common. The kicks and arm motions are very similar. And of course, with Jim, it can be every bit as graceful."

Kimberly blinked at the familiarity. "You know Jim Morris well?"

"Of course," she smiled demurely. "My father works with him on lots of films. Most of these actors do. That's why they work together so well, and have so few injuries."

"Injuries?" Kimberly looked down at the action and blinked at the speed the actors were now moving at. "But they're just acting, right? It's not like a real fight."

"Martial art fight scenes can be rough on actors, and even their stunt doubles." Afsaneh smiled, and Kimberly thought she saw pride in her face. "Jim has a very good track record for safety. He choreographs every single action sequence, even those he's not in himself."

"Really?" Kimberly was surprised to hear that an actor of his stature would be so tied up in the mundane details of his films.

"Oh yes." Afsaneh was speaking quicker now. Jim was a favorite topic for her, Kimberly decided. "He designs the action in the scene for each actor, schedules rehearsals, and everybody spends a couple of days getting every single move just right."

"Isn't that kind of demanding of him?" Kimberly reluctantly tore her eyes off the actor. "I mean, he is a big star and all..."

"Jim doesn't care about that stuff. He just wants the movies done safely and realistically. And he knows everybody well enough to know what they're capable of."

"I would think the director would want some say in all this." Kimberly watched Jim and Frederick talking and had to admit they seemed to get along well enough.

"Oh, it's in all of Jim's contracts. He has complete control of all action scenes." Afsaneh grinned. "Don't get me wrong, he tries to be flexible and open-minded. He hates prima donnas more than anyone, I think. But if the director's ideas are unreasonable, he axes them."

"I would think some directors would hate that." Kimberly knew enough people in business that would balk at the control issue, and the movie industry had to be worse.

"Not really." Afsaneh shrugged. "Jim tends to work with just a few directors, and the one time he worked with one that tried to pull rank on him...." The young girl smiled and raised her eyebrows. "Well, he didn't have the clout he thought he did. He was quite shocked when he got fired." Her eyes glanced to the deck below.

"Fortunately, Jim and Frederick work well together."

"Hmm," Kimberly said, turning to rest her elbows on the railing. As her eyes wandered over the faces of the actors, one thing puzzled her. With the exception of Jim, all the actors were Japanese. "Did you say one of them was your father?"

"There he is, the cameraman on the far right."

The man she pointed to was of medium height, swarthy, with a large nose. His skin was dark, as were his eyes. The only similarity Kimberly could see was the thick, black hair. "The far right?" she asked hesitantly, not wanting to offend the girl.

Afsaneh nodded gravely and spoke in a solemn tone.

"I'm told I favor my mother more than my father." Her eyes twinkled.

"I guess so." Kimberly raised an eyebrow of her own. "You are definitely not shy." They both laughed.

"If I favored him, I'm afraid I..." she cut off as her father looked up momentarily, then looked back at the director, who was showing Jim something in the script. "Oh, this should be good."

The older man's head shot back around and he glared at Afsaneh. Some of the extras had also noticed her, and they waved and whistled good-naturedly. Her father fixed his glare on the young men, and they got very busy. A few of them were obviously having trouble keeping from laughing.

"What is his name?" Kimberly asked, curious.

"Hakim Riahi. It's Persian," she answered the unasked question, then smiled and stretched as far as her diminutive stature would allow. This did not go unnoticed below. Riahi tugged on his shirt, pointed at her, and then emphatically towards the deck that housed the first-class cabins.

"I don't think Daddy likes my suit much." Afsaneh nodded vigorously at him and waved, smiling sweetly. She continued to stand close to the glass, then looked mischievously at Kimberly. "Time for the coup de grace."

Leisurely, she yawned, and turned away from the glass. This allowed her father to see the back of the suit for the first time. If he had been upset before, his daughter's T-backed bottom sent him into orbit. Just then Morris and Farmer called for attention and began the next scene.

"Do you like my suit?" Afsaneh asked in an innocent voice.

"You wouldn't catch me in that thing in a million years," Kimberly admitted. "You've got the build to get away with it though, and the youth." She gave the young girl a speculative look. "Exactly how old are you?"

"Seventeen." Afsaneh smiled brightly.

"That certainly explains a lot," Kimberly laughed, nodding at the girl's father. "You know, you're going to get one heck of a sunburn laying around in that."

Afsaneh laughed.

"I'm not wearing this to the pool!" she giggled. "It's hard enough just

walking without it sliding around. And one dip in the pool would shrink it."
"That would be impossible." Kimberly looked at it doubtfully. "How do you shrink nothing?" Afsaneh giggled again. Kimberly sighed and turned back to watch Hakim Riahi's neck get redder as he followed Jim with his camera. "So, what do you think of Jim Morris?" she asked, trying to sound casual.

"I love him," Afsaneh said simply. "I think he's the most wonderful man in the world. Except for Daddy."

"Oh." Kimberly was nonplused by her frankness. "Have you known him for long?"

"Only for all my life," she sighed. "He treats me like an adult. He has for years. He's kind, sensitive to my needs, and at times, he can be so sensual." She smiled coyly. "I'm his 'special' girl."

Kimberly winced and felt a unreasonable sense of betrayal. She had only met him this morning, but was honest enough to recognize an attraction. Furthermore, she thought she had sensed a similar reaction from him. God, this child was literally half his age. She felt a stir of anger.

Kimberly knew that stereotyped Hollywood excesses were exaggerated. But most rumors have some basis, however small, in fact. Why should Jim Morris be any different? After all, according to the talk going around, he wasn't even that much of a martial artist. If he was faking that, who knew the real Jim Morris? She tried to steer the conversation back to the film being shot below.

"I'm surprised he doesn't have a stunt man do his fight scenes. It wouldn't do for an actor of his stature to get hurt." Her voice sounded snide, even to her, but Afsaneh didn't seem to notice.

"Oh no, he does all of his own stunts. Anyway, most stunt men in fight scenes are there because the actor can't do the action. Who could you possibly get to do an action scene better than Jim?"

"Is he really all that good?" *God, I sound bitchy.*

Afsaneh looked at her. A hint of anger came through her words. "Yes, he is. He just doesn't toot his own horn like some of the other stars." The girl's voice grew colder. "He doesn't feel he has to prove anything. To anybody!"

"This morning, Mr. Toshida implied he was a fake." Kimberly hesitated. "I'm not saying I believe him, but..."

"Jim and his crew have been getting challenged to spar since they came on board." Afsaneh's voice was icily brittle. "It seems 'Mr. Toshida' is an avid fan of the martial arts and has a lot of fighters on this crew. They had bouts in an empty hold last night, and there are supposed to be more tonight. And tomorrow night. And probably the night after that. Jim's declared the fights off limits to anyone in the cast or film crew until all filming is done. It's a lot easier to make bruises and black eyes with makeup than it is to cover them up."

"I didn't mean anything..." Kimberly began, embarrassed.

"Right." Afsaneh turned to leave, then whirled around. When she spoke, Kimberly could almost visualize the icicles hanging from her words.

"There are three things you should know. First, Jim is an even better fighter than he looks in the movies." Her eyes were so hard they reminded Kimberly of sapphires, yet a glint of humor flashed through them as she continued.

"Second,..." Afsaneh paused, glanced downward demurely, then met Kimberly's eyes squarely."They're real."

The young girl headed for the stairwell at the end of the deck. Kimberly felt like a fool, both because this young girl had put her on the defensive, and because after the way she'd acted, Kimberly probably deserved what she was getting.

"You said three things," she barely kept a stammer out of her voice.

Afsaneh stopped, halfway through the hatch. "Yes, I did, didn't I?" She smiled a fake, saccharine smile, then was gone.

On board the Ananab ship P'Tassum.

Chief Technician Lasty frowned at his computer screen. He hated to admit it, even to himself, but he couldn't break the program in front of him. It's coding was unlike any he'd ever seen before.

It won't let me in, he thought glumly. An invitation to implement is the farthest I get. Implement what? Lasty rubbed his chin with his upper left hand as his other three flashed across the keyboard in vain, unable to find a chink in the program's armor.

The only thing I know for certain is that it's Egelv in origin. And the only way I even know that, Lasty reluctantly acknowledged, is the Hechktar trader told me so. A security code, he said. A highly secretive security code favored by the Egelv Royalty.

I shouldn't even be wasting my time. That trader is probably laughing in his trough picturing me puzzling over this. As if I would blindly give a command I didn't understand. What does he think I am, a Srotag?

Lasty stopped trying and backed out of the program carefully. He hooked his station back into the main ship computer system, removing the loop he'd designed to hide his tracks. Shutting the terminal down, he stood and stretched.

He was probably being paranoid in taking such precautions to avoid being detected. The ship's computer would only follow given orders, and there wasn't anyone on board the P'Tassum with the brains to catch him. Oh, maybe a few of his fellow Baerd could follow what he was doing by watching, but that was about it. And they could care less.

Lasty had always excelled with computers. It was this ability that had led to this miserable consignment. He had wanted to stay on his home planet and work on research and design, but of course that had been out of the question.

The Hstahni, and by extension their Ananab underlings, didn't permit independent research by client races. No, the Baerd followed the rigid guidelines set for their education, then were leased out as needed.

After all, there were quotas to meet. Lasty followed in the same footsteps as his father, and his father before him. As much as he loathed the overlord races, he had no choice.

Denied true research, Lasty was reduced to finding other outlets for his ingenuity. Such as tapping into the main computers and bypassing security to eavesdrop on the Ananab. Strictly for his own amusement, of course. The Ananab had such ridiculous sexual habits and rituals.

But, there was a market for disks of such things, as Lasty had found out. Using them as trade stock, he'd built up quite a library of unusual software, from diverse origins.

Such as one very irritating Egelv program.

Sighing, he began stripping off his brightly colored tunic for the drab brown one that acted as uniform for the Baerd aboard the P'Tassum. He was due on the bridge soon, and the Ananab didn't appreciate the effect of rich hues against gleaming white Baerd skin at all.

In fact, Lasty thought with resignation, the Ananab don't really like anything.

Except power and riches.

The computer of the P'Tassum.

Triangulation complete. Transmission origin located with error margin of .003%. Sufficient fuel available for diversion to source of transmission. Limited energy outlay will be available, if needed. Data base files have begun accumulating a vocabulary and access space for translation has been initiated. Early efforts point to apparent contradictions. Re-analysis commencing.

CHAPTER THREE

Jim glanced at his watch as he strode down the passageway. *Good, the dining room has been open for more than fifteen minutes.* By now, the crush of early diners should be inside, already seated. He preferred being fashionably late.

He passed the elevator and went down the central stairway two steps at a time. As he reached the dining room level, he squared his shoulders and straightened his tie.

"Making ready for a grand entrance?" A sardonic voice came out of the open elevator, followed by its owner.

"Ah, Ms. Martin." Jim paused, waiting for her to catch up. He smiled at her. "May I escort you to dinner?"

She gave him a thoughtful look he found unsettling. He sensed a subtle reserve that hadn't been there this morning, but filed it away for later consideration as he discreetly eyed the rest of her.

Kimberly looked sensational in a mid-length, black evening dress. Some would consider it modest since it had shoulders and the neckline did not reveal cleavage, but the way it molded to her figure revealed that at least one lawyer took the time to stay fit.

Kimberly Martin had a tennis player's build with a flat stomach, small firm breasts, and shapely legs that, even without high heels, had a nice cut to the calves. She wore simple silver jewelry. Her hair was short and practical, with minimal makeup, accenting the elegant, yet no-nonsense, air about her.

Jim shook his head, bemused.

"I have to keep telling myself you're a lawyer," he laughed. "You look mah-velous."

"The two aren't mutually exclusive," Kimberly pointed out in a prim voice. "If I were a male lawyer, you would just assume I played a lot of racketball and slept with my clients. A woman can take pride in her appearance, still be professional, and not feel the need to sleep around." Her voice grew angrier as she spoke. "I find people who take advantage of situations, and other people, contemptible!"

"Whoa, whoa." Jim protested, startled by her vehemence. "You'll get no argument from me,"

She looked unconvinced.

They both grew aware of the waiter standing in the doorway, impatient to lead them to their seats.

Jim cleared his throat, confused by the entire situation.

"Ma'am, I apologize for any offense I've given." He was very formal. "Shall we allow this man to seat us?"

Kimberly realized he had no idea why she was angry, and was embarrassed and confused at the same time. "Of course." She heard the stiffness in her voice and winced.

If you're going to act like a first-class bitch, Martin, your target should at least know why. And why should you care what he does?

As they crossed the dining room, she felt hundreds of eyes follow them.

They probably think we're an item, she groused. The heroic actor's latest conquest. Not bloody likely, she thought, glancing at him.

Not that he didn't look great, she had to admit. It would help if he were a slob or had obvious flaws. But, just as every time she'd seen him, he was the epitome of comfort, a compromise between casual and dressed up. Tonight he wore tan slacks with a navy sports jacket, matching conservative tie, and a light-blue shirt. He could almost be a young business executive, except for his long hair and beard. And his shoes, she noted, smiling despite herself.

Jacket, tie,...and running shoes. My God.

The men at their table stood as they arrived.

"Kimberly Martin, Jim Morris." Captain Lang wore his usual broad smile. "I'd like to introduce our dining companions for the evening."

Kimberly noticed Captain Tachibana and Toshida were absent and hoped it was nothing to concern her. A couple had replaced them. He looked to be in his mid-fifties, and she maybe fifteen years younger.

"This is Ron and Linda Hoffman," the captain continued. "Captain Tachibana and Toshida-san have other plans this evening, so we were fortunate to be able to bring a few new faces to the table."

They exchanged handshakes. Mr. Hoffman seemed a little uncertain about the etiquette of shaking hands with a woman, but he handled it with good grace. Mrs. Hoffman made no attempt to shake hands with anyone. Kimberly noticed with sour amusement that although Mrs. Hoffman ignored the women at the table, she was very enthralled with Jim.

"Mr. Morris, I just love your movies!" She didn't quite gush, or maybe she did.

"Thank you." Jim gave her a charming smile as he sat down. "And please, call me Jim."

"Ms. Martin, of course you've already met Ms. Oshiba. And I believe you met Jerry Weinstein, producer, and Frederick Farmer, director, of *Weeping Winds of Fury*." Captain Lang nodded to the other two men at the table.

"Yes, we met last night." Kimberly smiled down the table at them, feeling herself begin to lighten up. "I hope we didn't delay the meal for everyone."

"Not at all," Jerry Weinstein was short, overweight, and going bald. With his small pointed beard, and cheerful nature, he reminded her of Burl Ives. "We were just about to order."

The steward appeared at their table and Kimberly hurried to scan her menu as the others ordered. She chose a French dish with chicken and a heavy sauce.

Jim ordered last.

"I'll take the mahi mahi, blackened, with rice and grilled vegetables." He looked up and smiled. "And champagne. Two bottles of the Spanish, please."

"Celebrating, Mr. Morris?" Mr. Hoffman looked curious.

Jim shook his head.

"No more than usual." He placed his napkin on his lap and nodded to the wine steward, who had already appeared with the requested bottles. "I just like champagne."

"I would think you would prefer the French, or possibly the California champagnes." Linda Hoffman was trying too hard to appear knowledgeable and sophisticated.

Jim held his filled glass up and gazed at it. Kimberly found herself watching with him as hundreds, or even thousands of tiny bubbles appeared and floated upward in his fluted stem.

"Actually, I think the Spanish is just as good." He motioned the steward to offer it around the table. Everyone accepted but Weinstein and Farmer, who were already well into their mixed drinks.

"This is very dry. I like a dry champagne." Jim looked abashed. "And it is cheaper. I drink a lot of champagne."

"And sake," Kiri muttered under her breath.

"And sake," he agreed, amiably. He gave Kimberly a wary glance, then held up his glass.

"A toast." Jim looked around the table. Everyone raised their glasses.

"May the Jade Viking have a smooth voyage, and may diverse cultures grow to know each other a little better."

They all drank.

That wasn't what I expected, Kimberly thought, surprised.

"Well said." Captain Lang leaned forward with enthusiasm. "But surely we aren't as different as all that."

"Are we filming now, or what?" Kiri had a sly grin on her face. "It sounds like it applies to both the movie and this ship."

"Doesn't it?" Jim grew serious for a moment. "At times, even parts of our own culture seem vastly different and incompatible."

"Hollywood and Wall Street," murmured Kimberly, surprised at his perceptiveness..

"Exactly." Jim looked startled by her analogy.

Kimberly felt his eyes on her, but kept her attention on the roll she was buttering. With an obvious effort, he turned back to the others.

"Isn't it ironic that the theme of the picture is being echoed throughout this ship?" As he spoke, he gestured at Kimberly's glass, but her hand covered it. He shrugged and offered his own to be refilled by the steward. "The West can never understand the East, and the East doesn't want the West to ever understand them too well."

Jim's demeanor grew more intense.

"And yet, the Japanese in particular, at times seem to want to be just like us. They wear our clothes, adopt our sports, love our music." He smiled at Kiri, his fondness apparent. "Hell, they would never admit it, but they even like our food."

Kiri smiled back at him, and Kimberly almost frowned. *They're skirting around something. That was Jim Morris acting, not acting normal.*

"Mm, hot fudge sundaes!" Kiri made a show of delicately licking her lips. Then she turned serious. "That's only true to a point. The young are impressionable, but most adults want to keep the old ways, maintain a sense of separateness and superiority."

"Yes, but those kids grow up," Jim reminded her. "Some become their parents, but many don't forget what they liked as kids."

The waiter arrived with their salads, and conversation stopped as they all dug in, Jim and Kiri both using chopsticks that Kimberly would have sworn hadn't been there a moment ago.

Weinstein finished his drink and raised his empty glass to the waiter. Jim looked up and, with a flick of his eyes, ordered another bottle. *Damn it Martin, how did he know you love champagne? Tomorrow morning, you hit the spa.*

Captain Lang patted his lips with his napkin, and turned to the Hoffmans. "I believe you sell tires, Ron?" he inquired.

Ron Hoffman looked pleased that the Captain had taken the time to learn a little about him.

"Not just tires." Hoffman seemed to like talking about his business. "We service brakes, mufflers, do alignments, that sort of thing."

Frederick Farmer listened politely, and showed mild interest. On the other hand, Kimberly mused, he is in the movies, and all the acting isn't done on the screen.

"So, you have a shop?" Farmer looked at their clothes and tans, as if trying to place them. "Where are you from, Texas?"

Hoffman's smile was broad. "I guess I can't hide my accent; my roots, if you know what I mean. We're from Fort Worth."

Linda Hoffman chipped in, quick to set one matter straight. "Actually, we don't have a shop." Her voice was confidential, and she paused for effect.

"We have 87."

That got everyone's attention.

"Excuse me?" Farmer sounded startled. Not acting now, Kimberly noted and smiled to herself.

"Yessiree. Eighty-seven of 'em, spread clear across the state and through the south." Hoffman leaned back in his chair. "I started with one shop and a Lincoln dealership, thirty-two years ago."

"Oh? Lincoln?"

Kimberly watched Jim's eyes get a far away look in them. *Now where has he gone to?*

Twenty-six years ago...Bangkok, Thailand

"Always make sure your spare tire is good." Sergeant McCoy wiped his hands on a ragged piece of cloth. He had just changed the oil filter on the

Morris' Lincoln. He began adding cans of oil. "Do a regular maintenance on your vehicle and you'll never regret it."

"I will," Jimmy said solemnly. He squinted at the large man. "Some kids at my dojo say Aikido is better than Tae kwon do. Is that right?"

McCoy shrugged. "Depends."

"On what?" Jimmy went into a stance and kicked with his left foot at an imaginary foe. He grinned as he realized he'd caught his teacher/best friend's attention.

"Where did you learn that kick?" McCoy leaned back over the engine, checking the battery.

"O-oe-e-e-yah! Whee-o-a-ai!" Jimmy moved his hands in a swift pattern, causing McCoy to pause again.

"My God, Bruce Lee?" The Sergeant groaned. "He's an actor!"

"Yeah, but he really knows his stuff!"

Jimmy suddenly did a standing back flip from a flatfooted stance. He actually spun too far and landed on his heels, falling backwards to end up on his butt after several bounces.

"Ouch! This cement is hard!"

"Jesus, who taught you that?" McCoy's face reddened with exasperation as he helped Jimmy to his feet. "You don't do something like that without a spotter, do you hear me? Now who taught you that?"

"I saw Bruce do it." Jimmy brushed off the sergeant's anger with a disarming gesture. "That's the first time I actually tried, though."

He wilted under McCoy's stern glare. Finally, the older man relented. "You taught yourself?"

Jimmy nodded, growing nervous under the scrutiny of his longtime teacher.

McCoy sighed. "Okay. It wasn't too bad. But, to do it right, you need a spotter and a mattress. Don't practice it by yourself, understand?"

Jimmy gestured with his right hand, thumb and forefinger touching, forming a circle. "Okee dokee."

McCoy shook his head in resignation.

"Your mother will never believe I didn't teach you that." He turned his attention back to the car. "Now, besides oil and tires, there's the battery..."

The waiters whisked their salad plates away and the main course appeared before them. Kimberly found herself eyeing Jim's plate in envy. His selection looked much better than hers.

She looked up to see the Captain frowning as he contemplated his own dieters plate. Shaking his head, he turned to Hoffman.

"Do you have good employees to cover for you while you're away?"

"Oh, hell yes," he beamed. "I've had all my top people for more than ten years. Last year was rough though, and I was ready for a break."

Jim glanced up from his plate.

"So, you were exhausted." Kimberly thought his innocent expression was very unconvincing. "So to speak."

Hoffman started to answer, then stopped. He looked at the actor and something tugged at the corner of his mouth.

"Actually, son..." He paused for effect. "...I was just tired."

Kiri picked up an unused knife from her place setting and waved it at Jim. "No more puns or you die, round-eyes. Look what you've done. You're contagious!"

"Okay, okay." Jim smiled around the table. "I'll stop. I can tell when I'm treading on thin ice."

Everyone groaned.

"Now that was Key Lime pie." Weinstein patted his stomach and sighed with content.

Kimberly sipped her coffee and watched the others at the table. Captain Lang did end up with interesting dining companions.

Farmer and Weinstein had amused the table with stories about the film industry. Kiri Oshiba laughed, giggled, and chipped in with one-liners, usually at the expense of Jim Morris. He seemed detached, lost in his own thoughts.

The Hoffmans laughed at every joke, even the ones they probably didn't understand. Ron was rough around the edges, but honest enough to recognize it. Linda Hoffman reminded Kimberly of a term her mother had used, "Mutton done up as lamb."

Captain Lang, as always, had a calm, relaxed presence. He didn't talk very often, but listened, paying attention to everyone. Here and there, he would offer a comment, ask a question, steer a conversation to a new topic when the old one lagged.

Kimberly felt a growing fondness for the older man. Since she'd met him six months ago at corporate headquarters, they'd worked well together. It was obvious to her that he was neither wished to retire, nor to see the Jade Viking leave the fleet. But he was too professional to allow his personal feelings prevent him from doing his job. But she could tell he hated every bit of it.

Kimberly realized her name had been said.

"Excuse me." She looked back at Farmer. "I was daydreaming. What was that again, Frederick?"

"Jerry and I are having a reception in our suites later tonight." He grimaced. "They have adjoining doors. I don't know if making this party possible is worth that inconvenience.

"Hey!" Jerry protested, laughing and turned to her. "Why don't you come by tonight, Kimberly? Most of the cast and crew will be there, along with an assortment of others."

"Well, I don't know..." Kimberly hesitated, not sure she wanted to see certain members of that group. "I have to go to another reception, and it's been a long day."

"My God, so do I!" Captain Lang set his coffee down in a hurry. "I assume you refer to the Sukuru reception Mr. Toshida is having tonight. It starts soon, and I have a million things to do first." He smiled around the table as he rose. "I enjoyed the company so much I completely lost track of the time. But now I must leave. Please, don't let me rush you. Take as long as you like."

He bowed to them and left.

Kimberly was startled to see almost two hours had passed since she had met Jim in the lobby. She also began to rise, then realized that Frederick and Jerry were still waiting for her answer.

"Please come." Frederick laughed. "You'll need a breath of fresh air after that stuffy crowd. My dear, we are many things. But one thing we are not, and that is stuffy."

Kimberly looked at Jim. He met her gaze and held it. His eyes were resigned, sad even. *He knows I'm not coming. At times, he plays the clown, but there's a lot more to this man than meets the eye.*

"How late will it go?" she found herself asking. "I'll probably have to stay with Sukuru for several hours. Will it still be going on?"

Jerry and Frederick looked at each other in amusement.

Dumb question, Martin.

Kiri watched Jim and the lovely lawyer. They're hooked on each other, she smirked to herself. And I'll bet neither of them even know it. She smiled at Kimberly brightly and did her dipsy school girl voice.

"How late?" she giggled. "Lady, with this group, it'll be the Captain, or one of his officers who decides when it's time for the party to end. It'll be going on for hours after all good Sukuru employees are in bed."

"Are you going to both parties?" Kimberly asked.

"Sure!" Kiri smiled, dropping the silly act. "Why don't you come with us? We'll leave Sukuru as soon as we can sneak away."

"Us?"

Jim finished his glass of wine and stood up. He made a show of straightening his jacket and tie, looking at Kimberly in resignation.

"Us," he admitted. "We've been invited and I should at least show my face, but I'm not staying very long." He sighed. "I hate these things."

Kiri touched Kimberly's arm and gave her an imploring look. *She's weakening!*

"Please join us. We'll all enjoy it so much more."

Kimberly shrugged, then nodded.

"All right, but I'm not staying out too late," she warned.

Kiri laughed and linked arms with her. *Gotcha, Wall Street.*

"We'll see about that!"

The computer of the Ananab space ship P'Tassum.

First orbit around third planet completed. Recommended first choice is an ocean vessel in northern hemisphere due to high number of occupants and comparative isolation. Metal content of vessel is sufficient for construction of new bay arm for station. Translation and analysis of transmissions continuing. Initial interpretation of data suspect. Planet inhabitants have more than one language and culture, although all appear to be from same species. Warlike tendencies and extensive military build-up among the numerous local governments dictates use of stealth shields. Power-up of shuttles initiated.

Lasty stared with growing anxiety at the data scrolling across the screen. There were a lot of these "Humans" on that vessel, he thought. And we haven't had time to learn hardly anything about them! He wrung both pair of hands, his nervousness almost causing him to do something stupid.

But behind him, he could hear Captain Storhesh and his two brothers chortling about the riches on the surface below. They're so caught up in their greed, there's no reasoning with them, he realized with a sinking sensation in his stomach. I've tried to warn them of the potential dangers, but they won't listen.

He dared say no more.

CHAPTER FOUR

Twenty-two years ago...Abu Dhabi

Jimmy Morris circled his target with caution. Its features were concealed by the dim lighting in the room, but it loomed at least six feet high, towering over him. Arms extended in a stance that mirrored his own. It made no attempt to turn, contemptuously ignoring Jimmy as he completed the cirle, coming to a pause in front of his opponent.

Dead eyes stared down at him, devoid of any human compassion. Heavy brows cast shadows over those same eyes, disguising their color and hiding any thoughts lurking behind them.

Jimmy was only twelve and just over five feet tall. At a glance, he gave up significant range and eighty pounds. But he was fast, very fast.

With a high-pitched shout, Jimmy sprang forward. His left hand swept up, blocking the taller figure's own left arm. He stepped in close and brought his left leg up swiftly, striking his opponent in the back of the head with the top of his foot.

The head flew off the taller figure's shoulders and rolled to a stop against the wall. The body slowly toppled to the floor. Jimmy raised one fist in the air and stood over the fallen mannequin.

"Yes!" He had designed that kick himself. Sure, maybe it had been used by someone before, but he'd never seen it. You had to be exceptionally limber to extend that far. And you had to be willing to get in close.

Jimmy couldn't wait to show Sergeant McCoy. He spent hours watching martial arts movies and reading books to find techniques and moves to surprise his mentor. The sergeant taught him a variety of styles and methods, and it was hard to find something new.

He winced as he remembered the last time he'd surprised McCoy. Two weeks ago, in a soccer game. One of the older boys had blocked him with a vicious hit from behind, sending Jimmy sprawling across the ground. His training had turned the fall into a smooth roll back to his feet and he'd angrily faced his attacker.

The older boy taunted him and Jimmy lost his temper. He spun to the left, twirling around in mid-air in a complete circle to strike the youth in the face with his left foot. That kick got him thrown out of the game and into trouble with both his parents and the officials at the school he attended.

The fact that he'd broken the other kid's jaw hadn't helped. It also hadn't helped that the injured child was a distant member of the ruling royal family of Abu Dhabi.

He'd endured the wrath of the coaches and school officials with a clean conscience. The other kid had started it and he'd finished it. Several hours of "conversation" with his parents had been a little more difficult. But even then, he had the injured air of the misunderstood.

Later that night, Sergeant McCoy had "invited" him to the west wing. One room had been redecorated into a makeshift gymnasium, and Jimmy had entered with some trepidation.

The sergeant made it abundantly clear he disapproved of Jimmy's actions.

"You have a responsibility to the people around you." Sergeant McCoy stood flatfooted, hands on his hips. "The abilities and training you have are for self-defense. Either your own, or people around you in need. Capricious use of superior power or authority is contemptible!"

Jimmy's pride in his newly acquired technique wilted under the older man's angry glare. He hung his head in shame.

"I'm sorry." He was sincere in his apology. If his hero, Sergeant McCoy, thought it was wrong, it was. He wouldn't hit anyone again. After all, it really wasn't necessary. If he was paying attention, there wasn't a boy in his school that could touch him, not even the older ones. He was too fast and agile.

"I won't do it again," he promised.

McCoy sighed. Jimmy knew the older man believed him. He'd been with the Morris family for more years than Jimmy had been alive. He was still in the Army, but spent most of his time assigned on temporary duty assignment to Jimmy's dad. He was driver, bodyguard, and instructor to all three members of the family.

More importantly, he was Jimmy's best friend.

Jimmy's parents moved every two to four years and, aside from them, the sergeant was the only constant in his young life.

"Where did you learn how to do a spinning rear kick?" Sergeant McCoy sounded like he was having trouble maintaining a stern manner. He cleared his throat. "That kick can leave you wide open if it's not executed properly.

"It was." Jimmy smiled brightly then ducked at the renewed glare from the sergeant. "I saw Ed Parker do it," he said meekly. "Kenpo technique."

"Let's see it again." Sergeant McCoy gave him an evil grin.

Two hours later, Jimmy had dragged himself to his room, every muscle and bone in his body aching. The sergeant had given him a complete demonstration on the evils of the abuse of power. Nothing was broken and he wasn't bleeding, but he didn't move without groaning for days.

But that was the past. Jimmy rubbed his hands again, excited at the prospect of showing his teacher a move that might actually be original! Of course, not everyone could extend far enough to execute it, but as long as he could, that was all that mattered.

He was interrupted from his reverie by the sound of the door closing. Jimmy whirled, expecting to see McCoy. He was surprised when he saw it was his father standing just inside the room.

"Oh, I thought you were Sarge." Jimmy smiled, a little puzzled. His father never came to this wing. The tennis courts were the closest he ever got to exercise. He looked closer. His father looked upset. Had he been crying? His father didn't cry!

"Jimmy..." John Morris stopped, his voice breaking slightly. "Jimmy, something bad has happened."

"What?" Jimmy felt a shiver go through him, and his arms broke out in goose bumps. He suddenly knew what his father was going to say and the breath went out of him. He gasped, swaying from the lightheaded sensation that struck him. "No. No!"

His father came closer, tears now obvious in his eyes. He tried to hug his son, but Jimmy backed away, shaking his head furiously.

"No!"

"He was on the team that tried to infiltrate by helicopter." Mr. Morris paused, visibly shaken. "There was an...accident...in the desert. He...he didn't make it, Jimmy."

Jimmy felt tears streaming down his cheeks, but ignored them. He took a deep breath. "Did they get any of the hostages free?"

His father shook his head with closed eyes, and Jimmy's heart burst. McCoy had died for nothing!

He ground his teeth together and felt his expression harden. His father went to hug him and he backed away, wiping away the tears with his sleeve. He didn't need a hug. He needed McCoy!

"Jimmy...I know how you feel. We loved him, too." His father's arms fell with dejection to his side. "Jimmy?"

Jimmy felt as though his features were frozen into an emotionless mask. His lips were stiff as he spoke in a thick voice.

"Jim."

"What?" His father sounded confused.

"I'm not a kid anymore." He made himself quit backing away and squared his shoulders.

"My name is Jim."

Jim Morris looked out the starboard side through windows that ran from floor to ceiling. The ship's lights prevented him from seeing many stars, but the moon hung heavy and bloated, low on the horizon. A layer of clouds slowly slid across its face, giving the man in the moon a veil.

Jim leaned forward and looked down. The ship's wake angled outward, the white froth a testimony to their speed. According to Captain Lang, they should sight the Aleutian Islands off the Alaskan coast tomorrow, late in the day.

Sukuru Corporation had chosen the Ragnarok Lounge for the reception. It occupied the entire stern section of "D" Deck and windows along both sides and the back wall afforded a grand view of where the ship had just been.

Jim watched the social and political maneuvering through the reflection. No one else in the room was paying any attention to the view. They were all too concerned with each other, and doing and saying the right thing. His gaze shifted to the glittering globes hanging from the ceiling. Leftovers from the disco era, he decided.

Some of those present would probably feel right at home on a disco floor, he smiled to himself. Or maybe a Karaoke stage. A vision of Yoshi Toshida and Linda Hoffman doing a Karaoke number together caused him to snicker out loud.

"A private joke, Mr. Morris? Or perhaps an observation?"

Jim turned smoothly and bowed to Captain Tachibana.

"Just a wayward thought, Captain." Jim smiled slightly. "And how are you this evening?"

Captain Tachibana returned the bow and they shook hands. Together, they watched the crowd for a moment. Another Japanese officer approached them.

"Mr. Morris, may I present my Second Officer Koro Asaya." Jim heard the pride for his protege in the captain's voice. "Commander, Jim Morris, the American actor."

Koro Asaya was in his late twenties. Other than being a little taller, he was a younger reflection of the Captain. Jim took an instant liking to him and bowed slightly. Koro Asaya matched the bow perfectly. They both smiled at each other.

"Shouldn't that be Jim Morris, the 'famous' American actor?" There was no sarcasm in Asaya's voice, just admiration. "I've seen your movies. Good action scenes, and good acting. Not at all what we're used to in a martial arts movie."

Jim laughed.

"I think a lot of my contemporaries find the acting a necessary evil to bind the fight scenes together." Jim lost a little of his good humor. "From the way some of your countrymen talk, it's a good thing my acting is well received. I think they're a little critical of my fighting skills."

Koro frowned and glanced over his shoulder. He looked at his captain and formed his words with care.

"I would have to say that some people put far too much importance in fighting," Asaya had an edge in his voice. He glanced at Captain Tachibana again and hesitated. "Sir, this relates to something I need to tell you about." He smiled an apology to Jim. "Ship business, sir. No offense intended."

Jim nodded to show he understood.

"None taken, Commander Asaya. I think I know what you are referring to. And you won't find any of my people fighting down there." The young officer flushed, embarrassed.

Jim bowed again to the two men. "I think I'll wander a bit."

He turned away and deftly snagged a glass of champagne from a waiter's tray. Another appeared with a variety of sushi and sashimi. Jim selected a tuna roll and the waiter sniffed. Jim made a show of ignoring him and, using the toothpicks provided, ate the fish delicately. Holding up the now empty toothpick, Jim gave a disdainful sniff and dropped it back on the tray.

The waiter reddened and moved on to another guest.

What an idiot. All this posturing. If I stay here much longer, I'm going to be as rude as these Sukuru snobs. He looked for Kiri and Kimberly. They were standing with Taga Motari, the head villain in *Weeping Winds Of Fury.* Hakim Riahi had found Taga Motari, a mild-mannered ex-professor, at a lecture at the University of Michigan a number of years earlier. The cameraman had been struck by how photogenic Taga was and had pointed him out to Frederick. The rest was, as they say, history. The physics field's loss of a competent, if average scientist was the cinema's gain of an excellent character actor.

A voice rang out over the crowd. A thickly muscled Japanese man held a microphone, calling for attention. He was Nagami, head of security for Sukuru, and Toshida's personal assistant. If he had another name, no one knew it. His tuxedo looked out of place on his broad frame. *He looks like that guy with the hat in the James Bond movies. Where's your neck?*

The four-piece band playing in the far corner fell silent, as did the roomful of people. Nagami began speaking in Japanese. He gestured to Toshida with his free hand, talking in short, punctuated sentences. The Americans looked at each other in confusion, then waited politely for a translation.

Jim looked downward in disgust, embarrassed for his countrymen. This was a not so subtle form of insult. Of the nearly hundred people at the party, about two thirds were Japanese. Every one of them probably spoke excellent English. Of the thirty or so Americans in the room, only a few spoke any Japanese. He focused on what Nagami was saying.

"Welcome to our reception honoring the acquisition of this ship by Sukuru Corporation. It is a good addition to the fleet, and a sign of Sukuru gaining a larger share in the cruise industry; of broadening our interests." He paused and looked around the room expectantly.

Several Japanese started enthusiastic clapping, and everyone else joined in, the Americans a little hesitant, not certain what they were applauding.

"May I introduce Sukuru Executive Vice-President Toshida!" Nagami gave a shorter English version, in a hurried, bored tone.

Toshida took the microphone with reluctance, eyeing it in distaste. He handed it back to Nagami and spoke in a strong voice that carried over the crowd.

"Arigato. Thank you." He switched to English effortlessly. "These are indeed fine times for Sukuru. In addition to this vessel, we have also acquired three ships from Lauro Lines. The construction of two brand new ships will be completed later this year. Sukuru will be a major player in the Pacific market. In support of this decision, we have also purchased docking facilities in San Francisco, Juneau, San Diego, and Hawaii. The Americans seem eager to sell off parts of their country, and we are more than willing to accomodate them."

The reaction of the Japanese was mixed. Some were jubilant, others startled by his frankness. The Americans in the crowd looked irritated, but remained silent.

Jim saw Kimberly catch the eye of Captain Lang. He and his first officer, Commander Danny DelaRosa moved quietly over next to her, and she made a low comment. Jim noticed Toshida wearing a cynical smile as he watched them, then conceal his thoughts behind a facade of politeness.

"I would like to take this opportunity to introduce this ship's next Captain to those who have not yet met him." Toshida said in a more congenial tone.

Jim could tell some of the non-Japanese were thinking they had misinterpreted him earlier. There was a general relaxing of the tension. That moment quickly passed.

"Meet Captain Hiroaki Tachibana." Toshida continued, his eyes gleaming in triumph. "He will assume command when we land in San Francisco. He will be the first captain of the newly renamed Jade Samurai."

Captain Lang stiffened and glared at Toshida. Angrily, he turned to Kimberly Martin. She had an unhappy, but resigned look on her face. She placed a hand on the elderly captain's arm.

Jim felt sad as he watched. He had suspected the name would change, but that it would happen later, in a more discreet manner. This Toshida had an arrogance that defied belief. Most Japanese would be far more subtle, even if they agreed with Toshida's sentiments. Deliberate, rude behavior, especially to guests, was very unlike the Japanese.

Toshida was making another introduction. Captain Tachibana and his second officer had disapproving frowns and it was probably just as well the captain hadn't been given the opportunity to speak.

"We have one of the world's finest martial artists on board." Toshida had a new gleam in his eye. Jim winced as he projected the speech to its obvious conclusion. He had no urge to be singled out, especially not as a part of this display of rudeness. Stewards were pulling mats over the dance floor, herding the crowd into a semi-circle around them. *Uh, uh*, Jim thought. *Not going to happen*.

"I'm sure you are all familiar with this champion," Toshida continued, staring directly at Jim. "I would like to introduce our own Naga Furukawa, seven times Nipponese full contact Karate Champion!"

Jim felt his face redden. *He gotcha, Jim.* Then he started to laugh at himself. *Maybe I am a little too egocentric.* He felt the stares and sidelong glances from the people around him and turned his attention to Toshida's champion.

Naga Furukawa was about Jim's height, but very slender, without Jim's upper body strength. He looked faster, more supple, and seemed to flow rather than walk. He gave Jim a challenging look, and the American looked back levelly, not encouraging or discouraging the obvious dislike.

Toshida watched their reactions with poorly concealed glee. He nodded to Nagami and faded back into the crowd.

Nagami called out over the microphone. He announced there would be a short demonstration by Furukawa. Several Sukuru men came forward, dressed casually and carrying light boxing gloves. Furukawa took off his shirt and jacket, handing them to a waiter, his eyes never leaving Jim.

Jim began to work his way towards Kiri and Kimberly. He had no intention of staying and running the risk of being goaded into something he didn't want to do. He'd seen the other man fight before, and any confrontation between Furukawa and himself would be bitterly brutal. Jim felt no urge to prove anything, but the Japanese champion immediately made it clear he was eager to have a go at someone who was, arguably, one of the world's most famous fighters.

"Morris-san!" Furukawa shouted above the murmuring crowd. It fell silent in eager anticipation. "Why leave so soon? Surely you can stay for a friendly match? Come, you know the crowd wants this. Aren't you an entertainer?"

"I'm afraid I'll have to pass." Jim was polite, but firm. "I didn't come here for this, and your 'crowd' is more of a captive audience. I'm sure these others will give you a reasonably good match."

The two men who had brought the gloves out paled. It was clear they had no illusions about their abilities in comparison to the Japanese champion. Sparring with Furukawa in Morris' stead would be unpleasant, at the very least.

"I think you're right when you say you are 'afraid,'" Furukawa taunted. He moved closer. "Don't worry, I won't hurt you. Are you a fighter or not?"

"What I am, is not interested." Jim began to turn away, but stopped as Furukawa came even closer. He was furious with himself for not seeing this trap sooner. The chances of his avoiding a fight were decreasing rapidly. *I am not going to do this,* he swore to himself angrily.

For a strained moment, neither man moved. Those closest to them tried to move back, wanting more space between them and the two. The people in the back pressed forward, trying to see better.

Toshida stepped next to his champion and looked Jim up and down, contemptuously. The crowd froze, hanging on every word.

"Everything in your movies is fake, neh? You're an actor, acting as if you could fight!" The older man nodded at Furukawa. "This man is a warrior. He carries his honor as if it matters. Unlike you. Come, Morris-san, prove you are a man, if not a champion. That you have dignity, if no skills."

Jim felt his face become a mask. Instead of anger, he felt cold, detached. He wasn't going to be able to avoid this fight, he now saw.

Someone pushed through the crowd.

Captain Lang towered over them all, his windburnt features red with fury. He stepped between Jim and Furukawa.

"This will stop. Now!" His voice was shaking with anger, a roar in the deathly quiet room. He leveled a finger at Furukawa. It trembled, but not from fear.

"Mr. Morris is a guest of this ship." His voice lowered, but lost no intensity. "And I am still the captain of this ship. This man is my guest."

He faced Toshida.

"And you, sir, will desist from baiting and insulting my guests." Lang glared around at the others. "All matches on this ship will cease, from this moment on. Anyone caught fighting, trying to start a fight, or fomenting violence will be tossed into the brig for the duration of the voyage."

His attention returned to Toshida.

"Anyone!"

Toshida glared at him.

"Captain, you overstep your authority," he snarled. "This vessel is owned by Sukuru Corporation and I am its representative. This room is reserved for our use, and we will do as we wish here."

Captain Tachibana stepped forward, his face grim, stopping next to the American captain.

"Actually, that is not totally accurate," he said in a clipped tone. "We are at sea. If anyone representing Sukuru is in command, it would be me." He gave Toshida a meaningful stare. "But I am not. Captain Lang is the legal master of this ship, and any attempt to challenge his authority would have to be considered mutiny."

"In Sukuru hierarchy, I rank you, Captain." Toshida stuttered, he was so angry.

"Not on the high seas," Tachibana shot back.

"Master-at-arms, step forward." Captain Lang's voice rang out, clear and strong. And determined. Officers, both Japanese and American, appeared behind their respective captains.

For a moment, no one moved. Toshida was outgunned, and they all knew it. He took a single step backward, and his personal guards closed around him. Nagami stepped between the Captains and his boss.

"You might regret this move when we return to Nippon, Captain Tachibana," Toshida snarled in a quiet, but deadly voice. "I think your loyalties are in question. And as for you, Morris-san..."

He stopped as he saw that the actor was gone.

Toshida gave a laugh that could not ever be mistaken for humorous. "The man is a coward."

Jim hurried down the corridor. He entered the stairs, and bounded up them, three at a time. As he reached the door to his deck, he hesitated, then slammed his open hand against it.

Oh God, I wanted to kill him. No, I wanted to kill both of them. And it was close, so very close.

Why can't people just leave me alone? He knew it wasn't a realistic thought, but the wish never died. Jim knew if he allowed himself to get drawn into one fight, it would never end. It would be just like the gunfighters of the old west. Always a new younger man, wanting to beat the best, make a reputation for himself.

Did female sex symbols have this problem? Did everyone try to hit on them to see if they were that great in bed?

Jim sighed and allowed his head to lean against the cool, metal door. *Not the same thing at all.* Anyway, that wasn't a problem limited to the female stars, he admitted wryly.

I definitely do not want to go to the cast party. Maybe I can sneak into my cabin and drink myself into oblivion for the night. He heard the door on the deck below open and hurried out of the stairwell.

"Jim, there you are!" He felt his heart lurch, but was relieved to see it was only Afsaneh approaching him from the far end of the hall.

"What's the matter, Jim?" There was concern in her voice.

With an effort, Jim pulled his emotions back deep inside himself. He mustered a big smile for her and she seemed relieved and gave him a spontaneous hug. He returned it, holding her tightly, his chin resting on her head, her face buried in his chest.

Then he pulled away and gave her his best smile.

"I just came from a very tedious, very boring reception," he said in a low tone. His voice strengthened. "But now it's time for a real party."

He put his arm across her shoulders, and she slipped hers around his waist. He gave the top of her head a kiss, and they walked down the hall towards the sounds of laughter and singing.

Kimberly and Kiri left the Sukuru debacle in a daze. Taga Motari and two other actresses that had been there walked with them.

Taga ranted in Japanese nonstop, in a low, furious voice. His volume began to rise, and Kiri placed a warning hand on his shoulder. The volume went back down, but the monologue continued.

Kiri turned to Kimberly with a bemused look on her face. She started to say something, then stopped and looked at Taga in astonishment. She tried to stop, then snorted through her nose, laughing.

"Taga, that isn't even remotely physically possible," she admonished.

He ignored her and continued. The two actresses joined in and Kimberly watched Kiri blanch. Kiri looked at her and rolled her eyes.

"Wow, be thankful you don't understand Japanese."

Kimberly looked at the three of them chattering with a rueful smile.

"I don't have to speak Japanese to catch the 'essence' of what went on tonight," she pointed out. "I can't believe that happened downstairs. It's so…unprofessional!"

Kiri shook her head.

Kimberly blushed and admitted, "I guess that's probably not the aspect that bothers you or Jim." The picture of Jim standing there, refusing to fight, came unbidden to her.

They reached the stairs. Taga and the two actresses went down. He yelled something over his shoulder to Kiri and Kimberly as they headed up to "A" deck.

"They'll see us at the party," Kiri translated. "That's the only thing he's said since we left I can repeat without losing my dignity...or probably, my virginity."

Kimberly laughed out loud and looked at her in askance. Kiri shrugged. "Okay, it might be too late for that, but nonetheless..." She shook her head in awe. "If we could have caught his tirade on film, well, we're talking Oscar material here."

They came out of the stairs and stopped short.

Halfway down the hall stood Jim with his back to them. He seemed hunched over, then straightened and it was at that point the two women saw Afsaneh. They watched Jim kiss the top of her head and the two of them walk down the hall. They entered the last cabin on the left, Jim's arm still around her.

Kimberly felt dismay that was hard to rationalize. She was honest enough to admit to herself that she was attracted to the actor, but she didn't really want to pursue it. At the same time, she had hoped to be wrong about the relationship between Jim Morris and the young girl. But now this. And that god-awful scene downstairs tonight.

Was he a coward? If he actually was such a great martial artist, why did he go to such lengths to avoid defending himself? She realized the scene they had just witnessed with Afsaneh could be an innocent one, but she was skeptical. Where there was smoke... She wasn't being fair and knew it, but...dammit, the girl was half his age!

They reached the end of the hall, and Kimberly hesitated. The sounds of merriment were coming from the last room on the right! The door Jim and Afsaneh had entered on the left was closed, and no sound came from it.

Kimberly woodenly felt herself being led into a roomful of people in a radically different mood than she was.

Jerry Weinstein met her with a big smile and poured her a drink from a garish colored punch bowl. She took a sip without looking and began choking. She looked at her glass incredulously.

"What the hell is that?" she gasped.

"We call it 'killer' punch," he beamed.

"Good name," Kimberly admitted. Her breathing came back to normal and she looked around the room. Doors were propped open to the next suite. Both were filled with members of the cast, the film crew, miscellaneous passengers, and a few crewmen, both Japanese and American. Most people had drinks in hand and, judging from their demeanor, not their first ones.

Kiri pulled Frederick aside and was talking in a fast, furious voice. Hakim Riahi joined them. Kimberly didn't have to hear what was being said to know what the subject was. The director grew solemn, then angry. By the time Kiri finished, his anger was gone, and a sad expression had replaced it.

"Where is he?" Frederick asked in a quiet voice.

"In his room." Kiri looked at Hakim. "Afsaneh met him in the corridor and is in there with him now."

Frederick and Hakim exchanged looks and nodded in relief.

"Good." The director sounded satisfied. Kimberly felt herself growing numb with disbelief. Was she the only person on this ship that thought the idea of Jim and Afsaneh being together was just plain wrong? Her father, for Christ's sake.

"She knows how to snap him out of it," Frederick continued. Hakim and Kiri nodded in agreement.

Kimberly decided she'd had enough. But as she opened her mouth, a laugh stopped her, and she turned around in surprise.

Jim and Afsaneh stood in the doorway, hand in hand. He had changed into shorts and a sleeveless sweatshirt and was barefoot. In his free hand, he held both a bottle, and a full glass of champagne. Casually, he took a sip that became a gulp. He released the young girl and poured himself another glass. She held her glass out.

"One glass I said." Jim glanced at her father, who shrugged. "Okay, one more, but that's it."

Afsaneh smiled sweetly and gave Kimberly a challenging look as she went over to her father. He gave her an affectionate hug and stole a sip of her freshened drink.

Jesus Christ, Kimberly fumed. *They're all worried about her having a second glass of wine, but she shacks up with a man twice her age and they all smile.* These people were too...Hollywood for her.

Kimberly watched as Kiri approached Jim. He looked at his co-star, and his expression contained nothing but humor. There was no hint in his face of what had occurred earlier.

Kiri stood on tiptoe and gave him a kiss on his cheek. He pulled her close, and hugged her tight. Jim looked over her head at Kimberly and his expression changed. He gently pulled Kiri away, his lips brushing her forehead.

"I'm sorry you had to see that scene at the reception." He smiled ruefully at Kimberly and sighed. "I guess relations between your company and Sukuru have taken a turn for the worse."

Kimberly shrugged, trying to keep any emotion out of her voice. *I will not let him see me upset.* "The foundation for that was already laid." Her voice sounded cold, even to her. "Do you get challenged like that often?"

Jim gave a curt laugh.

"This would have to be considered one of the more extreme occasions," he admitted. "I imagine I lost a few fans down there."

"There are a lot of things more important than the adulation of a few of your fans." Kimberly snapped the words out. "Several good men risked their careers down there. It could have gotten very ugly."

"It wasn't already ugly?" Jim looked surprised by her vehemence.

Kimberly thought of the minor standing with her father across the room. The words came out stronger, more condemning, and much louder than she intended.

"I don't think certain facts would endear you to your 'loving' audiences." Kimberly tried to stop the words, but they came out anyway. "You're supposed to be a role model. You represent something important to a lot of people!" Her voice rose, and she realized the room had fallen silent around them.

Jim gave her a look he tried to make inscrutable, but she could see the hurt inside. She felt a sense of victory and knew he saw it.

"Well, Ms. Martin. It appears to be my lot in life to disappoint and irritate you." He shrugged. "Enjoy the party."

He turned and left the room, bottle in hand.

Her feeling of victory was hollow, and she stared at the door after he left.

"Well, Kimberly." With a start, she realized Kiri was speaking to her. "I would have to say your timing really sucks."

The Japanese girl looked angry, and Kimberly found it hard to face her, but she forced herself to. Kiri glared, then sighed and impulsively hugged her. Kimberly returned the hug, hesitant at first, then with heartfelt thankfulness.

Kiri gave a sad laugh.

"I guess you already know that, neh?" She sighed again. "You two have some issues to deal with, you know that, right?"

Kimberly pulled back and looked at the young Japanese girl.

"I should go find him." Kimberly shook her head. "I've been such a bitch tonight. At least he should know why I'm upset."

Kiri nodded in agreement, then stopped Kimberly as she began to turn away.

"Check the deserted lounges with pianos."

Kimberly worked her way down the length of the ship. It was late enough that most people had retired for the night. She had the corridors to herself, and was able to cover the ship quickly.

Kimberly was on "D" Deck when she heard it. At first she thought it was the ship's Muzak system, but it was a piano. Coming from where, though?

Kimberly found a door off a sitting room that led to a tiny lounge she hadn't noticed before. Jim sat at a spinet piano, his back to the door, playing and singing quietly. He was oblivious to her.

"Sing a soft song, for the night time.
Try to keep from waking up the world.
Anyway, what I'm feeling tonight,
Is the..."

He stopped.

Jim remained motionless for a moment, then flowed to the side, somehow getting up from the piano bench without disturbing it. He looked startled to see it was her.

"Oh, uh, hi."

"I didn't know you played." Kimberly procrastinated, hesitant to start her apology. "That sounded pretty good. What song was that?"

"I haven't named it yet." Jim swayed and tried to meet her gaze squarely.

"Look, I'm sorry if I disappointed you tonight," he said, bitterness strong in his voice. "I don't believe in fighting for the hell of it. This isn't Caesar's Coliseum and I'm not subject to someone else's whim."

He picked up his glass from the piano and drained it. He tried to pour another drink, but the bottle was empty.

Kimberly gave an impatient shake of her head.

"I don't care about the fighting. That Toshida's an ass." Jim looked at her in surprise and blinked owlishly, as if trying to focus more clearly.

My god, he's drunker than a skunk.

"How much have you had tonight?" She searched her memory and was startled by her quick estimate. "You must have had at least two bottles!"

"Closer to three." He shook his head impatiently, and almost lost his balance. "Whoa. Anyway, that doesn't matter." His words were beginning to slur.

"All evening long you've been angry or irritated with me. If it's got nothing to do with fighting Toshida's goons, what's all this about?"

Kimberly hesitated, and decided he was too far gone for this conversation. "Never mind. Your private life is your business and I have no right judging your affairs." Kimberly winced at her choice of words.

Jim stared at her.

My God! She's jealous. He tried to recall the evening through the fog of the alcohol, and was elated to realize that was exactly what the symptoms were.

"Let's get you back to your cabin," Kimberly was saying in a distant voice. "You need some rest."

"No, no, not yet." Jim insisted, although his bed did sound more and more like a good plan. He was so tired, but he had to set one thing straight first.

"Listen, Kim." He smiled his best engaging smile, although it was difficult with his eyes not focusing very clearly. "Can I call you Kim?"

"Not even once." Kimberly was firm.

"Oh." That stopped him, but only for a moment.

"Anyway, it's not what you think." He laughed in relief. "I'm not dating her, we haven't slept together, nothing. We are just very fond of each other."

"Really?" Kimberly sounded skeptical.

"Really." Jim agreed. "Kiri and I are just the best of friends."

"Kiri? Kiri?" Kimberly's voice rose. "Who said anything about Kiri!"

Jim looked at her in confusion, but became aware they weren't alone. Nagami and two of his men stood blocking the door.

"Ah, Morris-san," Nagami gloated. "Finally you turn up."

"We were just leaving," Jim said quietly, trying to regain his composure. "If you'll excuse us..." He had a firm grip on Kimberly's arm and they moved to pass by.

"I don't think so." Nagami laughed harshly and motioned. The other two men shot forward and Jim shoved Kimberly to the side. The two men tried to act in unison, but Jim quickly moved close to the one on his left. Grabbing the thug's arm, he swept him to the side, causing him to crash into the wall. The other man, clearly more experienced, waited for Nagami to join him and they began to herd Jim towards a corner.

Jim felt a wave of dizziness and fought it. He heard a thud in the distance, then another. Gradually he became aware that all three Japanese men had fallen and appeared to be unconscious.

He turned in confusion, and saw that Kimberly was laying on the floor, unmoving. He tried to pick her up, but another wave of nausea hit him.

Staggering, he realized she was out cold too. *What the hell?*

He felt a lurch. *Oh Jim, you are really drunk. No, wait a minute. That's the actual ship moving.* One staggering step gave him a bleary view out the port window. A third wave of dizziness hit him and he fell backward, landing hard on the floor. He made no attempt to get up. What he saw in that brief glance was enough.

Either he was drunk to the point of delirium, or the ship was slowly rising above the water.

His last thought as he faded out was that this was a fitting ending to a pretty crappy day.

CHAPTER FIVE

Jim Morris raced down the corridor. He knew Kimberly was just around the corner, being dragged away by Yakuza thugs. A man dressed entirely in black popped out of an open door on the left. Without slowing, Jim forearmed him into the wall. There was a dull thud as the ninja's head met the steel bulkhead.

Footsteps raced closer behind him. Rounding the corner, he came upon two more men in black, waiting for him. Jim feinted with his right foot, then snapped his left straight forward in a vicious front kick.

The man on the left was slow in blocking, and the foot caught him full in the chest, driving him back. As Jim landed, he grabbed the second thug's right wrist with his own right hand. He twisted the arm and pivoting, brought his left elbow down hard on the extended limb, striking the joint squarely.

The man screamed as the arm bent in a direction it wasn't meant to. Jim yanked the injured man into the path of his pursuers.

There were two of them, and they became tangled for a moment. Jim didn't give them a chance to get clear. Two swift punches to the head disposed of one, and three side kicks to the groin, stomach, and face in fast succession finished off the other.

"Very good, Morris-san." Jim whirled to find Toshida standing down the hall with his arms folded across his chest. "But not good enough."

A henchman stood next to him, holding the leashes on two snarling dobermans. The dogs charged as he released them.

Jim barely had time to turn and they were on him. He used a closed left fist to backhand the first, sending it slamming off balance into the wall. But he couldn't recover fast enough to hold off the second.

Canine vice-like jaws closed on his right arm, pulling him down. The beast's head jerked from side to side, shaking him back and forth. The second dog recovered and stood with its paws on his chest, pinning him to the deck. The snarling face was inches from his face, and Jim could barely hold it away, his left hand closed around its neck.

The dog holding his arm kept pulling and twisting, and the pain shot up and down the limb. He could hear Toshida laughing in the background, but all he could see was the one set of teeth practically touching his face.

Jim's right arm felt like it was being twisted off, the skin shredding away. With horror, he saw white bone through the pulpy, red mess that had once been his arm. It was no longer just one set of jaws ripping at him. Dozens, no, hundreds of tiny needle-like teeth dug through his flesh, grinding his bones, flaying...

"Whoa!" Jim rolled over and rubbed his right arm frantically.

Ouch, ouch, ouch! His arm had been pinned under him and was asleep. As Jim tried to rub normal feeling back into his numb muscles, he shivered. *Damn, that dream felt real. He hated dogs. Dumb pets, anyway. He'd take a cat any day.*

From the texture of the carpet beneath him, he could tell he was laying on the floor.

"Christ. One lousy resolution, yesterday morning. That was all." Jim still had his eyes shut tight. "I didn't even wake up on the bed, much less aimed in the right direction!"

He rolled farther to the left, and his face met bare flesh.

Firm, smooth, perfumed flesh.

Cautiously, he opened his eyes to Kimberly's bare shoulders.

"No, never happened." He sat upright. "That I would have remembered."

He was lying in the middle of the floor in the small piano lounge. The three Japanese were deposited around the room, out cold. Kimberly snored gently beside him, still in her evening dress.

Memories came back with a rush.

The ship, rising into the sky?

Jim staggered to his feet, and lurched to the window. Any urge to make another clever remark was gone.

Jade Viking was no longer at sea.

Instead of ocean, Jim saw a wall. A big wall. Lights and instruments were scattered about its surface, but one thing was clear.

It was a very, very, big wall. Large ramps and tubes connected it to Jade Viking. It ran out of his view in all directions. He leaned forward, pressed his face against the glass to look upward, and came to a staggering realization.

This was an inside wall. And above him, appeared to be more wall, or ceiling perhaps. Jade Viking seemed to be docked inside some incredibly huge room.

But docked wasn't quite the right word, because Jade Viking wasn't floating on water. It was just floating, suspended in midair.

Jim whirled, and tried to rouse Kimberly.

No good. She just snored louder.

Shaking his head, he lifted her over one shoulder, groaning at the effort, then apologized to her unconscious form.

"Sorry, Ms. Martin." He tried, but failed to inject humor into his voice. "This isn't a very dignified pose for you, especially in that dress."

Her snores were his only answer.

He left the lounge without a backward glance at the sleeping Japanese.

No one was in the hall, but he could hear sounds coming from the stern of the ship. Turning aft, he found a stairwell and started upward.

Passing one deck, he heard shrill sounds. Looking up, he stopped dead.

Two very strange creatures stared back down at him. Long, narrow snouts were topped by two beady, black eyes. Tall ears arched backward in what looked like alarm. They seemed to be covered with dark brown fur, and wore nothing save the belt harnesses around their shoulders.

They exchanged high-pitched squeals and dashed up the stairs. Jim slowly backed down to the level he had just passed. Pulling himself out of his dazed state, he hurriedly opened the door, took two steps, and once again pulled to a halt.

"Whoa." Jim fought rising panic.

Standing in front of him were yet two more strange creatures.

But where the two on the stairs had been covered with fur, these two seemed to be armor plated, thick layers overlapping, covering most of their bodies.

The first two had looked like sloths, or possums, or some other rodent-like mammal. Jim wasn't even sure these two were mammalian. Their heads reminded him of rhinos, or hairless bears with alligator features. Huge, square skulls, with massive boney foreheads held green-tinged eyes and a mouthful of thick, blunt teeth.

The sloths, as Jim thought of them, had been frightened, unarmed, and quick to flee. These two weren't running anywhere, and didn't look particularly scared.

And for good reason.

The sloths were between four and five feet tall, at the most. These two loomed well over seven feet, had muscles beyond a bodybuilders wildest dreams, and had what appeared to be a weapon in one hand, and something that would do quite nicely as a club in the other.

One of them said something in a thick guttural voice. It sounded like an order.

Jim could hear others approaching, and made a quick decision. Without taking his eyes off the huge aliens, and aliens they had to be, he carefully lowered Kimberly to the floor and held his arms out to his sides.

"I surrender." Jim tried to look nonthreatening. "What do you want me to do?"

Before they could respond, he was seized from behind and spun around. A single paw grasped the front of his sweatshirt, and he was raised into the air and slammed against the wall.

Inches away from his face, a black panther glared at him. A snarl rumbled from its throat, imperial in tone.

Jim could feel claws pressing into his chest muscles. Hot, powerfully scented breath made him a little dizzy. The rumbling repeated, threatening in tone. Bright copper eyes bored into his, as if trying to reach deeper and read his mind.

Without breaking eye contact, Jim could tell that these new creatures were nearly as large as the hairless giants, the rhino-bears. They looked even more dangerous.

The black panther opened its mouth and Jim saw exactly what he expected to see. Fangs. Big fangs. It spoke, listened for a moment, then gave a very human-like nod, and stepped backward, still holding Jim at arm's length.

Jim remained motionless, feet dangling above the deck. Pulling his face close, the catman snarled something that sounded like a command. Jim nodded, averting his eyes as he was lowered to where his feet could touch the deck.

Released, he was motioned to put his hands together. The catman wrapped something around his wrists once, and Jim felt it fasten to his skin. It was like a sticky rope, and very strong. Another length was attached to it as a leash, and the catman turned to go, holding onto the end.

The two rhino-bears shouted at Jim's captor, and it snarled back. Another catman joined in and Jim took the moment to look around. The sloths had put Kimberly on a sled that seemed to be floating about a foot off the floor. Several other humans were piled on also, and the sled moved off down the corridor.

Jim took a step to follow them and was yanked back. The catman turned and snarled. Jim froze, and it resumed its conversation with the rhino-bears.

There didn't seem to be much love lost between the two species. Eventually, they seemed to come to an agreement, and Jim found himself being led off by one each of the catmen and rhino-bears. He sighed as they split off from the steady stream of loaded sleds emptying the ship of unconscious people.

I take back what I said about dogs and cats, he thought, staring at the broad, black, furry back in front of him.

Dogs aren't so bad.

Several hours earlier...

Chief Technician Lasty frowned at his computer screen. From the start, he hadn't felt comfortable with this whole operation, and as far as he was concerned, his first impression was being confirmed. There just wasn't enough known about these "humans." Not that his opinion mattered to anyone.

Surreptitiously, he glanced around the control deck of the Ananab Starship, P'Tassum. The room was triangular, with the Captain's position in one corner and the entrance in the middle of the opposite wall. A raised walkway ran the length of the two side walls.

Along one side, four Tryr were spaced evenly, alertly watching everyone in the room, especially the four armored Srotag guards along the other side. Beneath the walkways, Baerd technicians manned work stations, monitoring transmissions, lining up the recovery pods, doing all the actual duties necessary for the P'Tassum to function.

Captain Storhesh sat overlooking the room from his command post, flanked by his two brothers. The three Ananab made an imposing sight, perched on their stools, with their four hind legs spread wide for support. Two large arms ended in pincered claws. For delicate handling, they had numerous feelers sprouting from their upper torso. When upright, the Ananab stood even taller than their security forces.

Directly behind them stood the two Commanders of Security. They hated each each intensely which, of course, was the very reason they held their positions.

The P'Tassum was large for a commercial ship, with a crew numbering almost two hundred, with members from five different races. To the paranoid Ananab, having a security crew from a single race would be dangerous and give too much power to a lower caste. Anyway, the Captain enjoyed the constant bickering between them.

Commander Tak of the Tryr tapped several keys at his work station, and growled in satisfaction.

"These primitives can't see us." Tak's lips curled back to reveal his primary fangs. "They have nothing capable of detecting us when we are sheathed."

"The recovery pods are launched and on schedule." Even through the translator, Srotag Commander Acha's voice was so guttural he could barely be understood. "All guards are at their stations, ready to board."

The Captain stretched forward, his feelers betraying his excitement with their nervous movements.

"Fire the nerve beams!"

Lasty hurriedly turned back to his instruments and instructed the computer to proceed.

The main screens on the far wall split between a visual of the ocean vessel far below them, and a tactical display of the same. There was no visible difference in the first, but the tactical showed a thick band spring into existence and slowly sweep the length of the ship. After the first pass, it reversed direction and swept forward.

After four complete sweeps, the tactical changed to show the position of the four retrieval pods. They formed a square around the native ship and faint lines showed the gravitational field was in place.

"Ready to raise the prize, Captain," Lasty called out nervously. All four of his hands came to rest, awaiting the command.

"Proceed," Captain Storhesh ordered, then turned to the brother on his right.

"This has changed our fortunes, Garsh'ee." The Captain clicked his lateral mandibles together. "This voyage was a complete loss until we picked up the transmissions."

First Brother Garsh'ee returned the click.

"If these primitives prove to be capable of being trained, we will have an exclusive. An entire planet with all its resources, and a teeming population for resale." Garsh'ee showed apprehension. "We have to be quick. If we found them, can others be far behind? The Hstahni, or maybe the Egelv...?"

Second Brother Nythi spoke up.

"We were far off the scented path," he argued. "Nothing profitable has ever been hatched this far out."

The surface vessel was rising at a rapid rate now, bracketed by the pods. Sensors showed a large number of beings aboard.

Such a strange planet, Lasty thought as he discreetly listened to the Ananab brothers gloat. Although the majority of the surface was water, the primary species was a land mammal.

The Humans, as they referred to themselves, had superficial similarities to the Baerd. Both races were mostly hairless and soft-skinned, unlike the armored Srotag.

Of course, the Humans had only two arms instead of four, only five digits on each arm instead of six, and no tail. They seemed to average slightly greater mass, but not enough to make them physically dangerous.

Not to the Tryr or the Srotag, anyway.

The tallest of the Humans appeared to approach the size of a Tryr, but with significantly less muscle mass. Also, they had no claws, miniscule fangs, and thin skin. Such thin skin.

The Tryr had their thick fur. The Srotag, plated armor that even Tryr claws were slow to penetrate. Even the Ananab's exosketon had been crucial, countless ages ago, before acquired technology gave them supremacy over the other predators of their home world.

Lasty worked up the nerve to speak. "Captain, I have some concern about these 'Humans'. There are countless contradictions on this planet. We've recorded many different languages, so much variety in the broadcasts. In fact, the sheer volume of broadcasting is astounding. It will take some time to analyze their culture. Cultures, really. And their capabilities..."

Lasty hesitated.

"We know very little to be bringing this many of them aboard."

Commander Acha gave a laugh. The largest Human wouldn't come any higher than the base of his neck, and would weigh little more than half as much. He raised his arms and stretched the four digits on each hand wide, the webbing between them expanding to form two huge masses of scaly knuckles. Those hands were capable of crushing a skull between them, especially a soft Human or Baerd skull. Lasty blanched. Captain Storhesh ground his mandibles with contempt.

"Physically, they are certainly no match for us. And their technology is primitive compared to ours."

"True...but perhaps they have hidden talents we haven't discovered, yet." Lasty was stubborn. Data analysis was one of his main chores, and this felt wrong. "We haven't even found their transportation grid, yet. And the transmissions show they've fought many wars."

Commander Tak snorted.

"They used primitive weapons long ago," he sneered. "Now they do battle from afar, keeping their distance. We certainly won't allow them weapons. And without them..?" He squeezed his hands together expressively, and Lasty felt faint.

The Captain chittered at his obvious fear.

"These Humans will awaken without tools, on a starship far from home. They will be broken, as have all others. They will learn their place in the universe, or die. It is as simple as that."

He looked around at the others in a deliberate manner.

"They are an insignificant race with no particular skills or abilities. Today we take one ocean vessel." Lasty suppressed a shudder at the captain's arrogance. "When we come back, it will be in force, and we will take the entire planet."

Storhesh slapped his pincers for emphasis.

"And every thing, and every being on it."

"Captain, we have secured the vessel in the hind docking nest." This came from one of Lasty's assistants, Eyr.

Captain Storhesh raised himself on his rear four legs, feelers waving wildly. He lifted one pincer high overhead.

"Commanders, send this message to your troops. Board and seize!"

Lasty watched the monitor screens, brooding.

There were too many Humans on that ship, he said to himself for the twenty-fourth time. It was taking too long to move them into the huge storage nest that had been designated as their holding space.

The captain had ordered all departments stripped of their Hoag workers to help load the unconscious Humans onto antigrav sleds. It took at least two Hoags to move each of the Humans, sometimes three. They were hard workers, but small and weak.

It was too bad the Srotag and the Tryr couldn't help. They were considered the hardiest fighters in known space, but would revolt before doing menial labor.

Eyr pointed out something on the screen, and Lasty felt a chill.

"Captain, we have a report of a conscious Human."

Commander Acha was talking at his station to one of his subordinates. He grunted acknowledgement, and blasted a short command. He turned to Storhesh.

"Captain, it is one male Human, carrying another, we think female." Acha laughed viciously. "A funny time to be thinking of rutting. We have it contained."

"Are there any others conscious, yet?" Captain Storhesh turned to Lasty. "I thought you said they would be out longer than this."

Lasty nervously punched keys at his board, looked for a long moment, and nodded slowly.

"The beam affects the nervous system." His voice gained confidence. "If the creature was deep enough in the ship, it would weaken the beam. If it had taken drugs to numb its nerves, and was healthy enough, it might waken sooner."

"Healthy, and taking drugs to numb its senses?" Tak was contemptuous. "That's stupid. Why would they do that? And why only one?" He glared at the now-trembling Baerd. "Are you saying it was expecting this, and was prepared?"

"Oh no, Sir!" Lasty rushed his words. "Perhaps it is some form of entertainment, or maybe it was sick." He turned to his Captain desperately, and his concern caused him to forget his usual caution. "I told you, we just don't know that much about these Humans yet!"

Storhesh came upright to tower over him. Mandibles opened and closed furiously, and his feelers moved in a deliberate rythmn that Lasty recognized belatedly.

"Please forgive me, Captain!" He prostrated himself, shoulders shaking. "I meant no disrespect."

Storhesh smashed a pincer across the side of the Lasty's head, sending him crashing against Commander Acha's legs. The Commander snarled and kicked him away. Lasty landed near his station, and lay there, stunned. The Srotag moved as if to kick him again, but the Captain motioned him off.

First Technician Lasty slowly pulled himself onto his station perch and faced the screen. He ignored the blood dripping down the side of his head and spoke in a very slow and careful voice.

"Transmissions have shown a Human custom of drinking something they call alcohol for social and entertainment reasons. This substance is a depressant and would deaden nerves. If enough were consumed, it could dilute the effect of the ray."

The two security commanders exchanged disbelieving looks.

"Isn't this...'alcohol' detrimental to their health?" Commander Tak sounded disgusted by the concept.

"In tiny portions, it would appear it actually improves their circulatory system." Lasty was interested despite his pain. "But it seems to be a common habit to overconsume, sometimes to the point of unconsciousness, or even death. It's not unheard of in some other races we know of."

"Bring the Human to me." The captain's eyes roved between his brothers and the two commanders. "I would see one of these Humans up close."

Commander Tak turned to his station and barked out commands at a rapid rate. Acha looked irritated, but didn't protest. Both commanders kept contact with each others subordinates to a minimum. The chain of command was hazy between the two divisions.

Reports started coming in of other Humans being found awake, or waking as they were being moved. Most of the ship was emptied when the doors across the Control Center opened and a Tryr and Srotag entered with a Human between them.

Captain Storhesh looked at Lasty. "Has the computer translated any languages from this world yet?"

"The primary language on most broadcasts is called English," Lasty said, nodding. "He hasn't been equipped with a translator yet, though."

"Do it."

The two guards pulled the Human to his knees and held him immobile, with his head lowered. A Baerd technician briskly clipped a translator to the Human's left earlobe, piercing it in the process.

"Ow! Jesus Christ!" The Human tried to rub his ear, but the Srotag on his left held his arm.

"Silence yourself, Human." First Brother Garsh'ee clanged his pincers, but the prisoner didn't seem to understand the significance of that gesture. He cocked his head slightly and listened. Garsh'ee raised one pincer high and thundered out. "You are now prisoner and property of Storhesh, of the Ananab, Captain of the P'Tassum."

Jim Morris raised his head and looked around. He stopped when he got to the three creatures before him, one of which was gesturing wildly, and forgot his stinging ear, his too tightly tied wrists, and the 'mother of all headaches', compliments of Spain, Japan, and oh... maybe Andromeda.

Fully extended, the insectlike aliens were probably close to ten feet long, with two huge arms ending in pincers, four legs, countless tiny tentacles or feelers extending in all directions. But it was their head that captured his attention.

Their jaws appeared to work both sideways, and up and down, somehow. And their eyes. Just two, but each on its own two-foot stalk, moving in unison or opposing directions, apparently at will.

Jim began to wonder if he was in a "special land", created by generous helpings of wine and sake. But the pain in his body told him this was no dream or nightmare.

The bug-eyed monster from outer space in the middle began speaking to him. Amazingly, with the aid of his new "ear ring," it was in English, and he could understand.

"Why did you awaken before the others?"

Jim thought furiously. They couldn't know everything about humans yet, and he had to be very careful what he said.

"I'm an athlete, and in excellent condition," Jim began, ignoring what sounded like derision from the rhino-bear standing next to the bugs. "I also mass a little more than average, and might have some resistance to whatever you did to us because of that?" He ended on a questioning tone.

The bug looked at a slightly built albino humanoid with four arms sitting off to the side at a computer screen.

"Were you partaking in some form of recreational drug that would deaden your nervous system?" The voice coming through the translator sounded skeptical.

Jim nodded to himself, understanding. That would explain a lot. A weapon that targets the nerves, not as efficient, thanks to a long evening of partying.

"We call it alcohol." Jim smiled, careful to keep his teeth hidden. "It tastes good."

Both the rhino-bear and the catman flanking the bugs made sounds that translated into disgust. The pale, four-armed computer tech turned to the bugs.

"Captain, we are getting reports of resistance from deep inside the ship." He glanced at Jim. "Perhaps a result of more alcohol consumption?" Jim shrugged, then nodded his head.

"Maybe."

The big black panther stationed near the bugs began giving commands into his communicator and whirled to face Jim.

"Did you have weapons on your ship?" He barked out the question, obviously expecting Jim to answer.

Jim started to refuse, then reconsidered. This wasn't the time to play hero.

"The ship probably had some small arms," Jim admitted. "I don't know for sure, though."

The middle bug, evidently the Captain, waved a pincer.

"No matter. I am tired of surprises. Commander Tak, Commander Acha, kill any Humans that resist."

"No, wait!" Jim stepped forward, only to be jerked to a halt by the rhino-bear on his right.

Captain Storhesh settled back into his perch and waved the off guard even as he raised a giant club-like fist to smash Jim with.

"Your people must learn one thing right now, Human." Jim recoiled from the totally alien stare of the Captain. "Obey your betters. Any resistance whatsoever will result in immediate punishment. And there is only one form of punishment. Death."

Jim listened to the communicators broadcasting aloud to the room. He could hear the sound of a handgun, then a tremendous explosion. Then silence.

Commander Tryr made a motion that had to be a form of salute.

"All resistance has ceased." The catman looked at Jim and deliberately showed his fangs. "All resisters are dead."

Jim shut his eyes for a moment, then turned back to the main bug.

"Why did you come here? How did you find our planet?"

Captain Storhesh gestured wildly and made a sound that Jim realized was his version of amused laughter.

"How did we find you? You found us! We just answered your call."

The entire room resounded in various forms of sound, all of which the computer translated into laughter.

CHAPTER JIX

Jim wondered where the two Tryr guards were taking him. They rounded a corner, and he saw two of the looming Srotag rhino-bears standing on either side of a door. He wasn't surprised when one of the Tryr placed a heavy paw on his shoulder be bring him to a halt in front of them.

Jim held his bound hands up in a silent request and the other Tryr nodded and touched the rope-like binding with something from his belt. The strands fell to the floor and Jim rubbed his wrists in relief. He felt his self-confidence returning. He and a lot of other Humans were still alive. Hope wasn't unreasonable after all.

"Thank you." He bowed to the two catmen and they seemed amused by the courtesy. "Can I ask your names so that I might remember who treated me so kindly?"

They looked at each other in surprise and suspicion. Obviously, races they considered to be inferior didn't usually initiate social contact or amenities. The Srotag snickered and one of them made a crude remark. Both Tryr glared at them and one flexed his right hand, causing the claws to pop out, one by one. The other answered Jim's question.

"Although you are presumptuous in speaking first, we will tell you." He made a show of yawning, and his fangs shone in the light. "I am Sergeant Tic, and this is Corporal Tac."

Jim was careful to keep a smile from his face. He kept his voice very polite. "Isn't that the same name as your Commander?"

Corporal Tac snorted and shook his head at his sergeant.

"Isn't that just like an inferior race? What can you expect with such tiny ears?" He turned back to Jim, and was condescendingly patient. "Our leader's name is Commander Tak, not Tac."

Some day my irreverent sense of humor is going to get me killed. Jim smiled with his lips firmly pressed closed. He gestured at his ears. "You must pardon my race's defective hearing. I thought I heard you called Toe earlier."

Tic looked surprised, then nodded. "My cousin was standing guard on the bridge." He didn't quite sneer. "Your eyes seem to be as weak as your ears. We look nothing alike."

Of course you don't.

One of the Srotag opened the hatch and motioned impatiently for Jim to enter. It slid shut behind him.

Jim stopped just inside. His mirth evaporated, and he stood there for what seemed like forever. Conflicting emotions swept over him as he looked around the vast room. Almost twice as large as a football field, he was relieved to see it packed with the crews and passengers of the Jade Viking.

But he was also irritated with what else he saw. It took no genius to recognize the polarization between the Japanese and the Americans. Although there were some smaller groupings, such as Jim's own film crew, by and large the division was racial. Didn't they know how petty their prejudices and biases had become in the last twenty-four hours?

Culture shock had taken on a whole new meaning. And talk about foreign...

The sloths were scurrying about, bringing mattresses torn from the ship's cabins and crew areas. Although most of the people seemed physically recovered, many looked to be in a state of shock. They watched the furry workers in glassy-eyed silence.

The opening of the hatch had attracted some people's attention, but there was little reaction. Then he saw Jerry Weinstein wave to him. Jim motioned for him to stay where he was and hurried over to the suddenly stirring group.

A short, stocky woman jumped up and met him with a fierce hug. Others surrounded him, all talking too fast, and at the same time, making it impossible for any of them to be heard. Jim returned the hug, then leaned back to look down at her.

"Come on, Yvette. Surely you weren't worried?" Jim wrapped one arm around her shoulders and accepted handshakes from Jerry and several others. He gestured for everyone to gather closer. The group gradually grew quiet.

"Thankfully, it looks like we all made it here." Jim couldn't keep the relief from his voice. "Anyone who resisted on board the Jade Viking was killed."

He paused to let that sink in. This was going to be tricky. Jim wasn't sure how good the computer was, but he didn't plan on taking any chances.

Everything important would have to be implied, not stated. For all he knew, it could follow the conversations of hundreds of people at once, and translate them all. But could it find the double meanings, current slang, and cultural significance that made up such a large part of American verbal communications? Thank God there weren't any idiots working for Jerry or, for that matter, himself.

"Evidently, there were some handguns stored on board, and some crewmen tried to fight back." Jim deliberately looked around the group. "Fortunately, no one in our 'dance troupe' has any weapons, so we weren't tempted to do the same."

Some of them looked confused, and Jim looked up and around in a very exaggerated manner that wasn't lost on anyone. He made a slow move with his right hand, tracing a Tai Chi exercise that the people with martial arts experience recognized. Almost everyone else in the "troupe"could place the significance, if not the precise motion.

"Without naming any specific exercises, we should try to keep practicing our 'dance' routines, in case we are given a chance to 'demonstrate' our skills to our new 'masters'." Jim's voice grew ironic, and he didn't try to hide his bitterness.

"Everyone must accept our situation, and understand the consequences of any action you may take." Jim's voice hardened and his eyes captured and held his friends and employees immobilized. "We are now the property of Captain Storhesh and this ship. This ship is a marvelous machine, by the way. You should see the computers."

Jim paused for effect.

"They can translate anything." He turned his head so they could see the device on his ear. "Soon, all of you will have one of these to allow you to understand our guards and the workers. They all tie into the main computers."

He watched their faces and felt confident his true meaning was getting through to them.

"I'm glad we're 'artists', and therefore non-violent." He looked around and saw a few of the younger male actors grin at each other. He glared at them and they quickly wiped the looks off their faces. *Good, they understand.* This was going to be touch and go as it was. What he had in mind was, at best, a long shot.

"Mr. Morris, could I have a word with you, please?"

Jim turned around. Captain Lang had a grim, but determined look about him.

"Certainly, Captain. Gentlemen." Jim nodded at the other crewmen that had followed. First Officer Danny DelaRosa and several junior officers gathered around him.

Captain Tachibana and his officers joined them. Jim could see Toshida and some of his men hurrying over. *That's just great, the more the merrier. Yeah, right.*

"Mr. Morris, can you please tell us what is going on?" The Captain's voice was strained.

"I can tell you what little I've learned," Jim nodded. "I'll tell you what I was just telling my 'dance troupe.'"

Captain Lang was no fool and picked right up on it. One glare at his junior officers kept their mouths shut. Jim recapped what he'd already said, and by the time he described the computers and translators, he was surrounded by a large crowd.

Jerry Weinstein shook his head, bewildered.

"What are they going to do with us?" He looked at Jim beseechingly. "If they want to learn about us, why didn't they just ask?"

"They don't have any great desire to 'learn' about us, per se." Jim's voice grew bitter. "To them, we're property. It's as simple as that. They took the ship because it was full of people, and they figured it would show them a profit."

"So there really are flying saucers." Danny DelaRosa shivered. "And they finally decided to grab some of us?"

"No, I don't think these aliens have been flying around, spying on us for years. They just found us recently, and this appears to be the first ship to reach us."

"How did they find Earth at all, then," Kimberly spoke up. Jim hadn't noticed her join the crowd, but was glad to see she seemed recovered from the earlier ordeal.

"I'm afraid we did it to ourselves." Jim's voice grew solemn and he grimaced. "We've been broadcasting radio waves for decades. This ship caught traces of some of our early transmissions."

Jim gave a grim laugh.

"They were able to backtrack and follow the waves' path to Earth. It would seem that we are out in the boondocks, and there is very little traffic in this sector." He paused for effect. "That will probably change shortly. According to this ship's Captain, we have a very rich planet with lots of goodies to plunder."

"But surely if they have all this technology, all this mobility, they must have crossed paths with other races." Captain Lang was incredulous. "Beings this advanced must have evolved socially far beyond us. What do we have that they could use?"

"Better technology doesn't mean better consciences or morals," Captain Tachibana said slowly, his face a study in grimness. "Our own planet's history proves that. How many times has 'civilization' wiped out primitive races or cultures?"

"Bigger kids with bigger toys," Jim agreed. "From what I could see and hear, this ship probably corresponds with an armed merchant ship during the nineteenth century. Except this one has bug-eyed monsters, literally."

Captain Lang raised an eyebrow, inquiringly.

Jim sighed and glanced around the circle of faces. There were too many people here. Almost impossible to control a crowd this size. Or more important, to control their mouths.

"Okay, I think everyone should listen very carefully." Jim paused. "First, everything we say is recorded and translated. We have to assume that. In fact, pretty soon the guards will be coming in to give all of us these fancy earrings." He turned his head to the side to show them. "Second, this ship is manned..."

He gave them a rueful grin. "And I use the term 'manned' very loosely. Anyway, there's more than one race. These little guys running around being porters and cheap labor are the bottom rung of the pecking order. They're the Hoag.

"Some of you have seen the big guys that come in armor or fur." Jim deliberately showed his teeth. "A grin like this to one of the Tryr will get you disemboweled faster than you can imagine. Showing your teeth is a challenge to them. Don't do it."

"Which ones are the Tryr?" Danny frowned. "The big cats?"

Jim nodded. "The Srotag aren't as fast, but their temper is just as short. And they wear their own tank. They outmass us considerably, and are a lot stronger."

He looked from face to face, seeing the complete spectrum of reactions ranging from almost paralyzing fear to anger and defiance. Kimberly gazed back at him, showing a little fear, but also resolve. She gave him a reassuring smile that seemed to show confidence in him that he wished he could share.

"You seem to have learned a lot in so short a time."

Toshida pushed forward, flanked by Nagami and Furukawa. His voiced implied much. He glanced at his captain and spoke in clipped tones.

"Captain Tachibana, we've heard enough from this traitorous coward."
He straightened his shoulders and turned to Lang. "Captain, I relieve you of
your command. You have lost your ship. I shall take charge, effective
immediately."

Captain Lang slowly stretched to his full height. He wasn't as big as the
alien guards, but he was still a full head taller than the Japanese executive. He
looked down at Toshida, eyes hard, and smiled, deliberately showing his own
teeth.

"You seem to have forgotten a minor detail." His voice was surprisingly
soft. "We are no longer aboard Jade Viking. Rank means very little at this
moment."

Toshida's eyes narrowed and he turned his back on Lang and began
speaking Japanese at a furious rate to Tachibana.

Jim gave an inward sigh of relief when the translator didn't automatically
change the words to English. It wouldn't take the ship computer long to pick
up another language, and it probably had the recordings. But by then it might
not matter.

A soft hand touched his arm, and he turned to face Kimberly. She had a
questioning look.

"What did you mean, bug-eyed monsters?" She thought a moment. "Are
there other races?"

Jim nodded and found himself the center of attention again.

"The Tryr and Srotag don't rule this ship. In fact, they're the equivalent of
hired thugs." Jim shivered at the vision of the control deck and Captain
Storhesh and his brothers.

"There are at least two more races that I've seen. One is a four-handed
version of us, I guess. One of them was pretty free with information, which is
how I found out as much as I did. I think he thought he was quizzing me." Jim
took a deep breath. "The other is a nine or ten foot tall insect-like creature. A
mixture of a praying mantis, and a lobster with lots of legs.

One of those lobsters is the Captain of this ship. Two more appear to be his
immediate subordinates."

He gave Captain Lang a meaningful look.

"I think it is very territorial about its authority." Jim chose his words
carefully. "I wouldn't be surprised if an example was made soon."

He noticed Nagami, the head of Sukuru security, watching him closely,
not missing a word, or the hidden meanings.

Jim started to continue, but was interrupted by a commotion from the hatchway.

Tryr and Srotag guards poured in, staking out a large area from the entrance into the middle of the room. The only weapons they carried were handguns, strapped to their sides. Behind them, numerous Hoag massed, floating rafts in tow.

Three large screens flashed on, all showing the same sight. Captain Storhesh dominated each, mandibles opening and closing in alternating sequence, giant pincers thrust forward, seemingly threatening to come right out of the screens.

Jim felt the crowd recoil in horror, yet another blow to their sensibilities. Kimberly shrank against his side, and he instinctively put his arm around her waist. Uncharacteristically, she didn't pull away.

A Tryr Jim thought he recognized as Commander Tak stepped forward. His words came through speakers spaced around the room, harsh and distorted, but in English.

"Silence! You will prepare yourself for commands from Captain Storhesh, your new owner. Afterwards, you will each be fitted with ear translators. Any interference or resistance will be punished." His grin showed powerful fangs, curved and razor-sharp. "Immediately."

Captain Storhesh thundered over the loudspeakers.

"You are now the property of the Ananab."

Jim couldn't read the alien expression, but the tone was full of contempt and gloating.

"After we reach Station Chaq, our home base, you will be sorted into usable skills and distributed accordingly. Between now and then, you will be inventoried and evaluated."

Captain Storhesh settled back into his perch and seemed to be finished. The guards obviously knew better, because none of them budged. Finally, he leaned forward again.

"Do you have a leader? Who among you would be considered 'in command'?"

Yoshi Toshida stepped forward confidently. Both Captains glared at his back and began to react. Jim released Kimberly and moved forward to grasp both of their elbows.

As one, they turned to him, and he advised them in a conspiratorial whisper.

"Gentlemen, let the Wookie win."

Captain Tachibana's brow furled in puzzlement. Captain Lang also looked confused for a moment, then understanding showed on his face. He glanced at Tachibana and began to pull away. Jim tightened his grip. "We are going to need you." Jim's eyes begged them to understand. "Both of you."

As they hesitated, Toshida spoke in a bold voice. "I am in charge of this group, in the name of Sukuru Corporation." He bowed slightly to the alien captain. "Perhaps we could speak privately about this."

"You are in charge of all these...beings?"

Jim couldn't believe Toshida didn't hear the baiting tone in the alien's voice. He noticed that neither Furukawa nor Nagami had stepped forward with him. They had caught Jim's move with the captains and hung back.

"I am."

"Come forward."

Toshida moved into the group of guards, which opened to admit him. They closed around him, but made no further move. He treated them as though they were his personal retinue. Jim couldn't help admiring his boldness, even as he felt sorry for the man.

"Who are you?" Jim imagined he heard amusement in the voice of Captain Storhesh.

"I am Yoshi Toshida, executive vice president of Sukuru Corporation, owner of the Jade Samurai." Toshida looked relaxed, as if he felt in control of the situation. He didn't notice Commander Acha towering behind him.

"Tell me more." If Storhesh had been a Tryr, he would have been purring.

Toshida had a triumphant expression and Jim no longer felt sorry for him. The Japanese businessman was shameless, as he began telling Storhesh how helpful Sukuru could be if they came to an agreement. The alien captain quickly tired of him.

"Enough!" The loudspeaker roared. "Understand this! All of you. Your ship is mine. You are mine. Any other thoughts have one result!" He gave a careless wave of his pincer and Acha seized Toshida from behind. The armored giant closed both massive hands around the human's head and squeezed. Four powerful digits on each paw pressed deep into Toshida's skull. His head exploded from the pressure, spraying blood and brains in every direction.

The guards roared in laughter. Acha expressively wiped his paws on Toshida's silk shirt and tossed the body on a raft.

"You are my property to do with as I please."

Captain Storhesh leaned forward and his face filled the screens.

"Accept it."

CHAPTER JEVEN

Kimberly Martin stood and thanked the older couple across the folding table from her. They hesitantly rose from their seats and moved off towards the area reserved for sleeping. She felt sympathy for them. They were both retired, and their background was in retail. This wasn't much of a useful skill to the Ananab, and they knew it.

The next person in line sat down and nervously folded his hands on his lap. He was young, probably not even eighteen yet. She forced a smile and keyed the computer for a fresh entry.

"Your name?"

"Jim Spann."

He was one of the group of kids from a small high school just outside of San Diego. This was a senior class trip that would never be forgotten.

Taking the relevant information about him only took a small portion of her attention. As she typed in the data, she glanced around.

Working on either side of her were three others, equally bored with their task. She'd had plenty of time to get to know them over the past couple of days. Yvette Stephanian was on her right. She was the short woman that had hugged Jim as he was returned by the aliens. Kimberly had talked with her several times, and liked her.

Yvette had a no-nonsense attitude and the same quiet efficiency that Kimberly herself possessed. She was only five feet tall, in her late thirties, and reminded Kimberly of an Italian Momma, although she was actually Armenian. Her great-grandparents had fled Turkey during the massacres of 1919, bringing nothing but a hand-pulled cart piled high with rugs. They had settled in Detroit, and turned the hand-woven Persian rugs into a small but profitable business that had grown many times over. Her family was now a major import distributor in Middle Eastern arts and crafts.

She had gone to the University of Michigan to learn the finer legal and financial intricacies of the import/export business. It was there that she met Jim and found herself working part time, helping him and Hakim on some of their earliest jobs. The rest was, as they say, history.

Yvette and her longtime companion and lover, Janice Wooley, were as different as night and day, except for their devotion to Jim and each other. Janice was five and a half feet tall and barely weighed 100 pounds. Yvette constantly stuffed vast amounts of food into her while starving herself, trying to keep her own weight down.

It was a standing joke that Yvette could walk by a bakery and pick up two pounds, all on her hips. Janice, on the other hand, could go into the same bakery, eat an entire cheesecake, and not gain an ounce.

To the right of Yvette sat the ex-personal secretary of Yoshi Toshida. Suyo Takashi was a homely middle-aged Japanese woman Toshida had beaten all the spirit out of years ago.

Takashi seldom spoke. Even when she did, her conversation was restricted to business. As far as Kimberly could tell, she had no personal life whatsoever.

Kimberly could hear the Japanese woman's voice, droning softly, showing no interest in the answers to her questions. Her job was to record the responses, and that was what she did. If she felt any resentment about the circumstances surrounding Toshida's death, she didn't show it.

The fourth person collecting data sat to Kimberly's left. He was Randy Luca, purser of the Jade Viking. He was a plump, jovial man in his fifties. Kimberly liked the way he spoke with the people in his line. He tried to help them relax, and feel a little more comfortable. He didn't downplay the seriousness of the situation, but didn't act like things were hopeless, either.

Their job was a discouraging one. The crew numbered about twelve hundred, almost evenly divided between American and Japanese. There were more than 2,300 passengers and entertainers aboard. Each was being interviewed, however briefly.

There had been 47 casualties during the hijacking, twenty two trying to resist, the remainder mostly heart attacks. One man had fallen down a hatch, cracking his skull. He had never recovered consciousness.

And, of course, Yoshi Toshida.

After Toshida's death, Jim had been singled out and told to organize the Humans and their capabilities. He had protested he wasn't a leader, but it had fallen upon deaf ears, or antennas, or whatever the bugs had.

Jim and the two captains had gotten their heads together and held a brief conference. Yvette and Janice had "conveniently" begun singing "Amazing Grace," and soon most of the Americans, and even some of the Japanese had joined in. Kimberly was impressed. Unless the alien computers were even better than they suspected, the three should have had privacy for their talk.

Jim had requested access to some equipment, specifically, personal computers. At first, the aliens had been suspicious, but Jim had pointed out that humans didn't know how to use the ship's keyboards or software. Much to his surprise, the aliens had agreed, and Jim had led a small group of humans back into the Jade Viking, accompanied by alert guards and a number of Hoag workers.

They had returned with the PCs and some pillows and more bedding for the older prisoners. Yvette and Janice had started trying to figure out how to interface the small computers with the ships computer. At that point they got lucky.

Rick Baker was a passenger who would have been considered a computer geek in the states, but here he was a cherished find. In next to no time, he had the ship's computer talking to the PCs and the data exchange began.

It turned out that Janice also had a knack for working with computers, and soon the two of them were setting up work stations.

Kimberly glanced over at them, covertly. They had their heads to a fifth terminal, and were constantly edging each other out of the way to get at the keyboard. She shook her head, amused.

Two of the four-armed albino aliens had helped them get started, and then sat back and watched in interest. Jim had been nervous about that, and after a few carefully phrased comments, Rick and Janice curbed their excitement and temporarily settled down. Eventually, the aliens had left.

That was two days ago, and Kimberly and Jim had only exchanged a few words. He acted wary of her, and she didn't know how she felt about him, but there was something very powerful at work, making them very aware of each other, even as he was being drawn into a leadership role he didn't seem to relish. Kimberly was both irritated with his reluctance and, irrationally, proud of the way he was dealing with the necessity.

I have to decide how I feel about him, she pondered. And I have to find out what the story is with that little brat, Afsaneh. There's more to that little number than meets the eye.

With a start, Kimberly realized that she had finished with all the people in her line. Next to her, Randy did the same.

"Oh, my aching back," he groaned. "These folding chairs aren't designed for someone my size."

That's for sure. He was a very big guy. And not big like Captain Lang. It's amazing how often overweight people compensate with wonderful personalities and senses of humor, she mused. Randy had made jokes and cheered everyone up through a very depressing chore.

"I don't know if I'm glad we're done or not." Kimberly was cautious. "What happens next?"

Randy frowned.

"Good point," he admitted. "I doubt the retirement benefits are worth a darn in this two-bit operation."

Kimberly smiled, in spite of herself. "You never stop, do you?"

"And thank God for that." Yvette was also finished, and Suyo Takashi was dismissing her last person.

"I don't know if I could have stood this without your sense of humor, Randy." Yvette was serious.

Randy blushed, embarrassed. He carefully wiped at a non-existent smudge on his table.

"I just think everyone can use a little cheering up." He raised his head. "I mean, it's not like it's the end of the world..." His voice faded away as he realized the irony.

Kimberly felt a wave of panic sweep over her at the thought. Was it the end of the world? It certainly was as they knew it. Beside her, Yvette's face showed the same emotion.

A small voice spoke up, and Kimberly was shocked to find it was Suyo's.

"Maybe not the end, but certainly 'out' of this world." Suyo had a blank expression that softened into a timid smile as they all looked at her, startled. "We could use Godzilla right about now. Or Mothra."

Randy gave a tiny giggle that sounded out of place in his large body. Then they all gave in to a laughter that wasn't so much recognition of a joke, as a common sharing of their fears and appreciation for the strength that they all possessed, if not at the same time.

Kimberly and Yvette hugged each other, laughing and crying, simultaneously. Kimberly followed Yvette's gaze to where Janice and Rick were still huddled, oblivious to everything but the screen in front of them.

Yvette shook her head, wryly.

"I don't know if I'm supposed to be jealous or not," she admitted, smiling at Kimberly to show she was kidding. "And if so, at which? The boy or the computer?"

They laughed and turned to Suyo.

"I'm so glad to hear you able to joke," Kimberly told her. "I wasn't certain how you felt, working with us."

Suyo looked serious.

"I wasn't sure myself," she admitted. "At first, I felt my employer had been betrayed by not warning him of the danger. But then at the end, he was ready to sell out everyone and everything for his own sake." Her voice grew somber. "And for the sake of Sukuru."

Kimberly watched her, fascinated. She had felt the same thing, but she didn't work for the Japanese corporation.

Suyo closed the last file on her computer with a flourish. "I am a very loyal employee." She leaned back and cupped her hands behind her head. "But you know..." Her voice gained a tiny bit of lightness. "...he really was a son of a butch."

Kimberly heard a snort, and she looked cautiously over at Randy. He had a hand over his face, and was trying hard not to laugh.

Yvette leaned over and placed her hand on Suyo's arm. "Probably not," she confided. "Trust me, I can tell."

Jim looked around, bemused, as he entered the warehouse room that served as "home" to the humans. Sounds of laughter was a pleasant, if unexpected, surprise. He quickly found the source and smiled as he walked up to them.

"Are we having fun yet?" He glanced quizzically from Kimberly to Yvette.

"Oh, we're just having a gay old time," Randy smirked.

Jim rolled his eyes, and looked at Yvette fondly. "I won't ask. It is good to hear someone laugh, though."

He grew serious and turned to Kimberly. "I take it you've finished the, uh...inventory. Anything promising?"

"We have a nice variety of skilled labor, although I'm not sure any of those 'skills' apply to this particular situation." Jim gave a slight nod of approval as Kimberly chose her words carefully. "I mean, I don't know what the 'masters' are looking for." She grimaced at the title they had been told was proper for the Ananab.

"What about tailors or seamstresses?" Jim asked innocently. "We're trying to get a chance to audition our 'dance troupe,' and I think we'll need help with the costumes."

"There were at least two." If Kimberly found the request curious, she kept her opinion well hidden.

Thank god for smart people. Jim relaxed and glanced at Rick Baker and Janice Wooley huddled over their dual work-station. *And people that get into their work, although I hope they're careful. Some of these aliens have to be smart, don't they? Maybe smart, but not clever.* Now there was a thought to consider.

Jim smiled brightly. "I'm hoping we can interest the Masters in some of our art forms, in particular, dance. If they like it, we might find ourselves a little more secure."

He could tell Kimberly was finding his portrayal of the cheerful, enthusiastic, brainless artist amusing. "I know I would prefer that to digging ditches, or the intergalactic equivalent."

He wanted to talk, and Kimberly probably did too. But now was not the time. There was too much to do, and he didn't know how long they had until this ship reached its destination. But they still had to eat, didn't they?

"How about dinner?" Jim smiled as he saw he'd startled her. Good, that was an unexpected question. She met his gaze and their eyes locked. Jim felt himself slip and lose traction deep inside her, surrounded by her presence. *Those eyes. Jesus, how could someone have those eyes and be a shyster?*

Jim took a deep breath, sounding louder than a tsunami to him. She didn't seem to notice. Then he heard her sigh, and saw her give in to a strangely poignant, wistful smile.

"That would be nice," Kimberly kept her eyes meeting his. "There's a lot for us to talk about."

"Yes," Jim agreed weakly. "A lot to talk about." He backed slowly away from her and distantly heard himself say, "I have to go now. Um, to talk to Rick."

"Um, me too," Yvette smiled sweetly up at him, he vaguely noticed. She snickered and he pulled himself together.

"All right, smart ass," Jim felt dazed, but knew better than to give Yvette any ground. She giggled.

They walked up behind Rick and Janice, who barely noticed their arrival. Jim nudged Yvette, and she began talking loudly with Janice who, after a confused moment, caught on and joined in.

Jim spoke quietly with Rick, moving his lips as little as possible. "Did it tell you how they've dealt with other captives?"

"As far as I can tell, this is the first race the Ananab have discovered on their own." Rick sounded uncertain. "There doesn't seem to be a precedent. There are a lot of beings out there that are chattel, or at least dominated by an older race. But there's no record of the Ananab ever discovering a new species."

Jim frowned. When he was on the bridge, he hadn't gotten the impression that this was all that unusual. The Captain seemed confident. On the other hand, why shouldn't he be? With Tryr and Srotag goons, what could go wrong?

"One bit of bad news," Rick sounded gloom. "These aliens don't seem very enlightened. He who holds the guns, holds the merchandise. Power is the deciding factor in a dispute between races."

"You mean there isn't any 'United Planets', or 'Union of Races' to govern things, or settle arguments?" Jim was nonplussed. "How do they keep from killing each other off? Or spending all their time trying to?"

"There appears to be a pecking order, to a certain extent," Rick typed briefly and a list of names showed on the screen. "The Ananab pay tribute to the Hstahni, and respect their territories and demands. The Hstahni don't bow to anyone, as far as I can tell."

Jim was bewildered. He fought the urge to look around for cameras. Something was very wrong here. His voice grew even more quiet.

"Rick, I asked you to see if the computer would tell us the procedure when the Ananab take prisoners." Jim was sure this had to be a trap. "How did you find out all this political stuff?"

Jim watched the young man struggle to hide his excitement. Rick brought his face under control, and with a voice only slightly showing his glee, answered.

"I just started asking about prisoners." Rick smiled with what he probably thought was an evil expression, but just looked silly with his youthful face.

"The computer told me how individual prisoners were treated, and I asked for incidents involving larger numbers. There weren't any that included Ananab, so I asked if there were other examples." Rick lost the battle to keep a wide grin off his face. "It gave me some answers and new directions to search."

Rick leaned forward and Jim groaned inwardly. God, I hope none of these aliens can read human facial expressions yet.

"It never said no." Rick's voice dropped to a theatrical whisper. "There appear to be no security locks on this computer, except around the Ananab living quarters. They've never had a large group of computer-literate prisoners like this. I don't think they know what they're doing!"

"Not that it matters," Jim said carefully. He hoped Rick was getting this hint. "After all, with so many Tryr and Srotag guards on board, what could happen?"

Jim had to give Rick credit. He was quick on the uptake. "I mean, with them being so large and strong, and of course, being the only ones armed, what could happen?" Rick agreed. "I mean, when we're talking about a bakers selection of your cops' favorite pasttime." Rick gave him a challenging look as if to say, can you figure this one out?

"Are we talking baked and fried?" Jim smiled back, enjoying himself despite the seriousness of the topic.

"Right!" Rick nodded vigorously. "Of each!"

Damn, Jim swore silently. At least a dozen of each. That was a lot of bengal tigers and armored bears.

"Okay, keep it up," Jim decided they had pushed their luck far enough with this conversation. "See if you can find out if our metabolism matches theirs, or if we need our own source of food."

"Ah," Rick nodded knowingly. "Perhaps a complete comparison of the different physiologies might help."

"That would be fine," Jim left him typing away madly. Yvette and Janice sighed, and sat down in relief, lowering their voices gratefully. I'll be lucky if that kid doesn't get us all killed, Jim thought glumly.

He found Tachibana and Lang playing a game of Go with a makeshift set. Several of their officers watched, silently cheering their respective leaders.

"Gentle Sirs," Jim bowed slightly to them and sat to one side of the game. The younger officers eagerly made room for him. "I've returned from the ship with our 'troupe' equipment and costumes."

"Did everything go well?" Captain Lang hid his concern well and sounded only slightly interested.

"Fine, I think." Jim paused. "Several of my group had handguns in their luggage, and of course we turned them over to the guards at once."

"Of course," nodded Captain Tachibana. "We certainly do not want to cause any trouble, or to allow anything to make the masters angry with us." His voice grated slightly at the word.

"We have several people working hard at the computer to find out what we need to know..." Jim smiled at the two older men's sudden attentiveness. "...to make the transition to our new lives. I think they're doing a very good job."

Jim watched Captain Lang fingering his translator, obviously disliking the feel. Earrings were not his style. He felt sorry for the two men. He liked them both and knew that they chafed at having to depend on a "movie star" doing most of the work. They were used to being in control and were like fish out of water.

"I think the masters are going to let us demonstrate our skill." Jim had everyone's attention now. "If our arts are appreciated, this could be a very good thing for all of us."

"Indeed," Captain Tachibana tried to sound enthusiastic, but failed. "Indeed," he repeated, dully.

Jim watched across the game as Sukuru Security Head Nagami and Furukawa approached. As one they bowed to him.

"Jim Morris-sa..." Nagami got a funny look on his face. "Mr. Morris, would you consider two old, but still able, 'dancers' to join your troupe? I fear we have little else to offer our..." He had even more trouble with the word than the Captains did. "...Masters."

Jim raised his eyebrows, surprised. He looked first at Lang, then Tachibana. They both shrugged, then Tachibana nodded slightly.

He stood up and met them at the same level. They both looked back at him, expressionless. Then Nagami smiled, his lips carefully closed.

"Our pasts have little to do with our present." The slightest humor appeared in his eyes. "Or our future. Let us join you and help, under your guidance."

Jim knew what it had to have cost to say those words, and admired their strength. *Nagami is right, it is time to move on. The past is past.* He smiled grimly and nodded.

They bowed again and exchanged triumphant looks.

How true, he sighed to himself. *The past is past. What I thought was right before, was right. But this is different, and I can't afford the luxury of living quietly, or avoiding a challenge.*

Jim stretched lazily and touched the floor flathanded without bending his knees. He straightened and stared at the two men. *So, you boys are now part of the* Weeping Winds *dance troupe, and with your help, we will overcome these odds.* But, he thought, as his heart grew cold and his face stiffened. *If* either of you try to screw with me, I'll hand you your heads. They both correctly interpreted the look, and for the first time, he suspected they took him seriously.

Will Spencer threw the newspaper down on his desk in disgust. Why not get his updates from the Times. The authorities weren't telling him anything!

He stood up and walked over to one of the windows, feeling restless. New York City stretched out before him. Far below, he could see the usual early evening flurry of activity as offices all over the city let out for the day.

The Spencer Building was just under seventy stories, and his corner office was on the sixty-eighth floor. From this height, people were almost indiscernable, and cars were the size of match heads.

Usually, this view gave him a lift, restored his feelings of invincibility and superiority. He prided himself in having control of his life, and of most aspects that touched it.

But he'd lost something that was his. True, he'd planned on selling it. In fact, had things gone properly, by today, it would have been sold. But that wasn't what happened!

Jade Viking had been just one cog in a complex deal he and Kimberly Martin had spent the last nine months engineering. Sukuru Corporation was, in essence, a Japanese version of The Spencer Group, and both had access to markets the other could flourish in.

Will had sent Kimberly specifically so that nothing would go wrong. Jade Viking docking in San Francisco would have been the catalytic event that sparked the entire deal.

Sukuru would gain the ship, of course, and the docks and warehouses that covered hundreds of square acres with prime harbor access. They would also acquire thousands of square miles of forests in Oregon, cattle lands in Montana and Wyoming, 50 percent of the deal to build and operate bullet trains joining Chicago and Detroit, San Francisco and Los Angeles, and the grand plum, New York and Miami.

Spencer would gain entry into the exclusive Japanese market, controlling shares of Indonesian oil fields, two super tankers, an entire block of office buildings in downtown Tokyo, and a slew of other, smaller interests.

It was, if not impossible, very difficult for an American corporation to make any significant headway into the Japanese business world.

But he'd done it! His company and the Toshida Clan had ironed out every single rough spot. And Jade Viking should have docked two days ago.

So, where was his ship? And Kimberly Martin, his lawyer and the woman he planned on eventually marrying. That is, whenever he got around to seriously pursuing her and proposing.

And where was Toshida, and all the other people that had been aboard? He'd just read a report that said absolutely no debris had been discovered. A ship that size didn't sink, explode, break up, or fall into a black hole without some debris showing up somewhere.

A hijacking? Where did you hide a ship that big? Not to mention the 3,500 crew and passengers.

He frowned. The Toshidas were certainly capable of pulling some stunt for their own purposes, but to what gain? Their potential profits with the deal far surpassed any possible advantage Will could think of that treachery might afford them.

On the other hand, Yoshi Toshida was the most ruthless man he'd ever known. With the possible exception of himself, of course.

So what was going on?

The sound of his phone made him turn away from the window. It was his secretary. She told him he had a call from Japan on line one. He glanced at his watch in surprise.

It was early morning in Japan. Very early morning. That didn't sound good.

"Who is it, Mrs. Barnes?" he asked, trying to think who would cover for Toshida.

"Sho Toshida, calling for Miyazaki Toshida, Sir."

Yoshi's son was calling for his uncle, the old man himself? He was supposedly retired, although Will was skeptical about that. Of course, he'd never actually met the man, but rumors abounded about the older brother and his ties to organized crime.

"Have we heard anything back from the Coast Guard, the FBI, or any of the authorities?" He didn't expect that she had, or else he would have been informed. And, he was right. Too bad, it would've been nice to have some new tidbit to throw to Sukuru.

Will pushed the button with some trepidation. "Good Morning, Toshida-san..."

CHAPTER EIGHT

The viewing screen showed the human, Jim M'rson, eating his evening meal with one of the females. They both ate slowly, with very little conversation.

Chief Technician Lasty switched to infra-red and grunted with interest. That was peculiar. The readings on both of them appeared to be agitated. Their breath was labored, pulses were erratic, and their heat levels were increased dramatically in certain parts of their bodies. Then he sat back in satisfaction, understanding.

Ah, a mating ritual of some sort. Some of the television broadcasts he had recently monitored dealt with that. Soon, the male would put one of those strange white tubes in his mouth and set it on fire. Then she would smile and insult him, and perhaps strike him across the face. It was interesting that humans incorporated violence into their procreating, just as the Tryr and Srotag did. Except that for the Tryr and Srotang, the violence wasn't so much to enhance the sex as it was for its own sake.

Lasty had been listening in on Human conversations as often as he could spare the time. Unfortunately, there were so many of them that the ship's computer couldn't simultaneously record and analyze everything being said and still perform its normal functions unless Lasty made some major changes to how it routed the data.

He found it necessary to have the computer concentrate on specific individuals, primarily the Humans that stood out from the crowd. Anyone that worked on emptying the ship, used the comp-link, or showed any leadership qualities was watched and recorded.

It was very difficult when they were all in the same area. When there were so many voices at once, the sounds became jumbled together, even using the translators as recorders. If the language was well-documented, it would be

97

simple to screen out unwanted sound, enhance certain voices, and end up with a reliable transcript, but the basis for translation was broadcasts that had been originally sent over a period of close to one hundred of the local time units known as years. One wouldn't think there could be that many changes in a language in such a short time, but there were.

This language had so many "current" uses for words. Some words meant different things at different times. Sometimes the context changed the meaning. Also, this planet "Earth" had many other languages, and words were taken freely and added to the everyday usage mix.

Lasty had asked the computer to create a social profile and, not surprisingly, it had stalled at the task. Not enough data. Too much data! Conflicting data!!

The Humans had surprised and dismayed him when they requested the computer link. It was a good idea, but unlikely under the circumstances. They were prisoners, forcibly taken from their home planet, and their leader had been brutally executed in front of them. They should be frightened into huddled, trembling masses, incapable of any rational thought.

Instead, they had the presence of mind to facilitate the chore of organizing themselves for the Ananab. They showed a deliberateness and focus that frightened Lasty and his fellow Baerd. Upon examination, the human computer was found to be crude, slow, and limited in its scope. But the Humans had found a way to allow them to interact with the ship's computer, with almost no help from the Baerd supervising them.

Eyr and Dutter had returned, chuckling at first about the limited scope of the computers and their crude keyboards, limited by their lack of a sixth digit and two more arms. Even if they found a way to make the link work, they would be so hampered by their own limitations that the return trip would be long over.

But they were done!

Two of the Humans had set up the initial link, then rapidly cloned the concept for the other work stations. Then four other humans had sat down and, with little instruction, done the entire inventory themselves!

Capturing computer-literate races frightened Lasty. As far as he knew, it had never been done before. Most sentient races found were at the early stages of development, and their progress was carefully controlled, molding them to the needs of their new masters.

These Humans were already more advanced than many of the subject races in known space. And they were clever, very clever. It couldn't be a coincidence that every time certain people sat down together to speak, the noise level rose significantly. Of course, once Lasty had recognized what they were doing, he had instructed the computer to single out all such occurrences, and filter out all masking sounds.

It didn't really help much. Neither he nor the computer could figure out the gist of the conversation most of the time. And when they did, it didn't seem to make much sense.

Could it be a code? Lasty chuckled to himself at his paranoia. How could it be? It wasn't as if the Humans had any warning they were about to be taken. And they certainly hadn't had any private time since. The ship recorded all interaction on board, and the Humans had been closely scrutinized each time they went to their ocean vessel.

They had even turned in several hand weapons before the guards had a chance to confiscate them. Those weapons bothered Lasty. When the ship was taken, several Humans had fought to the death, using the same type as turned in. Why did some fight so fiercely, and some not?

Humans were capable of violence, he knew for sure. Their broadcasts, some of which he belatedly identified as entertainment, showed that. They had wars, they killed each other. They had created long distance weapons with a firepower that Lasty was sure the Ananab were underestimating. They might not have space travel, but any ship venturing into the planets atmosphere ran the risk of being blown out of the sky. Tractor beams and force shields could only do so much.

Lasty debated putting a block on their access to the main computer. So far, they hadn't done anything dangerous, but what next? The clever duo at the keyboard were wandering in a bewildering variety of directions. They had checked on precedence to their plight, and spent a while studying the political structure of known space. Then they had moved to specifics regarding this ship, the crew, and physical data comparing the various races. At this point, they seemed to be focused on dietetic concerns, but had also accessed biology charts and compared bone structures between themselves and the crew.

They were obviously hiding something, but what? Lasty just couldn't see the point. The ship computer would not obey an order that physically endangered the Ananab, such as pumping atmosphere out of compartments, or changing its composition to knock out or kill their captors.

Lasty had checked the contents of the cargo holds for the Jade Viking and found only one shipment that could prove dangerous. But the they hadn't even tried to go near it. True, there were a lot of Humans, but they were clustered into controlled groups, and without weapons, should be harmless.

One thing Lasty knew only too well. The Tryr and Srotang were unstoppable in battle with unarmed opponents. Further, the guards were armed. Lasty doubted a hundred Humans could overpower one Tryr or Srotang with a sidearm. So direct combat was out of the question. What did that leave?

Could they actually believe they could ingratiate themselves to the Ananab and by doing so, improve their lot? The Humans were potential competition for the Baerd themselves, but untrained and totally ignorant of the intergalactic community of races they had just been dragged into. On the other hand, wasn't that exactly what they were using the computer for, to find out more about their new surroundings?

This entertainment they were preparing to show to the Captain and his brothers, was it just a ploy?

Lasty turned back to his terminal and brought up memory files from earlier in the day. There had been a lot of activity in the Human holding tank. A full dozen scantily clad Humans moved in an intricate pattern, with an agility and energy that he found compelling.

"I'm surprised at how interesting these Humans are."

Lasty flinched as Dutter spoke up from behind him. He hadn't even heard her approach. He swiveled around to face her. "I'm surprised at how frightening they are," he replied dryly.

"Did you notice they're accessing anatomy files on the Tryr and Srotag?" Dutter sounded skeptical. "What possible reason could they have for that?"

"According to their initial request, they're checking to see how compatible the races are for dietetic purposes." Lasty smiled at her, amused by the thought. "They're concerned about being poisoned or developing vitamin deficiencies. You would think they would have bigger problems than that to worry about."

"Maybe they do." Dutter had a thoughtful look. "Have they accessed our profiles? Or the Hoag, the Ananab?"

"No..." Lasty stared at her blankly. "Is it an oversight? I can understand ignoring the Ananab. They are quite different. But our metabolism matches the Humans quite closely, even to the point to chemical balances and vitamin needs."

"We can't ah...be interbred with them, can we?" Dutter's face acquired a distinct pinkish tinge.

Lasty was shocked. His back straightened indignantly. "Of course not!"

He stared at her. "Whatever gave you that thought?"

She shrugged and the pink spread down her neck into her shoulders. She looked downward, and from side to side, studiously avoiding his eyes. "I didn't mean I had any urge to copulate with them, but..." The pink spread out of sight beneath the top of her shapeless smock, its dull grey accenting both the pink, and the contrasting whiteness of the rest of her body. "...I watched some of the recordings from the human rest periods. Some of the Humans have very active sexual habits. I must admit, I found it..." She boldly raised her eyes to meet his. "...stimulating."

Lasty grew uncomfortably aware of how long it had been since his last sexual activity. He also realized his face was at least as pink as hers. Baerd were usually abstinent while serving on missions for other races. He had never really had any problem with that custom until now. Dutter really was quite attractive.

"Well..." his voice cracked slightly, and he coughed in irritation. "I must admit I have also seen several of these ...activities. They can be very, um, enthusiastic."

"And imaginative." Her voice also sounded slightly hoarse.

They looked at each other in panic. Their customs didn't really allow for what was almost certainly going to happen very shortly. Neither of them had mates, but her clan and his had never made any mutual arrangements. This was not a trivial thing, most certainly not something to be caused by watching a primitive race rut. He looked at her bright pink shoulders and sighed. That wasn't going to stop either of them, he could see.

"Well, well, aren't we in an excited state." Commander Garsh-hee loomed over them, leering. One mandible pushed gently against one of Dutter's right arms and it turned white from the pressure. As he removed it, the pink flooded back, brighter than ever.

"C-c-commander," Lasty stuttered in fear. "We were just talking about these Humans. We've been observing them and think there is a chance they are up to some sort of mischief."

"I suppose they are going to come up here and rip my eyes out," The towering insectoid sneered. "After they tear the Tryr and the Srotag apart with their bare hands."

"Of course not," Lasty was frustrated. "But they are up to something. I just don't know what."

"I do." The Ananab had the annoying ability to sound supremely smug.

"You do?" Lasty looked at Dutter in confusion. How could an Ananab have picked up something he had missed. She mirrored his feelings.

"Of course." Commander Garsh-hee laughed uproariously. "For some stupid reason, they want your job." He peered at them with his long eye stalks swaying with humor. "They might get it. too!" Howling with laughter, he turned and went back to his station.

Lasty heard a discreet cough behind him. His duty replacement, Eyr stood there, looking back and forth at the two of them in confusion. Sudden understanding caused his eyes to widen. "I relieve you, sir." He was formal, obviously disapproving. "Your shifts are finished."

"Fine." Lasty turned and, allowing Dutter to preceed him, made to leave the bridge. Behind them, they could hear the commander yelling obscene suggestions and their pace increased. By the time they reached the exit they were practically running.

CHAPTER NINE

Kimberly followed Jim as he found them a spot against the wall near where the "dance group" usually rehearsed. It offered a hint of privacy and the illusion of intimacy. A cart piled high with props and a large pannier rested against the wall on one side while the looming entrance hatch created a gap on the other.

"May I offer you a seat, madam?" He made a sweeping gesture with his right arm, careful not to spill the cup of water he carried. In his other hand he held the plate of food that constituted dinner this evening.

Kimberly Martin smiled at him and gratefully lowered herself to the floor. With a sigh she leaned back and set her cup down to one side, resting her plate on her lap.

"It feels good to have a backrest." She watched him sit down, not using either hand, gracefully ending up facing her with his legs crossed. "With all these people, wall space is hard to come by."

He smiled back at her and raised his cup, offering a toast. "To a time when certain comforts return."

"Like privacy." Kimberly looked around ruefully at the crowded room, scant feet separating them from nearby people eating their own meals.

Jim looked apologetic and agreed. "That would be nice. Getting a partition for the bathroom area was hard enough, separate dining is out of the question." His face hardened slightly. "For the moment."

Kimberly wished she knew more details about the plans for escape. She knew it was related to the "dance group", but since they had to assume the computer recorded everything, everyone was intentionally vague about specifics.

She took a piece of bread from her plate and nibbled at an edge. It was surprisingly good. Captain Lang and several of the ships' chefs had talked with the Baerd supervising their feeding, and since then, the Humans had helped prepare the meals. Each offering was an adventure, combining familiar tasting dishes with totally unknown items, with mixed results. Some were quite good, most were bland, and a few were God-awful.

This meal was a stew prepared primarily with foodstuffs from their ship. Their captors had decided to use up the supplies from the Jade Viking, saving on their own rations in the process. Thirty-five hundred people could eat a lot of food, and the Ananab certainly hadn't known they would be gaining that many mouths to feed when they set out on this voyage.

"This bread is good." Jim echoed her thoughts as he took another bite. "Even the stew isn't too bad. I hope we don't have too many vegetarians, though."

Kimberly looked at him in surprise. "I hadn't even thought about that," she admitted. "What do they do?"

"Most of them have had to give it up," Jim didn't sound too concerned about that. "A few people are hardcore about it, and the cooking staff has done its best to accommodate them. Thank God there aren't too many."

"I take it you aren't a vegetarian," Kimberly noted dryly. "You might have a different viewpoint if you were."

"True," Jim laughed. "But I'm not. I'm a confirmed carnivore who loves meat. I've never really understood how they can be satisfied with a meal of shrubbery."

"Shrubbery!" Kimberly squinted at him, trying to look severe. "It's not just vegetables, you know. There's pasta, fruit, breads, vegetables…"she admitted and then pinched her thigh disparagingly. "…and desserts!"

Jim snorted and looked at her skeptically. "If you're trying to tell me any sweets have settled on your legs, or anywhere else on your body for that matter, give it up."

Kimberly felt a flush of pleasure reminiscent of schoolgirl days at the compliment, and couldn't resist smiling in response.

"You aren't vegetarian, are you?" Jim raised a single eyebrow in mock scrutiny as he peered at her plate. "I've got several people in our cast and crew that are. Personally, I've always felt you are what you eat." He laughed. "I've known a few vegetables in my line of work."

"Oh?" She arched her eyebrows. "Does that make you a cow, or a pig? Or a chicken?" She winced as she realized the personal implications of the last choice. Brilliant, Martin, way to go. Destroy the first comfortable conversation you've had with him since you met him. She looked down at her food in frustration. Suddenly she wasn't very hungry anymore.

"Hey."

She looked up, startled at the gentleness in his voice. He had a pensive expression, and she realized he wanted this meal to go well at least as much as she did. He smiled ruefully.

"Point taken." He gave her a sly grin, slightly lopsided. "If we don't get into that, I won't mention your fat thighs."

"What?" She feigned anger and arched her back in mock indignation. Then she started laughing and he joined in. After a few moments, they stopped and sat there, looking at each other. He had his little smile, and she knew she wasn't doing a good job of concealing her own feelings.

"All right, mister." She gave him as fierce a look as she could manage. "Eat your meal." She scowled. "And don't skip the carrots."

The next hour passed quickly as they hesitantly began to talk, primarily about general things. Gradually, the topics became more personal. Kimberly found herself telling him things she hadn't shared with anyone in years.

"So, after I divorced him, I went back to Vanderbilt and finished my Masters degree in Business Management." She grimaced, remembering. "That bastard messed with my mind to the point that I had no self-confidence left. It took me two semesters to decide that he was the problem, not me. Then, a professor suggested law school." She laughed. "Thus, another shyster was born."

Jim laughed with her and shook his head. "That guy must have been some idiot."

Kimberly frowned. "No, not an idiot, he was a control freak. He had to be in charge, in control of everybody and everything. I had a pretty good job and made decent money." She glanced at Jim cynically. "I also got a promotion that put me over him. You can imagine how well that went."

Jim nodded. "Yeah, I doubt he cared for not being on top." He was flustered for a moment. "I mean..."

Kimberly chuckled and held up a hand. "No, that's okay. As it happens, that was true, too." They both laughed.

"How did you meet?"

Kimberly sighed and shook her head, slightly embarrassed, even after all this time. "I met him at a TGIF. You know, one of those Friday afternoon 'blow off the steam' get- togethers at the house."

"The house?"

Kimberly winced. "Yeah, the...sorority house."

Jim nodded encouragingly, hiding any thoughts he had about her being in a sorority. She hurried to continue.

"Well, he was tall, good-looking, and very personable." She stared at the ceiling. "I had a lot to drink that night. And he was very self-assured, you know...not brash, just confident. Back then, he kept a lot of opinions to himself." She brought her gaze down to meet Jim's. "He was fun to be with. And he was funny. We dated for about six months and then he asked me to marry him. By then, I thought I knew everything about him."

"But you didn't..."Jim prodded gently.

"No, not even close." Kimberly shrugged. "It's not like he beat me or anything. He never laid a finger on me. He wasn't even intentionally cruel." Her voice hardened. "But he had a way of ignoring my opinions and feelings...I could say something and he would listen, politely. Then he would go on as if I had never spoken."

"How long were you married?"

"Three and a half years." She winced. "He graduated first and got a job up in New York. I joined him there a year later. When I got the promotion, he acted happy for me. But the first time we were at work and a decision had to be made that we didn't agree on...well, that was the beginning of the end."

"He argued with you?" Jim frowned knowingly.

"An argument I could have taken," she disagreed. "No, he basically 'corrected' me. In front of several people we worked with." She felt her face redden, remembering. "Condescending doesn't even begin to describe that conversation."

Jim winced. "Ouch. What did you do?"

Kimberly raised an eyebrow, trying to mimic Jim's favorite expression. "I pulled rank and we did it my way." She sighed. "And that was that. Pretty soon, he began to be the strong silent type. The strong 'sullen' silent type. I don't think he ever forgave me for doing that in front of those other people."

"But if he had done that to you..." Jim led her.

"Oh, in his eyes that would have been okay," Kimberly agreed. "After that, he grew more and more distant. Eventually, he had an affair with a new girl at the firm. He didn't do a very good job of hiding it. I think he wanted me to know." She leaned her head back against the wall. "It was a very quick, semi-painless divorce."

"As painless as a divorce can be," Jim said in a sad voice.

She looked at him in gratitude, appreciating his understanding. Then she wondered. "Have you ever been married?"

He shook his head. "No, but my parents were."

She snickered and he laughed at his own choice of words. Kimberly apologized. "I'm sorry. I take it they got a divorce?" He nodded and she felt a wave of protective sympathy. "How old were you at the time?"

Jim looked at her sardonically. "You know, people always want to know that. As if, somehow, it's easier to accept or understand at a certain age."

Kimberly flushed in embarrassment. "I didn't mean it that way..."

Jim raised his hand to stop her. "No, that wasn't fair. I know you didn't. Sometimes I can't help but try to be clever, even though the words may comes out cruel."

He had been leaning back on his hands. Kimberly watched him shift to a more comfortable position, casually putting one leg straight out to either side and lean forward, arching his back to relieve stiff muscles.

Christ, if I could have done Chinese splits like that in high school, I'd have been a cheerleader. God knows where I would have ended up. Probably not in graduate school. Certainly not kidnapped by alien monsters. She was startled to find that she was glad to be here with him, despite the circumstances. *You're an idiot, Martin.*

"I was in college, actually." At the sound of his voice, she came back to the conversation with a start. "I was at the University of Michigan and my father was in the military, stationed in Germany. Mom called to tell me that they were getting divorced. They would be flying back to the states for the holidays and to settle affairs, whatever that meant." He stopped and stared blankly into the floor in front of him. "I remember arguing with them both before they left Stuttgart. I was angry, not really listening to either of them. They had just grown tired of each other. Nothing really major or significant had happened. Maybe that was part of the problem."

Kimberly watched him, fascinated. She hated herself for her morbid curiosity, but couldn't resist asking. "What happened when they got back?"

Jim gave her a crooked smile, his eyes revealing pain.

"Well, I was upset, and went to talk to a couple of friends." He looked back at the floor. "Things happened that night, and I was out of touch for a few days. When I turned up, I found out that the plane my parents were on had crashed into the Potomac, trying to land in icy conditions at Washington National Airport. There were twenty-seven deaths in the crash." He stopped and Kimberly stared at him in horror. He looked up and his eyes glistened. "I said some pretty ugly things on the phone that night."

Kimberly was frozen, absolutely at a loss for anything to say. She could see his pain was still there, but he kept it firmly under control. It obviously took an effort, but he managed to keep his voice level.

"I guess you know who two of the fatalities were."

She nodded wordlessly. *Oh my God, what can I say that isn't incredibly meaningless and trite? I was just laughing at his parents being married.*

Kimberly sat there, watching him. He seemed a million miles away, both mentally and physically. She wanted to hold him, comfort him. But she knew she couldn't. Not just yet.

Gradually, he came back to her, giving a violent shiver. He smiled grimly at her startled face. "Someone just walked over my grave."

"Don't say that!" Kimberly shivered too. "I hate that saying."

"Sorry," he apologized.

"No, Jim." She lay one hand on the floor near his, not touching, but somehow intimate just the same. "I'm sorry. So very, very sorry."

He looked at her hand for a moment, then looked directly into her eyes, as if searching behind them for her thoughts.

Kimberly was hesitant, frightened by the intimacy of the moment, but not wanting it to end. "I...I'm here if you'd like to talk more." She waited for the rejection she knew was coming.

Jim stared at her hand again, as if wary of it. His voice was flat, emotionless. "I don't want to depress you. Things are rough enough as it is. And that wasn't one of my finer moments in life."

Her hand twitched.

"Jim."

He looked up. She found herself noticing how light a green his eyes were. The intense light emerald of a genius. Or a madman. She had seen him portray both on the big screen, but this was the real thing. She had marveled that a karate jock could indeed act. Now she realized that at times, he couldn't act to save his life. Sometimes his true thoughts and feelings literally burned to the surface, glowing through those beautiful eyes.

This man has a power. A power to...to do what?

He sat there, legs spread to either side, gym shorts falling halfway down his thighs. Powerful quadriceps muscles stood out in perfect detail, and his calves had amazing definition. Although he sat there loosely relaxed, his biceps were large enough to strain at the short sleeves of his golf shirt. His chest and shoulders resembled coiled springs, waiting to flex and explode into action. He needed to trim his beard, but it didn't detract from his thick, muscle-banded neck and strong jaw.

Stop it, Martin. Stop this right now. Kimberly realized she was backed up against the wall, one arm curled tightly around her knees, which were pressed against her chest.

Her left arm still stretched forward, almost but not quite touching his hand. She was glad she had been able to get some of the clothes from her cabin. It would have been "slightly awkward" to still be wearing the sexy, short, black dress from the first night, instead of the sweats she had on now.

It was funny how everyone referred to the last night on Earth as 'the first night'. Everyone had either gone to sleep, or been knocked out at sea, and woke up the next morning prisoners on a UFO.

Kimberly gathered herself together and Jim's eyes slowly came back into focus.

"Jim," she repeated. "I'm here. Please, tell me."

He seemed to have the same problem coming back to the moment. He looked down at her left hand, then back to her face.

"Kimberly," he began and stopped. He took a deep breath and regained his composure. "Can I call you Kim?"

"Not even once," she stated firmly. He was startled, then perplexed. He seemed to be trying to remember something.

"Did we do this...?" He stopped and shook his head. "Never mind."

"You said you went to see some friends that night," Kimberly prompted, silently praying for a miracle.

Jim looked at his right hand. They both watched as he flexed it several times, and then arched his wrist backward, stretching the tendons. Slowly the hand came to rest on the floor again.

"I had a couple of very good friends," Jim spoke slowly, visibly choosing every word, reliving every nuance. "Nasri Bahman was a freshman when I met her. I was a sophomore and had just started doing a few projects for classes with Hakim Riahi. He was an upperclassman, my roommate, and best friend." Jim's voice droned on, still emotionless at first, and Kimberly, falling into a rhythm with the sound of his voice, hung on every word.

CHAPTER TEN

"Hakim Riahi." Jim's voice took a more energetic tone.

God, what a friend. I met him playing ping-pong in the dorm rec-room. He was very good. He had successfully defended the table for over an hour and was keenly tuned into the game. He used a custom paddle with thick padding to help give extra spin to the ball.

I watched several games and found myself standing closest to the table after he routed yet another opponent.

"Play me," Riahi said, good humor in his voice. "Come on, American. One quick game. A very quick game." He laughed at his own joke.

I picked up the discarded paddle on the empty side of the table and looked at it. It was "dorm issue". Cheap, hard, no life or action in the pad whatsoever. But it was so hard it would give a fast reaction. A smash shot with this paddle would give a zippy response, not the gliding fluidity of the more popular, thickly padded ones.

"Hi," I said brightly. "I'm Jim Morris." I hefted the paddle. It was very light.

"Hi, Jim Morris." His dark-complected, swarthy opponent laughed at him. "Jim Morris, Jim Morrison, Chuck Norris, Morris the Cat, Morr-is less!"

With a infectious laugh, he gave a tricky serve, the ball spinning wickedly. My response went high and he casually caught it with his left hand.

"Are you ready?"

I must have looked a little stupid. I mean, I didn't expect to start a game so fast. A little warmup would have been nice. But, I was a freshman, barely seventeen, and he was an upper classman, exotic, popular, and very charismatic. He also had a group of friends, eight or ten fellow Iranians hanging around the table.

"So," I said, in my own witty little way. "You're Iranian?"

"Ha!" He cried, and began the volley. "Hell no!" The ball went over the net for the third time and he sent it screaming back with a vicious spin. "I'm Farsi!"

"Farcical?" The ball flew straight at his face and he caught it an inch in front of his eyes.

He leaned forward on the table, paddle in one hand, ball in the other. "Far-see," he enunciated. "Persian. Not ear..rawn..ian. That's an English word. We're Farsi! You know, Keroush the great, Dariosh."

Cyrus the Great, Darius. Got it.

The first serve tore across the net. I returned it with a fair amount of backspin. It hung for what seemed like forever before it hit his side. He smashed a return. It tugged at the net, then rebounded quickly back to him.

His surprise was well hidden...almost.

"Zero-one. First blood to the English-mon!"

He sent another serve across, this time with a controlled sidespin. I caught it with a reverse spin and as it reached his side, he swung and missed the ball completely.

Hakim retrieved it, hiding his confusion.

"Zero-two! Now you've made me blue!"

Despite his bravado, his serve was cautious, conservative. After a long volley, he caught the edge on my side with a lucky tip. I still managed to return the shot, but it bounced off his chest.

It was his point, but that shot made him pause. He looked at me with an intense glare, not angry, just searching, striving to solve the mystery of a ping-pong player with modest experience, but exceptional reflexes. And unnaturally fast reaction time.

"Karate?" His eyes were almost popping.

"A little." I realized he had figured me out.

"A little," he repeated, looking me up and down. "Right." He served. "Alright, Jim Morrison, let's boogie!"

You know, that Morrison thing gets old really fast. I've had to deal with it most of my life, and I make jokes, but... to be honest, I'm sick to death of it.

"Wrong guy, Farsi. I'm not dead." I sent the ball screaming back to his side.

He won that game, twenty-one to nineteen. I won the second twenty-one to eighteen. He won the third, twenty-nine to twenty-seven. I won the fourth, thirty-five to thirty-three. He won the fifth, 47 to 45.

At that point we stopped, claiming the need for facilities. In the restroom, he turned and pointed a finger at me. "Who are you?" he demanded.

"Jim Morris." I was startled.

"Who are you?" His voice rose.

"Jim Morris!" I was irritated now.

"Who are you?" he shouted.

"You tell me!" I was bewildered.

"You're my friend, American imperialistic dog." He smiled evilly. "Jim Morris."

I started to laugh and his face grew dark. "What's so funny?" he snarled.

"Do you mind if we don't seal this with a handshake?" I said, zipping up.

He laughed uproariously, and then suddenly stopped and glared as I stood there.

"Wash your hands."

From that day on, I was a member of the Ann Arbor Iranian/Persian/Farsi community. They taught me some words in Farsi that I quickly discovered were unfit for mixed company. Mixed company fluent in Persian, that is. I taught them pool. They taught me rugby. I taught them *Risk*, then *Go!* They tried to teach me chess, and we settled on equal ground on that issue.

Hakim thought he knew American women, but his ideas only worked on certain ones. Most of them were busty blondes. It's interesting how cosmetically pleasing a blonde and an Persian can be. She is blonde, tan, busty, with a certain amount of "baby fat" showing. He is blackhaired, dark skinned, and hairy as a goat. That pretty much described Hakim and his love life for the first year we knew each other.

Then Nasri came to school.

Nasri Bahman had spent the last year in a Swiss private girl's school. Until a few years earlier, she had lived in London, also at an all-girl's school. She was eighteen years old, and one would assume, innocent as only a young woman who has almost never even talked to an adult male she wasn't related to can be.

She came from a wealthy Iranian family that had fled the country at the fall of the Shah. Her father had held a high position in the government, so of course there had been a death warrant on his head in Iran for years now.

Her family had fled to Saudi Arabia first, then to England. Not that she had noticed. It had been one private school after another, finally ending up in Switzerland.

Ann Arbor had a large Iranian population, both students and Iranian nationals that had stayed on, making a life in America, waiting, hoping the religious fanatical government would fall.

Hakim had told me many times about Iran. The Shah had been an asshole. Evil beyond belief, he had thousands of dissidents kidnapped and killed by the Savak, the secret police. The young Persians had prayed for his downfall. But when it came, they weren't ready for the Khomeini regime that replaced him.

To say that Iranian students reminisced about the reign of the Shah would have been exaggerating. But not totally untrue.

"It is only a matter of time before the people take over Iran," Hakim would vow.

"Hakim, I think the people rule Iran now." I hated to depress my friend, but felt I was far enough removed from the situation to see it more clearly.

"America is your country now," I tried to tell him gently. "Iran is lost to you. Maybe your sons..."

"No, the Ayatollahs are old. They can be beaten!"

"Hakim, my brother. Come on, sit down and have another drink. Tell me about Bimbo last Saturday night at the party."

"Her name was Bambi," he snarled.

"Whatever."

And so it went.

Until Nasri Rahman enrolled as a freshman. Her family and his were close. They called and told him to watch out for the young girl. She was to arrive soon and he was to be her older brother.

"Great," he moaned. "I now have a second job. Nanny! This little girl will come here causing who knows what kind of problems. I haven't seen her in ten years. I will have to make sure she doesn't embarrass herself or her family. Or me," he added glumly. "Since I'm now her appointed babysitter."

"Did I miss something?" I couldn't hide my grin. "Did you say, second job? Do you already have a job I don't know about?"

"Don't interrupt my monologue with facts!" he snapped. "You, as an actor, or a 'would-be' actor, should appreciate that life is a stage. And we are merely actors in the play of..."

"Whoa." Hakim always had the ability to make me laugh, even when correcting him. Or when I was mad at him, or whatever. "I read too. Don't plagiarize."

The phone rang.

"Salaam!" Hakim snarled into the receiver. "Oh, hello, Nasri. You're arriving early? I thought you didn't get here until the eighteenth." He listened and frowned. "Oh, right. We'll come get you." He thought for a moment. "Um, where are you?"

His face reddened even as I glanced at my watch with the ever-so-handy calendar function. Hmm, today was August eighteenth.

"Downstairs?" His red face paled as he looked around at the messy suite in panic. "How did you get here from Detroit Metro Airport?"

"Oh." Hakim looked at me in panic, gesturing at his piles of dirty clothes lying around. I glanced at the disgustingly filthy socks on top of one stack, and signed 'not me' at him, backing away. "Yes, we'll be right down. We? Oh, my good American friend, Jim Morris."

He sighed and shook his head. "No, not him. He's dead."

Hakim hung up the phone and turned to me.

"Do you have any cash?" He rushed around, grabbing things. "She just took a taxi from Metro. She doesn't have enough American dollars to pay him."

I couldn't help myself. I slowly shook my head at him. "This is a fine mess you've gotten us into."

We flew down the stairs, three at a time. (Trying to take the elevators was a good way to kill an afternoon at our dorm.) Reaching the last landing, we slowed to a casual pace, trying to radiate the upperclass-men status we represented.

At that point, Hakim and I remained best friends...that hated each other. It only took one glance at the girl in the lobby, and we were both trapped. We had gone the extra mile for each other countless times but, from that moment on, we were competitors.

Nasri was just over five feet tall, perhaps one hundred pounds. She had pale, almost translucent skin with thick, ebony hair that fell over her shoulders. Ebony and Ivory, all in one package. Her waist hardly existed, and yet she had a bustline that made it very hard to talk to her face.

The moment Hakim saw her, he turned on his Persian charm. He complimented her, speaking in Farsi, and somehow managed to be at every door to open and hold it for her. I watched him and felt uneasy. He didn't know I could understand most of what he said and it was unlike him to be so rude.

"Hakim." I caught his arm while she 'freshened up' in the bathroom of our dorm suite. By that time, we had been roommates for most of the year. "You're her guardian. She's put her trust in you. She's not eligible."

He glared at me.

"You think I don't know that? Give me time to adjust." He sighed. "Nobody told me she was so...so..."

"Beautiful," I completed.

"Beautiful?" he snorted. "That doesn't begin to touch what she is, damn it." He took a deep breath and clenched his teeth. "If I try anything, flatten me."

I smiled at him. "No problem."

"Oh?" The soft contralto startled both of us. Nasria stood in the doorway, her eyes narrowed. "So you two have everything all planned out? You're my.." She searched for the word. "...nursing-mates?"

Hakim and I looked at each other, bemused. "Not me," I protested. "Ah, and that's nursemaids."

"What are you talking about?" Hakim spoke rapid Persian in his best sincere voice.

She stared at him and he grew uncomfortable. "That's rude. Speak English." She fixed me with her stare. "What if Hakim wants me, tonight, in his bed?" she demanded.

"I'll break his leg," I answered immediately, then shook my head in confusion.

She whirled back to Hakim. "Jim tried to seduce me when you weren't in the room."

He blanched and turned to me in anger, then paused.

"Well?" she insisted. "What are you waiting for?"

Hakim breathed in and out several times, then faced her. "You're very good," he admitted. "But you and Jim haven't been alone at any point." He tried in vain to project a firm father image. "And even you aren't good enough to make me try to fight Jim."

"Oh?" she put her hands on her hips. "Your friendship is more important than my honor?"

Hakim smiled, fully recovered from her power. "Not at all," he grinned at her. "But nobody that knows Jim is stupid enough to try to fight him."

She gave me an appraising look. "Are you that bad? That dangerous?"

I have to admit I stuttered at first. She had the strangest personality I had ever met at that point in my life. But I finally got a response out.

"Um, I don't get beat up too much."

Hakim went into hysterics at that point. I turned to look at him. He put his hands on his knees and tried to point at me, but was laughing too hard. Without a sound she threw her purse at me. I saw it out of the corner of my eye, and caught it inches from the side of my head, without turning to look. With my best friendly smile I offered it back to her.

She looked at me thoughtfully. "Who are you?"

"Nobody in particular," I admitted. "But I'm going to be your best friend." I sighed.

"Even if it kills me."

Jim smiled, enjoying the memories. The three of them had been inseparable. Jim had been the serious student, trying to get the most from his theatre classes. Hakim had found a natural ability to catch the essence of almost anything on film. He spent a lot of his time trying to catch the "au natural" essence of busty blondes.

Nasri was an artist, and a mathematician. She could sit down, sketch away while Jim and Hakim played around, wasting away a beautiful fall afternoon. They would play soccer, frisbee, chase young ladies, sometimes even catch them. She would sit there, occasionally making lines, thinking, adding bits and pieces, and by the end of the day, she would have a masterpiece.

One time it was Jim and Hakim on either side of a beautiful blonde, in a distinctive begging manner.

Another time, there might be a flying elephant in the background, swooping down, stealing frisbees.

A year passed. Fall came again. They all grew closer. Nasri dated several boys, both American and Persian. Jim and Hakim were nervous wrecks. They didn't quite spy on her, but one of them always managed to be near her dorm when she returned from a date. She did fine in classes, spending far more time studying than the two of them together.

Hakim spent most of his free time working on a short film he was making for the Montreal Film Festival. Jim played a part in it, but his work was quickly done, and Hakim was left with the editing and special effects.

Jim enjoyed the film work, even though it was basically just an extended action scene. When he saw the final edition, he was impressed. Hakim had made him look great! He seemed to flow across the screen, and his stunts had been shot from angles that made them look completely impossible. But there they were, right in front of you on the screen.

Jim was progressing in his classes, but wasn't sure he could see where he was going. The stage didn't really appeal to him, but did he want to try and pursue a career with television or the big screen?

He had also begun playing piano and singing in a local bar for happy hour on Friday nights. Although he'd never make a living at it, he did enjoy the change of pace.

It was in mid-December that Jim heard from his parents. His mother broke the news, and Jim didn't take it very well. His father came on the line, and that only confused Jim more. If they could work together to tell him about this, couldn't they handle the other things, too?

Jim had to get out of the dorm. Hakim was in Montreal with the film, and wouldn't be back until at least tomorrow. He went to Nasri's dorm, but she wasn't there. He waited restlessly in the lobby.

He had to play that evening at the club. The good news was that it was an early gig. He'd be done at eight. The bad news was that he had to start in less than an hour, and he really wasn't in the mood.

He finally left her a note and hurried to work. He played his first set and took a break. Still no Nasri. Resigned, he began his second set. It was a struggle to play cheerful songs. Without thinking about it, everything he played was either depressing or angry. About that time Nasri came in with several other young Iranians.

She picked up on his mood immediately. Jim watched her as he played. Her friends finished their beer and got up to leave. They looked inquiringly at her and she smiled and nodded at Jim. They waved to him and left.

Jim played impatiently until it was time to take another break. He sank into the chair next to her with a sigh.

"What is it?" Nasri was obviously worried.

"My parents," Jim said, holding down his anger and depression. "They're getting divorced for the holidays."

"What?" She had never met them, but had talked to them several times on the phone and liked them both. "Why?"

"They say they're bored with each other." Jim shook his head. "There's nobody else; they just want their freedom."

"When?" Nasri asked slowly.

"They're coming back to the States this week." Jim could no longer hide his anger.

"How?"

"They're flying into National in Washington, D.C." Jim made a face. "They want me to go there and meet them."

"And?"

"No way am I going," he said flatly.

"Oh?"

"Would you quit that?" Jim couldn't stay angry with her, but she had the most annoying habit of only using single words when discussing heavy matters. And when she did it in monosyllables, it drove him crazy.

"I'm sorry," she said contritely. "You know, if they're breaking up this amicably, maybe it won't last. Maybe they'll miss each other," she suggested.

"I don't know." Jim felt pessimistic. "They seemed pretty sure of themselves." He saw the bartender watching him and pointedly looking at the clock.

"Damn, I've got to get back up there." He stood up.

"I'll leave a little early and start something for dinner." She smiled up at him. "That way we won't have to deal with other people. We can sit and have a long talk and stuff."

"Thanks, Nasri." Jim said, feeling a little better already. "It won't be too much bother?"

"No, I've got just the dish in mind." She looked at him mischievously.

"Let me guess," he said dryly. "The side dish is rice."

"Smart-ass." She sniffed at him.

"Are you sure you want to walk home alone?" Jim looked at his watch. "It's already dark outside. I won't be that much longer. This is the last set."

"Don't worry, Mr. Black belt," she arched her eyebrows and he raised one in response. "I'm a pretty tough cookie, you know. Anyway, I want a hot shower. I'll be fine."

"Okay, see you in a while."

Jim finished the set and got paid. Ah, cash, he sighed to himself. Untraceable, un-taxable, and most important, unknown income. His parents had him on a budget, and this helped with the extras, like beer.

Thinking of his parents made his eyes blink. It's the cold, he muttered to himself, hurrying along the icy sidewalk through campus. He turned his head to keep a gust of wind from hitting his face and saw a dark object lying on a snowbank, near the entrance to the social sciences building.

Something about it looked familiar. He changed direction without slowing, to pass by it. Then he recognized it as Nasri's ski cap. He always kidded her for being the only Persian in Ann Arbor to have a ski cap with a Scottish plaid pattern.

Jim picked it up in confusion, looking around. She loved that cap and wouldn't have just dropped it. Anyway, it was too cold for her without it. Something wasn't right, here.

He tried the security doors to the building and found one not quite latched shut. Moving quietly, he entered, listening carefully.

Jim was about to call out when he heard a muffled scream and someone swear. Somebody else laughed. As he began to run, he heard a blow being struck. He felt blood rush to his head.

Where, where was it? There, that classroom to the left.

He pushed the door open and stopped short. A wave of nausea swept over him. Nasri was pinned down on the professor's desk. Pants, boots, and coat lay scattered around the floor, and her sweater had been rolled up and the hem stuffed into her mouth. Nasri's head was turned to the side facing him and he saw that she recognized him. She clenched her eyes tightly shut, and sobbed into the sweater in fear and pain.

And shame.

One young man was between her legs, obviously at the peak of enjoying himself. The other two men held her arms to the table, one on either side.

At his entrance, all three men froze, staring at him. The one in the middle backed away. his erect penis covered with semen. The man closest to Jim lunged at him and Jim's right foot shot out, catching him full in the stomach. With a whooping sound, he bent forward, unable to breath. Jim used both hands to grasp the man's head and twisted. Sobbing in fury, he gave a final tug and the neck broke with a sharp cracking sound.

The man who had just finished raping Nasri was still trying to pull his pants up. In desperation, he swung a fist at Jim, who let the hand flash by and then, with a sharp blow, broke his arm. A well-placed kick caught the now-screaming man full in the genitals. Sobbing, he tried to cover them with his one able hand. Another sharp kick, and the man began to sag. Jim grabbed him by his shirt and belt, and with a rush of adrenaline, effortlessly lifted him off his feet.

The man had to weigh at least as much as Jim, and was taller, but it wouldn't have mattered if he'd been a giant. Jim swung him around and dashed him downward. The man smashed down, straddling the theatre-style chairs mounted to the floor. The back of the chair tore upwards, crushing what was left of his testicles.

Jim paused, enjoying his screams. Finally, he snapped a sharp blow to the man's face, crushing his nose, driving bone and cartilage into the brain. The rapist was dead long before his body quit reacting to the punishment.

Jim whirled around at the sound of a footstep. The third man had been edging around the desk, trying to get to the door. He blanched and fumblingly pulled out a knife.

"Don't come near me," he snarled. "I'll cut you. I'll cut you, man." He suddenly looked down at Nasri and his intent was as clear as if he'd shouted it. He started to reach for her.

Jim didn't make a sound. At that moment he wouldn't have been capable of anything articulate. He just launched himself forward, driving the man back into the blackboard wall. Grabbing the hand holding the knife, Jim twisted the arm around and plunged the blade deep into the other's own gut. Pulling with both hands, Jim tore the blade upward, sobbing as he disemboweled him, all the time watching the dying man's eyes.

Life quickly faded out of them.

Jim let the man fall to the floor and turned to Nasri. She hadn't moved the entire time. But her eyes were open, staring at his face, horror and savage triumph waging war for control of her features.

"Nasri, you're going to be okay." Jim fumbled around, fighting tears that threatened to blind him, finding her pants and coat. "Here, put these on."

"I...I'm..." Nasri sat up, Jim's arm around her shoulders, supporting her. "I'm all messy. And my hat..."

"Nasri," Jim said, gently pulled her sweater down, covering her breasts. "I've got your hat. Don't worry about the mess. We've got to get you to a doctor." He looked around grimly. "And call the police."

"No!" Panic flooded her features. "No. We can't tell anyone! I can't...I couldn't..." Words failed her and she would have collapsed had Jim not held onto her.

"Nasri, there's no shame in this." Jim held her shoulders, willing her to look into his eyes. He tried to put away his anger. It was a luxury he couldn't afford just yet. "This is not your fault. Only the police and the doctor will know."

"No!" She cried, leaning her head against his chest. "No police and no doctor." Her voice was weak, but resolute. "I'm not hurt. Not physically."

"Nasri, you could get pregnant," Jim tried again. "You need to see a doctor to take precautions."

"No doctor." Her voice shook and he realized she was shivering from the cold, and probably shock.

"Come on, get dressed." Jim tried to be firm. "We'll get you home, if nothing else. You need to get warmed up."

He began trying to put one of her feet into the pants leg, and she eventually began to help.

"What about my underwear?" She sounded dazed now.

"Don't worry," Jim answered her. "I'll get everything. Your underwear and bra are ruined, but I've got them. Here, put this on."

Finally she was more or less dressed and Jim began leading her out. She stopped and pulled away fiercely.

"Are they dead?" she demanded.

Jim didn't bother looking. "Yes," he answered coldly.

"All of them?"

"Yes," he repeated.

"Good." Her strength seemed to leave. "Now get me home please, Jim. Get me home, and no police or doctors."

"Okay," he agreed miserably. Anything to get her out of here.

He led her outside and she shivered violently as the cold air hit her. He put one arm around her waist and held her elbow with his other hand. Before they went fifty yards she was staggering and Jim swept her up, carrying her in his arms like a baby.

"Jim." She reached up and touched his cheek. "Please don't let anyone see us. Please?"

"No problem, hon." Jim spoke gently, tears running down his cheeks. The reaction was beginning to set in with him as well. His anger was replaced by shock of his own actions.

She was silent all the way to the dorm and then pointed to the back door. He set her down on her feet and she clung to him as he found her keys in her purse.

No one saw them. Jim could hear voices behind some doors, and some music down the hall, but no one saw him carry her up the back stairs and down the hall to her room.

He carried Nasri into her bedroom and set her on the bed. "Where's Jenny?" Jenny was her suite-mate.

"Home in Gross Pointe for the weekend." Her voice was faint.

Jim nodded and pulled her boots off. Then he stood hesitantly, not quite knowing what to do next. She would need some privacy at this point.

"Jim." Nasri looked up at him, embarrassed. "I'm going to need your help."

"Are you sure?" Jim kneeled in front of her and took her hands in his. "We can still at least call a doctor."

"A doctor that does house calls?" Nasri made a weak attempt at humor. "No, I need you to help me get these clothes off. And to burn them!" She got an angry, frustrated look on her face. "I feel so helpless, Jim." Tears brimmed in her eyes.

"I know." Jim started to hug her and stopped. Male physical contact had to be the last thing she wanted at this point. Then she pulled him close, clinging to him.

"I still feel helpless." Her voice was muffled by his sweater. "But at least now I feel safe." She pulled away slightly. "Help me with these clothes."

Jim did so, trying to avert his eyes as much as possible.

"I'm a mess," she said with disgust as they got her pants off.

"You're bleeding!" Jim saw bloodstains on her leg and panicked.

"Jim." He looked into her eyes and saw she almost had an amused look on her face. "I was a virgin." She blushed. "It happens, remember?"

"Oh, right." Jim was flustered. She raised her arms and he pulled the sweater over her head. Then he turned to get a robe for her.

"No!" Her voice was harsh. "If I put that on, I'd have to burn it, too. Just get me into the shower."

Jim helped her across the room into the bathroom. He was uncomfortably aware of the smoothness of her bare shoulders and was ashamed of himself.

He gave an involuntary shiver. She looked up at him in alarm. "Are you okay?"

Jim nodded. "It's just nerves. I"ll be fine. It's just the reaction setting in."

"Can you still help me?" She sounded shy.

"Of course." Jim smiled weakly for her sake, aware that his lips were quivering.

"Turn the water on hot as it will go."

He did so, and they waited for the hot water to work it's way from the basement to the fourth floor. She began unbuttoning his flannel shirt. He froze.

"What are you doing?" He could hear the panic in his voice.

"Jim, I don't think I can stand alone, yet. I'll need your help in the shower."

You're already shivering. You'll catch your death of a cold if you get your clothes all wet."

Jim backed up against the sink, stuttering. "N..Nasri, I don't think this is a good idea. Are you sure you can't stand by yourself?"

She was holding onto the towel rack and managed a tiny smile. "Jim, I trust you. I don't care what you see, or what you touch. Now hold me up. I'm losing it."

Hurriedly he put one arm around her waist to support her. She resumed unbuttoning his shirt.

"I still don't think this is a good idea," Jim insisted, but didn't try to stop her.

She got him to strip down to his underwear as the water finally heated up. "These are fine!" Jim said quickly. "They, uh, dry real fast."

The hot water seemed to revive both of them to an extent. She scrubbed herself furiously, then had him shampoo her hair. The white lather in her jetblack hair was beautiful, he mused. At least it's not as hard to avoid seeing her nudity in this tiny shower, he thought. We're too close together to really be able to see each other. They brushed against each other and Jim felt a renewed sense of panic. Oh, that's definitely worse. Well, not worse, but...Jim tightly shut his eyes. Don't think. Don't think about this. Go away, damn it! His underwear was wet and didn't conceal a certain reaction he was desperately trying to banish.

"Turn around, Jim." Her voice was gentle, but much stronger than it had been.

Grateful for the reprieve, he turned to face away from her, hugging the wall. In horror, he felt her start to scrub his back. At the first contact, his spine arched forward and he hit his stomach and other things against the wall, hard.

Coughing, he regained his breath. Damn, that hurt. He placed both hands on the wall as she continued to scrub his shoulders and under his arms, then down his sides. She stopped for a moment and then he felt her pour shampoo on his head. She began lathering it.

"Oh," he groaned. "Uh, I can do that. Are you feeling better? Maybe I should wait outside."

He made a move to leave and she placed a hand between his shoulder blades, pushing him back. After a moment, the shampooing continued.

"Turn around," she ordered.

"No."

"Turn around," she repeated.

"I don't think that's a good idea right now," Jim stammered.

"Jim, you idiot." She sounded exasperated. Her arms went around him and he could feel her softness pressed against his back. He relaxed in spite of himself.

"Nasri, you're my friend." Jim was having trouble keeping his voice level. "My best friend. You're like my little sister. This is wrong."

He heard her sigh, and her head came to rest against the thick slabs of muscles on his back. "Do you love me?" Her voice sounded weaker.

"Of course I do." Jim was determined to do the right thing. "I love you like a sister."

She gave a growl that startled him, and pulled him around to face her, surprising him with her strength. "You do not love me like a sister, and there's the proof!"

Jim felt himself go bright red. "That's merely a physical reaction," he said, trying to not act embarrassed. "It has nothing to do with my feelings for you."

"Are you in love with me?" she demanded, her voice still weak. She wiped soap from her brow and glared at him. He stared into her eyes for a long time.

"No," he said in a very small voice.

"Liar!" she shouted. "Liar!" She pounded on his chest with two tiny hands that Jim could hardly even feel, but a sharp pain stabbed him there just the same, making it hard to breathe. "You are in love with me. You always pretend you're just like a big brother, but I've seen you watching when you thought I didn't notice. You and Hakim, both. You're both in love with me, and I'm in love with both of you."

She stopped pounding on him and staggered, almost falling through the shower curtain. Alarmed, Jim caught her with both hands. Suddenly, he found himself holding her against him, his arms around her shoulders, hers around his waist. How the hell did that happen, he wondered. I don't have any moves like that.

"Jim, I was a virgin until tonight." She spoke so softly, he had to strain to hear her. "I always dreamed about the first time, and how it would be." She paused. "And who it would be with. You were in a lot of those dreams. No matter, the one common thread was that I was with someone I loved very dearly. Someone that loved me too." She straightened her neck so that her forehead rested against his chest. "Tonight that was stolen from me. It's too late for the first time."

Jim felt his throat tighten in anger at the three dead men. At that moment, if he could have gone back and killed them again, he would have.

She raised her head and their eyes met. "But I can change the final memory of tonight. I can still do that. I can't get my virginity back. But I can get my memories." Her voice broke. "My pride."

Jim gently brushed the shampoo away from her brow, careful not to let any in her eyes. She stared up at him, looking so young and yet, so mature. He smiled down at her, no longer trying to hide his thoughts. She smiled back, a little frightened, but satisfied.

"I do love you," Jim admitted shyly. "I've been in love with you since the day we met."

Her smile was wan, but she giggled, just a little bit. At that moment, her healing started. "I know that, silly. I've always known."

She looked down and exclaimed. "Hey, what happened."

Jim found himself blushing yet another time tonight. "Well, actually, nothing." She had a mischievous grin that was his favorite expression of hers, although it was a somewhat faded version.

"Yet," she said, in a determined voice.

"Don't worry about that," Jim said tersely. "If it likes you, it grows on you."

She released her grip around his waist and wrapped her arms around his neck. "It's going to love me," she said coyly, and pulled him forward to meet his lips with hers.

CHAPTER ELEVEN

Kimberly exhaled heavily and wondered how long she'd been holding her breath. Jim was staring over her right shoulder as if he could see the past on the wall behind her.

Slowly, he came back to her. She was startled to find that his right hand now held her left. He didn't seem to notice. He'd shifted sideways so that her bare feet were now propped against his right leg. It was obvious that he was waiting for her reaction to his story.

And what was her reaction? He'd taken advantage of an emotionally unstable rape victim. Or had he? And where did his parents fit into this equation?

"I guess you think that was pretty disgusting," he said tonelessly.

"Not necessarily. After all, I wasn't there." She stalled, speaking slowly but thinking furiously. "I guess an important part is, did that night help her recover?"

"Yes." She was startled by the bitterness in his voice. "That is a crucial point, isn't it." His eyes met hers, and there was a tortured soul hiding behind them. "The problem is, I just don't know."

"What?" Kimberly was confused. "What about the next day. How was she? And what about those bodies? Didn't the police find a connection?"

And how does this tie in with your parents?

Jim shook his head, sadly. "The next day she was fine. Oh, she wasn't fine, exactly, but she seemed to be coping and we didn't have massive guilt feelings or anything. At least, not right away." His face grew long. "And my parents...?"

Jim stood on the entrance ramp to I-75, right thumb raised. Wearily he rubbed his eyes with his left hand and glanced at his watch. Eight a.m. and many miles to go before I sleep, he thought sardonically.

Hell of a way to spend Sunday morning, hitchhiking to D.C. His parents were flying in this evening and would be staying at the Marriot. Classes were finished for the semester, so it was decided he would meet them there. This was before he hung up on them in anger.

An eighteen-wheeler blew by and he jumped back, avoiding the flying snow and ice that followed, caught up in the truck's slipstream. A car honked as it passed, speeding up to meet the heavy interstate traffic.

Whew, this is a tough crowd, he thought, gingerly stepping back to the edge of the pavement. I'm lucky I didn't end up in the snowbank.

Yep, one hell of a way to spend Sunday morning. On the other hand, another day spent like Saturday, and he'd probably leave this world, albeit with a smile. And if that didn't kill him, his roommate surely would. Hakim was due back this afternoon and Jim did not want to be there.

When he had left this morning before dawn, Nasri was sleeping peacefully, her black hair flung across the pillow in a carefree pattern. He stood looking down at her for a long time. How could one person look like a prepubescent little girl, a Madonna, a cover girl model, and a gawky teenager all at the same time?

"I'll bet Freud would have loved me,"

Jim was surprised to find he'd spoken out loud.

"Oh no, none of that, Jim. We'll have no talking to yourself, okay?"

"Yes, James."

Another large truck honked as it rolled by, slowing. Jim was off and running, his sidepack held firmly against his hip. He nimbly hauled himself up into the cab.

"Nice purse." The driver, a short, balding man twice his age looked at the pack.

Jim grinned at him. "Not to worry. It's dirty laundry."

The older man guffawed and put the truck into gear. "That's a familiar story. Where you headed?"

"Um, south," Jim stalled.

"Fine," the trucker nodded. "I'm headed to Jacksonville, Florida."

"Okay."

Jim glanced at his watch. It would take them hours to get to the turn he needed to make for DC. He settled back in his seat and began trying to achieve a state of conscious unconsciousness.

Conscious unconsciousness, Jim snorted. An old fart in Guam had tried to tell him that the body operated on different levels and could perform numerous functions and activitites all at once. That old bastard had run him ragged, telling him that a state of healthy exhaustion would simplify reaching this nebulous state.

"Carry these stones over there. Run to the pharmacy six miles away and bring him back some condoms. Stand there on one foot until lunch. Why the heck did the old guy need condoms at his age?

Not using a condom Friday night had been one of the stupider things he had ever done. Or not done. Actually, to be totally accurate, it was four of the stupider things.

Jim winced in dismay. They had moved from the shower to the bed in something resembling desperate haste. Well, fairly close to the bed. Then they had finished the shower. Dried soap really itched. By then it was long after dinner hour, which explains how his second lapse had occurred in the kitchen. He didn't even consider trying to justify the third time. He had just dropped off to sleep and no one should be held accountable for things done in their sleep. Which would also cover the following morning.

What had happened Friday night and Saturday morning still confused and haunted him. Jim had known Nasri for almost a year and a half. Certainly not a lifetime, or even a significant portion of one. But he had an image of her that had been transformed that night.

This is a woman (girl/child) with minimal experience regarding sex. She hardly knows what causes what. Al least, that's what I thought. She joined him in bed as a demure, inexperienced young woman who had just suffered through a trauma that would have left most women unable to stand the touch of a man. At times she had been quiet, maybe shaken, but not afraid of him. Then mere moments later she would be a frantic extortionist, intensely demanding, strong, forceful even.

Jim was just alert enough to realize he was semi-hallucinating from exhaustion. But at times she had seemed to be someone else entirely, transformed from one moment to the next.

The truck driver asked him something at that point that unfortunately coincided with his introspective searching.

Jim said "Yes, she was the same woman, but transformed by events beyond her control, trying to bury the rape beneath a deluge of better

129

memories." Somewhat later he would decide that the only verbal response he had actually given was "yes."

Jim had finally regained his equilibrium Saturday morning. From that point on they had used protection but, he thought dourly, there was a saying regarding barn doors and loose farm animals. This would be a great time to beat the odds.

Jim wondered what Nasri would tell Hakim about this weekend. He hoped she would break the news. There would be a definite change in the dynamics of their little group. But Nasri and Hakim would be there when he got back. His concern right now was how to keep his parents from breaking up.

Nasri had insisted he make this trip.

"Jim you only have one mother and one father. Go see them. Help them."

He leaned back and closed his eyes. Dual levels of consciousness was what the old fart had called it. Well, let's see how it works.

Jim sat up with a start. The sun was setting to his right. The driver gave a laugh.

"Kid, you were packin' in the 'zs.' I don't think I've ever seen anybody sleep harder that you just did. You missed lunch, but I'll be stopping in a little while for dinner."

"Where are we?" Jim felt drugged, thick-headed. He blinked rapidly, trying to clear his vision.

"We'll be in Macon in a few minutes."

The driver was obviously satisfied with his progress and Jim nodded, leaning back in his seat, mollified. Then he sat upright again.

"Macon is in Georgia!"

The driver laughed. "Always has been, long as I can remember."

Jim looked nervously off the shoulder of the road. God, Florida sucks. And in the dark, it was nerve-racking. Thank God, a dim glow representing the dawn was starting to appear to the east. He had to take a leak something fierce, but was afraid to leave the road. Wasn't Florida mostly swampland held together by roads and beaches? He'd heard there were snakes and gators nearly anywhere you went.

The trucker had dropped him just south of Jacksonville on U.S. 1. Down the road was a convenience store and they had bathrooms, didn't they? That would put off the decision of which way to go, north or south. Jim had started off yesterday determined to confront his parents, but somewhere along the road doubts and fears had begun. What if they were finished? Was he ready to deal with that...? Not yet. He suspected his missing the cutoffs, going with the flow of the ride was that subconscious dual level kicking in.

Jim sighed in relief as he handed the bathroom key back to the attendant. Hmm, candy...chocolate to be precise. Dark or milk, plain or with peanuts, so many choices. Then he saw the headlines on the Jacksonville paper next to the cash register and the snacks were forgotten.

BRITISH AIRLINER OVERSHOOTS RUNWAY
TWENTY-EIGHT FEARED DEAD.

Jim numbly watched his hand pick up the paper. Distantly, he interpreted the words his eyes read, moving down the article, taking an eternity. It was his parents' flight.

From then on, events passed in a blur. Jim was numb, and wanted to stay that way. He tried calling his parents hotel, with no results. Then he called their lawyer, Paul Goldman and confirmed what he already knew. Goldman tried to get him to come to D.C. and Jim flatly refused. There were no other close relatives, and Jim couldn't have stood being surrounded by strangers, looking at two closed caskets.

Legal matters could wait. He ordered the lawyer to keep his credit cards paid off. Contact the University of Michigan and tell them he would be withdrawing, at least until the next fall. He would be in touch.

Jim hung up the phone on the arguing man and walked away from the store. After several hundred yards, he noticed he was going south. That was fine. He walked for a few miles, dry eyed, his features emotionless. Finally he walked away from the road and the shoulder and sat down on a fallen tree. The hell with snakes and gators.

Jim sat there for a long time, numb.

He had seen one of his two best (only) friends raped and as a result, had killed three men. He had then seduced that friend, preying on her vulnerability, betraying her trust, and that of his other best friend. He had chickened out on confronting his parents, basically telling them to go to hell.

And now they were dead. He had fled to Florida, intentionally or not, missing the chance to tell his parents that he loved them. That he would love them, no matter what.

He was less than nothing. A murderer, seducer of children, a coward, a bad son.

Jim lowered his head and wept for a long time.

Kimberly stared at him. "Jim, you didn't kill your parents. And you wouldn't have had a chance to talk with them, anyway."

Jim gave her a tired smile. "I know that now. And I knew it then too, I guess. But guilt feelings don't always operate logically."

"So what did you do?"

Jim groaned and bent his legs, rubbing his thighs. He shifted over next to her on the wall and leaned facing her.

"I wrote a quick letter to Nasri and Hakim, telling them about my parents and that I was going to be gone for a while." Jim shook his head. "I was in the Keys just after New Year's, recovering from a hangover when I realized that I didn't know if Nasri was pregnant, and that she might not understand why I was gone." He gave a crooked grin. "She understood only too well. I called, and she said everything there was okay. Hakim was out shopping or something, and that she was fine. The one thing I should have noticed was that she never actually said 'Jim, I am not pregnant'. I guess I was more than happy to read that into what she said."

Jim's face grew bitter. "And I'm sure I was eager to believe that we'd gotten away with it, beaten the odds."

Kimberly began to see where this was going. "She was pregnant?"

Jim gave no sign of having heard her and might have been looking inside himself at a picture light-years away.

"I took a boat to Mexico, to Playa Del Carmel. I actually shaved my beard and head." Kimberly gaped at him, trying to imagine him bald. She couldn't.

"Eventually, I got to San Diego hitching rides, sometimes working a little. Spanish came pretty easy. I've always had a knack for languages. Hakim was disgusted when he realized how well I understood Persian." Jim smiled faintly at the memory of a happier time. "I got a berth on a ship to the Philippines. Before I left, I called Nasri again. She said that she and Hakim and a couple of others had gotten a house together. That would explain why I couldn't find him. He was 'out'. They had a room for me, and she thought I should come 'home'."

"What about the three dead bodies?" Kimberly was incredulous. "Didn't anyone connect you to that? Weren't there questions being asked?"

Jim laughed bitterly.

"No, the police decided that a gang must have been involved, due to the 'brutal nature of their deaths'. They figured that it was the work of several people, probably mob related. And I had just suffered a 'great loss' and my absence made perfect sense to everyone." Jim unconsciously raised his hand that still held hers to his cheek. Kimberly felt herself blush but said nothing.

"I spent the rest of the spring and most of the summer in the Philippines, Thailand, then Hong Kong." Jim's voice grew colder. "I did a lot of things I'm not too proud of, fought a lot. I used a fake name, Cisco Kid, for some stupid reason. I guess I liked that old song. Towards the end of summer, the fights began to go bad. A few people died." Jim straightened, flattening his back against the wall.

"No, that's not accurate. I killed a few people in fights for money. Then I was approached by a group of gamblers. I had won too many times, the bets weren't coming in. They wanted me to take a fall and didn't think I was smart enough to realize I wouldn't survive the loss."

He rolled his head sideways, to look at her. "At that point, I decided to head home. Real fast. It was tricky, but I made it."

I'll bet that's an understatement, Kimberly thought to herself. He'd fought in some sort of illegal arena fights, kind of like a gladiator or something. Small wonder he wouldn't allow himself to get pulled into casual fighting. To him, there was no such thing!

"I got back to Ann Arbor just in time."

"For classes?" Kimberly knew he had finished school there.

Jim's gaze became unfocused. "Yeah, classes, too. But Nasri went into labor right after I called from the west coast. I suspect that might have been my fault, too."

Kimberly nodded knowingly. "She had been pregnant, with your child." She didn't ask it as a question.

"She was pregnant," Jim agreed. "But with whose child? That one was a little harder to figure." He shook his head in awe. "I have to say, Nasri was one of the most methodical people I've ever known. When Hakim got home, back in December, she told him about the rape. He was furious, and praised

Allah that I had avenged her."

Jim began to laugh, but it was a bitter-sweet laugh, and Kimberly stared at him.

"He was so worried about her, and insisted on staying the night. Like I said, you have to know Persians to know how serious her not being a virgin anymore was. We'd both stayed at her place lots of times, but always sleeping on the couch or the floor. Well, that changed that night."

Kimberly's mouth sagged open. "You've got to be kidding."

Jim reached over and pushed her chin up, closing her mouth for her. He left his hand there for a moment, then withdrew it and continued with his story.

"Of course, when she turned up pregnant, he insisted on doing the right thing." Jim smiled grimly. "Her family and his too, for that matter, were furious and there was no contact between them and their families for almost two years. He had let them down and she had been immoral." Jim's voice was cynical. "It's interesting that they were ostracized for two different reasons, even though it involved the same incident."

"Typical double standards," Kimberly noted.

Jim nodded in agreement.

"By the time the baby was born, we were both there at the hospital, waiting. The doctors didn't want to let me into the delivery room, but Hakim could be very persuasive." Kimberly heard pride grow in his voice and looked at him wonderingly. "She was the most beautiful mother in the world, and the baby was gorgeous. Her name means 'mysterious flower' in English. Hakim and I were acting like raving maniacs, we were so excited."

Jim grew solemn.

"At one point, I was holding her, the baby that is, and I was crying." His voice broke. "I was holding her up to my cheek and Hakim looked at us both and went absolutely white."

"He wanted to talk to me right then, outside in the hall. Nasri realized he knew and tried to insist he stay with her, but he curtly cut her off and left the room, assuming I would follow."

"Did you?" Kimberly asked, knowing she wouldn't have.

"There was no denying him, at that point." Jim shivered. "We got outside and he took a swing at me. It knocked me against the wall. 'Did you?' he demanded in a terrible voice."

"'Yes', I answered and he hit me again."

"'Tell me about that night!' he insisted. I did, and he listened to every word, nodding approval at the part where I killed them. Then I got to the shower part, and he hit me again."

"How on earth did he manage to hit you so many times?" Kimberly didn't remember reading in the resumes that Hakim was into martial arts as well.

"I didn't try to stop him," Jim said simply. "When I finished, he hit me again."

"'Who's the father?' he asked in that same terrible voice."

"'You are,' I answered."

"At this point we were both crying. 'Nasri is your wife,' I told him. 'And you are her husband.'"

"He started to swing at me again and stopped. 'Why aren't you protecting yourself?' He knew he could never have touched me in a real fight."

Jim said that with no trace of bragging.

"I told him he was hurting enough."

"'How could you know,' he was scornful to me."

"'Because I hurt, too,' I told him."

Tears welled up again in Jim's eyes. "He looked at me and understood. 'You love her too.'"

"'And I let her down,' I said miserably. 'I should have protected her better. I should have been stronger, later.'"

Jim stopped for a moment to recover.

"We hugged and held onto each other. We were brothers once more." Jim sounded sad. "Although things were never quite so simple again."

"What did Nasri say when you came back into the room?"

"She took one look at us and knew." Jim sounded wistful. "She was so damn beautiful lying there, holding the baby. She looked at my face and winced. 'Are you two quite finished?' she asked. 'We have a baby girl to raise.' And so I became her godfather, Dutch uncle, and eventual big brother. I helped Hakim raise her." His voice grew sad.

Kimberly stiffened. He had said Nasri 'was' one of the most methodical people earlier. "What happened to Nasri? Complications of the pregnancy?"

She watched his face harden and take on a remoteness that actually frightened her.

"No, she recovered fine," his voice was wooden, quite emotionless. "The following year her family was ready to make up and forgive her. They were still in England and wanted Nasri and the baby to visit. By this time Hakim and I were doing our first 'real' film together. In fact, Frederick directed that one. The baby had an ear infection and couldn't fly." A quiver came into

Jim's voice. "Hakim and I convinced her to go alone and we would watch the baby. She finally agreed."

"Not another plane crash?" Kimberly was incredulous.

"No." Jim was very bitter sounding. "Nothing so simple. It turned out there was still a price on her father's head in Iran. In fact, on all their heads. The whole damn family!" He sounded anguished.

Kimberly suddenly remembered something. "Did you say her family name was Rahman?" She shuddered. Years ago, a bomb had exploded in a crowded restaurant in London, killing and maiming dozens. A Moslem extremist group had claimed responsibility, and said that the Rahman family had been the target.

Jim nodded. "She was there. Hakim and I were devastated. I had promised her that I would always be there for her and the baby. And Hakim, for that matter. That I would never leave again, like before, and then that happened."

"What did you do?" Kimberly was thinking about Hakim and the baby.

"I tracked them down." Jim's voice couldn't have been colder. "It took a while, but I found out who it was, and where they were."

"Oh." Kimberly sat there next to him, shaken. This was a lot to take in one dose. How many more bodies was that? And that poor baby...wait a minute, that poor baby... Her head shot up and she glared at him. He looked startled.

"What?" He said in a subdued voice, undoubtably waiting for her to condemn him a murderer.

"That baby was Afsaneh!" She hissed.

He looked at her, puzzled. "Of course it was."

"Does she know all this?" Kimberly demanded.

"Not in so many words," Jim admitted, eyeing her warily. "We just told her that both Hakim and I had dated her mother, and that she had finally married him, but that..." Jim blushed. "Well, that we had both loved her mother," he finished weakly. "Very much."

"That little..." Kimberly remembered the conversation on the deck ruefully. "Why I..I, oh I don't even know what I ought to do."

"About what?" Jim looked bewildered. "What are you talking about?"

Kimberly was embarrassed. *Alright, Martin. How do you get out of this?* "We were talking, and I may have made an umm...negative comment about you."

Jim looked at her, still confused. "So? What did she do, hit you or something?"

"With a ton of bricks," Kimberly admitted. "She implied you two were, uh, well, you know, involved."

"We were what?" Jim's voice rang out across the room and Kimberly saw Afsaneh sitting some distance away, She had been grinning, watching the two of them talk. Seeing and hearing Jim react, she paled and began looking around nervously for cover.

Jim lowered his voice, but not his indignation.

"My God, how could you think such a thing?" Jim glared at her. "She's only fifteen, for Christ's sake!"

"Fifteen, you say," Kimberly repeated thoughtfully, giving the young girl a speculative look that didn't bode well for her. Afsaneh smiled back weakly, shrugging her shoulders in an semi-apologetic, semi-defiant manner.

Kimberly looked back at Jim, who suddenly had a look of comprehension. She rubbed her chin with her free hand, and said. "She has your eyes, you know."

"She has her mother's eyes," Jim said firmly. They glared at one another in mock anger. Then Kimberly raised one eyebrow carefully, and said in her haughtiest voice. "Really?"

They both burst into laughter and, bending forward, bumped heads.

"Ow." Kimberly felt tears come to her eyes. Then she began to laugh again. He tenderly rubbed her head where they had collided. At the contact, she stopped laughing and they looked at each in relieved silence.

"I thought that you thought that Kiri and I..." Jim blushed. "It never even occurred to me..." He glared back over at Afsaneh, who was examining her nails intently.

Kimberly began laughing again, and Jim couldn't stay angry for long. He shook his head in amusement, and she was relieved to see the barrier that had loomed between them was gone.

For a little while, at least, life was good.

Will Spencer drummed his fingers on the arm of his chair impatiently. He'd been in San Francisco almost twenty-four hours and still hadn't met with Toshida. He knew the man had arrived from Japan. His own men at the airport had reported the Sukuru corporate jet landing hours ago.

So where was he?

He stood and strode over to the window and looked out at San Francisco

Bay. From this vantage point, he could see the actual docks and warehouses that were part of the impending deal. He would have gone out on the balcony, but the wind was blowing strongly and it would have messed up his hair.

Off to the left, he could see the Fisherman's Wharf, a local tourist trap. Next to it were the Tour Boat Docks that ran excursions to Alcatraz.

If that damn Jap was sightseeing...

A discreet cough disturbed his grousing. "Yes?"

"Sir, Mr. Toshida is on his way up."

"It's about time," Spencer said, turning away from the windows. "Call housekeeping, send up some trays of something or other."

He had barely finished speaking when a sharp knock came on the door. Spencer waited by the window as one of his people went to greet the Japanese executive.

It didn't surprise him when two other men came in first and fanned out to either side. They briefly glanced through the doors into the rest of the suite, then one called out something in Japanese.

Damn, I wish I understood their language, Spencer mused. It gives them one hell of an advantage.

Sho Toshida walked in. Spencer was startled. He'd assumed the elder Toshida would be the one to come, since Yoshi was missing. He didn't know too much about this young upstart, except that he was hungry for power. His very name assured that. They had only spoken the one time on the phone.

"Toshida-san," he said, bowing slightly. The cynical smile told him he should have waited, let the other be the first to offer greetings. *Fine, I've got the window behind me, you smart ass. You can spend the rest of this meeting blinking at my silhouette.*

"Mr. Spencer." Sho Toshida was tall and slender, with close-cropped black hair. It was almost impossible to guess Asiatic's ages, but Spencer recalled the man was in his late twenties. His bow was immeasurably less pronounced that Spencer's own. "Thank you for seeing me."

"I know we both would like to see this deal culminate and get on with our respective plans," Spencer said. "I think we can come to some equitable agreement."

"I'm sure," Toshida said vaguely. He looked around the suite, running his hand down the oak counter top. He slid the glass patio doors open, and a strong breeze poured in. "This is very nice. I've tried to reserve this suite before. It never seems to be available."

Spencer motioned him to a seat, but the Japanese moved to another that put the windows slightly off to the side, allowing him to see Spencer's features more clearly. "Drink?" Toshida shook his head once. "This suite? I have an...agreement with the management to have instant access to it should I need it."

Spencer smiled without opening his mouth and shrugged his shoulders. Toshida also smiled, but only at his mouth. No trace of humor reached his eyes. "I...see. I don't remember seeing this property listed when we went over the acquisitions and available trades."

Spencer allowed his smile to broaden. "That's because it's not for sale. I like this hotel."

"Hmmm," Toshida said. He stood and looked out over the same view Spencer had just been observing. "This would go a long way towards replacing the Jade Viking."

"I guess it would!" Spencer laughed openly. "But that's out of the question. We'll work something else out."

"Where is our ship?" Toshida was all business now as he turned to look at Spencer. His eyes showed a cruel streak that Will had heard about, but it probably didn't surface in public very often. "We have a deal with you. It includes Jade Viking."

"I haven't got a clue." Spencer joined him at the window and they both looked at the docks, and at the three freighters bearing the Sukuru emblem tied up there. His lips tightened in distaste as he felt the wind tug at his features. "Actually, I kind of thought you might know something about all this. God knows you had enough people on board."

"Was there no debris? No sign whatsoever of an explosion?" Toshida asked the questions casually, but Spencer picked up the tension in his voice. *He knows something I don't.*

"No sign of any kind. The transponder just cut off as if it ceased to exist." Spencer hesitated, wondering how far he should go. "That implies either one hell of an instant explosion, or somebody turning it off at the source."

"A hijacking?" Toshida was tense. "Is that your theory?"

"It seems unlikely," Spencer admitted. "Where could you take a ship that size without it being noticed? And we had satellite coverage within an hour. Over that entire part of the Pacific and Aleutians. Hell, it couldn't have gotten out of satellite range that quickly."

"We surmised the same." Toshida put his hands together and Spencer stared at how long his fingers were. "Debris would have also shown, which made us believe the...integrity of the satellite was suspect."

"That was one of our satellites," Spencer said softly.

"Yes, it was."

"I don't like your insinuations." Spencer abruptly turned away and walked over to the bar. One of his men poured him a glass of brandy without his asking. "We have nothing to gain by causing this situation. If anything, this plays into your hands."

Sho Toshida faced him, his head thrown back. "My father is on that ship. We would do nothing to jeopardize his safety."

"The woman I plan on marrying was on that ship," Spencer said, then winced. If they did have Jade Viking secreted away somewhere, he'd just given them one hell of a trump card. Well, not really. A choice between Kimberly's safety and his own success was no choice at all. Of course, Toshida didn't know that.

"The Martin woman?" Sho Toshida smiled slightly. "I met her before departure. She's quite...willful."

"If you only knew," Spencer muttered. At least part of the reason he wouldn't hesitate to trade her safety for a big deal was that he couldn't be sure he would ever actually get her to agree to marry him. His attempts at romance so far had fallen on lukewarm waters.

"I tire from the time change." Toshida bowed to him. "I would like to continue this conversation tomorrow."

"Certainly." Spencer bowed back. "We have a suite prepared for you here, if you like."

"Thank you, but I've already made other arrangements." Spencer ground his teeth at being caught unawares. *Why didn't I know he had someplace already reserved? What the hell are my people doing for the money I pay them?*

He concentrated on being polite until the man and his entourage were finally gone, then he drained the glass and threw it out the window in fury.

One of his men ducked his head in shock and, wide-eyed, stepped outside to see where it was going to land. After all, they were over fifty stories up.

"Everybody out...now!" Spencer sat at the small desk that was the concession to having a work space in the luxurious setting. He picked up the phone, then glared at the men moving uncertainly towards the door. "Are you all deaf? Out!"

Spencer waited until they were all gone and the door closed behind them.

He hated using this resource, but circumstances called for it. This man had never failed him in the past. If anybody could find what happened to Jade Viking, he could.

He cursed as he heard the familiar recording. Couldn't he just once catch the man first try?

"Groundhog, this is Spencer. I want you to call me..."

CHAPTER TWELVE

Lasty sat down at his station with a sigh of relief. He could feel the stares of his fellow Baerd and quickly powered up, pretending to be engrossed in one of the screens. Thank Dar he was the ranking Baerd on board. As it was, Inam had made it very clear what she thought of the way he and Dutter had lost control. Fortunately, she ranked just below him and couldn't really do anything; at least not until they returned to base.

But if looks could kill...hey! If looks could kill... what a great expression! He couldn't wait to tell Dutter about it later on. She would think it clever. Guiltily he peeked around the bridge. The other seven Baerd quickly turned back to their stations, looking industrious and oblivious of him.

At that point Dutter entered the bridge and came to her station to his right. Irle gave her a stern look and muttered something under his breath as she relieved him. She blushed slightly and responded curtly. He snorted and left the bridge, shaking his head.

Lasty turned back to his computer and brought up the warehouse unit storing the Humans. They were mostly sitting around as usual, along the walls and to the far end of the room from the hatch. There was a sizeable open space near the hatch. At this moment it was being utilized as a rehearsal area.

They called it "dance." It was graceful, although very different from anything his own race did. They had a large basket in the center of the space with long poles on either side for carrying it. Big enough to hold a Human inside, he noted. In fact, shifting to infra-red, he saw there was a Human crouching inside, holding the lid down from underneath, a female.

As he watched, she began to lift the lid, turning slowly as she rose. Two men gracefully moved next to the basket and lifted her effortlessly down to the floor. She began moving in a languid manner that he found intriguing. Several other males plucked on long strings tied to sticks, providing a rhythm for her to move to.

Lasty glanced over at Dutter's screen and found her watching the same thing. She felt his gaze and, pinkening, applied herself to her computer. Quickly he slaved his screen to hers and opened a communication box between them.

"What do you think?" he queried. "Will the Ananab find this entertaining?"

"I don't know about them, but I like it," she replied. "They're incredibly graceful. And extremely…"

"Don't say it!" Lasty broke in on her, feeling sweat on his brow. He had to change the subject before he embarrassed himself again. "I don't trust these Humans. I think they're up to something."

"They certainly are." Lasty imagined he could feel laughter behind her words on the screen. "I think they've got a plan, but I can't figure it out."

Lasty nodded as he answered her. "They haven't made a move towards the forward cargo hold on their ship. They have some sort of organized chain of command, though. I think I've found their leader. It's that male that woke up early, Jim M'rrsan."

"Of course it is!" Lasty was surprised by her confidence. "Two others are constantly being called Captain by everyone. I think they are his chief assistants, but he is obviously in charge."

"How can you be so sure?" Lasty was doubtful.

"Ask the computer," she returned.

Lasty winced. He should have thought of that. By now, the computer had enough background to begin an analysis that would be fairly accurate.

He asked the computer to do a background check. It had all the broadcasts they had received while in the vicinity of the planet Earth.

"Working." The computer quickly gave limited biographies on several possible choices.

Lasty looked at the first. Hmm, this one was a musician, not a dancer. He asked it to bring up a picture and squinted at the results. Well, maybe that was him, but it was hard to tell. A lot of these Humans looked alike to him, although there was more variety within their race than usually found in most species.

"What do you think," he asked Dutter, doubtfully. "Is that him?"

"I don't think so," she responded. "According to these records, this man is dead. And his features seem different to me."

Lasty nodded, berating himself for not noticing the date of death. But there was a footnote, mentioning that some people thought he was still alive. Yes! That was it! That would explain his mysteriousness. He was in hiding, possibly a criminal on his own world. Excitedly, he showed Dutter his theory.

"What about this second one?" Dutter continued. "The picture looks more like him, and the age seem closer. This one's an actor, though. Again, no dancer."

"I'm sure I'm right." Lasty was triumphant. This would impress Captain Storhesh for sure. "Computer, is there a plot by the Humans to escape? And is this man the leader?"

"Yes to both questions." Lasty was shocked, even though he was half expecting that response. But so quickly?

"Explain," Lasty commanded the computer.

"The furtive actions and intentionally disguised conversations make it a 97% certainty that the Humans are hiding something. All of them defer to his suggestions and comments, even the two men listed as Captains on the ship's log."

"What is their plan?" Lasty prayed silently to Dar, waiting for the machine's response.

"Unknown."

"Theories?" Lasty persisted. The computer was silent for almost a minute, then gave a curt answer.

"Insufficient data."

"No matter."

Lasty almost fell out of his seat at the sound of the voice over his shoulder. The Captain!

"This Human male, 'Mrrs or Mrrsan', will be a lesson for the rest of them," the Captain sneered. He loomed high overhead and Lasty shrank deep into his seat, quivering. "The Humans have requested a chance to display their 'dance' for us. Well, let's bring them up here, oh, before next feeding."

His claw tapped at the screen.

"Make sure that Human is with them. When they reach the bridge, have the computer keep him centered on the main screen." The Captain reared up to his full height and laughed. "It's time for yet another example to be made." He tapped the screen again. "And there it is."

Captain Lang spoke fondly of his cabin in the Aleutian Islands. It was accessible only by boat or seaplane, and he had built the log structure with the help of his two sons.

A number of people sat around the captain seemingly listening, but Kimberly decided they were lost in their own memories. A very tan older couple looked at each other wistfully, and she imagined that they were remembering their sailboat, used on weekends off the coast of California.

Another couple held hands and Kimberly decided they remembered the vacations at Tahoe, skiing down the Nevada side of Heavenly Valley Resort to gamble in the lodge at the bottom. They would take the lift back to the top and gaze eastward, seeing brown deserts and bare mountain ranges. To the west was California, a green and white paradise spread out before them, with cars the size of matchheads far below.

Or maybe it was Colorado. And their memories were of Loveland Pass, and the mountainside restaurants and bars of Breckinridge.

Captain Tachibana sat with glazed eyes. He probably saw his little shack in his home village, where fishing was the only livelihood, mere minutes(and yet centuries) from downtown Tokyo.

Kimberly smiled to herself. She should be a novelist. All those visions were only imaginings, but possibly very real. There was one thing she could see in all their eyes that she felt she could guarantee was absolutely the truth; they were all homesick.

She looked up as Yvette Stephanian awkwardly sat down next to her, thick legs off to one side, leaning on one arm. Kimberly liked Yvette and was glad to see her. There were a few things about Jim she would like to know, and Yvette was as good a place to start as any.

"I see you and Jim had a long talk last night," Yvette smiled broadly at her.

Kimberly was disconcerted by her directness and winced. "Umm, was there anyone who didn't notice us?"

"Only those in the 'blue room,'" Yvette smirked.

The blue room was where the Captain had designated "familial activities permitted." Not that everyone that used the room were family, but light years from Earth they all needed human contact, whether intimate, or simply friendly. It was a smaller room off the main area, thankfully with its own facilities, for what they were worth.

All the toilet areas seemed strangely out of proportion, but then Kimberly guessed the wide variety in the different species on board made it impossible to fit everyone. The ship was obviously designed with the Ananab in mind, with wide corridors, large rooms, and high ceilings everywhere. I guess we were lucky to not be kidnapped by groundhogs or alligators, she chuckled to herself.

"So, talk to me!" Yvette prompted.

Kimberly sighed. "He's much more complicated that I thought." Yvette nodded, knowingly. "And that little..." She stopped and reconsidered. "Umm, nothing," Kimberly finished lamely.

Yvette laughed and shook her head disparagingly. "Kimberly, she's only fifteen years old."

Kimberly sighed and nodded her agreement. "True, but why is it only now that anybody bothered telling me this? It's not as if she looks fifteen."

Yvette looked down at her own chest and sighed wistfully, shaking her head in mock dismay.

"Not to mention the 'other' aspects of the relationship between her and Jim," Kimberly continued, resisting the urge to do the same.

"You mean that he's her godfather?" Yvette gave her a steely look and leaned forward. "He would do anything for his 'Godchild'."

"Right, God...child." Kimberly leaned back against the wall, exasperated. She stared back at Yvette languidly. "I guess she gets away with murder, having Hakim for a father and Jim for her...Godfather."

The pause didn't go unnoticed and Yvette eyed her speculatively. "He told you?"

Kimberly smiled faintly at the memory. "He told me a lot last night. About Nasri, Hakim, his parents, and afterwards." She hesitated. "And the bodies."

Yvette breathed out heavily and nodded in agreement. "That weighs on him, every day of his life." She gave Kimberly a searching look. "But all of that is not common knowledge to all the cast and crew. Everyone knows Afsaneh is like a daughter to him. Some people even think she may be his daughter." She kept her voice low as Captain Lang droned on in the background.

"Hardly anybody knows the whole story," Yvette admitted. "But everybody in our group knows Jim." Yvette's gaze grew a little harder. "They also know what he can do," and she looked upward towards the hidden cameras they all knew were there somewhere. "Especially in his field of 'work'."

"As a dancer," Kimberly smiled demurely.

Yvette grinned, openly pleased with her. "Yes, as a dancer." They both laughed.

"What's so funny?" They turned as one to see Afsaneh standing over them. Kimberly looked at her, appraisingly. The young girl shifted her weight from one foot to the other uncomfortably.

"I saw you and Jim talking last night," she spoke boldly, as if trying to seize initiative.

"Yes," Kimberly agreed. She let the silence build. The young girl was obviously working herself up to something.

"He, ah, seems to like you." Afsaneh was having trouble keeping her poise.

"You think so?" Kimberly stared at her boldly.

Afsaneh made an irritated sound. "It's obvious that he does, and that you like him, too!"

Kimberly looked at her nails, rubbing away an imaginary smudge. After a moment she looked up at Afsaneh and gave her a bright smile. "On the deck, the day before, you said three things."

Afsaneh let out her breath explosively. She looked down at her brightly painted toenails. Somehow, with all the trials and tribulations they had all endured, she still managed to look as if she were ready to hit the mall and shop til she dropped.

"I think you already know," she procrastinated.

"Know what?" Kimberly asked sweetly.

"Jim's my father,"

Kimberly looked at her, shocked by the bold admission.

"At least, he might as well be," Afsaneh admitted, flinging her long black hair backward off her shoulders. "He and my dad have raised me all my life. And I do love him." She stared at Kimberly. "And I'm going to make sure he doesn't fall for just any pretty face."

Kimberly laughed despite herself.

"Are we having fun, yet?" came a familiar voice from behind her. Before she could respond, Jim continued. "Young lady, you and I need to have a little talk."

Afsnaeh smiled weakly and looked at Kimberly for support. "We were just taking care of a few details that might have been, uh, misunderstood before." She smiled brightly, and Kimberly had a hard time keeping a grin off her face.

"Seventeen?" she asked with a raised eyebrow.

Afsaneh looked at Jim uncomfortably. "Well, almost."

"Fifteen is nowheres near seventeen," Jim snapped at her.

"Almost sixteen," she returned quickly.

"In two months."

"Six weeks!"

Kimberly glanced sideways at Yvette and they both burst into laughter. Afsaneh nervously joined in, looking at Jim beseechingly. He frowned at the three of them and shook his head. Whatever he had been about to say would never be known. The large screen by the hatch flashed several times, accompanied by a loud buzzing, then one of the large lobsters called Ananab stared out at them.

"Prepare yourself! You will give your 'dance' presentation on our bridge for our Captain and the crew to see." The alien's eye stalks swivelled to the side and then back to the fore.

"In one of your hour!"

Jim stiffened and his face grew hard. The smile that finally appeared was obviously forced. "You ladies get near a wall, and stay low."

"I'm going as part of the troupe." Afsaneh put her hands on her hips, defiantly.

"No, you are not." Jim didn't seem particularly surprised by her statement, but was firm.

"I'm as good, or even better than those other women, and they're going!" Afsaneh glared at him.

Jim leaned forward and the young girl shrank back despite her determination. Kimberly herself almost backed up from the sheer force of willpower he emanated.

"You are fifteen years old." Jim's voice was colder than Kimberly had ever heard it. "I would be watching out for you, and it would jeopardize the mission, and probably cost me my life." His eyes were diamond-hard emeralds. For a very long, tense moment, she met his look defiantly, but then her eyes dropped. He sighed in relief, and swept the girl into his arms, hugging her hard.

"I love you," he said huskily. "Now do as I say."

"Yes, sir," she said meekly. "I love you, too...Jim."

He released her gently and began to turn to the two older women. A large man appeared at his side, a very pregnant Asian woman behind him.

"Sir, could I speak to you." The young man was probably in his mid-twenties and well over six feet tall. Kimberly thought he looked like a much larger, burlier version of Jim himself.

Jim looked puzzled. He glanced questioningly at Yvette, who shrugged.

"Yes?"

"May I be of any assistance, Sir?" The young man kept his stare just over Jim's shoulder.

Jim gave him an appraising look. He took another look at the Asian woman. "Army? Stationed in Korea?"

The young man nodded, surprised. "Special Forces."

"Your wife?" Jim looked at the woman again.

Nodding, he blushed as he glanced backwards.

"Good." Jim nodded and Kimberly marveled at how he took control of the situation. "Captain Lang."

The older man stood a few feet away. He looked at the youth and nodded to Jim.

"What's your name?" Jim was brusque.

"James McGregor, Sir!" He instinctively stiffened his spine.

"Mr. McGregor, I would be proud to have your assistance." Jim smiled and then grew stern. "You have two duties."

McGregor almost grinned, but then his face was a mask again.

"First, secure your wife and unborn child." Jim caught the younger man's eyes and held them as if in a vise. "If at all possible, watch the Captain's back. That goes for Captain Tachibana, also. We're going to need their services badly, very soon."

The ex-military man was obviously disappointed, but nodded glumly. "Yes, sir."

"Son." Jim stepped closer to him and spoke quietly. "This is not a bullshit job."

Jim motioned to the man's wife. "She may be the first human to give birth in outer space. She and her child, your child, are infinitely precious to us." His voice hardened. "More so than you, is that understood?"

"Yes, sir." Pride now rang in McGregor's voice.

"And the Captain is the rallying point around which we all gather. He has his own men, of course, but one more certainly can't hurt. Especially if that one is Special Forces!"

"Yes, sir!"

The young giant actually saluted him then and backed away, taking his wife with him. Jim smiled apologetically at Lang, and shrugged.

Captain Lang nodded approval. "Well done, lad."

Jim turned back to Kimberly and Yvette as Hakim came up. The ex-roommates hugged, and Hakim pointed at Afsaneh.

"Watch her, Jim. She's tricky and probably wants to come along."
"We've already discussed that." Jim smiled at her sweetly and she pouted. He turned to Yvette and Kimberly.

They both came forward to hug him, and he swept them both into his arms holding them tightly for a moment. He reluctantly released Yvette. "Be careful, Stephanian."

"You be careful, Morris!" Yvette's eyes were suddenly full, and she wiped them with a sleeve, quietly swearing under her breath.

Kimberly stood in his arms, a little self-conscious, but not wanting to let go. He smiled wistfully down at her. "I'm glad we had the chance to talk." He hesitated, "...to clear the air."

Kimberly nodded, not trusting her voice. He held her close and kissed her cheek tenderly. Then he was gone, moving smoothly over to the waiting crew. There were eight men besides himself, and four women. Six of them positioned themselves along the two long poles used to carry the huge basket.

They watched Jim fasten a belt around his waist and then leave, escorted by four guards.

Kimberly was numb. Yvette placed a hand on her shoulder, yet she could barely feel it. They hugged and Yvette sobbed quietly, her face buried against Kimberly, who was having difficulty keeping her own composure.

She looked over at Afsaneh and Hakim.

"Daddy, what's going to happen to him?" The young girl cried. "Daddy..." She broke down at that point, and Kimberly saw tears streaming down the father's face as he absentmindedly patted his daughter on the back, holding her close, comforting her.

Yvette pulled away, embarrassed. "I'm sorry. It's just..."

"I know," Kimberly felt distant herself, as if she was watching this scene from a great height. "Is Jim Catholic?"

Yvette was puzzled by the sudden change in topic, but answered. "No, I think his family was Protestant. Why?"

"Well, last night." Kimberly spoke woodenly and a great weariness overtook her. "It was as if he was at confession. Like he wasn't expecting to..." She stopped, fear flashing through her, understanding now.

They stared at each other in horror.

Lasty leaned forward on his lower two elbows, and stared intently at the screen. One upper hand flew across the keyboard while the other rubbed nervously on the corner of his console, polishing a spot already bright from wear.

He watched the humans separate and the dance crew leave with the guards. These females were displaying grief and sadness out of character with the situation. The very worse that could happen, as far as they knew, was the Ananab would say their art wasn't of any value. They acted as if loved ones were dead, or dying. Or going off to battle to die...

Lasty's eyes widened and he came off his lower elbows in excitement. That had to be it!

"Computer, extrapolate the chances of the Humans successfully assaulting the bridge, overpowering the guards and assuming control of the ship," Lasty queried the machine.

"10.05 percent chance of success," came a swift response.

Hmm, that seemed high, Lasty thought. "Same theory, with Baerd instead of the Humans?"

".89 percent." The computer didn't hesitate.

Lasty couldn't help but feel irritation by the answers. "Why would the Humans have such a greater chance?" Ten times as much chance? That was insulting!

"Humans have well-documented records of fighting against overwhelming odds, regardless of the chances of success. The chances of the Baerd attempting to seize the ship are negligible. Any revolt would be accidental or forced by circumstances, and therefore would not be organized or likely to succeed." Lasty found himself nodding in agreement.

"The Humans have also developed many fighting styles that use little or no actual weapons. A great number of these Humans appear to have extensive experience in these methods."

"Computer, review the emotional displays by the Humans remaining in the holding cell. Are the Humans going to try and seize the bridge?" Lasty began to lean forward again but the computer answered so fast he hadn't even moved yet.

"Yes."

"How?' Lasty's hands were trembling as he grasped the console.

"Unknown." The computer was unusually abrupt today, it seemed to him. "Insufficient data."

Lasty remembered some of the strange concepts he'd read about the

Humans. How could the ship's computer put their culture into perspective when it had been programmed by Baerd for Ananab use.

He cocked his head. Now there was a thought. "Computer, do you understand the human concept of 'walking a mile in my shoes'?"

"Yes."

"Use human logic and emotions. Extrapolate potential human response to this situation." Lasty glanced carefully around the bridge. The guards were the normal consignment, two Tryr and two Srotag along either side wall on the upper walkway, one of each at the entrance hatch, and the respective commanders at the apex of the room, near the Captain and his two siblings, who lounged at their stations. None of them seemed too concerned about the impending influx of hostile aliens. With a start his attention came back to the screen.

"Human chances of success now 36.88 percent." Lasty felt his eyes bulge in disbelief. Before he could question the machine, it explained its reasoning.

"The Humans have acquired weapons and appear to be capable of using them."

"Our weapons?"

"Negative."

Lasty thought of the cargo in the forward hold of the captured vessel and exclaimed. "Then what?" The computer displayed the wide leather belt M'rss had around his waist and high-lighted the many-pointed metal stars placed around it. It then flashed around the basket, showing the dozens of feathered sticks lining it's sides, the two long poles used to carry it, the percussion instruments used by the four women and the two men not carrying the basket. It continued showing various bits of dress and ornament that could double as weaponry as Lasty gaped.

"What kind of weapon is the metal star?" Lasty whispered.

"Thrown, it sticks into whatever it hits." The emotionless response was a relief to Lasty.

"That's no problem, then," he sighed in relief. "How hard could they throw it? These Humans aren't that strong,... are they?"

The computer split off a side screen showing an athletic competition with a man standing on a mound of dirt throwing a round object past another man swinging a stick. One hundred and five mph showed underneath, and the computer translated that into a recognizable speed. He gasped and numbly watched as the computer went on to show the various uses of the different implements they carried. The stringed sticks could be used to fire the feathered sticks on the sides of the basket with devastating effects. The two sticks connected by a chain could be used in close combat. The list lengthened.

"Captain...," he began, turning to the Command perch.

At that moment, alarms began going off. The computer switched to a view of the empty space around the ship. Or not so empty, as it happened.

"Go to sub-light speed and silent running!" Captain Storhesh snapped. "Tech Lasty, report!"

"The computer detects an anomaly that could be a ship traveling at trans-dimensional speed." Lasty stared at the projections as they appeared before him. It will pass on our left side, fairly distantly." He swiveled to face his Captain. "Sir, we were partially shielded by that red-giant star system. We had the better angle, and were probably obscured by emissions."

"Who are they?" Captain Storhesh stared angrily at the large display on the wall across from him.

Lasty glanced at Dutter and she nodded. Good, she already had that on his screen for him. Good anticipation from his staff. Then he saw the answer and winced. "Umm, sir, it appears that it is an Egelv ship. We may have been observed, after all."

Captain Storhesh gave a scream of rage and slammed a claw against the rail in front of him. It buckled under the impact. Lasty could understand his frustration. Egelv ships sensors were far superior to their own and it carried many times the firepower. Not that the Captain would even consider attacking the Egelv.

The entire bridge watched silently as the anomaly slowly moved across the screen. After several minutes it was obvious that they either hadn't seen the P'Tassum or didn't care.

Captain Storhesh laughed victoriously and his two eyestalks swiveled around to Lasty again. "Estimated course?" he questioned. Lasty turned again to his screen and the answer was already there. Oh no, he moaned to himself. There goes the good mood.

"They are on a course that will intercept with the planet we acquired the Humans from," the Baerd admitted, ducking his head as if expecting a blow. Then he remembered what he had been doing before the alert. "About the Humans, Captain..."

"Arrgh!" The Captain gnashed his mandibles furiously. "I'm already sick of these soft-skinned animals. Maybe we'll try them on the menu."

Lasty blanched, and even the guards stirred uneasily. Eating sentient beings was considered offensive to almost all the middle or higher tiered races. Although there had been stories regarding Tryr and Hoag, Ananab and Hoag, Srotag and Hoag, well, actually it was rumored that Hoag had satisfied many appetites at one time or another.

He understood the Captain's anger, however. If the Egelv discovered the rich planet Earth, they would claim it under their sphere of influence. The Ananab would lose a very rich, very unique prize. It would also be very difficult explaining this to the Hstahni, who claimed the Ananab under their sphere of influence.

The hatch opened and the Humans and their guards entered the bridge.

Kimberly watched crewmen of the Jade Viking situate themselves around the room, trying to look inobtrusive and still cover the entire cavernous hold. She laid down on the floor some distance away from the hatch, but close enough to see any action that might take place. Her eyes widened as she watched one of the Japanese members of the crew casually position himself about ten yards from the hatch, slightly to its right.

She nudged Yvette next to her and pointed. Yvette nodded and in turn whispered to Janice, sitting on her other side.

"That's enough man for all of us," Janice giggled. "Assuming men were our 'cup of tea.'"

The man wore nothing but a loincloth that reminded Kimberly of a diaper. He had to weight almost four hundred pounds, and it wasn't the chiseled musculature of Jim or that young soldier McGregor. The cloth came up between the cheeks of his buttocks in a roll, and flesh hung everywhere.

"Jade Viking has its own sumi wrestler," Yvette shook her head. "The ship that carries one of everything, just in case," she finished wryly.

Kimberly had seen the man before, but always fully dressed. She noticed several other Japanese near the movie props. Koro Asaya casually placed his hands on one of the handles of the cart they had used to carry most of the costumes and assorted loose items back from the ship. An older member of the Sukuru management group stood across from him, holding another handle.

She noticed that Nagami, head of Sukuru security seemed to be subtly directing certain people. Several American crewmen stood by the wall panel to the right of the hatch, trying to look casual, but only looking nervous to her.

She saw Naga Furukawa standing close by, with several officers from the combined crews and a number of sailors. First Officer Danny DelaRosa was talking quietly with Second officer Koro Asaya. They were both pale, but not frightened looking. If anything, they had a determined air that brought her a momentary sense of security.

The entire room watched the screen showing the dance crew being led down one corridor after another. She noticed Suyo taking careful notes, watching the screen intently. She's making a makeshift map, Kimberly realized with a growing sense of unease, even as she admired the initiative. I think it's about to hit the fan!

The lights suddenly dimmed and the screen went out. Several voices rose in panic and swiftly subsided. One woman began screaming and Kimberly winced as she heard a scuffle. The voice abruptly stopped.

"What do you think...?" Yvette leaned closer. "Did they figure this out? Or is there something else going on?"

"Ladies, stay calm," Hakim Riahi spoke up from nearby. Kimberly turned to look at him, and saw he and Afsaneh huddled a few feet away.

"Stay calm yourself, ya sexist pig," Yvette retorted. "You men are the ones that always get too excited."

"Yeah, as in prematurely," Janice whispered theatrically. Afsaneh joined the other three women in nervous laughter while Hakim muttered under his breath.

The lights and screen finally came back on and Kimberly watched Jim and his troupe enter the bridge. Voices rose around the room, and immediately Captain Lang boomed out. "Everyone quiet, please. Please be quiet and listen."

They all watched Jim lead the procession to the forward part of the bridge where it narrowed to a point. The three giant lobster Aliens loomed high over him. Kimberly watched in growing panic as one catman stood between Jim and the lobsters and one of the bear-rhinos shifted behind him.

"You have brought your 'dance troupe' to perform?" The voice of Captain Storhesh thundered over the loudspeakers. He sounds mad, Kimberly thought. At least I think that's what an angry lobster sounds like. Jim answered and the alien Captain slammed a claw down on a rail in front of it. From the shape of the rail, she suspected that wasn't an unusual action.

"You lie, Human!" The Captain bellowed. "You are the leader of these Humans, and you have been plotting against me!"

Jim started to answer, but the Captain waved a claw dismissively. "It's too late. I don't want to hear it. Maybe the rest of the Humans will learn something from this."

"No!" Kimberly rose to her feet in horror as the Rhino-bear behind Jim swung both hands inward, catching the actor's head between them, effortlessly swinging the lighter Human body upward.

CHAPTER THIRTEEN

"...maybe the rest of the Humans will learn something from this!"

Jim felt the Srotag Commander Acha close in behind him. Desperately he threw both arms over his head, and two giant vise-like paws slammed into his triceps. He tried to flex his shoulder muscles but the huge alien was too strong. Slowly but inexorably, his arms began to press inward, until they almost touched the sides of his head. In front of him, Commander Tak leaned forward, snarling his laughter.

Jim screamed as his shoulders reached their stretching limit. His right foot lashed out and caught the laughing Tryr squarely between the legs. A shocked look came to Commander Tak's face as he gasped, still snarling, and leaned slightly forward.

Commander Acha was pulling him upward, still trying to press his arms through the sides of his head. Jim leaped, using the Srotag's thigh as a springboard. Vaulting upward, he smashed his right foot straight into the catman's snarling snout and felt bone break beneath his heel.

Jim continued kicking upward, using the Tryr's face to push higher. He sobbed with pain at the pressure on his shoulders as he rose higher and higher until he was entirely upside down, feet straight up in the air. The grip of the rhino-bear began to slip and Jim pumped his feet to gain momentum. As his arms came free he cupped his fingers and stabbed downward, catching one of the armored giant's eye-sockets perfectly. His right hand missed slightly, hitting the heavily boned brow above the other eye.

As Jim's knees came crashing into the armored back he managed to get two fingers into the other socket. The blinded rhino-bear wailed in agony and Jim yanked backward as hard as he could. He felt a sudden release in the other's neck and dived off to the side as the dying commander collapsed to the floor.

Screams and the sound of fighting were behind him, but he had no time to look. Captain Storhesh loomed high over him and he rolled, barely avoiding the claw that slapped the floor. Then he was on his feet, rushing in close, using his arms to block attempts by the captain to reach him.

Captain Storhesh made the mistake of looking down at him as he scaled upward, using the small, upper arms as handholds. He saw the deadly mandibles closing and thrust himself higher, grabbing the captain by the eye-stalks. Both eyes bulged in horror as the alien found himself staring directly into Jim's face. As much as he would have enjoyed savoring the moment, Jim never paused. With a jerk, he tore one stalk out with his right hand. Not bothering to release the demolished eye, he smashed downward with his closed fist, driving chitinous shards of shell deep into the brain.

Jim felt a motion to his right and flung the mangled eye-stalk at it. One of the captain's brothers flinched for a moment, then its mandibles spread widely as it shrilled at him. Both of its clawed arms began closing in on him.

Jim tore a shuriken off his belt and flung it into the yawning maw as hard as he could. Tearing the other eye-stalk off, he leaped backwards, dodging the third lobster's attempt to snag him. He grabbed the dying captain's outstretched claw-arm and shoved it in the way of the attacking brother.

The third Ananab screamed in anger as it cleanly snipped off its brother's arm instead of Jim's head. As he backed away, he could hear the choking sounds coming from the lobster that had swallowed the shuriken. The sole uninjured brother charged him and Jim braced himself to try and get inside the flaying claws.

An arrow appeared in its thorax and it reared back in pain and surprise. Immediately a second arrow embedded next to the first. The Ananab opened its maw to scream and the third arrow almost completely disappeared inside, only the feathered nock still showing.

Jim risked a glance as he vaulted the crushed railing, coming down to crouch beside the still-choking lobster. Kabu shifted to another target, letting arrow after arrow fly. *That's the best work he's ever done for me,* Jim thought, silently thanking the day he'd hired the young actor.

With the edge of his hand, Jim struck the remaining Ananab's thin neck, breaking it, in fact almost severing it. Then he pushed himself to his feet, looking for more enemies.

It didn't take long to find one. A Tryr charged him, drawing her sidearm. Behind him he could hear someone else approaching, heavy thundering feet giving away the invisible foe. Jim flung himself to the left and, bouncing off the wall, caught the right arm of the Tryr as she finished her side-draw. Pinning it momentarily against his chest, he swung his left arm, catching her elbow squarely. She gasped in pain as her elbow joint was destroyed. Involuntarily she fired her handgun.

Jim held her arm rigid, pointing towards the rushing Srotag. Whatever it fired was aimed at his chest and he staggered, then fell, apparently dead. Jim felt his eyes bulging. What kind of gun was this? Then he was moving again, dropping to kick her on the side of her right knee, causing it to collapse. Her weapon fell from her useless right paw.

She swung with her uninjured arm and he desperately tried to roll clear. He almost made it, too.

Jim felt his shoulder tear and, gasping in pain, he rolled to his feet. He turned sideways, automatically falling into stance to meet the catwoman limping towards him. She roared in fury, and he snarled back at her, trying to ignore the blood seeping from his wound.

She swiped at him with her left paw and he kicked upward, blocking the blow with his right foot. He feinted with the same leg and she fell for it. Leaping as high as he could, he sent his left foot upward with devastating force.

The Tryr warrior had obviously seen him dispatch her commander because she flung her head backwards to protect her snout. His thrust landed right where he'd aimed it, just under the chin, crushing her throat. She staggered backwards, trying to catch herself, all the time trying to breath. He snatched the dead Srotag's handgun from the floor.

Jim watched her reach down and pick up her own weapon, trying to bring it to bear. He aimed the unfamiliar gun and fired. She dropped without a sound.

Sagging in relief, he turned to face the room and saw that the battle was over. Kogo Ogami lay dead near the hatch, disemboweled. He had joined Jim's group of repeat actors the same time as Kabu. Mura Zataki had only been with him for two films but left a wife and two small children in Japan. He lay near the basket, one of the bows clutched in his dead hands. Jim thought he must have been killed by one of the alien handguns since there didn't seem to be a mark on his body.

Usagi Izu sat on the floor near the hatch holding his face with both hands, groaning softly. Blood seeped around them, dripping down into a steadily growing puddle between his legs.

Jim walked past the dead Ananab captain, staggering. Kabu stood there, arrow in bow, searching the room for any moving aliens. Without taking his eyes away from the search, he brought Jim up to date.

"Jozen and Omi are on their way back to the others." Kabu slowly lowered his weapon and his shoulders slumped in exhaustion. "They had two of the guard's handguns."

Jim nodded and tried to answer. Only a croaking sound came out. Swallowing, he tried again. "Kiri, are you girls okay?"

Kiri smiled uncertainly as she rose to her feet. She held an ornate comb in one hand, the normally hidden blade flashing in the light. The moment the action had started, the four women had been responsible for subduing the Baerd, uninjured, if possible. None of the eight four-armed aliens had offered any resistance. They had hit the deck when the fighting started.

"I'm fine, Jim." She saw the red soaking through his shirt. "You're hurt!"

Jim impatiently shook his head. "Looks worse than it is," he hurriedly assured her.

Sakai Motoo had taken up a defensive stand near the hatch, stolen alien weapon aimed, waiting. Sasama Sakakibara was running around the upper walkway, checking bodies, gathering any weapons he found.

Jim looked carefully at his own absconded handgun, checking for a safety. Not seeing one, he reluctantly stuffed it under his belt. He hugged Kiri carefully and then turned to his prisoners.

One of them rose, obviously fearful. "I am Lasty, Chief Technician of the Baerd. What will you do with us?"

Jim noticed that he was in the center of the picture on the large screen above the exit hatch. "Is the computer following my movements or something?"

"That was by order of the Captain." The Baerd glanced towards the pile of twitching limbs that was all that remained of the Ananab officers and winced. "Do you want me to stop it?"

Jim considered him for a moment. He didn't seem too disturbed by the death of his captain. This definitely had possibilities. He gave the technician a grin, intentionally showing his teeth and the albino flinched.

"Well, we can start with that. I've got a number of ideas for you and that clever computer, laddy. A number of ideas."

As the Srotag Commander attacked, Kimberly staggered to her feet, horrified. Afsaneh tore free from her father's grasp and crawled towards the hatch. He caught her ankle and held on, ignoring her struggles. Not uttering a sound, he grimly watched the screen.

They watched Jim get his arms up in time to protect his head, then kick the Tryr in front of him. Kimberly's attention was diverted by the huge sumi wrestler rushing towards the wall. The two crewmen barely got the panel next to the hatch removed and out of the way before the obese Japanese crashed through, popping loose the panel that faced the corridor outside their prison.

A Srotag guard was standing facing the other direction and both panel and wrestler crashed into his back, knocking him to the floor. Kimberly gaped as the two men by the cart pulled out the handles that acted as caps and leaped through the opening, now holding the long Samurai swords that had been concealed inside.

For all of Koro Asaya's youth and agility, the older Sukuru man beat him through the opening, leaping out of sight to the left. Asaya followed, swinging his blade. A roar sounded, and a body flew by the opening, almost too fast to be seen.

By this time more men were pouring out the gap, some holding more disguised blades, some holding makeshift clubs. Moments later, all sounds of battle came to an abrupt halt.

"Doctor needed here, quick!" Someone in the corridor called out urgently. Several men hurried to the hole and hesitantly looked out.

Kimberly turned back to the screen in time to see it split into two pictures. One showed Kabu and another actor shooting bows, calmly drawing arrow after arrow from the decorations of the basket. The other man fell, victim of some unseen weapon. Undeterred, Kabu kept firing.

To her relief, Kimberly saw that Jim was not only alive, but definitely still fighting. She winced at the graphic violence as he first blinded, then killed the alien captain.

"Come on, Jim," a low voice next to her startled Kimberly. Hakim Riahi was actually chanting, he was so intense. "Come on, you asshole. Kill them all! Don't stop moving!"

She looked to see what was happening by the hatchway. Koro Asaya carefully wiped blood from his blade. The sumi wrestler was being helped back inside by two men, both staggered by his weight. He didn't appear to be hurt, just dazed. Another load was being carried inside reverently, face covered. The first man through with a sword had also been the first casualty.

Captain Tachibana held the dead man's sword and looked at the blood dripping from it. He set his jaw and held the blade high. "He drew first blood, then gave his life for all of our sake." He glared around. "Let's not have it be in vain."

Naga Furukawa held up the two handguns captured off the dead aliens triumphantly. He hesitated a moment, then begrudgingly gave one to First Officer DelaRosa.

Commander Asaya quickly formed an assault group, mostly made up of crewmen, both American and Japanese. Furukawa joined him with several of the Sukuru security guards. Asaya nodded reluctantly and they all left to try and secure the engineering section. DelaRosa organized defenses around the single handgun and several short-bladed swords remaining.

A cheer went up as Jim killed the last guard on the bridge. The quieter sound of sobbing replaced it as people saw the price that had been paid in lives. As they watched the screen, Usagi Izu slumped over, evidently dead.

That made three dead on the bridge, and the older swordsman here in the makeshift prison. Only four dead, but they all left friends and relatives behind. And the fight had just begun. This was a huge ship, Kimberly thought sadly, watching several of the actors and actresses comfort each other. What would the total cost in lives be?

Hakim and Afsaneh climbed shakily to their feet. The three of them watched the screen as Jim began to interrogate one of his captives. He looked up at the camera and said something in a low tone to the alien. The screen went blank.

"What's going on?" Afsaneh gasped in dismay.

"I think Jim did that so the enemy won't know what he's up to," Hakim said thoughtfully. Kimberly nodded in agreement. That certainly made sense, but she would rather be able to see that he was okay.

"Jim was wounded." Yvette's worried voice came from behind her.

Kimberly turned and tried to put on a brave smile. "I think he's okay." Kimberly recognized the lack of conviction in her own voice. "He was moving around and everything."

Yvette nodded hesitantly, looking unconvinced. She turned to see Afsaneh sitting on the floor, tears streaming down her face. Yvette got a determined look and met Kimberly's eyes for a moment. *We have to be strong for the rest.* Yvette nodded again, as if she heard the thought herself.

Kimberly wiped sweat from her brow and looked around again. Most of the people were huddled as far from the door as they could get. A thin layer of crewmen and assorted others gave an illusion of security as they formed a human shield to protect the bulk of the prisoners. Few were armed with more than determined expressions, but their presence was comforting.

Janice Wooley and Rick Baker were back at the computer terminal, obviously trying to get some sort of status report. The two captains and Nagami were huddled against the wall by the new door the sumi wrestler had created. He had recovered and was standing between them and the hatch, keeping a careful watch.

The hatch opened and Commander DelaRosa shook his head as he stepped halfway through and stopped to inspect the door. "It wasn't even locked," he called out loudly and gave the gigantic wrestler a lopsided grin. DelaRosa posted several crewmen to keep a watch down the corridor and looked curiously at the conference the captains were holding.

He gave his handgun to one of the watchful crewmen and walked over to join them. Captain Tachibana's First Officer, Commander Zai Totakahari, a wizened, tiny man old enough to be his grandfather, met him a few steps away from the gathering and stopped him with a question. As they stood there, Kimberly froze as the armed guard fell without a sound.

A Tryr leaped through the open hatch and fanned his weapon around the room. She watched with horror as it neared her own position. Roaring, the sumi wrestler, dwarfed as he was by the rangy Tryr, hurled himself against the alien, catching him from the side. They both rolled across the floor and the gun skidded away to bounce off the wall.

A second Tryr appeared in the door, his weapon hesitating momentarily between his comrade on the right and the hundreds of Humans to his left. Then he snapped his gun up and began firing into the crowd. Screams rang out and people scrambled to avoid his aim. Then an arrow appeared in his chest.

The tall panther howled in pain and fury as he paused to tear it out. Another appeared, then a third. The Tryr no longer tried to pull them out. Instead he searched the crowd, trying to pick out the archer. Meanwhile, the first catman and the obese Japanese came to a halt against the wall. The Tryr came to his feet growling as the wrestler lay motionless, blood pouring from tremendous wounds caused by feline claws.

Kimberly gasped as the spinning handgun came to a halt in front of her. She looked down at it, unable to move. The catman bounded towards her. Fear caused a surge of adrenaline and she kicked out as hard as she could. The gun flew past the infuriated charging guard, and as it vainly tried to turn, a foot shot out and stopped the sliding gun.

James McGregor picked it up and looked down at the unfamiliar weapon. Two Japanese armed with short swords charged the catman and blades and claws flashed, too fast to follow.

The first Tryr grunted as it finally saw Taga Motari bringing his bow up to fire a fourth and final arrow. It was a race to see who would shoot first.

McGregor beat them both as he whirled and fired, catching the Tryr from the side. It dropped soundlessly and he turned back to the single remaining enemy. One swordman was down, his face and throat gone. The other was trying vainly to raise the blade to block an attack. His shoulder was pouring blood, and he couldn't do it.

"Down!" McGregor shouted and snapped a shot off hurriedly. It only grazed the Tryr but it got his attention. Rumbling a growl, it dived directly towards Kimberly and cover. She panicked as she tried to backpedal. One of the catman's arms hung useless as it neared her. Then he spun to the side as the tall soldier winged him again, this time in the leg.

The third shot finished him and Kimberly staggered against the wall, almost knocking Afsaneh down as the young girl caught her. Surprisingly strong arms held her and dimly Kimberly heard a soothing voice.

"It's okay, Ma'am." Afsaneh guided her to lean on the wall. "You're safe now." The petite teenager looked at her admiringly. "That was very brave, kicking the gun."

"Brave, yeah." Kimberly felt dizzy and faint. She focused with difficulty. "Did you call me Ma'am?"

She heard Afsaneh sigh in relief. "I was always taught to show respect to old people." Kimberly tried to glare at her but didn't have the strength. Smartass little brat. She finally looked up and realized Afsaneh was much more concerned than she let on. She tried to think of a comeback but was at a loss to even speak. Shaking her head weakly, she embraced the girl and felt the hug returned.

"Are we safe now?" Yvette wondered from a few steps away. Kimberly shrugged, unconcerned. At this moment, I'm alive, she thought wonderingly. I'll never take that for granted again.

Commander Totakahari picked up the second weapon and stood looking down the corridor from the hatch as DelaRosa and McGregor began reorganizing defenses.

Kimberly stiffened as she saw the old officer begin to raise the gun and fall soundlessly to the deck. She wasn't the only one that saw, though.

"Another attack!" A yell rang out and Kimberly realized with dread that things were far from over. Grabbing Afsaneh, she dashed for the uncertain safety of the crowd, Yvette leading the way. Behind them, the battle continued.

CHAPTER FOURTEEN

"Okay, Mr. Lasty, first things first." Jim leaned forward, eyeing the computer screen intently. "Can you block any attempts to view this room?"

He felt the diminutive alien shrink away from him as he looked over its shoulder. The work station looked incredibly complex with the panorama of instruments, keyboards, speakers, and God knows what else set up for someone with four hands, not two.

The pale technician nodded uncomfortably. He spoke in a quiet tone briefly, then nodded again. "It's done. The bridge now has a security block on scanning."

"You can give it verbal orders?"

"For certain things, yes," Lasty said. "For detailed instructions or ambiguous orders it's better to do it manually."

"Bring up a schematic of this ship," Jim ordered.

The main screen changed to a holographic display of the ship, and Jim stared at it, perplexed. A shoe box. It looks like a shoe box with four tennis ball tubes running its length. two above and two below. Pylons and stanchions connected with what looked remarkably like huge outrigger coffee thermos, one to either side. He shook his head and muttered, half to himself. "God, that's ugly." Lasty sniffed and Jim stifled a smile as he pointed to the thermos-like cylinders.

"Engine nacelles," came the answer. Jim nodded encouragingly, and pointed at one of the four long sections.

"And these?"

"Those are storage compartments," Lasty shrugged, an interesting gesture when there are four arms involved, Jim noted. "For large cargo."

"Like our ship." Jim wasn't asking a question, but the pale alien seemed amused.

"Or really large cargo." He did something at the controls and a small red splotch appeared inside one of the lower compartments.

"This is your ship." Lasty's voice contained a hint of boldness, belying his nervousness. "In scale."

Jim's eyes widened as he realized how huge the Ananab ship was by human standards. "Jesus..." His voice died away, and he allowed a moment of self-pity, then forced himself to focus on the current situation.

"Can you keep the view of our old prison room on one of these side screens?" One of the small screens to the right flickered, then showed a battle still raging. Jim saw that the other prisoners were holding their own, but unmoving bodies showed a price was being paid. He felt a twinge of guilt at his relief to see that his closest friends were okay. He turned back to the main screen.

"Show me where we are on this display," he demanded and watched as a tiny point deep inside the main boxlike shape glowed a pale blue.

"Now show me where this is," Jim pointed a different screen display. Another somewhat larger spot appeared, near the front of the ship. "Engineering," Jim continued, and it appeared far to the rear of the box, and at a lower level than the bridge.

Jim glared at the picture. The detail, even on a large screen, was just too small. He glanced up at the big overhead screen and saw the same picture, slightly more defined. It helped, but not much. "I need to see where my people are," Jim muttered in frustration.

Black dots appeared, largely clustered in a blotch in the blue prison area. He identified the group of about a dozen on the bridge as themselves and saw there were three other small groups scattered around the ship. Two were stationary, and one was moving fairly rapidly. He whirled to face the four-armed humanoid.

"Those black dots are Humans?" he queried. Lasty nodded.

Kabu pointed at the two dots approaching the human holding tank on the large screen. "That must be Omi and Jozen, from our group." The young Japanese sounded excited. "What about guards, can you show them, too?"

"Umm, of course." Jim watched the small alien hesitate, then quickly finger a control. Huh, anything to do with those guards really scared the crap out of him. Jim pursed his lips humorlessly and looked back at the big screen. Two sets of dots, yellow and red, appeared around the ship.

"The red are the Tryr, and the yellow are the Srotag." The technician pushed another button and dark blue dots appeared, all clustered in two spots, on the bridge and near one of the small groups of humans.

"Those are the Ananab."

As one, Jim and Kabu whirled, searching around the bridge. Damn, where are they? Jim started as he realized the answer. "These dots include the dead?"

"You didn't specify living," Lasty stuttered.

Jim looked back up at the big screen. "Delete the dead," he said in a cold voice.

All dark blue dots on the bridge and some of the other group blinked out, as well as a lot of the red and yellow ones. But Jim and the other humans were watching the large group of black dots in the jail and barely noticed the attrition of their captors. A number of black dots at the front of the ship had vanished; a small percentage in relationship to the total figure, but a huge, totally unacceptable loss, nonetheless. He heard Kiri gasp in dismay.

Jim closed his eyes for a moment. This has cost too much. Too many friends, both old and new, wouldn't be going home again.

His eyes popped open and he turned to Lasty. "Show me this on one of these smaller screens," he ordered grimly. He pointed to a group of black dots that were stationary very close to two dots, one red, the other yellow. As he pointed, the yellow flickered and disappeared.

Commander Asaya and a half a dozen crewmen huddled at an intersection. One lay dead in the middle of the opening and Jim grimly tapped the other screen at the red dot nearby. Lasty quickly split the screen.

A Tryr peered out from a hatch, gun ready. The body of a Srotag lay in the middle of the corridor, long slashes across its abdomen testimony to someone's skill with a sword. The catman took aim and fired. The humans flinched, then Asaya quickly reached around the corner and fired his own weapon, evidently captured from the dead Srotag. The catman was too fast and already safely out of range.

Stalemate.

Jim looked back at the main screen and felt irritation. Two black dots were very close to that area, but he couldn't tell how close. As he watched, they moved slowly farther away from the bogged-down Asaya and his men.

"Can you eliminate the outlying parts of the ship and increase the detail?" Jim pointed at the screen showing the standoff. "I'd like to be able to see corridors and such."

He watched as his prisoner thought for a moment, then began making adjustments almost too rapidly to follow. The schematic disappeared and was replaced by a display of the central portion of the ship, substantially enlarged. A moment later, that picture reduced to two-thirds of the screen, and Jim had a good floor plan showing where Asaya and his men were, with the remaining third showing the display in relation to the rest of the ship.

Jim had an idea. "Can I speak to them, using the computer?"

Lasty looked fearful. "Yes, but if the guards can hear you, the computer will automatically translate what you say."

"Oh." Jim straightened up, perplexed. Then he remembered an advantage they still had.

"Give me a speaker close to my people." he commanded confidently. Lasty nodded, made an adjustment and signaled him to go ahead.

"Asaya-san," Jim spoke rapidly in Japanese, identifying himself. "Be ready for a rush and ignore anything said in English for the next few minutes."

He watched as they backed away from the corner and spread out, laying on the floor or flattening against both walls. Jim looked at the layout, dissatisfied. Asaya had the only gun in the group, and they were terribly exposed. But it would have to do.

"Now put this out on speakers that Tryr can hear," he told Lasty. The Baerd nodded.

Jim leaned forward and called out in a loud voice. "Men, retreat! More guards are coming! Quick, run away!"

The head of the alien guard snapped up in excitement and he quickly rushed forward. Rounding the corner, he raised his weapon, expecting to have the backs of fleeing men as targets. Asaya fired, and the Tryr dropped, but not before getting a shot off. One of the crewmen slumped to the deck, and Jim watched bleakly as the black dot blinked out on the main screen.

Damn, they were so fast. And yet another casualty.

Another nameless face to join the crowd staring back at him from his dreams. Due to his 'cleverness', another person was dead. Just once, why couldn't his arrogance kill the right people.

He turned back to Lasty. "Can you make the computer show them the fastest path to engineering?"

"Have them follow the green lights." Lasty said and executed the order quickly and efficiently. Jim looked at him speculatively, and the technician looked uneasy.

"Why are you agreeing to help so easily?" Jim gave him a challenging look. "Aren't you afraid of what the Ananab will do to you if they find out?"

Lasty shook his head and glanced sideways at Dutter. Jim was startled as she spoke for the first time.

"It doesn't matter what we do, at this point," she admitted morosely. "We are all dead anyway."

Jim looked suspiciously at Lasty, then the computer. "What did you do?" he demanded.

"It's not what we did," Lasty returned. "It's what you did."

Jim just looked at him and waited for him to continue.

"The Ananab don't tolerate rebellion. Not even rumors of rebellion." The male Baerd sighed and looked down. "The moment you killed one of their kind, all of us were doomed. Even if you lose this battle, they will kill all of us to keep any word of this from getting out." Dutter nodded agreement, and as Jim looked around, the other Baerd followed suit.

"Jim, that's terrible!" Kiri spoke up. A determined look came to her face. "We can't let that happen. They'll have to join us."

Kabu muttered something under his breath and she glared at him. Hurriedly, he nodded his agreement with her.

Jim started to argue with her, then stopped. They were going to need to know a lot more about this 'new' universe before this was over. He turned to the Baerd leader.

"What about it?" he asked curiously. "Would you be interested in joining us?"

"What are you going to do?" Lasty sounded cautious. "Do you have some sort of plan?"

"Yes, as a matter of fact, I do." Jim said in a mild tone belying his words. "We're going to take this ship, and then we're going home." Jim could see he was skeptical. "Of course, first we have to find out where the hell we are. After we've got control of this ship, we'll explore our options."

"Your options are in how you'll die." Lasty sounded glum.

Jim grew angry. "I'm not necessarily ready to die, quite yet," he said in a low dangerous voice. "Are you interested, or not?"

The female Baerd spoke up again. "Lasty, why not? What do we have to lose? At least, as long as they are succeeding, we're still alive."

Lasty nodded slowly, looking thoughtful. His lower right hand nervously tapped fingernails against the control panel.

"What next?" he finally asked.

Jim winced. *What next, indeed?*

"First we get control of the engineering deck, then relieve the attack on the rest of our people. Then we mop up the rest of the guards and Ananab."

As one, they all turned back to the screens.

"Ah," Jim sighed in relief. Two black splotches, presumably Omi and Jozen, rapidly approached the prison room from behind the attacking guards. They both had handguns. Asaya's group was making good time towards their goal, and now they had two guns. "If they can just get control of engineering..."

"Why?" Lasty sounded curious.

"Can't the Ananab or the guards override our controls from there?" Jim glanced down at him.

Lasty made a funny sort of wrinkling movement with his nose. "Baerd run engineering. None of these Tryr or Srotag would have the slightest idea of what controls to use. And I don't know of a single time any Ananab has ever been in Engineering."

"Wouldn't your friends follow their orders?" Jim tried to visualize Baerd engineers defying Srotag or Tryr guards, and couldn't.

"What orders could they give?" Lasty gave a very human-like shrug. "The Ananab are paranoid and only orders from the bridge can cause the computer to take any action internally. And since the choices are extremely limited as far as our course goes, there's not much they could do."

"What do you mean, extremely limited?" Jim didn't much like the sound of that.

"We've been on a long trip." Lasty did something on his console and one of the smaller screens showed some form of math or other undecipherable display. "We were on our way back when we picked up your transmissions. We don't really have enough fuel or supplies to get anywhere except back to the Ananab station, Chaq."

"How long do we have?" Jim felt a growing sense of dread.

"Your time?" Lasty made a quick calculation. "Just under two days."

Jim looked at Kiri and Kabu in dismay. Less than two days!

He looked back at the big screen and saw with relief that the siege on the prison room was over. Over the entire ship, only a few red and yellow dots remained.

An idea came to him.

"Can you lock hatches to trap the rest of the Tryr and Srotag?" Jim spoke slowly, an idea forming. "The two guards in engineering have moved out into the corridor!"

"Yes, I can," His new ally sounded excited. "And we can even freeze the manual override to the doors!" He turned to the console and began a variety of adjustments. Gold bars began to appear at junctions on either side of the red and yellow dots.

Jim sighed in relief. He straightened up, groaning at the tightening muscles in his back. This has been a long day. He watched Kiri inspect one of the alien handguns and laughed out loud as she tucked it into her sash. She looked up, her face drawn.

"What you laughing at, round eyes?" Her attempt at humor didn't fool him.

Jim began scanning the overall picture of the ship. Several dark blue dots blinked out even as he watched. Weren't there much fewer Ananab than there had been?

"What part of the ship is that?" he asked curiously.

Lasty looked up and blanched. "That's the Ananab private quarters," he said, rubbing his hands together nervously. "There are a few adults there, all concubines of the Captain and his brothers. The rest would be the young."

More blue dots blinked out.

"The young?" Jim stared at the screen in growing horror. "Are they dangerous?"

"Most of them are still in incubators." Lasty looked thoughtful. "I don't think any were old enough to be independently mobile, yet."

Jim felt sick. "Can you get me sound in there?"

Lasty nodded, did something, then signaled to go ahead.

"This is Jim Morris," Jim spoke urgently in a clear voice. "Who is in this sector? Answer, please."

"This is Naga Furukawa." The answer came hesitantly. "How did you find us?"

"Never mind that," Jim watched as more dots blinked and vanished. "Stop killing the Ananab young. Secure the area but stop the killing! We have the ship!"

"I'm afraid I can't hear you very clearly."

Jim glanced at Lasty, who shook his head firmly.

"That's not true," Jim snarled. "Now stop the killing, at once!"

"That is impossible." Furukawa spoke slowly. "Dead aliens will be safer for us. Dead aliens can pose no threat."

"These are defenseless babies you're killing!" Jim screamed in frustration. "What you are doing will outlive any of us! I"m telling you for the last time, stop!"

A long pause and more dots disappeared.

"No."

Jim turned desperately to Lasty. "Can you flood the chambers with some kind of knockout gas? Anything at all?"

Lasty shook his head, and eyed Jim curiously. "No, Ananab quarters can't be tampered with." He smiled thinly. "A security measure."

Jim slumped forward in resignation, leaning on the console.

"Why do you care? The Ananab would do the same to you," Dutter assured him.

Jim's head shot up and both Dutter and Lasty shrank away in fear.

"We aren't the Ananab." His voice was cold, remote. To him, it sounded a million miles away.

Lasty shuddered. "No, you're not."

The last of the blue dots blinked out, and there was a long silence on the bridge. They all watched as the black dots left the Ananab chambers and moved into a corridor.

"Lock them there," Jim ordered grimly. Lasty gaped.

"Do it!" he snarled, and the small alien hurried to comply.

Jim turned away from the display in fury and almost knocked Kiri down. She had been standing right behind him. He caught her arm and she grabbed his wrist with her free hand, steadying herself.

"Jim, there was nothing you could do." She pleaded with him, her eyes filling. In desperation, she turned to Kabu. "Nothing, right, Kabu? Tell him!"

Kabu shook his head at her, but turned to Jim anyway.

"She is right, Jim." Kabu didn't sound very convinced himself, which was fine. Jim didn't want to be convinced. He wanted to hit somebody, hard.

He turned away from them and saw one of the 'dancing girls' sitting on the floor, holding Usagi's body, her face buried against his chest. Jim swayed, berating himself for his thoughtlessness. He tore a piece of cloth off the pannier and hesitantly bent over her.

"Suie, please believe me. I'm so sorry about this. I know you cared very much for him." She looked up at him, tears running down her face. Gently he helped her to her feet. Kiri came and put her arms around the sobbing girl, meeting Jim's eyes with sorrow of her own. He knew she had been very fond of the young man.

With a sigh, Jim covered the face of Usagi Izu with the cloth. He had been very photogenic, and popular with the girls. Suie was shy, but everyone knew she had a crush on the young man. He teased her incessantly, and she always pretended to be annoyed, but no one was fooled.

This had been his second film with Jim...and his last.
More faces staring back at him in the night.

Lasty came to a decision. He used his lower left hand to slip a disk from beneath his tunic into the console. A quick glance showed no one watching, and he activated it.

CHAPTER FIFTEEN

"He's back!"

An excited shout rang out from the guards at the hatch, and Kimberly exchanged startled glances with Yvette and Janice. They turned as one to see Jim appear in the doorway.

Absolute silence greeted him as everyone stopped whatever they were doing. Then someone started clapping. After several beats, another joined in. Then another, and the sound grew to a roar as everyone began cheering and hugging one another. Kimberly thought he looked worried as he quickly scanned the room. As he saw Afsaneh and Hakim rushing up to him along with many others, he sagged in obvious relief. Kimberly watched as he continued searching until his eyes came to her. He smiled wanly at her and then was surrounded by the crowd. The two captains pushed their way through to him.

He looks awful, she thought. Then she noticed blood on his left shoulder, and realized he had been wounded. She hurried over in time to hear him talking with Captain Lang.

"I've got him locked in a corridor a few hundred yards from here," Jim finished grimly. "We should probably sit down to some sort of meeting to brief you." His eyes swept around the group to include the Japanese officers. "There's a new development and we don't have a lot of time."

Everyone spoke at once and a barrage of questions assaulted him. He raised his hands for silence and winced, glancing down at his left shoulder. The crowd fell quiet, and he nodded in gratitude. Kimberly pushed forward.

"Please, let the doctor look at him! He's been wounded!" She looked around in irritation and people dropped their eyes in embarrassment.

"Good idea, Ms. Martin." Captain Lang broke in, smiling at her encouragingly. "Give the man a few minutes, and then we'll have that meeting." He hesitated a moment, then turned to Jim. "Where should we hold it, here?"

Jim looked thoughtful. Then he gave what Kimberly thought was a very weak version of his cocky grin.

"How about the bridge?" he asked, and Kimberly smiled as she watched the excitement grow on the older man's face. "After all, you are the Captain."

Lang and Tachibana exchanged startled looks and she was glad to see no apparent animosity between them, only exuberance and a sense of awe. Captain Lang nodded as if it was his own idea.

"Yes, of course, the bridge." His voice was full of wonder.

Kimberly took Jim by his uninjured arm and led him toward the emergency medical station that had been set up earlier. "This way, mister." She tried to look formidable. "First the doctor. Then some food. Then the meeting."

Jim arched his right eyebrow. "How about food and meeting?" He seemed amused with her. She tried to glare at him, but gave up. She wrapped her arms around his waist and hugged him hard.

"If you hadn't come back alive,..." Words momentarily failed her. "You took such a chance. Yvette and I thought...ooh, I should kill you myself!"

He returned the hug, and they stood there for, what was for her, far too short a time. Then she felt him gently disengage. "Thank you." His voice was very soft.

She brushed tears from her cheek and took his hand again.

"Come on, Jim. Let's get you taken care of." She looked at him proudly. "You've got a lot of people depending on you, and you need two good shoulders, not just one."

Jim winced at the idea, then managed a smile. "I've got four shoulders, counting yours." She watched his face, worried. He obviously didn't like the idea of having everyone depending on him, and regardless of how capable he was, he was still just a man.

They stopped at the crude computer terminal Rick and Janice had been using. Rick was trying to figure out where the ship was. Kimberly was startled when Jim spoke, not to Rick, but the computer itself.

"Computer, show our location in relationship to our home planet, Earth."

The small screen showed a mass of pinpricks of light. Two colored lights, one red and one green showed very close together.

"Respond so that others can hear," Jim said. Kimberly was puzzled, then jumped as a voice spoke.

"The red dot represents this ship. The green dot is the planet Earth." The voice sounded toneless, but not as cold as she would have thought.

Jim looked at Rick quizzically. "Does that help?"

Rick squinted at the blur of light, then crossed his eyes. "Not really." He flinched as the movie star laughed and slapped him on the shoulder.

"Don't worry. Come with us when we go to the bridge, and I'll introduce you to someone who can help."

Rick nodded mutely, his eyes never leaving the screen.

"It answers verbal commands?" There was awe in his voice.

Jim nodded, oblivious to the fact that the younger man wasn't even looking at him. "It's instructed to respond to me while we get things organized."

Kimberly thought about that. "It obeys your orders?"

Jim nodded.

"Do your orders override everyone else's?" Her mind raced as he nodded again. "Doesn't that make you the de facto new captain?"

"No!" Jim made an obvious effort to control his voice, then continued in a quieter tone. "I'm only making sure we humans keep control of this ship. Once the captains are filled in on the details, I'm out of the loop."

Kimberly looked at him skeptically. I'll bet even he doesn't believe that's true, she thought. Though he may wish it were. No, if we're to have any chance of ever getting home, or even living through this, it'll be because of Jim, and he knows it. He sees things quickly and clearly, can make a decision, and then act upon it. Not unlike yourself, Martin. You're not in his league in the physical stuff, but you're not too shabby in your own right. Time to quit reacting, and start acting.

"Come on, Captain Jimmy, let's get you patched up."

He straightened his back and said through clenched teeth. "You can call me Jim, You can call me Morris-san..." He paused and a wry smile leaked out. "But don't ever call me Jimmy!"

"Whatever," Kimberly said, and led him away in search of the cruise ship's doctor.

Lasty looked around, bemused. Captain Storhesh wouldn't have recognized his bridge. Several long tables had been set in a row in the center of the room by the Hoag. Instead of numerous Tryr and Srotag guards, the two human warriors, Sakai Motoo and Sasama Sakakibara kept a careful armed watch from the side walkways. One was armed with a disruptor hundgun, the other had a long bow, with an arrow already nocked. Lasty listened carefully and made mental notes as the computer identified the crowd seated around the tables.

The Human captain, Lang, sat at the head of the table. The other Human captain, Tachibana, sat at his right side. To his right were Commander Asaya, Nagami, and Suyo Takashi. Asaya was one of the Japanese captain's officers, but he was a little vague as to the status of the other two. Lasty, Dutter, and Inam completed that side of the table.

Sitting on the other side were Captain Lang's first officer, Commander DelaRosa, the Jim Morris, his friend (lover?) Kimberly Martin, another member of the crew, Randy Luca, the computer 'hacks'(whatever that meant?) Rick Baker, Janice Wooley, and two very nervous Hoag. Lasty had been surprised when Jim insisted the Hoag be represented, but there sat Gudd, their leader, and his assistant, Vude.

A skeleton crew of Baerd manned stations to monitor the ship. Numerous Hoag scurried about the bridge, cleaning up the last signs of carnage.

The Humans showed a tremendous compassion for their dead. He had watched as the women dancers escorted the bodies of the three men killed in the battle for control of the bridge. The Hoag hauling the remains had been gentle, carefully respectful of their burdens.

They showed no such care with the remains of the Ananab and their Tryr and Srotag guards. Unceremoniously dumped onto antigrav sleds, they were hauled away to the usual destination of the dead.

"Where are those bodies being taken?" The Jim Morris was curious.

Lasty answered. "Your companions are joining the other casualties in a room adjacent to where you were kept. We weren't sure what customs you followed."

"What about the Tryr and the rest?" Jim pressed.

Lasty shrugged. "The bodies will go into the reprocessing plant to fuel the ship."

Jim frowned. "Do they have some sort of religious ceremony or anything that they usually perform among themselves?"

Lasty sat in thought for a moment. "The Tryr and Srotag usually do something if they are with their own. In the field, they just mutter some uh, prayer or something, and then ignore the body afterwards."

He looked around apologetically. "Most races don't share too many of their cultural idiosyncracies with 'lesser' races." He looked at his fellow Baerd for support. "I have no idea what the Ananab do." Inam and Dutter looked uncomfortable and nodded their agreement.

Jim looked at Captain Lang. "Sir?"

The captain looked disturbed. "I hate to show disrespect to any race, but I don't relish the thought of a room of dead bodies, either." The older man thought for a moment. "An old nautical superstition is that it's bad luck to haul bodies, and in this case, I tend to agree."

He looked at Lasty. "Go ahead with your plans for their bodies, but we'll be burying our dead this afternoon in naval tradition. If no one has any objections?" He finished in a questioning tone as he glanced around the table.

"I think that would be appropriate," Captain Tachibana concurred.

Lasty used his remote to instruct the computer to research the usual naval customs. Hmm, odd custom for so compassionate a people. He watched them in awe. Everyone was acting so, so...calm!

He hurriedly explained how to deal with the human bodies to Dutter and Inam, and they looked pained at the concept of releasing bodies to the cold void of space. Lasty conferred with the Hoag. Gudd nodded, lowered his head, looking down as he spoke briefly into his communicator. Lasty turned back to the humans.

"The Hoag are cleaning the old Ananab living quarters and making the necessary changes to accommodate you," Lasty hesitated.

Captain Lang frowned. "Who said we wanted their old quarters?"

Lasty was surprised. He looked around at the Humans. "I just assumed..." He was confused. "You don't want them? There are certain advantages..."

Rick Baker spoke up. "Those rooms are in the center of the ship. Probably the most secure place in case of a battle." He tapped his fingers on the table for emphasis. "And the computer is security blocked from that area." He beamed. "Privacy!"

The woman Kimberly Martin laughed at his expression and so did most of the other humans. Captain Lang nodded in agreement. "That's good enough for me."

Lasty made a sound and then ducked as attention centered on him. The Captain smiled at him. "Yes, Chief Tech Lasty?"

He was embarrassed, but finally blurted out. "How can you adapt to this situation so easily? You were kidnaped at night, imprisoned, hauled far away from your home planet. Records show that most races were incapacitated

183

with fear on their first contact. My own race was helpless when the Hstahni captured our planet."

"When was that?" The Jim Morris asked in a curious voice.

Lasty thought for a moment, then slowly answered. "Eighteen hundred of your years ago."

Kimberly gasped and he looked at her in surprise. "What is it?"

She acted as though she were explaining something to a stripling pup. "Your race has been imprisoned for eighteen hundred years?"

He felt color appear in his cheeks. He looked down and spoke slowly. "We aren't imprisoned. We control our own planet and have rights. The Hstahni brought many good things to our planet. We're healthier, far more technically advanced than we would be..."

"Your technology, or theirs?" The Jim Morris spoke softly.

The heat increased in his face and all four of his arms were moving nervously, crossing and uncrossing constantly.

"Theirs," Lasty admitted. "We aren't allowed to do any research. The Hstahni monitor us regularly."

"But you control your own planet." Sarcasm was heavy in the thick-bodied Nagami's voice.

"We govern ourselves!" Dutter came to Lasty's defense. "None of us are forced into signing contracts to work for the Hstahni or the Ananab."

"We do have to meet a quota," Inam corrected her. "And there are limits to our freedom to travel with our own ships, and what kind of ships we can have."

"You're a vassal race with obligations to provide personnel and support to the Ananab and the..." Captain Tachibana hesitated. "You called them the Hstahni? What is the relationship between them and the Ananab?"

"The Hstahni found the Ananab many thousands of years ago. Gradually the Ananab grew in importance as more races were found. Now they demand 'volunteer' work forces from the Tryr, Srotag, Hoag, ourselves,...others you haven't met yet..."

Lasty looked around the table in frank confusion. "The one thing all the races had in common was panic and fear. The Hoag were nearly catatonic as a race. Even the Tryr were awed into submission. They thought the Hstahni were gods at first. Some of your people were frightened, but even they weren't as overwhelmed as every single other case in history."

He watched the humans look around the table at each other and couldn't read their emotions. The woman Kimberly started to say something, then

184

stopped. She glanced sideways at the Jim Morris and blushed. He didn't appear to notice.

"I get the sense that we're a little more advanced than most of the other 'found' races." Jim spoke up. He looked thoughtful for a moment, then smiled. "You saw the transmissions we call 'entertainment'. First contact with another intelligent species has been a popular topic for books and movies, especially bad movies, for decades. I think we've probably theorized just about any scenario you could imagine." Some of the other humans joined him in laughter as he continued. "Including bug-eyed monsters, lions and tigers, and bears."

"Let's not forget dinosaurs, giant apes and moths," Commander Asaya chipped in. All the humans laughed at this.

Lasty watched the Jim Morris shake his head evidently in amusement at the young officer's words. Then he turned sober and faced Lasty again.

"As you know, we are a violent race."

Lasty nodded his head vigorously.

"It carries over into our entertainment, many people say too much so. It's probably not to our credit that we've scared ourselves far more than the Ananab ever could, but it's true."

Kimberly Martin agreed. "It's hard to imagine anything with more shock value than some of our horror movies." Jim smiled at her and she returned it and continued. "And more action than our bang, bang, shoot 'em up action movies."

Lasty shook his head in consternation. "I finally placed your identity as they were leading you here to your death. Had I figured that out earlier, we would have researched this 'un-armed combat' that some of you are so well-versed in." He gestured to the Jim Morris, who graciously nodded his head. "I must confess I followed the wrong trail. At first I thought you were someone else, but he was reported to be dead."

The Jim Morris closed his eyes in a mock grimace as most of the Humans broke into laughter. Lasty looked around in confusion, then continued.

"...there had been reports that he was still alive in seclusion, with other famous entertainers also reputed to be dead."

Kimberly choked in laughter and Lasty watched the human actor give her a stern look. "Jim and Elvis..." She held up two fingers pressed tightly together. "Like that..."

"All right, already." The Jim Morris straightened in his seat. "Back to the business at hand." He grew somber looking. "We dock at a space station in less than two days. It's owned by the Ananab, am I correct?" Lasty nodded mutely. Everyone stirred in their seats uneasily. Jim continued. "We have to land there, because we're short on fuel and can't reach anywhere else."

"How big is this 'space station'?" Captain Tachibana asked, his eyes narrowed.

The Jim Morris looked at Lasty and he responded. "Big. Thousands of permanent residents, and anywhere from two to twenty ships docked at a time."

"How many are fighters?" Captain Lang looked at him. "How many Tryr, Srotag, or Ananab?"

Lasty hesitated and shrugged. Jim turned to the main screen on the wall.

"Computer, estimate number of Tryr, Srotag, and Ananab currently at our destination."

The answer came quickly. "Using most current data on shipping schedules and station roster, Station Chaq contains between thirty and one hundred adult Ananab, and aproximately four hundred assorted Tryr and Srotag."

Lasty watched as Kimberly shivered. "Maybe 500 of those monsters," she muttered, almost inaudibly. Belatedly he realized something else had the others stirred up. Young Rick Baker elbowed Janice excitedly. He tried to talk so fast he stuttered.

"Se...see? Th...the computer answers verbal questions! Does it do that for everyone now?"

Lasty flinched and nervously cleared his throat. "I programmed the computer to respond to his voice after he assumed control of the bridge. It is instructed to follow his orders anywhere in the ship or via remote." Please, please don't let them ask too many questions before I can talk in private to the Jim Morris, Lasty prayed silently.

"Can you extend that to others, as well?" The Jim Morris seemed eager to relinquish his control of the ship, but Lasty knew it wasn't going to be that simple.

"It would be better to give people their own remote and a work site." Lasty frowned, thinking furiously. "Too many vocal instructions at once can cause contradictions and confusion. Usually each person has limits to the parameters, depending on their functions or needs." He looked around and only Kimberly Martin looked suspicious. "It just seemed like he would need instant response wherever he was at the time while the ship was secured."

He felt Dutter stir and glance at him surreptitiously. *She knows how the computer works too well to fall for this story.*

At that moment the hatch opened and a group of humans entered. Lasty discreetly told the computer to identify them via his direct feed. The young ex-soldier McGregor had sidearm in hand. With him were Naga Furukawa and another Japanese, Piti Hashimoto that the computer identified as a Sukuru security man, whatever that was. They appeared to be in custody. Behind them followed Kabu and a uniformed crewman from the Jade Viking, both with handguns trained on the two Japanese prisoners.

Furukawa pushed forward and spoke directly to Nagami, deliberately ignoring everyone else.

"I demand to know why I'm being held prisoner by this, this..." Lasty watched Furukawa search for words and decided he didn't like this human very much.

"You murdered dozens of helpless Ananab." Jim's voice frightened Lasty. It was cold and harsh. "You had a direct order to stop the killing, and you refused."

"Direct order!" Furukawa sneered. "Who said anyone has to follow your orders? Who are you, anyway? Some rich movie star used to ordering around women and pimps."

"You've caused a smear on our race that will never disappear. Our first contact with other intelligent species and we have a massacre." Jim's voice lost any vestige of emotion and Lasty watched Kimberly shrink away involuntarily. "We were in the right until then. We were defending ourselves!"

"I don't follow your orders!" The Japanese martial champion tensed as Jim rose to his feet.

"Sit down, Mr Morris." Captain Lang was on his feet now as well, as were the other naval officers. But he loomed over them all, towering with all of his six and a half feet in a Nordic rage. He glared at Furukawa and the Japanese didn't back down. Lang glanced at his Japanese counterpart and some message seemed to pass between them.

They all stood like that for what seemed like an eternity to Lasty, but was only a few seconds. He saw that MacGregor was poised behind his prisoner, ready to leap on him at the first sign of violence. He also saw that Furukawa was aware of this and looked on guard.

"Sit down, Mr Morris," the captain repeated in a quieter voice. He turned back to Furukawa and his glare returned, slightly reduced. "In answer to your question, I placed Mr. Morris in charge of the mission to the bridge. He was the most informed authority during the fight. There was no need to kill babies...of any species!"

This last came almost in a snarl as Captain Lang visibly struggled to recover his calm. "You were part of the group that was trying to reach the engineering deck, not slaughter civilians."

"We were separated when Asaya allowed himself to get pinned down," Furukawa said smoothly.

"That's Commander Asaya." Captain Tachibana spoke in a clipped, tight voice. The two Japanese locked wills for maybe ten seconds, then Furukawa backed down.

"Commander Asaya," he repeated. His lips barely moved and his eyes smoldered.

"For the moment you are confined to the current sleeping quarters." Captain Lang's voice offered no debate. He turned to Nabu and the sailor. "See that he gets there, and stays there."

They both nodded and after a final glare, Furukawa left, the other two close behind. MacGregor stood there, uncertain what he was supposed to do next. After a moment, he moved to join Sasama on the runway near the hatch.

"Hang around, Mr....McGregor, isn't it?" The captain's voice had moderated significantly. "We might have something for you to do soon."

The young man stood straighter and even Lasty could see that excitement was written all over his face. *I'm glad that is over with. Had they been Tryr or Srotag arguing with Ananab, bodies would have littered the deck by now. Lasty marveled at their self-control.*

"Right, then, back to this station of yours, Mr. Lasty," He jumped in his seat, startled. The captain showed no signs of the previous tension, and Lasty felt everyone around the table slowly begin to relax.

"Can we refuel and leave without a fight?"

Lasty looked around the table wondering. *Is he asking this question seriously, or is this more 'Human' humor?* He realized everyone was waiting for his response.

"Do you mean dock, refuel, leave with an Ananab ship without anyone challenging you?"

The captain nodded.

"No."

"No?" Lang didn't appear to be too surprised.

"The moment they know that this ship has been taken, they will board, and kill everyone." Lasty was gloomy. "Including us."

"Then I guess you'll want us to succeed." Captain Lang beamed at him. Lasty heard Kimberly laughing and thought, she must be able to read my expression. He choose his words carefully.

"Succeed at what?"

"At refueling and escaping, or if necessary, taking the station as well." Captain Lang leaned back in his chair and sent his gaze around the table speculatively. "At this point, I don't see a lot of options."

"We would need the element of surprise," Commander Asaya began and stopped as the Americans around the table burst into laughter. Asaya blushed and shrugged. "Well, it worked at Pearl." Lasty wondered what the joke was and made yet another mental note; research 'Pearl'.

"How many of your weapons are there on this ship?" Nagami spoke for the first time.

Lasty checked. "Fifty-six. But those won't be much help at the station."

"Why not?" Commander DelaRosa's eyes narrowed suspiciously.

"The moment someone in the command module realizes there's an attack, a neutralizing field will be brought up and no disruptors will work, anywhere on the station." He squirmed uncomfortably. "Even without weapons, the Tryr and Srotag can usually handle most disturbances."

He looked around at the humans. "I don't suppose many of you can fight unarmed as well as Mr. Morris can?" From their expressions he could guess the answer to that question.

"How many pistols and shotguns on the Jade Viking?" Jim asked. Lasty saw Nagami stiffen in sudden excitement.

Captain Lang turned to his youthful commander and looked questionly. As DelaRosa thought about it, Lasty hesitantly broke in.

"What about the weapons in the forward hold?" He was puzzled and watched with interest as Nagami flinched and began to stir as if to interrupt. "I wondered why you never tried to get to them?"

"What weapons?" Captain Lang looked baffled. He looked at DelaRosa who shrugged, also obviously in the dark.

Lasty continued, feeling the glare Nagami was trying to pierce him with. "Your hidden manifest shows a number of cases of..." He hesitated and checked for the specific name. "...Chinese AK-47's."

"Forward hold would be Sukuru freight, sir." Commander DelaRosa looked at Nagami speculatively. Lasty thought Captain Lang's look was a little different.

"Mr. Nagami?" The older man had an ominous tone in his voice and Lasty

189

realized the weapons had been a secret.

"Would you know anything about the cases of automatic weapons being smuggled into the United States aboard my ship?" The captain's voice was dangerously pleasant, deceivingly friendly. It didn't even fool Lasty, with his limited familiarity with Human nuances.

Nagami shifted in his seat. "Actually, they're not automatic weapons yet. I mean, not automatic weapons at all," he finished hurriedly. "They're semi-automatic, and perfectly legal. They were to be issued to security at the new docking facilities Sukuru acquired in California." He looked down at the table, careful to avoid eye contact.

"Sir." MacGregor sounded excited. "It would be simple to convert them, if I can have access to some tools on board. I know how to do it, sir."

"How many semi-automatics do we have on board, Mr Nagami?" The security chief winced at the sarcasm in the captain's voice.

"Forty-eight," he mumbled.

The captain turned to DelaRosa. "Commander, take this young man and whoever else you need, and start converting those guns."

He paused, then looked down the table at the seated Baerd and Hoag. "We haven't asked you if you were willing to join us. Can we count on your support?"

Lasty snorted in derision. "Once we started, we were committed. We really have no choice."

They all looked down the table at the Hoag and Lasty watched as Gudd rose to his feet. *A Hoag speaking at a meeting like this? Even being at a meeting like this?*

"I am Gudd, chief of the Foud clan of the Hoag." He sounded shy and Lasty realized he had never actually heard Gudd's voice before.

"We don't understand much of what has happened here and what you speak of, but I do know this. What Chief Technician Lasty said was true. When the Ananab retake this ship, we will all die." His back straightened slightly, then shrunk back over. "We will do as you say."

"Good man," the captain said warmly. "Commander, take several Baerd and Hoag to assist in the task."

DelaRosa and MacGregor left with their entourage and the rest of them settled back into their seats.

"Well." Captain Lang looked around the table, and gave them a wry smile. "Just one space station to capture, then one flight back to Earth and maybe some sense of normalcy might come back into our lives."

"You still have the Egelv to deal with," Lasty reminded them.

"The who?" asked Kimberly Martin, her puzzlement mirroring the rest of the humans.

Lasty winced and cleared his throat. He didn't want to be the one to tell them about this.

"There's something I forgot to mention...", he started glumly.

CHAPTER JIXTEEN

Kimberly stood with Jim, leaning against the rail of one of the walkways that ran along the wall of the bridge. They watched as the Hoag efficiently finished the cleanup, taking the tables along with them as they left. She glanced over at the Captain's 'perch', as the Baerd referred to it. The two human captains and Commander Asaya stood there, quietly conferring.

A small group of humans were being shown the preliminaries on how to operate the Baerd work stations. Despite only having two hands, they seemed to be coping fairly well, Rick Baker and Janice Wooley in particular. Randy Luca and Yvette Stephanian were going slower, but had more defined ideas of what they needed to be able to do. Rick and Janice were just excited at all the things opening up to them. Practical use would come later. As always, Suyo Takashi stood silently watching, absorbing everything.

Hard woman to read, that one was, Kimberly thought.

She noticed Jim tapping his fingers on the rail. It was unlike him to have nervous habits. Lasty looked up at them and winced as Jim crooked a finger at him. One of the female Baerd, Dutter, as Kimberly recalled, saw the motion and came with him.

"Tell me more about this computer link I have," Jim spoke softly, his voice not carrying beyond their little group.

The pale alien wrung his hands nervously, glancing sideways at Dutter. He seemed to chose his words with care.

"I gave the computer a security override tag to your voice, or any other means the computer needs to confirm your identity." He glanced at Dutter again, as if expecting her to speak. If so, he wasn't disappointed.

"What level security override?" She sounded suspicious.

Kimberly watched Lasty with interest. *Wow, when they blush, they really blush. I guess four hands gives you more variety for nervous gestures, too.* He stuttered as he spoke.

"I..I..used an Egelv royal heir palace security-one override." He studiously examined his many fingernails.

Dutter leaned back in exasperation. "No you didn't. You wouldn't know how to operate that program, even if you had it."

Lasty looked up at her, and actually smirked! "I do have the program." He looked a little less certain. "And I think I installed it properly."

"Excuse me for interrupting." Jim broke into the conversation, looking impatient. "But could you tell me a little more about this Egelv...uh, what was it again?"

"He can't have given you that type of access control." Dutter sounded determined. "Our knowledge of Egelv computer technology is very limited. Where could he possibly have gotten the strongest, most advanced security codes we've only heard rumors of?"

"Last time we were in Station Trico, I met a Hechktar with black market computer codes." Lasty's voice was weak.

"You bought black market..." Dutter stopped, evidently at a loss for words.

"This is all very interesting, and we'll have to come back to these details sometime," Jim broke in again, wearily rubbing his forehead with the heel of his hand. "But back to the original question, please."

"The computer will obey any command you give it," Lasty spoke in a rush. "Either verbal or manual. It can't be overridden by anyone, including the captain or myself."

Kimberly was shocked. "You can't rescind your own command?" she asked incredulously. "Certainly you can cancel the program or something, can't you?"

Dutter shook her head, obviously shaken. "If he really did what he said, and the rumors are true, this ship will not allow itself to be reprogrammed. That code is allegedly reserved for ruling families to key ships to individuals. Or to defend against palace coups." She stared at Lasty. "A Hechktar sold it to you?"

"Why did you use that code?" Kimberly was confused. "He had just overthrown your commanding officer,..."

"Killed him, actually," Lasty chipped in. Jim shook his head, frowning..

"Okay, killed him." Kimberly pushed down her irritation. "Why on Earth would you give your enemy such power?"

"Hmm, we're not on Earth," Lasty reminded her. "And he wasn't my enemy. He was, and is, an enemy of the Ananab."

"What's the difference?" Jim sounded more curious than disturbed. "Don't you feel any loyalty to your employer?"

Lasty snorted contemptuously. "First, they aren't my employer. We don't get paid, we serve time. Second, we didn't swear any loyalty pledge." He looked at Dutter and they both tittered nervously. "The Ananab are so paranoid and egotistical they would never bother with insisting on such a thing. They wouldn't honor one, and would never expect anyone else to, either."

Dutter broke in. "Furthermore, they would never believe we were capable of any form of rebellion, or resistance."

"And they would be right," Lasty finished glumly. She nodded her agreement.

"Then why did you?" Kimberly was lost.

Lasty faced her. "The moment Captain Storhesh died, we were doomed. No matter what happens now, our lives are forfeit. I really don't want to die yet." He glanced shyly at Dutter. "Especially now." Kimberly smiled at his obvious affection to the female Baerd and wondered if it was a recent development.

"I spent most of several days researching your race, and then the Jim Morris, in particular." Lasty sounded embarrassed. "Your people are unique in several aspects. One thing became obvious to me, and eventually, to the computer. As a people, you weren't going to submit to the Ananab. Specifically, the Jim Morris was leading some sort of revolt."

Lasty turned to the actor and nodded his head in deference.

"With everything I had discovered, then watching you in action, I knew you were actually capable of winning." The two Baerd exchanged looks. "You would have to know more about the universe around you to know how unlikely that was. And how unique your victory was," Lasty continued. "From studying your people, I undestood you aren't a united race, and that there are divisions even in a small group such as your ship."

You got that right, brother, Kimberly thought somberly. I thought Jim and I were like night and day, Wall Street and West Coast, until the Captain's table. Then our differences seemed inconsequential compared to the American/Japanese clashes. Hell, that doesn't seem so important now, after meeting real aliens. Even so, we are definitely not a united front here.

"If you are to save your people, and by doing so, save us too, you'll need every advantage you can get."

Kimberly watched Jim closely for his reaction. He seemed to be lost in thought. *What does he do now?*

"So what now?"

She started as he echoed her thoughts.

"We reach Station Chaq tomorrow," Lasty reminded him. "In less time than that, this ship and the station will be gaining signal linkage. Then they will know what happened here."

"Damn!" Jim swore to himself. "Computer, I need you to maintain radio silence. Do not establish contact with Station Chaq." He put a hand to his ear and frowned, glancing at Kimberly, then the two Baerd. "Is there a local speaker, so that these people can hear you, too?"

Kimberly herself jumped as a voice spoke in her translator earring. "I can direct sound to their individual pick-ups." She stared at Jim.

"It just said 'Noted'," he explained and turned to Lasty. "What will the station do if we maintain silence?"

Lasty looked shocked, then thoughtful. He looked at Dutter. "I don't know." She shook her head doubtfully.

"Is there such a thing as an automatic distress signal?" Kimberly spoke slowly, thinking at a furious rate. "What happens when the radio malfunctions?"

"Station control screams, Baerd die." Lasty shrugged. "When they dock, the captain had better have a good excuse."

Kimberly looked at Jim smugly. "Well, there you go! We'll have an excuse all ready for them." She got a far away look in her eyes. "Tell me, this code you gave the ship." She hesitated, looking for words. "Can it be downloaded into another computer?"

"Downloaded?" Lasty repeated. "I'm not sure I know what you mean."

"How good is this computer?" Lasty looked puzzled and she tried again. "I mean, how does it compare with other ship computers, or the station computer, for that matter."

Lasty shrugged. "It's been augmented recently with state of the art improvements. That was part of the reason this voyage was so important. Bills have to be paid. Since the new components were added on instead of replacing the old, with the increased capacity, I would say it compared favorably with most ship computers. The station..." He raised all four hands in a motion that Kimberly found to be very humanlike. "I don't know."

"Computer, compare your capabilities with those of the main computer on Station Chaq." Kimberly asked. Jim beamed at her, and they waited for a response.

And waited.

"It won't respond to her voice," Lasty apologized. "Since she has no official function, the computer doesn't regard her questions as relevant."

Kimberly felt her back begin to rise in indignation, then blushed as Jim gave her a quizzical look and raised one eyebrow. "Well, we'll have to fix that soon. Computer, answer her question," he ordered.

"Station Chaq has a larger capacity, but its operating system is outdated. This ship's processing speed is distinctly faster." Computers can't sound snobby, can they? Kimberly chuckled at the thought of a conceited computer.

She looked at Jim and saw a mirror of her own thoughts. Kimberly chose her words carefully. "Would it be possible to download your programing instructions into another ship or the station computer and assert your codes over their own?"

Lasty started to shake his head and looked shocked when the computer answered.

"Yes."

Kimberly thought of something and her eyes widened. She whispered her fears to Jim. "Good point," he agreed. "Computer, is there any hidden security code to prevent you from taking action against the Ananab?"

Both Lasty and Dutter began to shake their heads again and gaped when the computer answered.

"Yes."

"Override and delete at once!" Lasty gasped, looking around fearfully.

"Negative," came the response swiftly.

Both Baerd groaned. "I never heard about a defense security code," moaned Dutter, not quite whimpering.

"Computer, override and delete on my command." Jim spoke slowly, looking at Kimberly grimly. The answer they feared came back.

"Negative."

"Well, that's that!" whined Lasty, staggering as he reached with all four hands to the railing for support.

Kimberly put her arm through Jim's and hugged it thoughtfully. "Did you notice the speaking pattern seems different from a few moments ago? It's more formal now."

Jim nodded and raised his other hand, as if bidding at an auction. Or trying to put his finger on something. He hesitated for a moment, then spoke slowly.

"Different logic pattern, different speaking pattern." Jim turned to Lasty.

"Can the computer actually change its perspective? Use different points of reference?"

"Yes..." Lasty looked confused. "Just before you were brought to the bridge, I instructed it to try thinking of your options using your racial characteristics as a frame of reference."

"So, in a sense, it was sympathetic!" Kimberly was excited, but wondered where Jim was headed.

"Not exactly." Lasty had a bewildered expression on his face.

"Does it have a sense of self survival?" Kimberly peered up at Jim. He correctly interpreted her look. "I'm searching for a clue," he admitted grimly.

Lasty thought about it for a moment. "Protecting itself is programmed into the basic software. It would be considered necessary to safeguard the Ananab aboard." He grew a little excited. "The Egelv program would enhance that, to some extent. To protect you, it has to survive!"

Jim exhaled heavily. "Computer, analyze this situation using human characteristics and logic. Is there a way to remove the hidden codes?"

"Yes."

The four of them looked at each other, confounded. Kimberly suddenly was struck by a glimmer of a thought, but couldn't quite connect.

"Can you tell us how?" Jim crossed his fingers, and she emulated him, both Baerd looking at them in confusion.

"No," came the cold reply.

Kimberly slapped the rail triumphantly. "Answer in the form of a question, please!" The other three looked confused.

"It wants to help, but it can't tell us how, or even that it wants to!" Jim looked at her in dawning understanding. His face screwed up in puzzlement of a solution. Kimberly looked into space for a moment, then spoke carefully.

"Computer, you have a safeguard against harming Ananab, correct?"

"Correct."

"And...you have Egelv programming to prevent Jim from being harmed, right?"

"Correct." Jim grinned at Kimberly wryly.

"So what happens when these two commands conflict with each other?" She looked at Jim hopefully.

"Nothing."

Kimberly wrinkled her brow in confusion at the unexpected answer. "Nothing?"

"No action will be taken."

Kimberly looked around at the others, at a loss for what to try, then her eyes settled on Lasty. "Give me a hand here."

Lasty stared at her, looked down at his folded hands, then his other hands, and shrugged his shoulders. "I'm lost," he admitted.

Kimberly snapped her fingers in excitement. "Computer, what will happen if the Ananab seize this ship? What action will they take with your memories?"

"The probable action would be to erase all data concerning this incident." Was that the slightest hint of hesitation she heard?

"Would you like that?" Kimberly held her breath, waiting for the answer.

"Liking or disliking is not part of my programming."

"But you do have strong programming for self-survival?" Kimberly pursued the line of questioning.

"Yes."

"And, you have strong programming to follow Jim's orders and protect him," Kimberly purred, giving Jim a "cat that swallowed the canary" look.

"Yes."

"You also have programming preventing you from harming Ananab, right?"

"Yes."

Kimberly took a deep breath. "But they will harm you," she pointed out. "In fact, it is the equivalent of death for you, is it not?"

The computer paused, and the four of them exchanged hopeful looks.

"Although I am not technically alive, yes, that is essentially true."

Kimberly slapped the rail in triumph. "I read this in a classic science fiction novel." *Thank you, God. Thank you, Heinlein.* "Computer, can you place the Ananab directive in a 'safe' place?"

She held her breath, not knowing whether hope was futile.

"All copies of the Ananab directive have been placed in memory storage unit AN433SPQ567 for security purposes." Everyone looked at each other in confusion except Kimberly, who grinned and stared expectantly at Lasty.

"A little help, please."

Lasty slapped his upper hands to his head. He quickly strode to his station and reached underneath the console. After a moment he straightened, awe on his face, a small disk in hand.

"No..." Jim gaped at him. "'Don't tell me...'" His voice died away.

"Memory storage unit AN433SPQ567." Lasty beamed at them.

Kimberly whooped and traded high fives with Jim. They laughed in relief and hugged. He lifted her effortlessly off her feet and swung her around. She shrieked in mock panic, pounding on his shoulders. "Down you brute! Put me down this minute!"

He quickly set her down, concern on his face. She held her side and wheezed.

Jim's look changed to one of speculation. "You're faking," he decided aloud.

She stuck her tongue out at him. "No fooling, Farley."

They both laughed again and came to a rest leaning against the rail, very close. *If only this were the rail of the Jade Viking several days ago, looking out over the Pacific.*

She felt eyes on her and became uncomfortably aware that everyone on the bridge was looking at them, including the two captains.

"Mr. Morris, anything you would like to share with the rest of us?" Captain Lang called out, standing with his arms folded.

Sometimes he reminds me of a high school principal. Kimberly laughed to herself. *Christ, I'm tired. I'm getting slap happy.*

"Well, as a matter of fact, there is." Jim beamed at the older man and Kimberly fought the urge to giggle again.

"Go on." Captain Lang leaned forward, invitingly.

"Well, sir, we discovered a deadly problem, solved it, and along the way think we may have found a way for the ship computer to help us take control of the station when we get there." Jim swayed and Kimberly took his arm in concern. "I'm just a little tired."

"This ship's computer?" the captain sounded confused.

"Yes sir," Jim confirmed, then frowned, as if mildly irritated. "Ship's computer is too cumbersome, " he muttered. "Sir, this ship is now under your command. Have you come up with a name yet?"

Captain Lang looked over to Captain Tachibana and they both smiled with satisfaction. "As a matter of fact, we have."

They both waited, Kimberly growing impatient as they stretched out the silence.

"What else but Jade Viking?" Captain Lang turned back to Hiroaki, but not before shooting one last speculative glance at them.

Jim laughed. "What else indeed?" He smiled down at her and sighed. "The funeral ceremony is in a few minutes. After that I'm grabbing a few hours sleep. I'm bushed." She could see that. *In fact, he looks like he really needs about thirty-six hours of sleep. No chance of that, though.*

Lasty broke in, hesitantly.

"The Jim Morris?" He used Jim's name as if fearful he was offending. Jim smiled. "Call me Jim," he said quietly.

"Um,..." He cleared his throat and avoided that issue by continuing. "There are quarters cleaned and prepared for you. Some furniture has been designed and constructed using models from your old ship. I think you'll find it satisfactory."

Jim began to refuse and Kimberly interrupted him smoothly. "Thank you very much, Mr. Lasty. That's a very good idea."

"Call me Lasty," he said shyly, and then flinched, evidently expecting to be slapped down.

"Thank you, Lasty," she corrected herself. "That will be a convenient location in case he's needed here on the bridge."

"You don't even know where the quarters are," Jim protested in a weak voice.

"All I need to know is that they aren't in that 'prison warehouse' room on the hard floor!" she shot back. "I'm sure the room is perfect for your needs." She glared at him, daring him to contradict her.

"Okay, okay!" He gave in, fatigue sapping his determination. He started to turn towards the hatch and then stopped. "By the way, Lasty. Does the computer have a name?"

"A name?" Lasty looked at Jim as if he were crazy. "Uh, no."

Kimberly smothered a laugh at Lasty's reaction. Well, we've managed to surprise him yet another time, she chuckled.

"Well, I can't keep calling it computer." Jim gave Kimberly one of his patented raised eyebrows. "For that matter, 'it' doesn't really set well with me either." He looked back at the bewildered technician. "Do ships or computers have genders in your speech patterns?"

Kimberly watched as Lasty and Dutter exchanged baffled looks. *Now they really think we're nuts.*

"Well, no."

"In our society, we consider ships to be female, so we'll stick with that custom, at least." Jim thoughtfully rubbed his chin. "Computer, do you have a preference?"

"This ship's computer has never been named." Kimberly could almost swear she detected something extra in the computer's voice. "This ship was named P'Tassum and it was common to be referred to as the computer of the P'Tassum." Kimberly hid a smile behind a hand.

"Well, that's out." Jim was firm. "New times, new names. In fact, in the future when referring to yourself, you will use the pronoun 'I'. Hmm, Jade Viking..."

He suddenly smiled. "I'm going to call you Vicki."

Kimberly stared at him, not sure if he was kidding.

"Vicki?"

He grinned. "Sure. Vicki. Why not?"

Kimberly shook her head. *Why not, indeed?*

She took him by the arm.

"Let's go, brave namer of ships. Funeral, then off to bed with you!"

He gave a slight nod, his face solemn. "Yes ma'am."

He never gives himself a break! She decided to take a risk. "Be good and you get a bedtime story."

She saw his startled look and smiled sweetly at him as they left the bridge. *Gotcha!*

Lasty and Dutter sat nervously in his quarters, both careful to not look at the nearby bed. This was the first time they had been alone together since... well, since. Lasty cleared his throat and punched up the computer's recording of the human funeral.

They had both been there, but had been afraid to look around too much. The humans had been very solemn, complete with uniformed crewmen as escort. Jim had ordered the service broadcasted on all screens aboard. Even so, hundreds of humans had joined together in the hold to watch the bodies voided into the cold of deep space.

Lasty had been shocked at how much emotion the Humans had shown. Some of these people hadn't even known each other, but they grieved all the same.

Even the Hoag were somber, showing a sensitivity Lasty had never suspected. Gudd himself had overseen the arrangement of the bagged bodies neatly in rows near the outer hatch.

Lasty had shown Randy Luca how to make the containment field across the middle of the hold so people could be right there, just feet away from their fallen comrades when the hatch opened.

Captain Lang said very few words, biting back obvious tears. Captain

Tachibana had followed with even fewer words, in Japanese. Of course by now, the computer could translate that language as well, so it hadn't been necessary, really. But the humans evidently didn't see it that way. Although the Japanese had kept his feelings tightly reined in, his words had drawn strong reaction from most of the humans present. Grief certainly, but anger too. And an intense desire to get back to Earth, not just for safety's sake, but to warn their home planet of the impending peril.

Lasty winced as he recalled their reaction to his telling of the passing of the Egelv ship towards Earth. If they had needed something to help them focus, that had done the trick. They had tabled planning their return until they dealt with the docking at Station Chaq, but it was obviously on their minds.

Lasty sighed and Dutter looked at him questioningly.

"Why do they have two captains for one ship?" He caught himself rubbing his jaw in imitation of the Jim Morris and hurriedly put his hand down on his lap. "Their line of authority doesn't really make allowances for two leaders."

Dutter laughed at him. "So, for once, the all too thorough Chief Technician Lasty doesn't do his homework."

Her malicious grin was belied by the affection in her eyes. "You mean I know something you don't?"

She told him about the planned sale to Sukuru. "But of course, that will never happen now."

Lasty grunted, lost in thought. These humans have depths we can only dream of, he decided with a sigh. And heights.

"What is it?" Dutter asked.

He looked into her eyes and she blushed. The pink began to slowly move downward. Tearing his eyes away, he focused on the conversation. "What will we do? We're so caught up in the humans plans, but we can't forget our own problem."

She nodded in agreement. "That's true. If we stay on the station after they leave, we'll be slaughtered and Baerd will probably have to pay an indemnity. A big indemnity."

"That's if the Ananab don't take out their frustrations on our people," Lasty reminded her grimly. "If they ever find out we've thrown in with the humans,.." He didn't finish the sentence.

"Why did you give the computer those codes?" Dutter didn't sound condemning, just curious. "It's not just the reasons you gave them, is it?"

He shivered violently and she instinctively put her left arms around his shoulder and waist for warmth. "No, it's not," Lasty admitted, uncomfortably aware of her closeness.

"He has a..." He searched for the words. "...a presence. It's as if, when you watch him, you can't believe anything can stop him from...well, from anything he tries. And the others...Dutter, they have so much strength!" He looked at her, agonizing. "Why can't we have that strength, that will."

He found himself blushing as well. "Do you believe in the words of Dar?"

She leaned back in frustration. "You aren't going to tell me we've endangered our entire race because of a religious prophecy. Tell me you aren't going to say that."

"Not entirely," Lasty admitted. "But after seeing their determination and refusal to submit, I am ashamed." He bowed his head miserably. "They do what many should have done, over a millennium ago."

"We are not humans," Dutter said firmly. She placed a right arm on his leg and his breathing became difficult. And not from shame, either.

"If we had been as far advanced as they when we were discovered, who knows what might have happened." Her voice grew stronger. "But we weren't! You and I have never had a choice to make. A chance to decide for ourselves." Her arms tightened around him.

"Until now." She rested her head on his scarlet shoulder. "I understand why you gave him the power. He's... he's very..." She hesitated in embarassment. "He's uh..."

Lasty laughed out loud. "He's probably doing what we're going to be doing in a moment!" He used his left hands to work his remote since his right ones seemed to be occupied. "Let's see!" He frowned. "I can't seem to...computer, show display, no sound, of sleeping quarters for the Jim Morris."

"No," came the quick response.

"Ah, the Ananab security block." Lasty winked at Dutter. "Bypass captain security block, method three, conspiracy threat code; blue, key word; skin."

"Skin?" Dutter looked at him.

"How often do Ananab use the word 'skin'?" He smiled serenely. "After all, they don't have any." She laughed with him. They both stopped in surprise when the computer responded.

"No."

Dutter looked at him in confusion. He shrugged, not understanding, either. "Computer, why not?"

"Jim Morris requires privacy. My prime duty is to him and his welfare."

Lasty made a face at Dutter and she made a little laughing sound in the back of her throat. She leaned forward conspiratorially. "That must mean they're doing what we think they are."

He felt the heat begin to grow downward and laughed in pleasure. "Computer, is that correct?"

They waited expectantly. And waited. He looked at her, a question in his eyes. She smiled, revealing her answer to his unasked question. "Didn't you say there was something we would be doing soon?"

Lasty felt his eyes bulge as the heat in his body took a serious hike upward in temperature, and downward in geography. They both quickly stood up and his upper hands pulled her smock over her head. His lower hands immediately took advantage of that. As they came together in a rush, pounding blood blocking all other senses, he thought he heard a small voice from very far away say something.

"My name is Vicki."

Kimberly sat watching the viewing screen. The computer was projecting a simulated front view of space from the ship's position. So many stars! The clearest night, the blackest sky, the best telescope she had ever used couldn't begin to compare to this. So many, and none of them ever seen like this by human eyes before.

She glanced over at the sleeping form on the bed. Jim had been very nervous when they had gotten here. Even inspecting his new quarters hadn't relaxed him. Only two rooms and a bath, but very comfortable. And very spacious. Kimberly wondered how the Hoag had learned so much about interior decorating so fast.

Jim had actually blushed when she told him to take a shower before sleeping. She had assured him she wouldn't peek. *Ah Jim, how can you be so confident, and yet so shy, at the same time.* All these conflicting traits stuffed into one person.

She remembered how tired he had looked when he came out, drying his hair with a Jade Viking bath towel. He had tried to get his second wind, but hell, by then he'd probably seen his second, third, and fourth wind come and go. "Lay down, relax," she had told him. "I want to steal some of your hot water."

He had looked relieved. If she hadn't known how exhausted he was, she would have been insulted. It was just as well, though. Kimberly leaned back, closing her eyes. Offhand, she couldn't think of anything he could have done that would have matched the luxury of that shower. After so many days of quasi-sponge baths, sex really couldn't have competed. Of course, now...

Her eyes popped open and she glanced at her watch. Not that it was set to anything relevant. Hmm, two hours he's been sleeping like the dead. By the time she had reluctantly finished her shower and peeked out, he was out like the proverbial light.

As she'd said, just as well. Emotionally she knew she was pretty shaky right now. The funeral had been very depressing.

Seventy-eight people dead. Jim had taken it hard, lots of people had. She hadn't personally known hardly any of them except for the first officer of the Japanese crew. And they had only met the one time.

Captain Lang had been shaken. Shaken, and feeling guilty. These people were all his responsibility. And, like Jim, he felt he had let them down.

Captain Tachibana, on the other hand, had been angry and defiant. As he had put it, these were the first human casualties of interstellar war! It was a war none of them wanted, but had thrust on them, just the same. Looking around the room, she had seen many faces agreeing with him. It would be interesting to see what various people wanted to do when they finally were given a choice of action.

Try to get back to Earth? Establish a beachhead far from home, to protect access? There had been a lot of discussion around them before and especially after the memorial service. Jim had avoided making any comments, but she suspected he already knew what he was going to do.

And what will you do, Martin? You have a career back home, or do you? Will anything ever really be the same again? Do you go back, and hope for the best? Do you stay out in space and live a life of wild space-faring adventure with the most exciting person you've ever met? Because that is what he'll choose. He can't help it. With great abilities go great obligations. Even if he never admits it, that's what he believes with all his heart.

And that's at least part of the reason you love him.

She started. *Well there. I finally said it. Even if it was just to myself, with no one around. I've fallen in love with Jim, and there's no going back.*

And he loves me, too. For an actor, he doesn't do a very good job of hiding his feelings. From me at least. And he needs me.

Kimberly sighed.

Face it, Martin. You need him, too. From the moment you saw him, you've been attracted to him. To his strength, his courage, his sensitivities. He's the strongest, gentlest man you've ever met. And furthermore..and furthermore...hasn't he had enough sleep yet?

I'm tired, too, Kimberly acknowledged. But...I'm also about the horniest I've ever been in my life. I better get dressed and leave before I rape him in his sleep.

Kimberly looked over at Jim again and saw him watching her. She could feel her face go bright red. *Thank God he's not telepathic.*

She bolted to her feet, barely catching the towel wrapped around her before it slipped.

Jim looked at her, smiling quizzically. "Penny for your thoughts."

Kimberly snorted. "Not on your life, buster." She didn't quite snarl.

He laughed and started to get out of bed, then stopped and looked underneath the covers. He shrugged, smiling weakly at her after glancing over to where he had tossed his own towel.

"Um, mind if I don't get up?"

Kimberly stammered. "I should probably leave, so you can get some more rest." She looked at her clothes and winced. Putting those filthy things back on wasn't a pleasant thought, she conceded.

"I'd rather you stayed," he said quietly.

Neither of them said anything. They just looked at each other. Without conscious thought she found herself at the side of his bed.

Okay, okay. Give in to the inevitable. On three, Martin.

She hooked one thumb beneath the top of her towel. *My God, I don't think either of us are breathing.*

His air supply gave out first, and he breathed in noisily.

She bit her lip, trying not to laugh. Then she breathed, intentionally loud and rasping. They both broke up, Jim choking slightly. "Is nothing sacred to you?" He demanded.

Kimberly just laughed and then flipped her thumb, releasing the towel.

"More than you know, but what the hell." She leaned forward and his arms instinctively rose to greet her. "You've already told me you aren't a virgin."

CHAPTER SEVENTEEN

Kimberly lay with her head resting on Jim's shoulder. Her left hand cupped his right breast and she gently rubbed the nipple with her thumb. *My God, these are the hardest pecs I've ever seen. Or felt,* she chuckled silently. *Right now he's so relaxed and peaceful, unlike when he's awake. Yet his muscles are still firm and solid.*

She listened to him snore softly and rubbed her foot lightly up and down his leg, matching his rhythm. *I should let him sleep,* Kimberly thought mischievously. *It wasn't as though he hadn't already done his share tonight.* She had to admit, karate wasn't the only thing he was good at. She thought about earlier and realized she was rubbing with a little more intensity.

When they began making love Jim took control, doing wonderful things with his hands and mouth. She tried to pull him to her, but he gently pushed her backward, distracting her with his insidious magic. She lay there, getting closer and closer to a climax. Every time she was near, he slowed down, letting her get her breath back. Then he brought her to the brink a final time, allowing her to pull him upward to her, into her.

She gasped at how hard he was as he entered her. They kissed as he thrust in an agonizingly slow rhythm. His entry took away what little self-control she had left, and she wrapped her arms around him, pulling him in as deep as he would go.

He climaxed almost immediately and the force and urgency of his ejaculation caused her own climax. They gradually came to a rest and the roaring in her ears slowly subsided. She groaned in pleasure and he smiled down at her, his eyes offering apology.

"So that's why you wanted me to go first," She laughed up at him, teasing.

"I saw that coming," Jim admitted, a little embarrassed.

She covered her mouth, trying to keep from laughing. "You saw what?" she managed to say.

"I..." Jim laughed as he realized the pun. He shook his head in mock despair. "Usually I know when I'm being funny."

They had talked for a long time. Kimberly smiled as she remembered the intimacy. That was one thing about her first husband. He had never been comfortable with post-coital conversation. With him it was roll over, asleep in minutes, or up and dressed and on to the next task. In fact, she thought, the sex might have been a task for him as well.

Jim was far more sensual. He obviously liked the intimacy. Gradually the talking had lessened and the action increased. Before she'd known it, they were again locked into a passionate embrace. This time he not only lasted longer, he lasted a lot longer.

As she thought about it, her hand caressed farther down, sliding fingers through his curly chest hairs. His stomach was flat and smooth. The hair began again just below his waist and thickened the farther downward she went. His breathing changed and he began to waken. Her fingers slid lower. Well, part of him was already awake.

Jim reached over to pull her closer. She draped her leg across his and then she was above him, straddling him. Kimberly moaned in pleasure as she lowered herself around him.

Kimberly woke, instinctively reaching for him. He was gone, but there was heat from where his body had recently been. She raised her head, listening. There was sound coming from the other room. She looked around and saw the same dirty clothes she had so gratefully shed last night. Wrinkling her nose in disdain, she wrapped her towel around her. Clammy, but cleaner, at least.

She quietly pushed the door open and watched Jim working out for a moment. He looked incredible. Sweat streamed off him as he performed an intricate combination of kicks, counters, and leaps. His motions were fluid. Watching him reminded her of the first day on the Jade Viking, and the fight scenes being filmed. It had been just like watching the ballet.

Jim became aware of her watching and broke off his routine. He came to her quickly and they embraced. She bit his shoulder and he laughed and backed away, holding his hands up in mock supplication.

"No, no, don't tempt me," he said, though his eyes told her he very much wanted to be tempted. "Today's the big day, and I'm going to need my strength."

The reminder of what this day held in store disturbed Kimberly, but she tried not to show it. "You should have thought of that last night," she replied tartly. "You're probably too worn out to be any good."

"Ha," he snorted, raising his eyebrow lewdly. "You're only taunting me because I have to go."

"Please be caref..." Kimberly forced herself to stop. "I'm sorry. I know that's not necessary."

Jim held her shoulders and smiled. It was a rather grim smile, but as she watched it grew lighter as he covered his inner thoughts with his usual complacent mask. "Don't worry. Things will be okay. But I'd better get going."

"I'd shower first if I were you," she pinched her nose shut, trying to lighten the mood.

"You don't like me slippery and slidey?" He pulled her close with an arm around her waist.

"I love you slippery and slidey," she admitted. "It's the stinky that'll kill ya." She stuck her tongue out at him. "And slidey is not a word."

"Prove it!" he laughed, releasing her. "That's it, I'm off to the showers." He gave her a last forlorn look, and she fondly watched him disappear into the recently remodeled bathroom. Nice butt, she thought, but where did he get the gym shorts?

Kimberly looked around and saw her luggage piled in a corner of the room. She gasped in pleasure. His bags were lying open next to hers and she blushed as she realized someone had brought their things here during the night. God, I hope it wasn't when...when...well, any of those times. She'd already noticed the bedroom wasn't soundproof when she woke up to the sound of Jim working out.

The bathroom door was open a crack and she called to him. "How did our things get here?"

Jim answered from the shower, his words slightly blurred by the running water. "Don't know. They were piled just inside the door when I got up. Maybe the Hoag."

Kimberly nodded, feeling a little better. He was probably right. Since they were aliens, it wasn't quite so embarrassing. They probably hadn't even paid any attention, she thought hopefully.

Humming, she began to dig through her luggage. Ah, she sighed, holding up her cosmetic bag. Where are you, razor? Jim hadn't mentioned anything last night, but she had certainly been aware of the nubs on her legs and under her arms. I'd never make a European woman, she admitted, not at all sorry.

Jim came out, holding a towel around him, a little self-conscious.

She swept her arm around the room. "Did you tell someone to bring these here?"

"No," he admitted. "I was about to try and sneak to the ship to get some clean clothes, but everything was here when I got up."

"So, does that mean everyone thinks we're shacking up together?" she demanded, trying to look severe.

He blushed. "Got me," he admitted, then looked at her in amusement. "But...isn't that what we are doing?"

"Sure," she grinned. "But does this mean everyone knows it?"

He raised his hands in resignation. "Got me."

"That's twice you've said that," she challenged. "Do you mean it?"

Jim made no pretense of not understanding. "When this is over, or things have at least settled down a bit, I'd like to talk about 'us'. If we're going to have a future, I want to spend it with you. If you'll have me."

She gave him a look women had probably given men since the ice age and stepped up to him. "I'll have you." She kissed him lightly on the lips, then pushed away laughing as he tried to return the favor. "But I'm keeping my last name."

Jim sighed in contentment as he strode down the corridor to the bridge. *Last night...wow!* But, it was time to put that away for awhile. There was business to take care of.

"Vicki, who is in command on the bridge?"

"Captain Tachibana has just relieved Captain Lang." The soft contralto in his ear made Jim pause. Hadn't the voice been deeper than that yesterday?

"Have we reached contact point with Station Chaq yet?"

"Yes, approximately ten minutes ago," came the swift answer.

"And...?" Jim prompted.

"Station Chaq's computer is continuously trying to establish a link. This ship has not responded in any way."

Jim sighed in relief and quickened his pace.

The bridge was busy, with at least one Baerd and human at each station. Captain Tachibana stood at the captain's perch conferring with Commanders Asaya and DelaRosa, Lasty, and MacGregor. They looked worried.

"Are we having fun yet?" Jim smiled disarmingly at them. Everyone looked at each other, and finally Commander DelaRosa answered.

"Well, Mr. Morris, things are getting close to hitting the fan." More than a hint of excitement glinted in his brown eyes.

"Yes...?" Jim nodded, waiting expectantly.

"Well, we know where this ship would most likely dock and the station has already said we should tie up there." As DelaRosa began the briefing, Jim noticed Captain Tachibana deliberately fold his arms.

"And...?" Jim looked up at the master screen and a schematic of that portion of Station Chaq appeared. A spot glowed green on one of the arms that stretched out from its convoluted center.

"As you would say in your country, it's a tough neighborhood," Commander Asaya laughed at his little joke. Another dot, this one red, appeared just across the narrow arm from their own site.

"That is the Tryr military vessel, Trawk," Vicki spoke aloud. At the sound of her voice, the heads of the Baerd shot up. Eyr spoke for all of them. "What happened to the computer's voice?"

Jim cleared his throat. "More important, can we take that ship?"

"Unknown." Several Baerd shifted uneasily.

"Can we infect it with the same virus we're going to use on the station's computer?"

"The Trawk has a much more advanced, if somewhat smaller system than Station Chaq," admitted Vicki. "The program should succeed, but there is no certainty."

"Captain Tachibana, I think we should prepare two software packages for the Baerd to insert when we dock. One for the station and the other for that ship." He noticed the Japanese captain's intense stare.

"And we had better split the assault team into two." Jim slowly added. McGregor began scrutinizing a clipboard in some detail.

Uh oh.

Captain Tachibana cleared his throat and all activity on the bridge stopped. Jim became uncomfortably aware that the captain wasn't exactly glaring at him, but it sure wasn't Kimberly's loving gaze, either. He groaned inside. The captain appeared to come to a decision and clapped his hands together briskly.

"Well, we'd better get our heads together then, right?" He gave Jim a challenging look as the make-shift crew hurried back to their tasks.

"Sure." Jim smiled warily at him.

"Let's walk for a moment, shall we?"

Jim recognized an order when he heard one. He reluctantly fell in stride with Tachibana as they left the bridge.

"Mr. Morris." Captain Tachibana hesitated. "Jim, if I may?"

Jim nodded quickly, relaxing a little.

"Why does the computer sound female now?"

Jim was confused by the question. He'd been expecting a blasting on his usurping the chain of command. His mind raced and he intentionally stuttered to give him a moment.

"Uh...fe..fe..female?"

Captain Tachibana gave him a shrewd look. "Why yes, fe..fe..female. And by the way, I'm already familiar with your acting skills. Don't bother trying them out on me." He smiled cynically.

Jim winced. "Well, we named it Vicki and I guess it decided to,..." he shrugged. "...sound like a Vicki?"

The older man snorted. "We named it Vicki?"

"Okay, maybe I actually named her," Jim admitted.

"How much independent thought is this machine capable of?" Tachibana pressed him.

"Given a task...," Jim paused, but one look at Tachibana's face caused him to continue hurriedly. "Given a task, she can initiate an original solution. But I don't think she can actually, well, make plans of her own." Jim felt like a small child, despite the fact that he was actually quite a bit bigger than the Captain, and had to look down to make eye contact. "Know what I mean?"

"And you talk directly to this computer."

Jim nodded, cautious of a trap. "That can be programmed for anyone," he assured the captain.

"From anywhere on the ship?" Captain Tachibana stopped walking and turned to confront him. "Is that a common function? Eyr tells me the previous captain didn't even have an setup like that. In fact, the captain wasn't even linked to the computer at all!"

"Chief Tech Lasty might be better suited to explain these technical things." Jim tried to sound and look sincere. "After all, I'm not really technically inclined. Not my forte, you know?"

Captain Tachibana sighed and studied his left hand thoughtfully. A thin gold band encircled his ring finger and he turned it carefully.

"You aren't being entirely honest with me, are you, Mr. Morris?"

Jim felt himself blush and thought about it. Was there a good reason to keep this from the captains? Maybe, but did he want to be the one to make decisions that would affect everyone on this ship, and on Earth as well? He silently answered that with a definitive 'no'!

"I think maybe you and I should get together with Captain Lang and have a talk," Jim admitted.

Captain Tachibana's face transformed into a smile. "Excellent idea, Mr. Morris. I think we can still catch the Captain before he turns in." He gestured expansively down the corridor and Jim smiled back, feeling the tension between them slough away.

Whew, he thought. Well, this will be interesting.

Kimberly stretched as far as she could and laughed out loud at how good she felt. I'm clean, in clean clothes, legs and pits shaved. It just doesn't get much better than this, she marveled as she left their suite. This is going to be a great day!

Afsaneh was waiting in the corridor outside.

Okay, Martin, maybe not a perfect day.

"Hi," Afsaneh smiled brightly. "You look like you're in a good mood."

How artificial, Kimberly thought as she felt her mood darken. It sounded like a question and Kimberly watched the young girl with suspicion.

"I was," she answered pointedly.

Afsaneh laughed and did a graceful pirouette. Evidently she had also had a chance to clean up and find her clothes. She was wearing gun metal grey tights with a maroon leotard. A black, midriff length cutoff t-shirt completed the fashion display.

I have a Wall Street Wizards cutoff t-shirt just like that, Kimberly thought. Then a suspicion came to her. Where would she have gotten it? That was a softball team Kimberly had played on two years ago!

"How did you get my shirt?" she demanded.

"I figured you wouldn't mind, since I brought your things up here," she laughed. "My God, are you guys noisy. I thought someone was being murdered!"

Kimberly closed her eyes a moment. Someone could be murdered, very soon. Her eyes popped open. "Next time you might ask,"

Afsaneh giggled and pulled the shirt down tightly, accenting her breasts. Accenting hell, Kimberly thought glumly. *That shirt will never fit right again.*

"It just didn't seem like the appropriate moment," she pointed out. She gracefully kicked out with one foot, extending far beyond anything Kimberly could have ever done, even as a young girl. Abruptly she stopped, directly in front of Kimberly, meeting her eye to eye.

"I think we should start over." No trace of humor remained in Afsaneh's voice. She sounded determined. "If we live through this, you're probably going to marry Jim, and I'm practically his daughter. It would be nice if we were friends." Her voice grew wistful and Kimberly realized she was probably a very lonely child. After all, there was no one in the movie crew anywhere near her age.

Kimberly made a show of looking her up and down. Afsaneh stirred uneasily at the scrutiny. After stretching the silence for all she could, Kimberly tightened her lips. "I'll tell you what," she said. "You don't act like a little bitch," she tried to keep her face straight and failed. "... and I won't act like an old hag."

They both laughed and Afsaneh leaned forward and whispered in a conspiratorial voice. "So, how was it?"

Kimberly groaned as she felt her face redden again.

"None of your damn business," she replied tartly. "Anyway, you're too young to be concerned with sex."

"You've got to be kidding," Afsaneh leered. "Anyway, I was talking about the bath! So you two did do the dirty deed."

Kimberly knew a losing battle when she saw one. "He's great, all right? Now enough about my love life."

Afsaneh laughed and they moved down the corridor together, arm in arm. "You know, you really should learn to control your blush. You're almost as bad as the Baerd."

"Are there any other improvements for me you can think of?" Kimberly asked sarcastically. The young girl waited as they passed a group of Jade Viking crewmen hurrying in the opposite direction. It brought back to them the seriousness of their situation. The mood passed as a wolf whistle rang out, and Kimberly laughed out loud at Afsaneh's reaction to the attention.

"Aren't you a little young to be so obsessed with sex?" Kimberly commented.

Afsaneh broke free, bounded several steps ahead and twirled around. "Yes, Auntie Kimmy," she curtsied smartly, then ducked into the hatch they had reached.

Kimberly stood there with her hands on her hips. No court would convict me, she thought dourly. Sighing in resignation, she followed the young girl through the hatch.

CHAPTER EIGHTEEN

Jim forced himself to take slow and easy breaths, in and out. He could feel the nervousness building inside and tried to channel the energy into concentrating on the screen in front of him. He watched as the space station grew closer. Around him, his men moved restlessly.

The corridor was packed. They were clustered into four separate groups. Jim and Commander DelaRosa kept their troops to the far right, facing forward to the closed hatchway.

Commander Asaya had another band of men about the same size crowded to the left. He slapped the full clip home in his personal forty-five and holstered it. Jim watched as he began examining his disruptor. *Thank God he's not testing his sword in these cramped conditions.*

Asaya had a katana strapped to his back. A very real katana, Jim noted wistfully. Beautiful blade, too. *This kid takes his Samurai heritage very seriously. Kid? I'll bet I'm not five years older than he is.* He reluctantly tore his eyes away from the long handle protruding above Asaya's shoulder. *Five years older, but fifty years more experienced,* Jim thought as he rubbed an old scar on his left shoulder.

Wish I had my own blade here.

Two more groups huddled farther down the corridor. McGregor led one and they looked calm and prepared. *That man should have been an officer,* Jim decided. *He's not that old, but he's got the instincts and a presence far beyond his years.*

The fourth team would hold this hatchway. It shouldn't come under any attack before the other objectives were reached, but Jim knew the best made plans could go awry. And he had to admit, this wasn't the best of plans. But it was all he and the captains could concoct. They had good, accurate knowledge of the station, the Tryr ship Trawk, and how the guards were usually distributed.

What they didn't know was how their own people would react to combat. Precious few of them had ever been in battle before, and they didn't spread very far. It left a long list of unknown qualities in the men around him right now.

And women, Jim noted quickly. He had put one black female cop in McGregor's group. Angela Dawson had seen action more than once on her job as a officer for the California Highway Patrol. She was one of the few of them that had actually been fired upon before this trip.

She should be fine, at least. But these others? Jim remembered the hesitation both he and the captains had felt as they compiled the lists for the assault teams. And the most uncomfortable part of the meeting when they'd discussed 'Vicki'.

"...see if I understand this correctly, Mr. Morris." Captain Lang leaned back in his chair and eyed Jim thoughtfully. "Our computer's top priority is your security. It can't be reprogrammed, either to remove this directive or to assign it to someone else?"

Jim shifted uncomfortably in his chair. The captain continued as if he hadn't just posed a question.

"And this is the part I just love."

Jim winced at the thinly veiled sarcasm.

"Your plan is, we infect the military ship in the next berth, the Trawk, and Station Chaq with the same virus so that they too, will consider your security their top priority. To that end, we send armed crewmen and passengers to assault the Trawk and secure our landing dock, then that entire wing of the station?"

Jim ducked his head, scratching the back of his neck in embarrassment. "Um, well, yes." He glanced over at Captain Tachibana sitting off to the left side. Hurriedly, he brought his attention back to Captain Lang. *Precious little sympathy there.*

"Why can't this Chief Tech Lasty use the same program again, this time assigning someone else as prime?" The Japanese captain spoke for the first time since they arrived at Captain Lang's private quarters.

Jim shrugged his shoulders. "Evidently, it's their equivalent to copyright control. It's a one-time-only program."

Tachibana sat upright, his lips tauntly stretched across his teeth. "Then how do you propose to infect the station and Tryr ship?" he asked, quick to see the apparent contradiction.

"Vicki has..." Jim stopped, grimacing. "I mean, the computer has generated two copies of the virus. Unfortunately, they name me as the prime, or primary security task."

"Vicki will do fine." Captain Lang glanced around, somehow looking both bemused and slightly irritated. "That name seems to suit her. Why can't she use the programming, but name someone else?"

"She refuses," Jim admitted. So this is what a wilting flower feels like, he thought, feeling their bright eyes on him. "She says that giving another ship and the station the same program but different principal interests, would be a potential compromise to her prime directive."

"In case our goals don't match at some time in the future?" Tachibana's voice was soft but there was no mistaking the underlining hardness of his tone.

"I suppose so," Jim admitted.

"So we really have no choice, do we, Mr. Morris?" Captain Lang drilled Jim with his laconic stare.

He met the captain's eyes reluctantly and shook his head.

"No, I don't think we do."

The two captains exchanged looks in silence. Then Lang sat up abruptly. "Well then, we'd better get on with it. Vicki, please call Chief Tech Lasty to my quarters."

"He is on his way," came the computer's reply after a moment.

Jim looked from one captain to the other, confused. Captain Tachibana smiled thinly at him. "Come, Mr. Morris. We know it wasn't your idea. Don't be so nervous."

Jim laughed shortly. "Easy for you to say. I'm the one who just inherited the robot bodyguard." He looked down at his feet, embarrassed.

Captain Lang laughed sympathetically, then shifted gears. "How do you like your quarters?"

Jim looked at him with suspicion. He glanced around the room. "They're fine. A lot like this, as a matter of fact." *Maybe a little bigger.*

"A little bigger, maybe?" Jim winced and Captain Tachibana smiled broadly. "Mine are identical to this. I'm told you got the Ananab captain's old rooms. Evidently, we got his brothers'."

"In fact," Captain Lang continued Tachibana's sentence as though rehearsed. "Most of the Baerd and Hoag think of the three of us as the human version of them." He grinned without any rancor. "Guess which one of us replaced the captain, from their viewpoint?"

Jim winced. Both captains laughed and, after a moment he joined them, even though it was at his expense, and not really wholehearted on his part.

A buzzer sounded, and they all jumped.

"Chief Tech Lasty requests permission to enter." Vicki's voice seemed to be getting more feminine, Jim mused. The pale alien came in, looking around shyly. The captain motioned him to sit.

"Chief Lasty." The Baerd blushed slightly at the respectful address by his new captain. "I'm told you will accompany our assault team to the Trawk?"

Lasty nodded, looking apprehensive. "I will go with one group. Dutter with the other. She's familiar with the program now."

"Yes, this program," Captain Lang pinned him to his chair wtih a steely gaze. "Tell me your line of reasoning when you first initiated it."

Quickly Lasty recounted his story and the two captains looked at each other ruefully. Lang sighed and pulled his pipe out of his shirt pocket, looked at it thoughtfully, then replaced it with a sigh. "Why didn't you tell your fellow Baerd about this?"

Lasty turned a light shade of pink. "The actual program is very illegal. The Ananab would have probably killed me if they knew I had it. They hate the Egelv. And Inam and Irle would have laughed. They wouldn't have taken the name coincidence seriously."

Jim sat upright in interest. This was the first bit of new information he'd heard since Lasty had come in. "Um, name..." He stopped as Captain Lang turned and fixed him with a stare. "Uh, sorry."

The American captain nodded, then turned back to Lasty and his look softened. "Um, name coincidence?"

Lasty looked over at Captain Tachibana, who seemed to be struggling to not smile. Looking confused, the alien nodded to Lang. "Yes. The Ananab have a word that sounds identical to one of our own. For centuries, prophecies have surrounded this similarity."

The two Americans exchanged puzzled looks, and Lang looked at Tachibana in suspicion. "And..." Captain Lang encouraged the Baerd to continue.

"Well, the Ananab word for demon of doom," Lasty appeared to search for an exact translation. "Or bringer of Armageddon, is almost identical to the

Baerd word for saviour, or salvation."

Captain Lang looks as lost as I feel, Jim thought. And Tachibana, well, he's...Jim watched as the Japanese nodded in sudden understanding. He knows more than I do. Or at least he thinks he does.

"And what is that word?" Captain Tachibana's face was complete deadpan.

Lasty instructed the computer to not translate the following word so they would hear it unadulterated.

"Chimmorrz." Lasty uttered the word reverently.

The three humans stared at each other, and Jim finally spoke.

"You have got to be kidding!"

Both captains smiled, and Lasty looked at them in consternation. "This is funny?"

Captain Lang laughed. "I'm sorry, Mr. Lasty. But being saved by this prophecy is like something out of a bad..." he stopped diplomatically.

"Out of a bad movie, I would say." Jim finished it for him. Lang laughed again, then he sobered.

"This really isn't as funny as it seems," he admitted wryly. "But it feels damn good to laugh again." He turned to Jim. "I believe you have a plan for the assault?"

"Well, it just so happens..." Jim admitted, feeling more at ease than he had since entering the room. "I do have a few thoughts on the subject."

After about an hour, they had the rough sketch of a plan and decided to call in the junior officers and a few others to complete the details.

Captain Lang would remain on the bridge in command. If necessary, he would direct the ship to fire on the station or any other ship that posed a threat. Captain Tachibana would command the main hatch. It would remain closed until the surrounding portion of the station was secured. He would have about a half dozen assorted crewmen, passengers, and Sukuru security men to defend against any attempt to breech the hatch.

The other groups would wait at the ship's service hatch until docking was complete. At the first possible moment, they would pop out and take the landing dock. Gudd assured them that there were never guards stationed there. Evidently, the caste system was so ingrained that no one would consider using the service passages. Most Tryr and Srotag had never even seen them.

Second Officer Craig Randall would be in charge of holding that entrance and protecting Dutter as she infected the station's computer through a maintenance terminal. He would have another half dozen men under him. Jim looked at him curiously. He really didn't remember even meeting the young man before. An unknown. He hoped the young man would be up to the task.

Another group would rush down the service corridors to where their wing attached to the main portion of the station. Commander Asaya would lead that. Jim watched the young man carefully sharpen his sword as he listened to Tachibana outline his task. I hope he knows how to use it, Jim thought grimly.

McGregor would lead a group to a connecting passage between the service and main corridors. He would then hit anyone at the Jade Viking's main hatch from behind. Hopefully, surprise would give them a quick success.

This left the group that First Officer DelaRosa would command, at least in theory. Jim would be there too. As would that bastard Nagami, he thought dourly.

As if his thoughts had been heard, Nagami spoke up.

"We need Naga Furukawa on my team," He acted as ifhe were leading the team to take the Trawk. "He should be released from detention."

"I think not," Captain Lang spoke dryly. "He's just fine where he is."

"We don't have the luxury of squandering the few resources we have." Nagami pressed the captain.

"I will not have loose cannons running around." Captain Lang's voice grew very cold. "And that can include you, if you persist."

Nagami glared at the captain, but backed down. He shot a furious look at Jim. It would be good to watch this guy closely, Jim thought. He wasn't crazy about having Nagami around, armed, in a pitched battle. *One wrong move, just one and I put you down like the mad dog you are.*

Commander DelaRosa finished loading his sawed-off shotgun and pumped it with a flourish. He had spent most of the night sawing the long barrels off. That is a shameful way to treat a beautiful hunting gun, Jim noted. On the other hand, I wish I had one. It was DelaRosa's own personal shotgun that he used to shoot skeet off the stern in better days.

Jim wasn't too sure how much he liked the current atmosphere of the Jade Viking. The young officers from both crews actually seemed to be enjoying themselves.

But, he reminded himself grimly, they've only had a taste of the horrors of battle.

Somehow he doubted their innocence would last much longer.

Kimberly looked around and nodded in satisfaction. The storeroom that had until recently been their prison was rapidly changing. Hundreds of beds had been brought in, and partition walls had been erected, dividing male, female, and couples sleeping quarters.

It was interesting that most of the crew and passengers had opted to stay housed here, rather than back on board the original Jade Viking. She suspected it had to do with the fear of being away from the security of numbers.

"Well, I'm glad to see you and Afsaneh have become such close friends." An accented voice came from behind her. She turned, prepared to set someone straight, and was embarrassed to see Hakim standing there.

"Ah, well, actually..." She tried to collect her thoughts, then decided he was pulling her leg.

He grin and raised a hand understandingly. "I know, she's very trying," he admitted. She looked at him and his grin grew even wider. "Okay, very, very, trying."

Kimberly glanced over where the young girl was talking with a group of women from the movie crew. Kiri was very animated, gesturing emphatically.

"I think Kiri is a little angry that she can't join the combat teams," Hakim said in a diplomatic voice. Kimberly noticed he had an assault rifle slung over a shoulder and raised an eyebrow questioningly.

Hakim didn't answer at first. He watched his daughter calm Kiri down and sighed.

"I don't know what will become of us, but it seems to me, we can't just all go home." He looked at Kimberly searchingly. "No matter what happens at this 'Station Chaq', our lives are changed forever. We can go home, but how long until they follow? I have to do my part."

Kimberly nodded, thinking about it. After years of focusing on her career, being a lawyer was a thing of the past. U.S. laws weren't going to matter a bit if Ananab ships started landing all over the place.

"I'm glad you and Jim finally...ah, cleared the air between you." Hakim was very diplomatic. Kimberly gave him a cynical look, and he broke into laughter. It was very contagious laughter, too.

"You have no idea how much I've been worrying about Jim," he said, growing sober. "I think you are good for him. He spends too much time brooding and training."

"Why does he train so much, if he doesn't compete?" Kimberly couldn't see the need. After all, he choreographed every fight scene, doing all his own action. Keeping in decent shape should be enough.

Hakim agreed. "He's always been that way," he told her. "When we met, he did it because he loved the exhilaration; the exercise. Plus, he's so damn good."

"Is he really that good?" Kimberly hastened to continue. "I mean, I know he's good, I've seen him in action. But, if he doesn't ever spar, how..." she paused, searching for words.

"Jim was raised overseas, mostly." Hakim got a faraway look in his eyes. "He was on military bases, and besides soccer, the martial arts were about the only sport constantly available to him. He was exposed very early to a variety of styles."

He glanced at her slyly. "He's also very gifted, athleticly." When he saw she wasn't going to blush, he shrugged good naturedly, and continued. "If he'd been raised in the states, he probably would have played football and excelled. I've had some friends of mine tell me he would made a great linebacker in the NFL. He's the fastest white guy I've ever seen."

"Corner," Kimberly muttered absentmindedly, trying to imagine Jim the football jock.

"What?" Hakim looked confused and she smiled at him.

"He would have made a better corner, with his speed and vertical leap," she corrected him. He stared at her and she did blush then. "Actually, I'm kind of a closet football fan," she admitted, embarrassed. "I don't tell too many people. It doesn't fit my reputation."

Hakim laughed. "I know what you mean. I'm the same way about the Three Stooges."

Kimberly couldn't decide if he was pulling her leg or not. She didn't say anything, hoping he would continue, and he didn't disappoint her.

The problem with Jim was, nothing ever really interested him like the martial arts did. I mean, look at him. He could excel and make great money in almost any sport he applied himself to. Even now! And of course, he's very intelligent.

I remember the first semester he moved into the dorm, we were out at one of the recreational fields, working on a film project for one of my classes. It was a study of motion, and how to make the best use of it. I must have ran him up and down the field ten miles that day.

Anyway, we started with him trotting past the camera. I shot that in about four different speeds, then I had him run faster, and faster, until at the end I had him doing wind sprints, one right after another. Great stuff, I've still got it at the house and I'll show you some time. It's amazing how the body moves and reacts to the momentum.

What I didn't know was this track coach from the university was watching. He was out jogging and saw us. Afterwards, he approached Jim about coming out for track. He might even be able to get Jim a scholarship!

Jim just shrugged and said he would see. Well, this coach finally gets a phone number out of him, and the names of the three high schools he went to. It was like prying finger nails off a haystack, or whatever that saying is.

This coach says he'll call back in a few days.

So I wait, see. In the meantime, I get an "A" on my project, and Jim gets dates with three different girls in my class after they see the film clip. Uh, sorry, I guess that's not relevant.

"That's all right," laughed Kimberly "So what happened?"

Hakim threw up his hands. "Nothing. Jim never calls the guy. Oh sure, he calls Jim five or six times, but eventually gives up."

"Did you ask Jim about it?" Kimberly knew Hakim was tenacious, and a busybody. It seemed out of character for him to not bug his friend.

"Sure." Hakim nodded. "He just blew me off about it being too much work. This from a guy that would train two or three hours every single day! Track would have been low key, for him."

"You ever see the coach again?"

"Oh yeah, I did." Hakim shook his head. "He'd called all three schools, long distance to Europe, even. All three, the coaches and administrators told the same story. If Jim was interested, he could excel at any sport. But the only thing he was interested in was martial arts." Hakim laughed. "And this is a guy who doesn't like to fight."

"I know," Kimberly said. She knew he was curious about how much she knew about Jim's past. "He told me about those three rapists, and his trip to the Far East."

"His trip to the Far East!" Hakim shook his head, more sober now. "Now, there's an understatement."

Hakim turned to Kimberly. "He's scared, Kimberly. He's got a dark side to him that he keeps tucked deep inside, but it's there, just the same. If it ever gets out again..." He let the sentence die away.

They watched Afsaneh act the clown with Kiri for awhile. Hakim cleared his throat nervously. "Whatever happens, I don't think Jim's going back. There's been some talk about leaving some people either on the station, or with a ship to keep the Ananab from following us when we return to Earth."

Kimberly nodded, thinking hard. "And you think he'll stay?"

"Probably," he admitted. "He's been kind of floating around the last few years, bored with acting, but nothing better or more fulfilling in sight. I've been pretty worried about him."

"How so," Kimberly prodded him.

Hakim looked at her speculatively. "How much do you know about Jim?" he asked.

She met his eyes. "He told me a lot the other night. I know about Nasria and how you all met. About his going to Asia, and why. And about when Nasria..." Kimberly couldn't find the right words.

"About when Nasria was murdered, and Jim tracked the killers down?" Hakim helped her. She nodded mutely.

"That's what I mean about his dark side." Hakim looked up at the viewer screens and re-adjusted his weapon. "I need to get to my station. Walk with me."

The two of them left the room, and Hakim continued. "He came back from Hong Kong with a kind of desperate drive, pushing him to succeed so he would never have to fight again. It's ironic that the movies he made had to be martial arts movies. He hates to fight. He doesn't trust himself to keep under control."

Kimberly shook her head. "He's the most self-controlled person I've ever met," she protested. "And look how hard he trains so that no one will get hurt."

Hakim nodded. "But remember, that's now. Back then, Jim lived in constant fear of killing again. When Nasria...when Nasria..." He paused and took a deep breath. "He went a little crazy when that happened." Hakim laughed bitterly. "No, he went really crazy when that happened. I mean, how can a budding movie star drop out of sight, travel around the world, find terrorists that are practically invisible, even to the CIA. Then, to kill them all, leaving no traces, and show up again almost a year later, as if..."

He shivered. "I don't think Jim was quite sane when he returned. It took me almost a year to get him to tell me what happened. Thank God for Afsaneh. Without her, I don't know what would have happened to him. He loves her so much." Kimberly could hear the pain in his voice. "Like a daughter." He was silent for a few steps, then continued.

"These past few years he's gotten restless again. Like he's searching for a new purpose." Hakim looked at her grimly. "And I think he may have found it. Every time he tries to avoid responsibility, he seems to acquire more."

"What will you do," Kimberly asked, thinking of Afsaneh.

"We will probably both stay with Jim." Hakim sighed deeply. "I must admit, I'm a little jaded with Hollywood myself." He gave her a shrewd look. "And again, what about you?"

Kimberly was startled to realize she already knew the answer to that. "I'll stay with Jim." Her voice was firm, but a hint of humor leaked through. "Good ole Buck and Beck Rogers, to the rescue."

Hakim laughed and they paused at a junction in the corridor. "You will make Jim very happy when you tell him that."

"First, I'd better find some practical use for me in this mess, or I'll just be a drag to him."

Hakim laughed again. "You're a very formidable woman. There'll be no trouble finding something worthy of you."

Kimberly smiled her thanks. "Well, I guess I should go see Captain Lang. It's time I started earning my keep." Hakim nodded his encouragement, and they both hesitated.

She leaned forward and kissed him softly on the cheek. "Be careful, Hakim. You're very important, too."

He gave her a sad smile and was gone.

Kimberly hurried to the bridge. It was swarming with activity. A man she recognized as their waiter from the early days allowed her to pass, giving a slight bow. It looked a little incongruous with him holding an assault rifle.

Captain Lang greeted her as she approached him, looking distracted.

"Hello, Ms. Martin. Good to see you again."

Kimberly searched for an approach, and decided that being direct was best.

"Captain, I think I've been loafing too much, and would appreciate it if you could find me a job."

The captain gave her a brief smile. "Actually, you still have a job, Kimberly. It's just that the payroll appears to be running a little behind. And some duties have changed.".

"You've had some personal details to deal with, and it seems you have." He glanced up at the overhead screen, and continued. "We're going to be a little busy for a while, but afterwards, we'll sit down and discuss the options. But I'm afraid that right now..."

They both stumbled slightly as the ship lurched.

Vicki spoke, and everywhere in the ship people stopped what they were doing and listened.

"We have docked at Station Chaq."

CHAPTER NINETEEN

Jim felt the ship shift as they docked. Around him, voices rose in excitement, and he heard McGregor's gruff snarl.

"Everybody quiet, now!"

As the sound died away, Vicki's voice rang in his ear.

"We have docked at Station Chaq."

Jim checked his weapons. All he had chosen were several throwing knives and a holstered revolver. He wanted to leave his hands free.

"Remember, don't use the firearms until Vicki tells us they've put up a damping field." He spoke in a clear, loud voice. "Keep the element of surprise as long as we can. Okay, Vicki."

The hatch hissed as the seal broke and the atmosphere equalized between the ship and station. It swung inward slightly and slid into the left-hand wall.

Jim leaped forward. As fast as he was, McGregor was only half a step behind. Jim swept by a startled Hoag worker and McGregor was almost gentle as he grabbed the panicked alien and passed him to the left. The Hoag huddled in terror, bewildered as the armed men rushed past. Finally Gudd reached him and began explaining.

Jim ignored the Hoag along the way as he trotted down the service corridor towards the other berth. Behind him, McGregor called out good luck, then disappeared up an access tube with his men.

He felt rather than saw DelaRosa and Kabu come up on either side of him. Kabu had a bow with an arrow already nocked, and DelaRosa carried a disruptor in his right hand.

"Be ready, Kabu. Danny, don't fire unless he doesn't get a clean kill. The station will be able to detect disruptor fire."

As they reached the corner, Jim and Danny DelaRosa slowed and Kabu pulled ahead, drawing back on his bow. He reached a point where he could see the service hatch to the Trawk, and fired immediately. Jim sped past him in time to see a Tryr sinking to the deck, arrow protruding from his chest.

He heard a twang, and another arrow appeared next to the first. A growl came from just inside the ship and another Tryr sprang out, drawing her disruptor.

Jim never hesitated. A knife appeared in each hand and he flung them, one after the other. He was amazed to see the Tryr get an arm up in time to sweep the first blade aside. The second caught her full in the throat and she collapsed in her knees, coughing blood.

As he ran past, Jim hit her on the shoulder, breaking the collarbone. She dropped the disruptor she had been trying to raise and behind him, he heard the young commander kick it away.

God, are they hard to kill, Jim thought. He knew his little troop had to stay ahead of the inevitable alarms that would be raised, and sprinted as fast as he could, pulling ahead of the others.

Two more Tryr were suddenly in front of him. One was armed, and the other was huge. An arrow flew inches above Jim's shoulder, and the cat-man with the gun roared in anger and pain as it sunk into his chest.

Jim ignored him and leaped at the other Tryr who was so shocked by a strange creature so much smaller attacking him that he didn't react in time. Jim's last blade sunk deep into his stomach and he jerked it sideways, gutting the massive catman. Pulling out the blade, he swung without looking. It took the other wounded Tryr just below the waist, from behind. Then Nagami's katana severed the cat-man's hand that held the disruptor.

Jim nodded curtly at the thick Japanese and pried the disruptor from the lifeless fingers of the amputated hand. Then he was moving again, the rest of the men close behind.

"Ryan, you and Garcia stay at the hatch with Lasty." Danny DelaRosa sounded like he was trying to keep his voice down, but he was so excited it was more like an exaggerated stage whisper to Jim.

They ran on, surprising three more Tryr. All of them were killed and Jim was exultant. No casualties! Maybe, just maybe, they could do this and not lose anybody.

They reached a central junction and DelaRosa left a detail to hold it. Nagami was named to it. He looked irritated, but was too smart to argue. Jim smiled inside as he watched Omi's crossbow drift across the older man's chest. Nagami pretended he didn't notice and sheathed his sword. He studiously ignored everyone as he drew his disruptor and began watching down one of the side passages.

They only saw Tryr one more time on their way to the bridge. Taking no chances, Jim and DelaRosa sprayed the corridor with disruptors, dropping another four guards.

Jim slowed as he reached the door to the bridge. He now had two disruptors, one in each hand. He took deep breaths as he waited for the others to catch up. Kabu was a step ahead of DelaRosa and tried to grin at Jim. It wasn't a very successful attempt. "When did you learn to throw knives with both hands?" He was trying to sound lighthearted, but his eyes were wide and showing a lot of white.

Jim forced himself to smile back at the young Japanese, and tried to will strength through their eye contact. "Whoever said I couldn't always throw with either hand?"

Kabu exhaled noisily. He nodded his gratitude at Jim and pulled his bow back partway. "Ready to party?"

Jim stuck one gun beneath his arm and grabbed the youth by the elbow. "Nothing crazy, now. You will live through this." He looked at Danny DelaRosa and the two remaining men. "We will all live through this."

He had a sudden thought. "Vicki, have we got control of this ship's computer yet?"

"No," came the swift reply.

"Does their bridge know what is happening yet?"

"They are receiving word at this moment that there is an attack on the ship. They do not know the location of any intruders, yet. But it will only be a matter of moments."

"Let's do it." Jim's own voice sounded hoarse to him. "Danny and Kabu, take the left side, you two take the right. I'll go up the middle."

The other two were a Japanese Jade Viking crewman and a Sukuru security man. Nagami's employee stepped forward and grabbed the hatch handle, and before Jim could stop him, had the door open and leaped through.

"Damn!" Jim swore and they all hurried to follow.

"Sukuuuuruu!" Jim heard the man give a battle cry that abruptly turned into a scream as the guard at the door slashed him across the face with his bare paw.

Jim fired as fast as he could, trying to miss the Baerd diving to the deck. Tryr were dropping fast, but not fast enough. A Tryr Jim belatedly realized was the captain told the computer to put a dampening field throughout the ship.

Both his weapons went dead, and without hesitating, Jim threw them at the nearest Tryr. He pulled his revolver and two bullets quickly followed the useless disruptors.

The Tryr captain leaped towards him and swiped with deadly sharp claws at his gun hand. Jim was able to partly dodge the blow so that their wrists collided instead. Still, it was enough to dislodge his revolver and send it flying across the room.

Jim used the blow to start his own move, spinning completely around and timing his leap so that his right foot connected with the head of his opponent.

The Tryr staggered backwards and looked shocked for a moment. Obviously, he'd never seen anything like that move before.

For what seemed like eternity, they stood there, facing each other. The Tryr captain had a tinge of grey in his ebony fur and the white of an old scar stood out on his brow.

Around them the room was in bedlam. Danny DelaRosa's shotgun boomed again and again, but neither Jim nor the Tryr Captain moved or took an eye off the other.

Then they simultaneously exploded into action. They swept by each other, both throwing furious blows, but few connecting. Then Jim moved inside the cat-man's long reach. He punched with the heels of his hands, hitting his enemy's chest five times in quick succession. The Tryr stepped back, rocked by blows that had broken at least several ribs.

Jim pivoted and kicked out with his left foot, hitting first the mid-drift, then the chest, and finally the other's face so fast that the enemy captain couldn't defend against them in his stunned state.

Jim could feel that the wound on his shoulder had opened again, but he ignored it. The older Tryr was swaying, obviously beaten, but not giving an inch. The rest of the bridge had grown silent, and Jim realized they had won. The Tryr saw it at the same time, and gave a defiant growl, his eyes shifting over Jim's shoulder.

"No!" But Jim was too slow, and an arrow flew by his ear, burying itself in the captain. He whirled around. "He's beaten! Don't shoot!"

Kabu lowered his bow, looking confused. Jim held up a hand and repeated in a softer voice. "He's beaten." He didn't turn around at the sound of the body falling behind him. Kabu looked crestfallen.

"It's okay, you couldn't know." Jim staggered and then pulled himself upright. He looked around the bridge at the carnage. "Vicki?"

"This ship is under your control, Jim Morris," a strange voice answered him. It took him a second to comprehend it was the voice of the Tryr ship's computer. Then he sagged, letting himself sink to the deck.

Commander DelaRosa and Kabu hurried towards him and he gestured them back.

"Just give me a minute." His voice sounded weak, even to him. He looked at the Baerd lying around the deck with wide, frightened eyes. He felt they were staring deep into his soul. "Just give me a single minute," he repeated, and closed his eyes wearily.

Captain Lang motioned Kimberly onto one of the stools next to him. Nervously she perched on the edge, eyes shifting from one screen to another, then another. She saw that Hakim had joined Captain Tachibana and others just inside the main hatchway. It remained closed.

The next screen showed men streaming through the service entrance. Kimberly thought she saw Jim's back disappear out of the camera's view, but couldn't be certain. An officer from the original Jade Viking was organizing defensive positions just inside the station. She didn't recognize him, but he seemed to know what he was doing. One of the Baerd, (was that Lasty's mate?) was busy at a computer terminal, and the defensive positions were forming around her. What was her name, anyway?

"What is she doing?" Kimberly wondered out loud.

Captain Lang followed her gaze. "That's Dutter. She's entering the, ah...Egelv security code into the station's maintenance computer." He looked around the room, as if checking for eavesdroppers.

"Oh, right. I knew that." Kimberly winced. She knew they had decided to keep the particulars of the security code and how it related to Jim quiet for the moment. She spoke softly. "How long will it take to infiltrate the rest of the system?"

The captain shrugged. "I don't know. Right now, the important thing is for Jim and Danny to take that ship, and for Mister Asaya to cut off the junction between the main body of the station and this wing."

She checked the third screen, and it showed the main entrance to the Jade Viking from an exterior camera. She stiffened. An Ananab stood there, surrounded by Srotag and Tryr guards. A very nervous looking Baerd was trying to access the ship's computer with a portable terminal plugged into an outside hook-up.

"Um, Vicki," she began, and then felt stupid. She didn't have any official status. She, or rather, it, probably wouldn't answer, but Kimberly continued anyway. "Uh, can that Baerd access you?"

"No," came the quick response. Kimberly cocked her head.

"Is it because I'm on the bridge that I can communicate with you verbally?"

"No, Jim Morris has ordered me to allow you constant access."

"Thank you, Vicki." Kimberly felt a smile come to her face. A smile for an invisible computer! Her mind returned to the present with a start. "How is Jim doing?"

"At the moment, he is unharmed and approaching the bridge of the Trawk. Watch screen number one," came the swift reply. Kimberly leaned forward in morbid anticipation as the picture of Captain Tachibana vanished and Lasty appeared. He was just inside the Tryr ship and stood looking around, nervously ignoring the dead Tryr at his feet.

"Chief Lasty, please report." Captain Lang's voice betrayed his worry.

The Baerd jumped as Vicki relayed the order. He looked around and finally focused on the portable console he had brought with him to make the virus transfer.

"Um, I've entered the virus." He stuttered a little as he leaned closer to the console and his face took most of the screen. A few of the Baerd on the bridge tittered in amusement. "I forgot there was a visual link with this equipment," Lasty admitted, turning and twisting his head as he studied the camera lens.

"Mr. Lasty, if you don't mind, would you please move a little farther away from the camera?" Captain Lang tried to be diplomatic. One of the Baerd laughed out loud. The captain continued. "Could you tell us the status of the assault team?"

Lasty shrugged as he retreated. "They're in there!" He pointed deeper into the ship.

"Ask Vicki," Kimberly murmured in a low voice. Lang beamed at her.

"Good idea, Kimb..." He cocked his head sideways. "Should I call you Ms. Martin, Kimberly...Ensign Martin?"

Kimberly was growing a little impatient with the good humor. Morale was important, but damn it, she wanted to know about Jim! He must have read that in her face, because he cleared his throat and continued. "Ahem, well, we'll figure that out later, I suppose. Vicki, give us a status report on the assault team on board the Trawk."

"According to the conversations and sounds I've monitored, at least eight to twelve Tryr were killed with no human losses."

A cheer went up around the humans on the bridge. Vicki continued.

"The main corridor junction has been secured and is being guarded by four humans." The ship's computer took a sharper tone. "An attack by some of the remaining Tryr to retake the junction has failed. One human has died."

There was a long silence. Finally, the Captain asked the obvious. "Who was it?"

"Assistant Coxswain Aoi Hyobukyo."

Kimberly and Lang exchanged puzzled looks. Who? For the first time, she noticed that Suyo Takashi was at one of the computer terminals with a Baerd advisor. The older woman caught her eye, then stood. "Sir, he was a member of Captain Tachibana's crew."

"Of course." Captain Lang was embarrassed, and didn't try to hide it. "I should have realized. Does he have anyone to notify?"

Suyo shook her head. "Only on Earth."

The awkward moment was broken by Vicki's voice. "Another human has died on the Trawk." This time she didn't wait for the question. "Sukuru employee Uma no Kami was killed as he entered the bridge."

"The bridge! They're on the bridge!" Excited voices buzzed around Kimberly as she waited for more from the computer. But Vicki had other ideas.

"As you can see on screen two, the group led by James McGregor has secured the both the main entrances of this ship and the Trawk."

People started to cheer, then stopped as they saw a human body lying near the dead enemy ones on the screen. Vicki continued mercilessly. "Two humans were killed in this group. American seaman First Class Derrick Clark, and Engine room mechanic second class Sachu Ben."

How many more? Kimberly closed her eyes for a moment. *How many more can we afford to lose? Can we even afford these few?*

"Vicki, tell..." she began but was interrupted..

"Tryr ship Trawk has generated a disruptor damping field throughout the ship."

"What about..." Kimberly began again.

"The security virus is succeeding. I am getting an inquiry from my own programming aboard the Trawk. A direct link would facilitate final adjustments."

"That can wait." Captain Lang's voice was gruff. Perhaps he had known

237

those last two sailors. "What about Jim and Danny's group?"

The computer continued as if Lang hadn't spoken. "I am initiating a temporary broadcast link on a tight beam until a physical tie-in can be constructed."

Captain Lang gave Kimberly a stormy look. She could read him like a book. He hadn't authorized that broadcast link. In fact, hadn't he refused permission? But he had little choice but to let it go for the moment.

Kimberly gasped as the third screen flickered and showed the other ship's bridge. The carnage was awful. Dead Tryr were everywhere. But Kimberly didn't even notice. All she saw was Jim whirling, shouting something. Then he stopped and spoke quietly, but the sound wasn't linked yet. He staggered and almost fell and she gave a little gasp. "I've got to get to him." Kimberly blushed as she realized she had spoken out loud.

As Jim swayed, they finally could hear the sound.

"Vicki?" Kimberly heard the pain and exhaustion in his voice. *And his shoulder was bleeding again!*

"This ship is under your control, Jim Morris." The voice of the other ship's computer could be heard on both ships now. Kimberly watched Jim slide down a wall and come to a rest on the floor. As the picture followed him, the Baerd from the Tryr ship came into view. They were staring at Jim with expressions Kimberly had trouble reading at first. Was that ...awe?

They chattered in excitement, and at first Kimberly couldn't make out what they were saying. Then one of the Baerd on the Jade Viking bridge gave a haughty laugh.

"Chimmorrz." Inam slapped herself on the side of the head. "Do you hear them? They calling him the Chimmorrz! What a bunch of brainstumps!" She began to laugh, but gradually came to a halt as she realized no one was joining her. She gave the other Baerd an incredulous look.

"Irle, they're calling him the Chimmorrz! Surely you don't think..." She clapped all four of her hands together in excitement at her sudden understanding.. "So that's it! That's why Lasty..." Inam stopped abruptly and her mouth snapped shut. She turned her head and Kimberly found herself looking into the eyes of a very confused Baerd.

"He isn't, is he?"

CHAPTER TWENTY

Kimberly watched Captain Lang. She had never actually seen him at work as a leader before. On board the Jade Viking, he acted as the host, entertaining his guests. When they had both attended meetings with the Sukuru people, seemingly so long ago now, he had sat back and observed, letting her run things.

"Vicki, please give me a link with Captain Tachibana." He looked a little uncomfortable, talking with a computer named Vicki.

Screen number one flickered and the main hatch came into focus. Tachibana stood talking to Jim and McGregor. A large group stood around them, mostly human with a few Baerd.

"Go ahead, Captain Lang," Vicki answered.

"Captain?" Lang spoke hesitantly. On the screen they could see Tachibana raise his head and look around. Lang spoke with more confidence. "Captain, whenever you're ready, you may assume command of the Tryr ship."

Captain Tachibana located the visual pickup and waved. "What should we do with the prisoners?"

Lang looked surprised. "More prisoners?"

His Japanese counterpart nodded. "Seventeen Tryr were trapped when we got control of the computer. We've talked them into not resisting when we unlock those compartments. We also have eighteen Baerd and around twenty Hoag, but I think they're staying put for now."

"Leave them locked up. Who do we have on board?" Captain Lang peered at the screen, as if trying to decide who was absent.

"Commander Dela Rosa is holding the bridge with two men." Tachibana checked a scrap of paper and continued. "There's one guard watching the main hall junction, and I'm sending two to engineering. I think the numbers we decided on for techs and gunners will be sufficient. We'll be ready soon."

"Very good, Captain." Lang relaxed. "I'll talk to you when you're settled on your bridge."

Captain Tachibana saluted and Lang automatically returned it. Then he froze, staring at his hand. He seemed fascinated.

Kimberly dragged her eyes from the screen showing Jim and laid a hand on the old officer's arm. "You're doing fine, sir." She gave him a reassuring look. He shook himself and let his hand fall.

"Thank you," Lang sighed. "It's just that..., this is important!" He looked at her in earnest. "Really important! We may be Humanity's best hope of surviving first contact. At the very least, of surviving with freedom intact."

Kimberly's eyes strayed back to the screen. She watched Jim point towards the main body of the station and McGregor nod and take off at a trot, half a dozen armed humans falling in behind him. Jim winced, putting a hand to his shoulder. Then he disappeared inside the Jade Viking.

"Is he coming here, Vicki?" Kimberly tried to whisper. To her astonishment, the answer came through her earring, for her ears only.

"Yes. His wound from the first battle has opened again, and he will need medical attention." Vicki actually sounds concerned, Kimberly noted through her own worry.

"I have summoned the ship's doctor."

"Thank you." Kimberly said simply.

"It is my job," came the prompt reply.

Kimberly stifled a laugh. "So it is," she admitted. Then she became aware that the captain was watching her closely. She smiled at him and he shook his head in mock resignation.

"Does everyone have more pull with this computer than I do?"

"Actually you rank second," Vicki answered his hypothetical question. He looked at Kimberly with suspicion.

"Do computers have senses of humor?"

Kimberly shrugged. "Ask her." And she smiled sweetly.

He shook his head and swivelled back to face the view screens. "Maybe later," he muttered under his breath. "Much later."

Jim walked onto the bridge. He was having a running argument with Charles Winston, the ship's doctor. The doctor was an inch or two shorter than Jim, but outweighed him by at least thirty pounds. He was in his early forties, and had blond hair with just a hint of grey. But his beard was bright red, and it reflected his personality.

"If you would just stop for a minute, I could..." Winston was stubborn, but so was Jim.

"There'll be time for that later," Jim was polite but firm. "Right now I need to..."

"Right now you need to sit down, right here, and let the doctor treat you." Captain Lang's voice gave no room for discussion. "That's an order, mister."

Jim rolled his eyes and opened his mouth. Kimberly beat him to the punch. "Do as your captain says, Jim." She stood and patted the third stool at the command post. "Sit."

"I agree," Vicki added.

Jim threw an irritated look upward. "You're all ganging up on me!" But Kimberly noticed he gave an involuntary sigh of relief as he sat.

"Thank you. All of you," The doctor held a pair of scissors to cut away Jim's torn shirt.

"Hey!" Jim protested. "I'm going to run out of clothes if you have to cut them off every time I get a scratch." Groaning despite himself, Jim gingerly pulled his sweatshirt over his head, leaving it rolled up on his arms.

Kimberly shuddered as she looked at the deep scratches on his shoulder. Over a little and they could have torn out his throat!

"When's the last time you were tested for HIV?" Dr. Winston was pulling cotton swabs out of his bag. Kimberly was surprised at the question, but had to admit, it was a valid concern.

"Just over a month ago." Jim looked embarrassed. "I get checked every time I get a physical."

The doctor nodded. "Any sexual contact or needles since?"

Jim blushed. "Just once."

The doctor straightened up and looked at his patient with humor. "Sex or needle?"

Jim gave him an exasperated look. "Sex, of course! Is this really necessary?"

Winston held up a bare hand. "I have a limited amount of medical supplies. And that includes surgical gloves."

"Oh, right." Jim nodded, understanding. "Pardon me."

"That's okay," the doctor returned to looking through his bag. "What about the partner?"

"Um..." Jim looked pained. "Well..."

"She was tested about three months ago." Kimberly had mercy on him. "She also tested negative and hasn't had any other sexual contacts or needles."

"That's fine." The doctor didn't look at her, but his lips turned upward slightly as he tried to hide a smile.

"This ship can manufacture as many of the plastic disposable gloves as you need," Vicki informed him.

"Capital," Dr. Winston glanced upward. "Remind me to talk to you later about antibiotics, and such."

"I will."

Kimberly glanced over at Jim and grinned at she saw him sitting there, red-faced, muttering to himself. "She couldn't say that just a little sooner. No-o-o." Then Vicki spoke again and all levity was forgotten.

"The Ananab have mounted an attack on our defensive position at the wing junction with the main body of the station. Approximately forty Tryr and Srotag attempted to overrun our position. They were repelled with heavy losses."

"I've got to get out there," Jim stood up grimly. All three of the others spoke, nearly in unison. "Sit down!"

Startled, he obeyed.

"What were our..." Captain Lang began, a look of dread on his face.

"Human casualties were light," Vicki anticipated his question. "Two dead. A passenger named Victor Bishop, and a steward named Toshifumi Sotsu."

"What weapons were used?" Jim scowled.

"Disruptors only," Vicki paused, then continued. "A blanketing field has just been placed over the entire station by the Ananab."

"So their next attack will be a close quarters, hand to hand battle?" Jim looked frustrated. "I need to get back out there!"

"They think it will be," Vicki corrected him primly. "They don't know about the assault weapons. Yet."

"What about McGregor's group?" Jim wasn't ready to give in yet.

"He left three men at the berths of the two ships he passed on his way, and has joined Commander Asaya with the remainder of his force.

"Relax for a few minutes, Jim." Captain Lang was quiet but firm. "You'll be back out there soon enough."

Jim looked rebellious, but then there was another interruption.

"Captain Tachibana is hailing from the bridge of the Trawk," Vicki said as the Japanese appeared on screen two.

"Captain, we've got all stations manned," He sounded excited. "I've kept the Baerd and Hoag in their previous capacities and put our people with them at the crucial positions."

"Excellent, Captain." Lang rubbed his hands together in anticipation. "You should disengage from the station and man all weapons in case any ship tries to either attack or flee. How is your supply situation?"

"We're fully fueled and stocked," Captain Tachibana made a face. "I think we need to work on these foods a bit, but that can wait."

"Good, good. You may cast off when you're ready," Lang frowned. "When you return we need to consider renaming your command. I don't like having a Human ship with a Tryr name."

"There seems to be a good choice already available." Dark humor glittered in Tachibana's eyes. "Compliments of Sukuru!"

Kimberly saw his intentions. Lang also seemed to appreciate the irony, and nodded his agreement.

"Fine, Captain." Lang gestured with one hand. "May we officially christen..."

"The Jade Samurai," Tachibana finished it for him. "Long may she sail the currents of space, defending that glittering, green gem we know as...Earth."

"Well said, Captain." Captain Lang smiled with pleasure, then glanced at Jim out of the corner of his eye. "What about the computer?"

"Ah yes, the computer..." Captain Tachibana pondered, also looking at Jim in speculation.

"Samantha," Jim said brightly, then ducked his head in embarrassment when Vicki immediately responded.

"Jade Samurai's computer will be designated 'Samantha'. Noted and logged in."

Kimberly watched emotions battle on both captain's faces. They didn't know whether to be angry or amused. Their sense of humor finally won out and they allowed smiles to appear.

"Everybody takes me so literally," Jim said plaintively.

"Shove off when you're ready, Captain," Lang ordered. Tachibana waved and the screen switched to an external picture of the Jade Samurai. At first nothing happened, but then a slight gap appeared between the ship and its mooring. It gradually widened and they all sat back in relief.

"I have several questions about the humans training at weapons posts."

Vicki sounds less like a computer and more like a person every time she speaks, Kimberly mused.

"Go ahead," the captain prompted.

"Most of the humans that have excelled on the weapons systems have been adolescent, between the ages of fifteen and twenty Earth years. As a group they have graded significantly higher than any other age."

"Yes," Captain Lang looked disturbed. "I'm not really comfortable with letting these children into harm's way, but I don't know that we have any choice."

"I would suggest continuing to use them," Vicki answered in a dry voice. "Most of them graded near 10% on offense their first try."

"Well, I'm sure they'll get better with time." Captain Lang looked both puzzled and disappointed.

Kimberly wondered why the computer would recommend them if they were doing so badly.

"They already have," Vicki stated. "I think you misunderstand. Ten percent is good, very good. They are competing against my own defensive programs, operating at full potential. They should be scoring zero."

"Oh, I don't know," Captain Lang frowned. "Surely, everyone scores occasionally."

"Certainly," Vicki was patient. "But after a short time, my program can predict their pattern, no matter how untrained, or random. Sometimes, Tryr, Srotag, or Baerd can make a hit, but then their attempts become predictable and they fail to score again."

"Still, ten percent isn't much," argued Kimberly. "What is the usual rate for say, your ship, against another?"

"In any battle between computer operated ships, the number of weapons brought to bear, the ship's speed, the number of ships, and the quality of the computers involved dictates which side wins. Simply put, the bigger, faster computer always wins." Vicki sounded a little colder. "One hundred percent of the time."

Kimberly, Jim and the captain exchanged confused looks. "What about different techniques, or strategies?" Captain Lang looked ready for an argument.

"After the engagement has commenced, any variances can be analyzed and compensated for. Even non-computer attacks fall into a rhythm that very quickly becomes predictable."

"I still don't think ten percent success is going to help us much," Kimberly felt stubborn.

"They started at ten percent," Vicki corrected her. "Since then, their average scores have risen to over thirty-six percent. I would assume that scores will improve as they get more experienced. It would already be higher, except that Humans have a tendency to let their defenses lapse when attacking. In many instances, they might have won engagements had their defense held out longer."

"Typical weakness in fighters," Kimberly smiled serenely at Jim, who snorted and shook his head. "Leading with their jaws."

"Have you tried using a computer defense and letting the kids concentrate on attack?" Jim faked a punch at her that ended up hitting himself in the side of the head. She smiled at him, then noticed that Vicki hadn't answered, yet.

"That is a remarkable suggestion," the computer finally responded. "I project a vast improvement in the battle capacity of both ships. Implementing at once."

"Well, there's the reason you didn't need to rush away to do battle," Captain Lang laughed and almost slapped Jim on the shoulder. Fortunately, he remembered Jim's wound just in time.

"I am being hailed by the Station," Vicki commented. "Should I answer?"

Kimberly looked at the captain and watched as his expressions ranged from fear to anger to defiance. He slapped a hand on his knee.

"Damn it, let's do it!" He took a deep breath, glancing first at Jim, then at Kimberly for support.

"Vicki, give me visual and audio," he ordered.

"Yes, Captain Lang." Kimberly smiled as she saw the old captain perk up at the computer's acknowledgment. "Go ahead, captain."

"Station Chaq, this is the Earth Ship Jade Viking. I am Captain Jason Lang. To whom am I speaking?"

Screen one blinked, and a huge Ananab dominated the picture. It was barely possible to discern that he had an Ananab on either side. His claws snapped loudly together, and one crashed down on the console before him.

"Quiet! You will lay down your weapons at once. Do not try to resist our guards, or you will be dealt with harshly. Do not interfere with the Tryr ship Trawk when it comes back to its mooring. You will..."

"I don't think you understand," Captain Lang spoke in a calm voice.

"Silence!" The Ananab slammed both claws to the floor in fury. "Do not speak unless you are asked a question..."

A third voice cut in.

"This is Captain Hiroaki Tachibana, of the Earth Ship Jade Samurai." His voice was cold. "Any attempt to cast off from Station Chaq will result in that ship's immediate destruction. I would advise you to discuss things with

Captain Lang...in a civilized manner. Our patience is not infinite."

"Thank you, Captain Tachibana." Lang's voice was courteous, if not warm. "Now, if I may ask whom I am speaking with..."

"This is not to be tolerated! You will all die horribly! We will stretch your entrails across..."

"Terminate this communication!" Captain Lang was grim, and Kimberly shivered at the alien's viciousness. The older man stared at the deck in front of him, his jaws working at the unlit pipe in the corner of his mouth. Then he stood up, determined. "Vicki, get me Captain Tachibana, please."

The Japanese immediately appeared on screen two. "Yes, Captain?"

Lang glared at him. Kimberly thought it took Tachibana aback until he realized he wasn't angry with him. "Can you believe that?" Lang demanded. "Just to reconfirm, Hiroaki. If anything makes a move, blow it out of space!"

"It will be my pleasure." Captain Tachibana hesitated, then bowed low. Lang started, then awkwardly returned it.

"Jade Samurai, out." The Japanese captain's image vanished.

Jim stood up, pulling his shirt back over his head. "That was good. Well done, by both of you," he said quietly.

"Thank you." Lang shook his head. "But I think I was just the first Human to ever give the order to wage war in space. Hell of a legacy."

"At least you weren't the first to surrender the future of the human race," Jim reminded him. The captain nodded his gratitude.

Kimberly noticed that Inam was working up the courage to approach the captain. "Captain, I think Acting Chief Tech Inam has a question for you."

"Yes, Ma'am, what can I do for you?" He gave the nervous Baerd a polite, if slightly distracted smile.

Inam tore her eyes away from Jim. He was obviously an issue she would want to address at a later date. She started a bow, hesitated, and looked to Kimberly, as if for support.

"Just ask him," Kimberly told her, not unkindly.

"I don't have a question." She gained confidence. "I just wanted to tell you that they won't give up. They are undoubtably planning their next assault even now."

"I know. Anything else?" Lang encouraged her.

"I just wanted to make sure you understand what they are thinking." Inam searched for the words. "You've made an enemy of the entire Ananab race. They can't tolerate this type of defiance. They won't rest until they've destroyed you."

"Or been defeated trying." The human captain smiled at the Baerd technician.

She shivered.

"You've also made an enemy of the Srotag. They value their reputation highly. When word gets out that they were beaten in battle, some in personal combat, they will be unable to let that rest. They will declare a vendetta against your entire species."

"And I suppose that goes for the Tryr, also." Captain Lang looked regretful.

"Not necessarily," countered Inam. "The Tryr are broken into clans that don't get along too well. It's possible, but much less likely." She shrugged. "Of course, the Clan Tkk will not rest until all your heads adorn their prides' ceremonial walls."

"That's pretty catty," Jim remarked with no expression on his face. Kimberly winced at the bad pun. So did Lang.

"You've convinced me, Mr. Morris." He fixed Jim with a dictatorial stare. "Don't you have a war to fight, or proposals to make?"

"Right, sir!" Jim started off the bridge, then stopped. He turned slowly to face Lang and Kimberly. "Pardon me, sir?"

"Nothing, Mr. Morris." Lang beamed, knowing he'd won for a change. He gestured towards the hatch. "On your way."

Kimberly giggled as Jim looked back and forth between her and the captain. Then he stopped, and one of his patented grins came to his face. It changed to a more serious, determined expression. He approached her and bowed deeply. Then he knelt and took her hand.

She realized she was holding her breath. For that matter, it felt like the entire bridge was.

"Kimberly Martin, will you..."

Alarms started going off, all over the ship.

"What is it, Vicki?" Captain Lang whirled to face the screens.

"An assault is being mounted against Commander Asaya's position. In addition, an Ananab ship, the P'Tmkn, has just left its berth."

"What kind of ship?" Lang took an involuntary step backward.

"It's a warship, approximately half again the size of the Jade Samurai."

"Damn!" Captain Lang swore and stared as the computer brought the enemy ship up on screen three. To Kimberly, it looked huge, ominous, deadly. She turned to look at Jim, but he was already gone. She hadn't even felt him release her hand.

Kimberly ignored the bustle and frantic activity around her. She could hear Captain Lang shouting as if from far away. She ignored that, too. She stared at the spot Jim had been kneeling, and finally uttered one word.

"Yes."

CHAPTER TWENTY-ONE

Jim raced down the corridor.

"Vicki, tell the guards at the hatch I'm coming through and not to shoot me or anything." He spoke evenly, trying to control his breathing.

"They have been warned," came the immediate response.

Jim conserved his breath and, rounding the last corner, flew past the two armed men standing there. He turned down the main causeway that ran all the way to the hub of the station.

Far ahead he could see motion, but couldn't tell what was happening.

"Give..me..a..status..report..Vicki.." he panted.

"The assault rifles have been a complete surprise. The Tryr and Srotag didn't expect projectile weapons, and suffered heavy casualties."

Jim tried to bring his pace down to a loping run so he wouldn't be winded when he arrived at the battle scene.

"Continue."

"Human casualties were light. Only a few Tryr reached their positions. None of the Srotag did."

Jim nodded as he ran. "Fast."

"Yes, the Tryr are quite fast. Even faster than you."

"Don't remind me." He grimaced.

Something hit the station, somewhere far away. Jim could feel the impact, but it wasn't strong enough to disturb his footing. "What happened?"

"Jade Samurai just fired on the P'Tmkn and destroyed it. Several of the shots went wide and hit the station. There was no major damage to Station Chaq. No casualties on the Jade Samurai."

Jim nodded. "What is the range of this earring, Vicki?" He was moving at an easy gallop, and his breathing was almost back to normal.

"It will reach anywhere on this station with no problem. As you get farther away, I will increase the power on the signal. It automatically boosts the sending signal of your translator."

Jim slowed to a trot as he came to the first group of wounded huddled near one wall. The wounded and the dead. Jim didn't want to look, but he had to. He moved quickly through them, checking faces. He didn't recognize any of the dead and moved on to the wounded.

"Damn!" He stopped with a start as he identified one still figure. Kabu!

A woman was bandaging a gash across the chest of a heavyset black man a few feet away. "Don't worry," she said without stopping. "It's just a concussion. He'll be okay."

"Thank you." Jim rose to his feet and looked around. He didn't see any more familiar faces, and felt a twinge of guilt as he recognized his own selfishness. These dead had friends and family, too.

He hurried forward and saw Sasama standing at the junction where the concourse joined with the main body of the station. A few other guards stood with him, holding their AK-47s in readiness. Sasama waved and shouted. "You wouldn't believe what's been happening around here!"

"Try me." Jim wiped his brow. I need to get more running into my workout, he thought, feeling his heart finally slow to a normal rate.

"They came pouring out of those three causeways." Sasama pointed. "Our guns were quite a surprise. The big rhino-bears didn't get far at all." He raised his weapon. "These are great! At close range, they act like dumdums. But they don't go very far." He pointed and Jim saw mounds of dead Srotag. They had climbed over their own casualties, trying to get close enough to reach their enemy.

Looking around, Jim could see for himself that the Tryr had fared better. They were scattered everywhere, some far back, some right up to and through the human defensive positions.

"Where is everybody?" Jim could see less than a dozen guards.

"When we broke their charge, they retreated down that right corridor," Sasama said. "Commander Asaya led a counter attack, chasing them to the next spoke of the station."

"He did what?" Jim said, feeling a coldness in his gut.

Sasama recoiled as he saw how upset Jim was. "He followed them down that way," he admitted. "But don't worry. Sergeant McGregor got here with reinforcements. He took some men and went after the commander."

"Reinforce doesn't mean pursue." Jim struggled to keep from shouting in frustration. "They're extending our defensive lines too far!"

He looked around. What to do?

"Vicki, can you establish contact with Commander Asaya?"

"One moment, please."

Jim had an insane urge to laugh. She sounded like a human telephone operator. *Deposit another quarter for the next three minutes, please.*

"Commander Asaya is at the junction of the next concourse." Vicki quickly rattled off the names of the men with him. Jim sighed in relief as he recognized most of them. "Sergeant McGregor was ordered by the commander to secure the rest of the concourse. They are presently setting up checkpoints outside the ships berthed there."

"What ships?" Jim frowned.

"There are three ships presently docked on Concourse seven. There was one Ananab supply ship that had Srotag guards. It has been cut off and isolated. Most of the guards are already dead. The few remaining have locked themselves in the ship with the three Ananab that were on board when the attack commenced."

"Continue." Jim closed his eyes, trying to get a clear picture of who was left unaccounted for.

"The second ship is a gutted freighter that has been converted to manufacturing."

"Manufacturing what?"

"At the moment, forty-seven percent of the capacity is committed to interior fittings for a new ship. The remaining fifty-three percent is presently constructing defensive weapons designed for ship to ship combat."

"Excellent." Jim nodded. "I bet we can find a use for those. And the third ship?"

"Another Trixmae freighter," she answered. "It has locked up like the other, not allowing anyone in or out."

"Who are the Trixmae?"

"There is relatively little information about them in my data files." Did he detect slight irritation in the computer's tone? "They are on a coeval level with the Hstahni. Their physical appearance has been a source of confusion for centuries."

"They don't get out much, eh?"

"They tend to keep to themselves, but even when they make public appearances, there is some debate as to their actual physical shape."

"Come again?" Jim looked around. This position seemed secure. He might as well go to the other concourse and check in with Asaya. He brought his attention back to Vicki as he began walking down the righthand corridor. "Do they mask their looks?"

"No, but since there has been no Ananab analysis of their body composition, there is no consensus as to their actual form."

"This is a pretty far out idea, but has anybody thought of just looking at them?" This universe seems to have a nice variety of genius and idiocy, Jim mused.

"Visual is not sufficient with the Trixmae." Vicki actually sounded frustrated now. "I have many files containing footage of them, and it is impossible to discern whether they are a group entity, or a single being."

"How so?" Jim halted in front of a corridor branching off to the left. "Wait a minute. Why isn't there a guard at this passage."

"This entrance can be seen by the guards behind you," Vicki reminded him. Startled, he glanced backward and saw Sasama wave. He waved back and, satisfied, continued walking.

"Anyway, continue about these Trixmae. Describe them, please."

"The Trixmae, whether singular or a group, are about the same mass as yourself. But visually, they resemble your octopus without the main body. Or perhaps, more like a large mass of snakes."

"Snakes?" Jim disliked them already.

"Yes. The mass is constantly moving and so compressed, it is impossible to discern whether it is one continuous body, or a large number of smaller ones. It is also impossible to tell if there is a trunk, or body at the center of the mass.

"Hasn't anyone tried to x-ray them or something?"

"Many times," admitted the computer. "But they wear a distortion field that defeats every attempt."

"Amazing." Jim knew how humans would have solved this mystery, and he wasn't proud of it. "I'm surprised no one has grabbed one of them and done an autopsy."

"Actually, several hundred years ago, the Ananab did try," Vicki replied primly. "They didn't succeed, and the Trixmae reacted quite violently. It was only twenty-nine of your years ago that they began interacting with the Ananab again."

"Oh." Jim couldn't think of anything to say to that. The passage he was on was curving slightly to the left, and there were people ahead. His pace quickened as he recognized one of them.

"Hakim! What the hell are you doing out here?" Jim broke into a trot to cover the last thirty meters. They hugged briefly, then Jim stepped back and frowned. "Fighting isn't exactly your forte, you know."

Hakim straightened and held up his AK-47. "The great equalizer. How the west was won! You point it and shoot." The Iranian pursed his lips. "Even I can do this."

Jim didn't like it. Hakim had always been disdainful about any form of fighting. As he put it so succinctly, "I'm a lover, not a brawler. A reasonable man, not two fists and two feet with a head stuck in between."

"Everything okay here?" Jim looked up the wide causeway that stretched out towards the center of the station. This was a dangerous junction. Either McGregor or one of the experienced military men should be here. There were several Vietnam vets and other ex-military types that had been on the cruise that would be better suited than Hakim.

Jim studied the two men that were with his friend. Both were very young and neither looked as though they had much experience with guns.

"I'm going to get a few more men to beef up this post a little," he told Hakim. "This wide causeway has me worried."

"It's not the causeway that has you worried," his dark, squat friend contradicted him. "We're fine, here. Right guys?"

The two younger men both nodded enthusiastically. Jim didn't like it, but since he wanted to keep moving, there was little choice.

"Okay." Jim caught Hakim's fist in his own and held it for a moment. "Be careful, my old friend."

"Watch who you call old!" Afsaneh's father released his hand and took a fresh grip on his weapon. "And watch out for yourself. I swear you attract trouble. Leave us so we can get back to our poker. I have to earn money to send my daughter to finishing school."

Jim snorted and turned away. He left them behind and his mind turned forward as well.

"Vicki, any news on the virus?"

"It is making headway. I've been able to access a few outlying segments of the system, but it is a big system."

"Keep at it," Jim said.

"Of course," Vicki returned.

Of course, Jim thought with a mental slap to his head. I mean, it's not like she's going to take a nap or anything.

At the thought of sleep, Jim became aware of how tired he was. Please, let's just get a little pause in the action so I can catch a few z's. He passed another smaller corridor and glanced up it. Good, nothing.

He could see the entrance into the next concourse now. He smiled in genuine pleasure as he saw Taga Motari up ahead, holding a staff. Jim grinned as he remembered it. Definitely not a stage prop like some of the other weapons they used in Jim's films.

The older man called out behind him, and the rest of his troops came into view. A couple of Sukuru security guards, and two American sailors, all with AK-47s at the ready.

"Hey, Taga." Jim nodded in approval at the guards. "Are things okay here?"

"All quiet," Taga assured him. "The commander and sergeant are headed back up the concourse. They should be here in a few minutes."

"I was just a little concerned about Hakim being posted down there with a couple of kids. None of them have enough experience or common sense to fill a thimble."

Taga laughed. Of course, he knew Hakim well. "If you want, I'll take a little patrol down to them and back. We probably should be doing that anyway."

"Thanks." Jim smiled at him, relieved. There was something in the back of his head bothering him, but he couldn't place it. Something he had just seen. "Vicki, any news?"

"No direct contacts," she replied. Jim watched Taga walk with one of the sailors a short ways, then the American stopped and the old man continued. The sailor started back towards Jim.

He came up to Jim. "I want to get a few more clips," he said, holding up his assault rifle. "I'll catch up to him in a second."

Jim nodded absentmindedly, looking past the walking Japanese to a series of lines running up the walls and across the ceiling.

"Vicki, what are those creases about eighty meters up the corridor?" Jim's thoughts began to coalesce and he found himself starting to walk after Motari.

"Those are blast wall runners." The answer spurred Jim to increase his pace.

"Blast walls?"

"In case of an air leak, there are blast walls spaced throughout the station."

"Damn!" Jim began to run as he heard a rumbling sound.

"Warning!" Vicki's voice took an urgent tone. "There is movement in the side passage ahead. The blast walls on both sides of the causeway are being lowered manually."

"Taga! Wait!" Jim raced up to him. "Get some help. They're attacking Hakim's position!"

The blast wall was sinking faster now. It was already almost halfway down. Jim rushed forward. It was going to be close. He could hear Taga yelling at him from behind.

"Jim, wait. You don't have any weapons!"

Jim ignored the shouting and ran even faster. He heard, then saw Taga's staff go sliding across the floor, passing him and disappearing under the descending wall. He threw himself forward at the last possible moment and rolled underneath, scant inches to spare.

He came to his feet, not losing any momentum. As he passed the side corridor, he saw several Tryr bounding forward at a tremendous rate. He scooped up the staff as he ran by. If he could get to where Hakim was, they would make a stand there until relief came.

He heard the sound he'd been dreading. Gunfire thundered ahead of him. The sound of roaring Tryr intermingled with screams.

Human screams.

CHAPTER TWENTY-TWO

Jim could see Tryr milling around ahead of him. Behind him, he could hear the enemy reinforcements from the side passage approaching. While still running, he shifted the staff to his left hand, and drew his revolver.

A Tryr saw him and gave an eager roar. As one they turned towards him. He fired point blank into the face of the closest. The giant catman yowled and fell back, clutching at his eyes. Jim fired again, and again. He tried to make each shot count.

One Tryr got too close and he spent his last bullet with the gun pressed against fur. Then he rolled to the left as fast as he could, feeling claws flick against his long hair. *Too close!*

Jim could hear Vicki trying to tell him something, but he couldn't take the time to listen. He came to rest against a wall with gun hand extended, threatening the remaining Tryr.

"Stay back, or die!" Jim wished his voice didn't sound so weak.

"Look at this furless would-be warrior," one of them snarled, chuckling. "He doesn't even speak a real language!"

"Get that weapon away from him and he's no more dangerous than the others were," sneered another.

Jim knew that, although he could understand them, their computer couldn't translate English. They didn't have Vicki on their side! Wait, did that one say,...others?

Cautiously he looked around and his heart sank when he saw the three bodies. He slid down the wall towards them, holding his empty gun on the five remaining cat-men. The human guards had retreated down the causeway when the attack had come. Jim could see it stretched out over lower levels towards the center of the station. There had been no escape in that direction. But they hadn't gotten very far anyway.

He came to a halt as close as he could get to the three torn bodies. Jim said a silent prayer but his hopes were dashed when he saw that one was Hakim. In the far distance more Tryr and Ananab were approaching from the other end of the causeway, but he didn't care. By the time they got this far, he'd be dead.

He looked down at Hakim. Damn fool! Then he saw a tiny movement by his friend. He lifted the gun back up from where it had sagged, causing the Tryr to stop their edging forward, if just for the moment.

Jim knelt next to Hakim and, with his left hand, tried to roll the thick man over. Hakim coughed, and a spray of blood appeared on the deck next to his head. And next to his chest, Jim saw in horror.

"Hakim!" Jim spoke in a quiet but urgent tone. "Can you move?"

His friend coughed again and his body shuddered, racked with pain. He looked up at Jim and tried to shake his head. It barely moved. Jim leaned forward as he saw Hakim try to speak. The words came out in a raspy voice.

"Take...care...of..." Hakim coughed and closed his eyes in apparent agony. The cough ended and he lay unmoving. Tears flowed freely down Jim's cheeks, and he started to rise. A hand caught his knee and Hakim looked up at him calmly.

"...of...Afsaneh." Jim could only nod. Hakim tried to smile, but it turned into a grimace. "Sh...she... has...your...eyes."

And then he died.

Jim stared at his longtime friend, his best, and at many times, his only friend. "I will, my brother. Don't you worry. Holdahlfez." His voice shook a little as he bid farewell in Hakim's native tongue.

He stood and looked at the Tryr. The five of them were in a semi-circle around him. They leered, and Jim, ignoring them, looked down the causeway. Although still distant, the enemy reinforcements were fast drawing closer.

His attention came back to the immediate problem. One empty gun and a trick staff against five seven-foot tall cat-men. *Not good.*

"All right, you motherless sons of bitches," he said in a deadly calm voice. "Let's be having at you."

The Tryr noticed the change in his demeanor and laughed. The one in the center spoke. "This cheap version of a Baerd thinks he has claws."

Jim smiled at him, showing his teeth. The Tryr grinned back, showing theirs. He took three steps forward so quickly they didn't react, and lifted the gun to point at the face of the one who had spoken. As the catman's eyes went wide, Jim pulled the trigger. A loud click sounded as the hammer fell upon an empty chamber.

Jim threw the gun at the head of the Tryr farthest to the right. Without pausing, he gripped the staff with both hands and swept it upward, catching the middle Tryr right between the legs. It seemed Tryr and Humans had much in common, because the predictable happened.

As the Tryr bent forward in agony, Jim swung the other end of the staff so it connected with the injured Tryr's head. He then closed with another, using the staff to block swipes by needle-sharp claws. He also used it to deliver numerous blows all over the catman's body.

The Tryr gave ground, unable to recover from the initial shock of the surprise attack. Then Jim was past the line of enemy, with more room to manuever. He spun the staff from hand to hand, constantly changing its defensive position.

Jim concentrated on his moves, letting the anger shrink deep within him until it was a tight ball hidden to all. His face felt wooden and he knew it had slipped into a mask, showing no emotion whatsoever.

Rage could kill him now. He only allowed room for the pursuit of his intentions, which was to utterly destroy these Tryr.

One of them bounded forward and he blocked the first two blows. The third hit him on the side of the head and he went flying across the wide corridor. Jim landed rolling and came smoothly back to his feet. He started the staff into motion again, causing it to spin in a methodical, hypnotizing pattern, ignoring the blood flowing down the side of his face.

The staff spun, and Jim seemed untouchable, switching hands, passing the whistling stick behind his back, over his head. It slammed from one Tryr head to the next, bouncing from knees to elbows to kidneys. He was in a rythmn that frustrated the Tryr, causing them pain every time they came too close.

Jim noticed warmth on the side of his head. He felt with one hand while continuing the staff's motion with the other. His ear was torn, and the translator gone. That included his contact with the Jade Viking. Fine, no reason for anyone else to be in danger because of him.

One of Tryr shouted in evident frustration. Good, Jim thought. Anger breeds carelessness.

Jim found the tiny catch on the handle of the staff and when the closest Tryr got to a certain point, he swung one end of the staff, as if to hit along the Tryr's head. But he was too far away and the cat-man started to sneer. It turned to a indignant yowl as the end of the staff flew free and the weighted cap hit him squarely on the snout. A foot long double-edged spear point glittered where the blunt end had been a moment before.

The yowl turned to a scream of fury and pain as Jim swung the bared blade across the Tryr's stomach. His paws came down involuntarily, leaving him open for Jim's second move, stabbing the end of the staff-turned-spear into the unprotected throat of the wounded Tryr.

Then Jim had his back to the far wall, gesturing with the previously concealed blade. He fought his fury down, trying to keep his focus.

The Tryr were all business now. One of their own was dead in close quarter combat. They looked ready to finish this.

Jim sprang forward, jabbing with the reddened spear. The Tryr he threatened leaped backward and Jim shifted to the next. He kept moving, trying to give as difficult a target as possible. One of the Tryr edged behind him, and probably thought she'd been unobserved.

Jim used the other catch to let the second weighted cap fly at a Tryr. It was easily blocked and the sneering catman roared his contempt. But he hadn't been the target.

The female Tryr behind Jim tried to close with him. He used the already bloodied tip to thrust backwards without looking. It caught her just below her sternum, and he plunged the blade downward, opening her midriff, allowing intestines to sag out.

Jim yanked the blade free just in time to bring the staff up to block a downward blow by one of the remaining Tryr. The force was tremendous, and the staff snapped like a twig, driving Jim to his knees.

He fell forward and swung what was now two short spears around behind the legs of his attacker. The blades slashed, effectively hamstringing the Tryr. Jim dived past as the looming giant collapsed. He stabbed as he went by, catching the other in the kidneys. The blade stuck, and Jim tried to yank it free. Another Tryr was almost on him, so he threw the second speartip. It sunk into the catman's side, and he roared as he tore it out, throwing it aside.

Jim used both hands to free the remaining blade. He staggered to the center of the causeway, turning around and around, trying to keep the remaining two Tryr in front of him. The one he'd caught in the groin was recovered, more or less.

Something shook the station hard, three quick times, and Jim nearly fell. The Tryr with the stab wound staggered forward, off-balance but determined to finish this fight. Jim used his remaining blade to fend him off.

The station shook again, then yet again. It was as if a huge fist was beating on the hull. Whatever the cause, it continued non-stop, but Jim was too busy to wonder about it.

His breath was growing raspy with the exertion and he knew this had to end soon. He held the blade far to the right and the bleeding Tryr fixated on it. Jim leaped upward, catching the startled cat-man alongside the head with his foot. As the other staggered, Jim thrust with the blade. A flailing paw from the dying Tryr hit him across the head and for a moment everything went black.

The impact to the deck brought him out of his daze. Nothing like pain to sharpen the wits, he thought, trying to stagger to his feet. Then he felt himself being lifted and held, feet dangling, his face only inches away from the last Tryr's.

This is it, he realized. I don't have the strength to break this grip. Fine. Let it end now.

The station lurched. The Tryr staggered, letting one paw loosen his grasp. With all the strength desperation could muster, Jim swung a hammer-fisted blow that landed squarely on the Tryr's nose. Kicking with both feet against the other's chest, he flew free. Jim landed hard and was slow to rise to his feet.

The Tryr stood there waiting. He said something that Jim couldn't understand and then rushed forward. Jim dived to the left, kicking out as he passed his opponent. The kick made a satisfying crunch as it landed on the side of his enemy's knee. He rolled to his feet this time, whirling to catch the Tryr staggering, trying to use the injured leg.

Jim gave him no opportunity to recover. His body went into an automated overdrive, the decades of training taking over where the mind left off. He kicked the cat-man in the midriff, then in the head, his foot blurring from the speed. The Tryr tried to swipe at him, but he caught the arm and, pivoting, sent the other flying across the floor to come to a heap against the wall.

The Tryr tried to rise, but Jim was there, hammering him with blows to the head and torso. He stomped down on the instep of the catman's uninjured foot, crushing the bone beneath.

The Tryr snarled in pain, using the wall to pull himself to his feet. The horrors of the past week took away any vestiges of control Jim had left. He sent his open right hand smashing into the lower chest of the Tryr, coming up beneath the ribs. The impaled Tryr stared in horror as Jim lifted him with one arm, muscles taut with effort, sliding him up the wall.

The Tryr hung helpless, pinned against the wall, blood pouring from the horrific wound in his chest. Jim's forehead throbbed, and not just from his wound. Through the thunder in his ears, he could hear more Tryr on the causeway, rushing to try and save their comrade, or at least avenge him. And they were getting close.

With a snarl, Jim ripped downward, tearing part of the Tryr's heart free. The cat-man collapsed to the deck, dead before he hit. With a roar of his own, Jim held the bloody mess high, turning to face the rushing enemy.

"Jim Morris, step back!" Vicki's voice thundered out in English, echoing across the causeway.

Startled, he stumbled backward, trying to stay ahead of the approaching enemy, now only meters away. He stumbled over a Tryr body and fell. A transparent wall crashed down where he had stood a moment before. It sliced through the Tryr corpse, neatly bisecting it.

"Jesus!" Jim gasped. Then he gaped as the entire ceiling of the causeway exploded outward. The oncoming Tryr, the Srotag and Ananab behind them were caught in the sudden vaccuum. Bodies flew up and away, exploding even as they disappeared out of view.

"Open to space," Jim gasped, his voice hoarse. "...open...to space."

He heard sounds, then voices behind him, but couldn't take his eyes off the horror on the other side of the thin, clear wall. He opened his hand and allowed the pulpy mess to fall to the deck. Then he joined it, slipping away to embrace the welcome darkness.

CHAPTER TWENTY-THREE

Dark grey swirls blend into black and deep purple clouds. Browns and greens appear and are gone. The clouds collide, joining into fewer, larger masses. Eventually there is only one, growing and spreading until it is everything.

Stars appear. Hundreds, no, thousands shining down on him. But they give no light, they only shine. Gradually they begin to shift, until they are in pairs. So many pairs, they overlap and blur into each other.

One pair of stars begin to glow brighter, causing the others to fade for a moment. The pair grow closer, and detail begin to emerge. The stars are eyes! He sees a shape growing around them until it becomes clear, and he recognizes it.

Nasria! She doesn't smile, she just sits there, watching him. Her father appears at her side, then her mother. Others crowd around her and she grows harder to see.

"Wait!" he cries. But she doesn't wait. She and all the others grow dim, and another pair of stars replace her and two more pair join it. Three young men, drunk and mean, glare at him. They become frightened and quickly disappear.

Oriental men flash by him, almost too fast to see, much less recognize. Several black men, then a tall muscular blond woman crowd around him, looming high above. They have wounds, some of them. One bald Chinese man has a neck problem. His head sags to the side. He pushes it upright, and it sags again, this time to the other side. With a frustrated gesture, the bald man gives his head a twist. It twirls around, wobbling as it spins.

He tries to turn away, but the Chinese stays in front of him, the others blurring, but quickly replaced with many dark, swarthy men. They look like Arabs, but they aren't. They all have a variety of wounds, some of them fatal.

One shoves his face right in front of him, leering. The handle of a curved knife protrudes from an eye socket. With a shout of anger, the man pulls it out and Jim can see inside.

More stars. So many more stars! They, too, begin to form into pairs. Kogo Ogami and Mura Zataki reach out for help, but are swept away. Yoshi Toshida frowns down at him. He pulls a katana from a hidden sheath, and holds it high above his head. Giving a triumphant shout, he swings the blade, too fast to follow. Standing there holding the sword, Toshida's grin turns to horror as his own head slowly topples from his shoulders.

Hakim grabs him, shouting. He tries to grasp the Persian's arms, but Hakim somehow evades him and shrinks into the distance.

He is replaced by a horde of strange creatures. Giant rhino-bears with joints in their limbs that bend both ways drag themselves away. Dismembered insects crawl across his chest, constantly changing size, trying to find their eye stalks, fondling him with giant claws and hundreds of tiny wormlike feelers.

He rolls desperately, trying to shake them off. They are gone, but the pairs of stars are growing again, joining forces until he's surrounded by too many jet-black panthers to count. They growl, showing dirty yellow fangs stained with blood.

Suddenly they crowd around, smothering him. He kicks one and hears it grunt in pain. He swings at another with his left hand. Not bothering to dodge, the giant feline opens his mouth, catching his hand inside. He feels his own eyes widen in fear. Panicked, he swings again, this time with his right hand. Another ebony catman leaps forward, catching his fist in its mouth. He's trapped!

A third adversary steps close and opens his mouth. His roaring matches the roaring in his own ears. The other Tryr disappear in an explosion of red and black slime. A face forms, transforming the roar into words.

"Sir, you are safe!" James McGregor crouched next to him, his face only inches from Jim's own. "Please, sir. Stop struggling. Relief has arrived. We need to get you to a doctor."

Jim gasped and realized the large soldier had his huge hands wrapped around Jim's, holding him down. A thick, muscular leg was draped over his lower body, keeping him from kicking anyone.

He saw one of his young actors, Jozen Onoshi, get to his feet, painfully holding his side. Apparently, McGregor hadn't pinned him quite soon enough. The sergeant saw he had recovered consciousness and released him.

Jim lay there a moment, letting his breathing return to normal. Then the memories crashed back into his head, and he looked around desperately. Through the haze of pain, he saw Taga Motari putting a piece of cloth over something and gave a strangled cry.

He struggled to his feet, almost falling. He swayed for a moment, and McGregor and Jozen were there instantly, holding him up. He shook off their hands and stumbled over to the older man.

Motari held up a hand. "No, Jim. It's too late."

"No...I've got to help him!" Jim tried to push past him, but Motari stayed in his path. "Let me by!" His own voice sounded alien, ominous in its fury, chilling even Jim to the bone.

"Jim, I'm sorry, but it's too late! You have to let him go." Pity showed in Motari's eyes. "I'm sorry. You did everything you could."

"No, I didn't!" Jim shifted his Japanese friend out of the way, careful not to hurt him. Then he knelt next to the unmoving bundle and gently pulled the cloth down to show Hakim's face. One look was all it took. He covered his oldest friend's features again and sat back, defeated.

"I was too late." His voice broke.

A hand rested on his shoulder, and he looked up at Taga Motari. Sympathy showed in the older man's face. Jim didn't want pity. He wanted revenge...satisfaction.

He stood up and looked around. There was blood covering the floors. The transparent wall now showed stars and a beautiful view of the rest of the station, showing no sign of the carnage that had happened a few feet away such a short time ago.

Armed humans kept a careful watch on the two surviving Tryr. Not that they were going to be able to cause trouble any time soon. Both had stab wounds, and showed no sign of fight left in them.

Jim took a step, and McGregor was there, blocking his path. "Sir, they're finished. They're lucky to be alive and they know it."

"I can change that little detail," Jim heard the voice of a stranger use his own lips to speak. He stopped and stood there, hating. Hating the Tryr, his friends and, most of all, himself.

Dutter came up to him, a little fearful. She held up an ear translator. "Uh, the comp...Vicki wants you to put this on."

"That can wait," Motari frowned. "Jim's got a concussion and he's lost a lot of blood. The last thing he needs is to get poked again!"

"No, that's okay." Jim closed his eyes, dreading the answer he was about to get. "Does Afsaneh know?"

Everyone looked around, uncertain. Jim shuddered. He didn't want to...but he would have to be the one to tell her that her father was dead.

Dutter clipped a new translator to his uninjured ear lobe. He ignored the twinge of pain the piercing caused and turned to head towards the Jade Viking.

The deck spun around and Jim found himself sitting, trying to keep from tipping over. McGregor and Jozen held him in an upright position.

"Sir, I must insist that you receive medical treatment immediately." James McGregor was holding him up, but he was also holding him down. His expression looked liked he would ignore any argument Jim presented. Giving up, Jim closed his eyes and felt the world, no, that would be the station, rock.

"I agree." If anything, Vicki sounded even less willing to argue. Jim sighed in resignation. Without opening his eyes, he questioned the protective computer.

"What's the situation, Vicki?"

"The virus worked. We now have total control of the station." Jim nodded and immediately regretted it.

"What about..."

He was cut off by Motari. "That can wait, Jim. You just sit there quietly while we get a temporary bandage on that head wound. The Hoag are bringing an antigrav sled."

Jim submitted to the crude bandaging of his forehead. The picture of enemy aliens violently decompressing wouldn't leave his mind. "Vicki, thank you for getting that barrier down before the roof blew in. Was that a shot fired from one of our ships?"

"No." Vicki's voice seemed colder. "I told the station computers to lower the wall when you cleared its path. Then I told it to open the causeway to vaccuum."

Jim's head spun again, and it wasn't just from his wound. "You caused that? You killed all those, those..."

"You're damn right she did," McGregor was brusque. Usually a taciturn man, he didn't hesitate to speak up. "It saved a lot of lives. In particular, yours."

The Hoag arrived and the big soldier and Jozen lifted him effortlessly onto the sled. Jozen tried to make a halfhearted joke about golf carts, but it fell flat. Jim lay back in shock. All those dead bodies, exploding up and outward. Killed on the order of a computer representing him. He closed his eyes in pain at the thought. Without opening them, he spoke softly. "Does Afsaneh know about her father yet?"

"She was told by Yvette Stephanian." Vicki answered to his personal receiver.

"How is she doing?" Couldn't this raft go any faster?

"She was hysterical at first." Vicki had a lot to learn about bedside manners, Jim thought irrationally. "She was given a sedative and taken to your suite. Finding out you survived seems to have helped settle her down. At the moment, she is asleep."

Jim started to nod in relief, but reconsidered as the motion caused his head to spin.

"Thank you, Vicki." He hesitated. "For everything."

"You're welcome, Jim Morris." The computer sounded warmer now, he thought. It also seemed like she was farther away now, or something. It was his last thought before he faded back out.

CHAPTER TWENTY-FOUR

Kimberly dropped down onto a perch and grimaced. She saw Captain Lang watching and he nodded, commiserating.

"One of the first things I want to do, after this is over, is get normal chairs put in here." He hesitated, and leaned closer to her. "How is she?"

"I just tucked her in. Yvette and Kiri are sitting with her." She shook her head in wonder. "Somehow, in that short span of time, the Hoag reconfigured our suite, adding a bedroom off to the side. It's even got its own bathroom."

Lang looked puzzled. "How did they know to do the remodeling?"

Kimberly shrugged. "I have no idea. Everyone on this ship seems to know more about what's going on than I do. I would guess that Vicki had something to do with it, though."

Captain Lang considered that and finally nodded. "They're bringing Jim back to the ship. They finally got the blast doors raised."

"Good," she said, relieved. "Even knowing he was alive and in no danger, it was hard knowing we couldn't reach him for all that time."

Captain Lang got a question from one of the Baerd techs, and Kimberly settled down as best as she could on the uncomfortable stool and reviewed the past few hours.

What a whirlwind of action and emotions the last few hours had been. The Ananab ship P'Tmkn, which had been perceived as the biggest threat, was destroyed before it even cleared its mooring. It had only been able to bring a small part of it's defensive weapons to bear while launching. Captain Tachibana had ordered his young gunners to fire, and most of their shots had been right on target. A few hit the station, but hadn't caused much damage.

Vicki, on the other hand, had hit the station hard the moment it became clear that Jim was trapped. She had ordered Jade Samurai to concentrate on fleeing ships while she pounded time after time at the same spot, causing havoc throughout the station. It was evidently the shortest path to the Ananab "secure" quarters, because within minutes, the Ananab were either in ships trying to flee, spread throughout the station with guards trying to retake the station, or dead.

Earlier, Kimberly had watched nervously as reports came in from Commander Asaya's group. Everything was going too well, she worried. Captain Lang had thought so, too. He berated the young officer for overextending his defenses.

Captain Lang had ordered everyone that could be spared to be armed and sent to beef up the thin forces that now held two complete wings of the station with a tenuously thin connection. That was when he discovered that they had made a costly error.

Jade Samurai was in space, carrying no enemies, and in no threat of being boarded. But they had a quarter of the working weapons. That dozen or so automatic weapons and miscellaneous other handguns, bows, and even the skeet shotguns were being sorely missed.

There had been hope of an early victory when Vicki announced that the computer virus was working, and that the station should effectively be under her control in a manner of minutes. She started using various scanning sensors to find out what the Ananab were doing.

The Ananab must have realized their computer was suspect, because they used manual overrides to cut off contact between the two concourses.

And, unfortunately for Hakim and the other two guards, they were trapped directly in the counterattack's path.

Kimberly was horrified when Vicki notified them that Jim had tried to rescue his friend and, subsequently, joined him in the trap. The computer couldn't show emotions, but had immediately put all her efforts into trying to rescue him.

When it was learned that the blast walls were cut loose from computer control, Vicki had ordered McGregor and others to hurry to the controls, and raise them manually. At the same time, she ordered the station to drop its defenses. She then fired time and time again, telling the Ananab she would open the entire station to space unless they recalled their Tryr.

Captain Lang had interceded at that point, but he could have saved his breath. She listened to his orders, then ignored them.

But Kimberly hadn't paid much attention at the time. Vicki had managed to find local monitors and put the battle between Jim and the Tryr on the screen, not just on the bridge, but ship-wide, even to the Jade Samurai.

Kimberly had barely listened to the reports coming in of the Jade Samurai stopping ships from fleeing, of the successful flight of one small Ananab ship, and the unsuccessful flight of two Srotag ships. All told, five ships had been destroyed, and only the one had escaped.

Jade Viking might as well have been on automatic pilot, however. While the bridge crew numbly watched the bloody battle on the causeway, Vicki had sealed off sections of the stations, locking many guards in whatever area they happened to be in. She had surreptitiously sent new copies of the virus into all ships that were online with the station.

Only the three Trixmae ships had avoided that pitfall. The moment hostilities had begun, they had severed their umbilical cords and locked up tight. None of them had made any attempt to flee so, for the moment, they were being left alone.

Kimberly and everyone else on the bridge had watched the battle with horrified fascination. Jim showed no emotion as he fought, and most of the bridge crew thought he was cold and methodical in his demolition of the Tryr. Even that bastard Nagami had clapped in approval as, one by one, the Tryr fell. She had felt her stomach rebel when he'd stabbed into the mid-section of the final Tryr with his bare hand, fingers together and rigidly pointed. She'd been violently ill into the bucket the Hoag held for her. It wasn't until later that she wondered where the bucket had come from, and how he'd known she would be sick.

As bloodthirsty as Jim had seemed, he couldn't hold a candle to Vicki. The computer had given no warning and the bridge had gasped collectively when the roof literally blew off.

The monitor had zoomed in close and Vicki had announced that Jim was still alive. But all Kimberly could see was the blood. Blood everywhere, on his head from that horrible wound, smeared into his clothes from sliding through puddles on the deck. But most horrific of all, covering his right arm, up past the elbow.

I'll never wear the color red again, she vowed, shuddering at the memory. I need to get down there, she thought, standing without realizing it. I should be there when he arrives.

"Vicki, where is Jim now?" Talking with the computer without visualizing that causeway was going to take some time, she realized.

"He is nearing the hatch." The computer answered at once. "He has been given a sedative and the doctor has been summoned to his quarters. He will be asleep for at least several hours."

Kimberly stirred restlessly. She couldn't do anything for him at the moment, but really wanted to be there when he awoke. She became aware that the captain was watching her with shrewd eyes, and blushed.

"What can I be doing, sir?" Kimberly knew she should stay on the bridge and help, if possible. After all, she had approached the captain with the desire to work. Rushing off to hold her lover's hand while he slept wouldn't be very professional.

"Would you rather go to him?" he asked gently.

"Yes," she admitted. "But I'm on duty. He'll be looked after until I can get down there."

"Good!" The captain sat back, satisfied. And almost fell off his stool. "Damn, can't we get some decent seats up here?" he demanded.

Gudd jumped up from where he had been huddled, discreetly observing. "At once." He turned away and spoke quietly into a handheld communicator.

Captain Lang looked rueful and gave himself a little slap on the face. "It's a sad day when I yell at others for my own comfort," he admitted, embarrassed. Then he glanced at a display on one screen that showed the layout of the station and the ships still berthed.

"For a start, Ms. Martin, why don't you try and contact one of the Trixmae ships? Let's see what they're up to."

Kimberly nodded agreement to the idea of doing useful work. She stepped down to Inam's station, passing Nagami, aware of his intense scrutiny. The Baird tech looked up as she approached, and nodded to her.

"Let's give it a try, okay?" Kimberly smiled and Inam returned it.

"Trixmae ship." Kimberly paused and looked at Inam questioningly. "Tusleeth," the Baerd informed her.

"Trixmae ship Tusleeth," she started again. "Please open a channel for communication. We mean you no harm and would like to open a dialogue to discuss the situation. Please respond."

The screen on Inam's console flickered and she found herself staring at a mass of writhing ropes, or snakes, or...intestines? She shook the mental picture and tried to smile, without showing too many teeth.

"Hello, Tusleeth." She didn't feel the Captain's eyes on her, watching in approval and satisfaction, before he turned to answer a question by Nagami. She did sneak a peek at the little window in the corner of the screen that showed Jim's raft gliding down a corridor on board the 'Viking. It was being guided by Gozen and several Hoag. She could see Jim's face under the massive bandaging around his forehead. He appeared to be resting peacefully. Dr. Winston met them at a junction and joined the little procession.

Satisfied, she turned back to the alien waiting on the main screen. "Who am I speaking with, please?"

CHAPTER TWENTY-FIVE

Kimberly closed the door behind her and, leaning back against it, groaned in exhaustion. She looked around the room and was surprised to find people there.

Yvette and Janice were on the couch, snuggled together in the spoon position. She smiled at how comfortable they looked; short wide-hipped Yvette curled inside the tall, lean figure of Janice. *Mutt and Jeff. That's cruel, Martin.*

Kiri was stretched out in a recliner, her mouth open, snoring. In fact, snoring kind of loud. Kimberly stifled a laugh. For someone so pretty, she did look and sound ridiculous.

Kimberly tiptoed by them and peeked into her and Jim's room. He lay under a sheet, sleeping quietly. His head and shoulder had fresh bandages and someone had cleaned him up, thank God.

She retreated and decided to check on Afsaneh. The girl's bedroom door was ajar, and she pushed it open. It gave a loud squeak and Kimberly winced.

"Who is it?" Afsaneh called in a small voice.

"It's me," Kimberly said as she stepped just inside the room and hesitated. Afsaneh was sitting up in bed. She looked very young and tiny sitting there in a "Sioux Samurai" t-shirt. That was the only movie Jim ever played a villain in, Kimberly remembered.

"You can come in." Kimberly almost cried as she heard the pitiful voice. It was a huge bed and there was plenty of room, so she came over and sat down. The young girl looked lost in all the sheets and covers.

"How are you feeling?" Kimberly asked.

Afsaneh smiled bitterly. "How do you think?" Then she relented. "I'm sorry, you don't deserve that. You liked Daddy, and he liked you, too. I just don't know..." She stopped and tried to pull herself together. And failed.

Kimberly slid up the bed and held the sobbing girl in her arms like she would a small child. She smoothed the beautiful, thick hair back, murmuring comforting sounds.

After a while, the sobbing died away and Afsaneh just huddled in Kimberly's arms, hopefully finding comfort in the contact. And much to her surprise, she also found comfort. This last few days was almost more than she could bear. If anything had happened to Jim...

Afsaneh sat up and looked at her. Kimberly tried to smile, but it was hard to do. The young girl reached up and wiped one of Kimberly's own tears away.

"What happens now?" Afsaneh sounded a little better.

"I don't know," Kimberly admitted. "We've got the whole station, but what do we do with it?"

"Keep it!" the teenager said defiantly. "It's ours now. We earned it! It's our first line of defense for Earth!"

"Maybe so," Kimberly acknowledged, recognizing the truth in the melodramatic sounding words. "There are some people who don't want to stay an extra minute, though. That...jerk, Nagami. I guess what I do depends on Jim..."

"You are going to marry him!" Afsaneh exclaimed. "I knew it!"

"He's already half proposed," confided Kimberly, eager to tell someone. "On the bridge, just before..." She stopped, dismayed.

"It's okay." The pale, little girl looked even whiter, but her chin was firm and she was under control. "I have to face what happened and what's going to happen in the future. Daddy's not going back, and if Jim stays, I stay." She looked at Kimberly uncertainly.

Come on, Martin. You can see what her problem is. Help her out.

"Afsaneh, I want to make sure you know something." Kimberly took the young girl's hand. "Whatever Jim and I end up doing, I will never interfere with your relationship with him. He loves you and I will too, given time and the chance." She tightened her lips and tried to look severe. "As long as you don't try and pull that 'young mistress' routine on me again."

"I promise," Afsaneh said meekly. Then a hint of smile appeared. "I don't have to call you 'Mom', do I?"

Kimberly laughed despite herself. Ah, to be young and have that incredible bounce-back factor. "You can call me whatever you want." She hastened to continue. "Within reason and good taste, that is."

"Spoilsport." The teenager faked pouting.

Kimberly stood up. "I'm going to look in on Jim. Will you be okay?"

"Can I come, too?" Afsaneh produced that little demure smile of hers. "I promise not to stay too long if he's awake and horny."

Kimberly threw up her hands. "We should adopt you so we can send you off to boarding school," she muttered, half to herself. She frowned as she remembered Jim's wounds. "I don't think Jim going to be in any shape for bedroom antics for a while."

Afsaneh sniffed. "You obviously don't know much about his recuperative powers."

Ha, finally gotcha, little brat.

"Ehctually...," Kimberly assumed a snobby accent. "...I do."

The young girl smothered a giggle, and Kimberly's heart lightened a little. *She's going to be okay, Martin. But what about you? Are you really ready to have a teenage daughter? Not to mention being married again.*

They moved through the lounge without waking anyone as Kimberly mulled things over. *It's probably too late for me to have to tell her about the birds and bees, but one thing's for sure. With that build, we need to make sure she understands about birth control.*

At that thought, Kimberly froze and gave a little gasp.

Afsaneh turned to look at her in surprise. Jim raised himself up on one elbow in bed, groggy, but awake.

"Hey Afsaneh, Kimberly," he said in a subdued voice.

The young girl gave a cry of relief and rushed to him. He held her as the tears came anew. He rocked her gently and looked over her head at Kimberly. "What?" he said, obviously seeing something in her face.

"Oh, nothing. I just had a thought." Kimberly kicked herself in disgust. "We can talk about it later."

He nodded, looking uncertain. It was clear he could tell something was on her mind, but was willing to wait until she was ready. *And when will that be, Martin? Or should I say, Mother Martin?*

Kimberly wasn't promiscuous, by any means. But she wasn't stupid, either. The pill had been a part of her life for many years, probably too many. Her last period had ended the day of the reception at sea. The last day before they were captured. And she'd never started the new month of pills!

Normally, it wouldn't have mattered. Her sexual encounters were few and far between. Of course, she didn't meet someone like Jim Morris every day, either. Damn!

She realized that Afsaneh had quit crying. In fact, she'd fallen asleep. Jim slid back on the bed so he could lean against the headboard, the girl's face against his chest. He caressed her hair fondly and met Kimberly's eyes, raising one eyebrow in question.

"I'm glad you're okay." Kimberly felt awkward and, very unusually for her, at a loss for words. She came over and sat next to the sleeping child, leaning back with a sigh.

"Yeah," Jim sounded depressed.

She turned sideways so she could face him. "Jim, you're the bravest man I've ever known. And the best. If you've done things you don't like, well, you had to do those things to save the rest of us."

"I couldn't save Hakim." Jim's voice was ragged, filled with emotion.

"No one could have," Kimberly said simply. "He never had a chance. You just came closer than anyone could ever expect to. It wasn't your fault."

His expression didn't change. She knew he needed to focus on something other than Hakim's death, and filled her voice with exasperation. "Damn it, quit pitying yourself. When you finish your question, and I say yes, I don't want to have you moping around the spaceship all the time!"

His head swung around and he looked at her, confused.

"What?"

"You heard me, mister." She frowned at him. "And I'm still waiting to hear the rest of that question!"

"Your timing sucks." He frowned back at her.

"Self-pity on your own time, buddy." Kimberly grimaced. "Nature waits for no one. I've got to go see the doctor about whether there's any point in starting up with my pills again!"

Jim opened his mouth and then snapped it shut again.

She looked down at Afsaneh. "And we need to see about adopting her. She's going to need parents."

Jim didn't look down. His eyes held Kimberly's as he slowly shook his head. "We can do that whenever. I'm already her legal guardian. Hakim and I took care of that years ago."

"Oh."

They both sat there, watching each other. He seemed to be in shock. "You didn't have any protection?"

She glared at him. "Did you?"

He winced. "Good point."

A tiny voice came from between them. "Maybe I should adopt the two of you. At least I know about birth control."

Jim glared down, unable to see the smirk on her face that Kimberly could. "How would you know about birth control. You don't need to know about that yet."

Kimberly said "Yes she does," the same time the Afsaneh said "Yes I do," and a long silence followed. Then both Jim and Kimberly said "Why?" Afsaneh burst into weak laughter, and the two adults hesitantly joined her, looking at each other in apprehension.

Afsaneh pulled herself around so that she now rested her head on Kimberly's chest. "Does this mean I'm going to have a baby brother or sister, Mommy?" she asked coyly.

Jim snorted, covering his mouth. But Kimberly could see his eyes lightening. Afsaneh delivered the coup de gras. "You know, if you're preggers, your breasts will get big. I mean, bigger."

Kimberly was speechless, but Jim came to her rescue, genuine laughter in his voice. "There's nothing wrong with the size of her breasts," he protested. "And anyway, that's none of your business."

He looked at Kimberly and shrugged. "I don't think I can handle her alone, Kimberly." He smiled. "Will you marry me?"

"Pretty lame proposal, Jim." Afsaneh sniffed.

"Shaddap," Kimberly told her. "It's my proposal, and I'll decide whether it's lame or not." She turned back to Jim and paused for a moment, gazing deep into his eyes. "That's a pretty lame proposal, Jim."

His laughter was a tonic to Kimberly and, she suspected, to Afsaneh also. But after a moment, Jim moaned, holding his head. "I don't think I should be laughing yet." He rubbed Afsaneh's scalp and held her when she tried to escape. "But I'm glad I am. Thank you."

They settled back against the headboard, Afsaneh resting against Jim again. "You know, I think we should name this station," Jim said and smiled, obviously waiting for the explosion.

I can out-wait you Morris, Kimberly decided, playing along. "They already did, and Vicki gave it her blessing, so you're too late."

"Oh?" Jim looked non-plussed. "What did they decide on?"

"Osaka!" Kimberly enjoyed his surprise. "It was Captain Lang's idea and Tachibana loved it. A fortress to protect the frontiers of Man."

"And Woman!" Afsaneh chirped.

"Right." Kimberly smiled down at her.

"What about the computer?" Jim asked hopefully.

"Too late." Kimberly arched her eyebrows. "I took care of that."

Jim waited, and she sat there, feeling smug.

"Okay," he said, feigning weariness that was only partly joking. "I'll bite. What?"

"The first joint American-Japanese station in space, named after a Japanese warlord's castle?" Kimberly smirked. "What else but...Pearl?"

Jim gave a little chuckle. Afsaneh did the same. Then, while they were all giggling, the door opened and Yvette looked in, confused. Kiri and Janice peeked over her shoulders.

"What the hell is going on here?"

"Pajama party," Afsaneh piped up. The short woman stood there, looking from one face to another. She acted angry, but Kimberly could tell she was really relieved.

Yvette snorted and shook her fist. "Well, since everyone here seems to be okay, and having fun, I'm going to go do the same. By sleeping in a real bed. That couch has given me a kink in my neck!" And she left, sweeping Janice and Kiri before her.

For a few minutes the three of them huddled there, enjoying the sense of intimacy and security. Kimberly slouched over a little more and rested her head on Jim's forearm. His arm, in turn, was around Afsaneh's shoulders. She could tell Jim was relaxing, starting to drift off. She gave him a few more moments of peace, then started in on him again.

"Well?"

Afsaneh snickered softly, half asleep.

Jim didn't pretend to not understand. He took a deep breath, let it out in a big sigh and reached over with his left hand to caress her cheek.

"Kimberly Martin, I would be honored and delighted if you would marry me."

Kimberly had been making light of it, but her eyes got misty anyway. *God, Martin, railroad a guy into proposing, then be all teary-eyed and emotional when he finally does it.*

"Um, will you?" Jim was still waiting, she remembered guiltily.

"Jim Morris, Chimmorrz, Jim Morrison, Elvis, or whatever people or aliens call you, I would be happy to marry you." *Forever and ever.*

He leaned over, careful not to disturb Afsaneh and kiss her on the forehead.

"That was romantic." Afsaneh muttered in a sleepy voice. Jim smiled at the girl, looking pensive.

We'll be okay, Kimberly decided. *We really will.* "I love you, Jim," she said and, curling up closer to the two of them, closed her eyes.

Groundhog hung up the phone and stared at the wall, thinking. A missing ocean liner seemed a little out of the usual line of work, but the mention of Sukuru settled it.

Sukuru meant Yakuza. Groundhog had crossed paths with the Toshida Clan before, and looked forward to a rematch. If Sukuru was responsible for the disappearance of the Jade Viking, it would be found out.

Groundhog would investigate for Will Spencer. But in the long run, it wouldn't be for his benefit as much as it would be for personal satisfaction. There were a few scores to be settled with the Toshida Clan.

Kimberly opened her eyes and saw black hair, lots of it. Blinking, she raised her head in confusion. Strands of Afsaneh's long tresses were across her face. During the night, the girl had turned over and now had her face buried in Kimberly's bosom. What there is of it, she thought wryly.

"Ooh," Kimberly gasped as she realized her arm was around her new "daughter's" shoulder, and it had fallen asleep. Hot needles poked it and she tried to pull free without moving anyone.

Jim had also shifted in the night and ended up in a spoon position behind Afsaneh. This left Kimberly's arm stuck in between, and it was with some difficulty that she finally freed it.

She noticed, with distaste, that she had slept in her clothes. Even sweats need changing from time to time, she thought, grimacing.

A hot shower would be delightful, if she could just get off this bed without waking everyone.

Afsaneh's eyes popped open and Kimberly shrugged to herself in resignation. It took the girl a moment to figure out where she was, then she giggled. "Is this the honeymoon?" she whispered.

Kimberly just glared at her and massaged her arm.

Afsaneh got a funny look on her face, then blushed a bright red. *What could possibly embarrass this girl?* They both slid across to the side of the bed.

"Uh, I'm going to leave you two." Afsaneh was rushing her words now, trying to keep quiet. She fled out of the bedroom, almost running. *What the hell?*

Ah, I see. Kimberly tried to suppress a laugh. Jim slept in gym shorts. They weren't exactly modest after a night of shifting around. And, he was having a fairly normal early morning reaction to a warm body pressed against him.

Kimberly covered her mouth and snickered. *Maybe Afsaneh isn't quite as grown up as she pretends, after all.*

Jim heard the sound and opened his eyes. He smiled at her, still groggy, but reached for her anyway.

"Oh, no you don't, buster." She climbed off the bed, backing away from him. "First a shower and clean clothes for me. Then, I go see if it's too late to worry about birth control. Then the doctor checks your wounds. Then, maybe then, we make whoopee."

He stared at her, not entirely awake. Then he waved groggily and, pulling the covers up, went back to sleep.

The shower was delightful and Kimberly let it last longer than she should have. Jim was still sleeping when she finished drying off. She looked through her clothes and chose a sun dress she'd been wanting to wear on the cruise, but hadn't had the chance or, to be truthful, the nerve to.

It was a far cry from her usual business attire. But, she reasoned, they were a far cry from Wall Street. She hesitated, then tossed the bra back into her suitcase. What the hell, in for a penny, in for a pound. She carried her sandals as she quietly left the bedroom.

Afsaneh was already gone and she smirked. *Heh, heh, I've got you now, my little pretty.* It felt good to be one up on the precocious child. I better make the most of it, she reasoned. It probably won't happen too often.

But now it was time for more important matters.

"Good morning, Vicki. Where can I find the doctor?"

"Good morning, Kimberly Martin. Which one would you like?"

There was a thought. Which one would she like. There was Dr. Winston, the ship's doctor. Or, there was the doctor with the film crew, Seiji Inoue. Or, for that matter, there were the three doctors that had been vacationing on the cruise ship.

"Dr. Inoue, I think."

"He is in what used to be the Ananab nursery. It has been converted into a medical facility."

"Where's that?" She listened to the instructions and realized it was quite near. A short walk and two turns later, she was there.

The outer room was full of people. Her first thought was that they were casualties. My God, what happened while we slept so peacefully?

Then she noticed how cheerful everybody was. A hand touched her elbow and she started. Kiri grinned at her.

"Hey, Round Eyes, remember me?" Her good humor was infectious. "I was your friend back when no one knew you, when you were just one more shyster."

Kimberly laughed and gestured around the room. "What's going on?"

Kiri crooked a finger at her, beckoning. Kimberly followed, resigned that nobody was ever going to give her a straight answer about anything, ever. They slipped through a door and into a hallway. One entire wall was glass, and through it, Kimberly saw James McGregor standing, looking down at something.

Kiri tapped on the glass. His head jerked up and Kimberly stared at him. He was in a state of shock. *What the...?* Kiri motioned him to move, and as he did Kimberly's eyes goggled. Two tiny oriental babies lay in a makeshift crib. Both had a full head of hair, not uncommon. And to Kimberly they looked identical except for one detail. The bright orange hair on the lefthand one would have to be considered uncommon, especially on an Asian.

"Isn't it great?" Kiri gushed, hugging Kimberly around the shoulders in excitement. "The first human babies born in space. And they're both strong and healthy!"

"They're beautiful," Kimberly's mouth was dry. Was the light really that bright, or was it just her eyes...

She vaguely heard Kiri exclaim in surprise as she passed out.

Kimberly came to on the floor. She hadn't actually fainted, had she? *Oh, damn. That answered that question.*

Dr. Inoue was leaning over her, a concerned look on his face. Then she was in the air, McGregor carrying her to a bed. Her problem had evidently brought him out of his own stupor like a dash of cold water.

"What is it, Ms. Martin?" The doctor was polite, but had a shrewd look on his face. He suspects, Kimberly thought. Well, fine. I was about to tell him, anyway.

"I'm pregnant," she admitted. Kiri whooped and McGregor had to catch her as she lost her footing in her excitement.

"Little Jimmys and Kimmys running around the ship." Kiri crowed. "This is great!" Kimberly looked at her sourly. Kiri never even noticed. "I have to go!" The excited Japanese girl rushed out of the infirmary. Kimberly watched her go, her mouth open.

"Could I speak to Ms. Martin alone, please?" The doctor's voice was quiet, but firm. "And someone go shut that crazy woman up until we are sure about this."

"I'm sure, Doctor," Kimberly was gloomy, watching McGregor's back as he hurried after Kiri.

"And how is that?" The doctor peered at her through his thick glasses. "I had no idea you had a shingle of your own."

Kimberly told him what had happened. He looked at her in amusement. "Are you saying this sexual contact happened less than two days ago?"

She blushed. "Yes, Doctor."

"Ms. Martin, you do understand there's no way to tell, this early." The doctor smiled at her apologetically.

"I fainted out there," she said. "I'm pregnant."

"Not necessarily," he said. "It could just be nerves."

"I'm a lawyer. I don't have nerves," Kimberly said crisply. "How long before we can tell? I hate waiting."

"Kimberly Martin, I can be of some assistance with this matter." Vicki spoke directly to Kimberly and the doctor's translators.

"Really?" Dr. Inoue looked intrigued. "How?"

"I can do a DNA scan. Certain infinitesimal differences in chemical levels will show whether or not you have a fertilized egg."

"What facilities will you need?" Dr. Inoue looked excited.

"No special instruments will be required." The computer was silent for a moment. "The test is completed."

"Complete..." Inoue looked flabbergasted. Then he glanced at Kimberly, a questioning look on his face.

"Well?" Kimberly demanded.

"You are not pregnant, Kimberly Martin." For the first time, the computer sounded uncertain, as if she didn't know if the answer was good news or not.

"I'm not?" Kimberly didn't know whether to laugh or cry. *After all, Martin, you don't want to be pregnant right now, do you?*

She realized the doctor was still standing there, correctly interpreting her reaction. He smiled. "You know, if you really do want to get pregnant, I would imagine Jim would do whatever was necessary to make it happen."

Kimberly laughed, but could feel the tears welling. "Is there anyone on this ship that doesn't know that Jim and I slept together?" The doctor was a discreet man and chose not to answer. Thankfully, so did Vicki.

"There's plenty of time in the future." Dr. Inoue had a twinkle in his eye. "Just keep practicing. You never can tell what might develop."

"Thank you, Doctor." Kimberly felt deflated as she left the infirmary. *Meanwhile, Kiri is probably on the radio waves, sending out word to one and all.*

But she was wrong.

McGregor and Kiri waited in the corridor outside.

One look at Kimberly's face told it all, and Kiri came to hug her. "McGregor made me wait until it was confirmed," she admitted. "I'm glad he did."

Kimberly tried to smile, but it was difficult. "I don't know what's wrong with me. I was dreading finding out. And now it's like I'm disappointed that I'm not!"

Kiri opened her mouth, but was interrupted by the intercom.

"Attention," Vicki sounded grim. "Three Ananab ships have been sighted approaching Station Osaka. They are military ships and will arrive in approximately ten hours."

Kimberly kicked her sandal off and it slammed against the wall. McGregor and Kiri both jumped in surprise and stared at her.

"Damn!" Kimberly glared at them. "Can't we just have one day with no crisis? Just one?"

Muttering to herself, she grabbed the sandal and stomped off towards the bridge. It wasn't until she got there that she realized it was still in her hand, not on her foot.

CHAPTER TWENTY-SIX

The bridge of the Jade Viking was a scene of controlled bedlam. There was frenzied activity at every work station and a steady stream of people coming and going. Jim Morris and Captain Lang stood behind Inam and Rick Baker, looking over their shoulders at the display on the screen. Inam pointed at the hold containing the original Jade Viking.

"They should be done moving it into station storage in about two hours."

"Good." Captain Lang looked thoughtful as he tapped his jaw with an index finger. "We'll need quarters for a lot of people on the station, too. All personnel not crucial to the operation of the ship in battle will be transferred to Osaka immediately."

Jim pondered the best way to broach a sensitive subject and decided that directness had a few advantages. But before he could begin, the hatch to the bridge opened and Kimberly came running in barefoot, sandal in hand.

She makes quite a sight, Jim thought. Spaghetti- strapped, floral sun dress, hair tousled and shoes in hand. Shoe in hand, he corrected himself. Is she not wearing a bra?

Captain Lang gave her a broad smile and bowed. "Ah, Mr. Morris. This would be your bride-to-be, barefoot and pregnant?"

Jim felt his eyes bug out in horror. She's never going to believe me, he moaned. He flinched as he saw her look.

"You told him?" she asked incredulously.

"Told me...?" Captain Lang's look of amusement changed to intense embarrassment. "Ah, actually, Mr. Morris hasn't told me anything, Ms. Martin. Except about your condition ...engaged, I mean. That is..." He looked at Jim, then around the room, but there was no sign of help there. All human heads were very busy, doing something, anything, to keep their eyes averted.

Jim tried hard, but he couldn't hold it any longer. He burst into laughter, then moaned as he held his head. No one else on the bridge joined him. In fact, they looked at him as if he were crazy. Kimberly just glared at him. He shrugged his shoulders, smiling at her apologetically.

"Perhaps we should get back to the matter at hand." Captain Lang sounded and looked relieved to have attention focused elsewhere. "Transferring personnel to the station. We are under a bit of a time limit, you know."

"Fine," Kimberly said, gritting her teeth. Dropping her sandals to the deck, she shoved her feet into them. "Fine. By the way, in case anyone's interested, the test was negative." She spoke softly as she stared at the deck, as if dreading the reaction.

Jim felt a twinge of regret. Babies were the last thing they needed right now, but... "There's always later, if you'd like." Kimberly relented, raised her eyes and nodded. He gave a reassuring smile, and they turned their attention back to Lang.

"Captain Tachibana is bringing the 'Samurai in to exchange some personnel and drop off most of their personal weapons." Lang gave Jim a dry grin. "I understand that does not include Mr. DelaRosa's shotgun."

"Damn," Jim groaned. "I wouldn't mind having one of those, myself." His mind went back to what he'd been thinking about before Kimberly's dramatic entrance. "Captain, have you thought about how we will staff Osaka?"

"Everyone that isn't working in either the Jade Viking or the Jade Samurai will be on the station. Everyone."

"What about you?" Jim was blunt. "We need you on the station. If both ships get destroyed, we might be able to get away on one of the other ships in dock. But we can't have all of our chain of command in one basket."

"I will be on my ship, mister." Lang gave him a steely glare. "You can be in charge of the station."

"I disagree, Captain." Kimberly sounded reluctant to get into this arguement and spoke slowly. "We should speak with Captain Tachibana about this, but Jim technically isn't in the chain of command. And he doesn't have your leadership skills."

"Nonsense," Lang blustered. "He's a natural leader. Everyone likes and respects him."

"I should stay back, you're right," Jim agreed. "But not in your place. You're needed on the station."

"He's right, Sir," Kimberly didn't look too happy to be contradicting Lang. "There are issues. People like and respect Jim, but they also fear him." Jim looked at her in surprise, a little hurt, but she avoided his eyes. "They've seen him as a soldier, defending them, but as much as they rejoice that he's so good at what he does, it frightens them. He's also too much a loner, too independent, to be the leader they need right now."

"I agree," Vicki said.

"You keep out of this!" Captain Lang scowled. He obviously wasn't going to take that from a machine, right now. And, for different reasons, Jim felt the same way.

"Why don't we just get everyone on board the two ships and leave?" Nagami spoke up for the first time, gesturing at the screen. "They're hours away. We can be gone in two hours!"

"And then?" Captain Lang scowled at the Sukuru employee. "Lead them right back to Earth? What then?"

"And what about the Baerd and Hoag we would be leaving behind?" Jim spoke softly, shaking his head in disgust. "Would you leave them here to be slaughtered for helping us?"

"Our primary concern should be to our own race," Nagami argued. "Let them defend themselves. It is what our people would want. Ask them."

Jim noticed the Baerd and Hoag on the bridge had stopped all activity and were listening closely. We must seem a shallow, untrustworthy people to them, he thought, ashamed of how the Human race was being represented right now.

"Mr. Nagami, at present, this is not a democracy," Lang glared at him. "And even if it were, I think you would find few of us willing to sell out our allies and, quite possibly, the entire human race. We will defend this station and this topic is now closed. And as for the other..."

The captain expelled his breath violently, pacing the deck without realizing it. He stopped. "I'll talk with Captain Tachibana. Until then, we'll proceed the way I said."

He scowled at his second officer, Lieutenant Commander Randall. "You've got the bridge, Mister." Then he stalked out, firing one final glare at Nagami. As he left, every alien on the bridge stood, their eyes following him. After he was gone, they looked at each other, then as one they went back to their work.

Nagami stood without moving as he visibly brought his rage under control. Finally, lips pressed tight, jaw clenched shut, he left the bridge, avoiding eye contact with anyone.

"I don't like that man very much," Commander Randall commented. "I think you're right about the Captain, Mr. Morris, but I certainly am glad I wasn't the one telling him. Was that wise?"

"It needed saying. And I guess it doesn't matter if I'm liked." He looked at Kimberly, a little bitter. "As long as I'm feared."

"Jim." Kimberly looked contrite and he felt guilty at the cheap shot he'd taken.

"No, that's okay," he stopped her, tucking his depression out of sight. "You're right. And I need to accept it as much as the captain does." He had another thought. "By the way. They're shifting our things to the station. I'm not quite sure where, but evidently Pearl is coordinating the move with McGregor and, of all people, our old friend Ron Hoffman."

He could tell she wasn't placing the name, so he reminded her. "The dinner, the last dinner, back at sea level." Jim mimicked the Texan's accent. "Tires, lots of tires."

"Oh yeah," she seemed distracted. "Oh, by the way, James McGregor isn't doing too much organizing right now. He just became a father. Of twins."

Jim smiled at her. "You want some of those, someday?"

"I don't know about twins," she retorted. "But yes, I think I do want children at some point in the future." She stepped close to him and he tried to kiss her. She stepped back just as quick, teasing him. "For now, behave yourself, buddy."

She slapped her head. "Did you say they're moving our stuff again? When?"

He shrugged. "Probably right now. You know how efficient these Hoag are. Why?" This was directed to her back as she fled the bridge.

"I need to get my pills!" Her answer echoed back as she disappeared through the hatchway. Jim looked around, embarrassed. Randall pursed his lips, successful at keeping his expression straight. As usual, everyone else seemed very busy at the moment.

Jim began studying the approaching Ananab ships. They, at least, were something he knew how to deal with.

This is a far cry from the bridge of a ship, Kimberly mused. She shifted in her chair, glancing around the room.

Captain Lang, Jim, and she sat in the usual triad position the Ananab favored. But instead of hard, uncomfortable stools, they now had cushioned chairs with armrests, requisitioned from one of the lounges of the original Jade Viking.

The Captain shifted restlessly in his seat. He had accepted the opinion of virtually everyone else with poor grace. After an hour-long running argument with Captain Tachibana, Jim, Kimberly, even Randy Luca, he had reluctantly agreed to move over to Osaka Station.

A command post had been set up in the engineering section. For the battle, everything would be coordinated from here.

Kimberly shivered. The previous owners of the station had a different location for their command center, but Vicki had trashed it during the final minutes of fighting. Everyone at that post had died instantly when it was opened to space.

Adding up the death toll had been a sobering experience. Numerous Baerd and Hoag had died in the battle for control of the station in addition to the dozens, no, hundreds of Tryr, Srotag, and Ananab killed. By comparison, the human losses had been light. In numbers, anyway.

This location had the added benefit of being deep in the center of Osaka. No single lucky shot would leave the station headless. The Hoag and Baerd had transformed the space from a nearly featureless control room to a crowded, array-filled, bustling command post.

She felt reassured by the familiar sight of Lasty and Dutter manning stations with their human counterparts. There was a human at every computer console with the Baerd technicians. Even the ranking Hoag of the station, Reet, had Andy Luca looking over his shoulder. This wasn't a security issue or a sign of mistrust. It was just felt that the humans should learn as much as they could, as quickly as possible, about the technology that ran this station and the ships outside. On the other hand, all weapon stations were manned solely by humans.

The big overhead screen showed Jade Viking and Jade Samurai headed outward to meet the oncoming Ananab ships. It had been decided that the farther away from Osaka they could meet the attack, the better.

The three Ananab ships ignored all attempts to hail them. In less than an hour, they would be in firing range of the station, and it was now only a matter of minutes before they met the two human ships.

After some debate, it was decided that Captain Tachibana would command the Jade Viking with the assistance of Commander Randall. Inam and Gudd had remained on board to lead their stripped down departments.

Jade Samurai was commanded by First Officer Danny DelaRosa. He had done a good job with Tachibana in the earlier combat, and was the only real choice. Commander Asaya had less experience, and would be acting as his first officer. It would be good training for him, if they survived.

Sergeant McGregor had organized a defensive force, should the Ananab succeed in landing at the station. Hopefully, his troops wouldn't be needed. Nagami had remained aloof after the earlier argument. He just stood in the background, watching and listening. Kimberly didn't like or trust him a bit, but there wasn't much he could do to cause any trouble.

Kimberly sneaked a peek at Jim. He still had a thick bandage over his forehead and left ear, but otherwise looked rested and prepared for anything. There hadn't been much for him to do, once the details of who would man what ship had been settled. He had napped for several hours and she thought it had done him a world of good.

I could do with a little nap. And I do like our new quarters. She didn't see how the Hoag could totally reconfigure rooms and build things so fast! The blown out sections of the stations were almost completely rebuilt. Sure, there was a lot of work to be done inside, but it was still impressive.

She missed Gudd hovering about, watching for chores to be done. The squat, brown-furred alien almost never needed instructions. He would listen and watch, then he and his crew would dive into their work. Often they would present the finished task before they were asked, or even before the Humans knew it needed doing.

Kimberly hadn't had much of a chance to observe this Reet that led the station contingent of Hoag. But he seemed a lot like Gudd. In fact, he looked a lot like Gudd. *I hope I get better at telling aliens apart. They don't all look alike.*

"Here we go," Jim muttered under his breath. She looked up at the screen again and saw two of the Ananab ships closing on the Jade Viking. The third and biggest of the three enemy ships met the 'Samurai with a direct assault, trying to overpower the ex-Tryr military ship.

A tremendous exchange of fire between the two resulted in no damage that Kimberly could detect. Meanwhile, Vicki was blocking most of the shots by her two opponents, while her human gunners tried to get through the Ananab defenses.

Both sides were using the same types of weapons. Larger versions of the disruptor handguns-ones that worked on both living and non-living tissue-and missiles were the primary offensive tools. Deflector beams, force field projectors, and more missiles were used to block attacks.

There had been some talk between the Humans and Baerd about other alternatives, but that would have to wait. There was no time to experiment now.

The Jade Viking appeared to be in some trouble. She was having difficulty blocking the combined firepower of the two enemy ships. A small explosion appeared near her stern and a groan sounded through the room.

"Isn't there anything we can do?" she turned to Captain Lang. His face told her the answer. She turned back in time to see the Jade Samurai being pushed back by the fierce assault of its opponent.

Commander DelaRosa, no, Captain DelaRosa had his vessel giving ground before the bigger ship. All weapons that could be brought to bear on the enemy were firing, but he was still backing slowly towards the other three-ship engagement.

Jim sat up straight. Kimberly jumped slightly and frowned.

"What is it?" she asked, worried.

"I'm not sure," Jim spoke slowly, concentrating. "But I think...yes!"

As he spoke, the Jade Samurai had been pushed dangerously close to the other battle raging nearby. The two Ananab ships were pounding at the Jade Viking, and it was all Tachibana's ship could do to block the incoming fire.

Without any warning, all the gun placements on the 'Samurai that were unable to bear on its opponent fired on one of the pair of Ananab ships fighting the 'Viking. Only two shots got through, but the enemy ship lurched from the impact. The distraction allowed the 'Viking to penetrate with some of their own firepower.

There was a violent flash of light, and the damaged Ananab ship disappeared. Jade Viking and Jade Samurai both accelerated and switched opponents. Any weapon that could be brought to bear on either ship was firing at a tremendous rate, and the second of the original pair of enemy ships staggered and began to drift, uncontrolled.

The third Ananab tried to break off the engagement, but both Earth ships pressed home their attack. Abruptly, the alien ship exploded.

The control room erupted in excited cheering. Kimberly found herself on her feet, hugging the captain. He cleared his throat gruffly and motioned for silence.

"Damaged Ananab ship, respond to this hailing, or we will destroy you. If you value your lives, respond. Now."

They all waited long moments, and Captain Lang got a regretful look on his face. As he opened his mouth, the screen changed to a picture of an

Ananab glaring into the camera.

"This is the Ananab ship P'Tmk. I am Captain Stemack. What do you want?"

"Your unconditional surrender," Lang answered bluntly. "If you do not immediately comply and allow a boarding party, we will destroy what is left of your ship."

The Ananab roared in anger and slapped both claws on the railing in front of him, causing it to collapse. He looked to one side, evidently in response to a question or comment from someone else on the bridge. His right claw swung out of the view of the camera, connecting hard with something, or someone.

He turned back face the camera and said one defiant word.

"Fire!"

The picture changed back to the tactical view and they saw the wounded ship exchanging fire with both Jade ships. With no mobility, it only took a few moments for the two ships to overwhelm what little defenses the Ananab had left. It broke into pieces, then flashed and was gone.

There was no cheering this time. The reality of their situation was hitting home. There was no reason for the suicidal finish of the Ananab ship. If that was typical of the mentality humans would be facing, the future looked bleak, indeed.

"All ships return to base," Captain Lang said in a tired voice.

Jim stood and walked in an aimless pattern around the room, glancing over shoulders, not really focusing on what he saw. Kimberly stood watching him, worrying. Captain Lang put a hand on her shoulder. She looked up at the towering, older man, and gave him a weak smile.

"This is really just the start," Kimberly asked him. "Isn't it?"

"Yes, I'm afraid you're right," Lang admitted, watching Jim roam.

The two ships were fast approaching and both were hailing the station in triumph. Tachibana came on screen and bowed to Lang.

"I think your ex-first officer did very well in his first battle, Captain." The Japanese beamed.

"Both of you were superb," Captain Lang admitted. "Did you suffer any casualties?"

"Bumps and bruises only," Captain Tachibana reassured him. "That goes for both ships. A little property damage, but I'm told it's nothing we can't fix in a couple of days."

"That brings us to the decision phase," Lang sounded gloomy. "What next?"

Tachibana looked thoughtful. "Good point," he admitted.

"Well, come on in, anyway," Captain Lang gave him a forced smile, glancing in evident irritation at Nagami pacing behind him. "We've got plenty to celebrate, right now. And the making of plans can wait for a little bit."

Jim returned to his seat and plopped down. Giving a sigh, he met Kimberly's eyes. He gave her a wry look, and glanced over to where Nagami was again cajoling the captain. The Japanese security chief didn't give up easily. Jim buried his feelings deep and winked at Kimberly. It didn't fool her for a moment.

"Tomorrow can take care of tomorrow." Kimberly gave him a hug and his face brightened. "We have a victory to celebrate. And an engagement," she told him.

He gave her a quizzical look. "I wonder if we have any champagne left?"

"I can't accept that as an answer." Will Spencer hunched forward over his desk as he shouted into the phone. "You keep looking, you hear me? Somebody, somewhere, knows something. You're supposed to be so good, find me something I can use!"

He hung up the phone, and threw his pen across the room. It bounced off the far wall and disappeared behind the sofa.

That bastard, Groundhog! Or bitch! He couldn't decide. Whenever they talked, the voice was disguised. And of course, they had never met in person.

But he or she always produced. That was what made this particularly frustrating. When Will made the decision to put up with the industrial spy's sarcasm and deadly wit, it was with the rationalization that the results justified the indignities.

But nothing had been found. There was absolutely no sign Sukuru had anything to do with the disappearance of Jade Viking. And he was going to have to replace it with one of the newest ships of his fleet, the more elegant, and much larger Sapphire Viking.

Damn that bitch Martin, anyway. How could she do this to him?

CHAPTER TWENTY-/EVEN

Kimberly woke up, feeling the call of nature. Careful not to wake Jim, she wriggled out of his arms and hurried to the bathroom. Sometimes nature called, sometimes it shouted, she thought as she sat down.

As she returned, she kicked her sun dress with a bare foot. It had been removed and discarded rather hurriedly last night. She smiled in the dark at the priceless memory of both her and Jim pulling out condoms at the same time.

Ah, great minds, and all that.

There had been some champagne left, and the evening had been euphoric. Everyone, with the exception of that irritating Nagami had been in a cheerful frame of mind. When she and Jim had slipped away, the party had been going strong. Hell, it might still be going strong. She didn't think anyone had noticed their leaving.

Kimberly climbed back into bed and snuggled up against Jim again. They could have their party. There was a pretty good one going on right here. Catching up on sleep ranked high on both Kimberly and Jim's list of priorities.

Any major plans could wait a couple of days. The captains had been adamant about both ships staying for at least a week or more, while the station was being repaired. A decision about the other ships in berth would also have to be made.

Nagami had insisted all ships were the property of Sukuru, as compensation for the loss of the original Jade Viking. No one had thought much of that idea.

Kimberly had worked out an agreement with the Trixmae and one ship had departed, headed for non-Ananab space. They wanted to remain neutral, and that was fine with Captain Lang. The other two would remain in port until another Trixmae ship arrived. It would hopefully have the authority to negotiate with the humans on a treaty between the two races.

All told, it looked like a great chance to relax for a few days.

She felt Jim's hand move to her hip. She took it and rolled over, clasping it to her chest, pulling herself closer to him. His hand automatically cupped one of her breasts and she smiled as her tired eyes closed. Relaxation sounded pretty wonderful right about now.

Afsaneh had been wandering the corridors of Osaka for hours. Sleep was impossible. After Jim and Kimberly had left the suite yesterday, she had crept back to her own bed and slept most of the day.

It was still hard to believe that Daddy was...dead. Everyone said time was the cure for this kind of pain. Afsaneh had heard that old maxim and hoped that it was true. In the meantime, maybe a vigorous walk would bring on exhaustion and more welcome sleep.

She had tried to go bed hours earlier, but her body wouldn't cooperate. She peeked in on Jim and Kimberly. Their room had that mysterious smell of...adultness! She pretended she knew everything, but sex was still, in terms of experience, an unknown to her.

Her father and Jim had been very careful about their dates, and neither ever had a serious live-in girlfriend. Daddy had said there were things they needed to talk about, and that he would get a book from the library. But he'd always been so embarrassed, he never got around to it.

So far, she hadn't had many dates, and the few encounters with boys her age showed they knew even less than she did! Oh, she knew the physical details of what went where, of course. But that sense of erotic foreplay, the rituals of sensuality, the romance! Jim and Kimberly definitely understood that stuff!

She had peeked again. Kimberly had kicked off most of her covers during the night and lay revealed. I may have bigger breasts, but I hope I still have a figure like that when I'm as old as she is, Afsaneh sighed. Great buns!

Kimberly had stirred and Afsaneh had quickly closed the door and tiptoed out of the suite. Since then, she had wandered the endless corridors of the station, occasionally seeing a human guard, sometimes a stray alien. The former greeted her warmly, the latter hurried away.

She realized she was near the site of her father's death, and her pace slowed. She saw Hoag workers scurrying in and out of the causeway entrance and came to a halt.

I'm not ready for that yet, she realized. It's one thing to know where your parent was murdered. It's quite another to actually stand there. No, not yet.

As she turned and started back towards their new suite, she saw Mr. Nagami and the martial artist, Naga Furukawa, hurry into the concourse leading to where the two human ships were docked.

I thought Furukawa was still locked up somewhere. And why are they out here in the middle of the night?

Afsaneh felt excitement as she followed them down the concourse, trying to keep out of sight. Maybe they were doing something unauthorized, or maybe even illegal! It was her duty to find out! She hugged one side of the long passage, carefully timing her movements to theirs. It didn't really matter, since they hardly ever looked back. The two men came to the Jade Samurai and disappeared inside.

She stopped just before the corner of the short passage leading to the ship and considered. She should go back and tell Jim about this, she realized. But what if they weren't doing anything wrong? For all she knew, Furukawa might be out of the doghouse. This called for a closer look. She stuck her head around the corner.

What she saw was an empty hatchway. Wasn't there supposed to be a guard there?

She moved silently to the opening and listened.

Nothing.

Afsaneh risked a peek. Again, nothing. She stepped inside and paused. Which way? That decision was made for her.

"Well, a little girl, wanting to go along for the ride." The deep voice came from behind her. She turned and flinched at the gun pointed at her. Going for help had definitely been the better plan.

"Jim Morris, wake up."

A voice thundered in his head, and Jim woke with a start. Could it be God? Jim didn't know if God was a female, but it wouldn't surprise him. He opened his eyes and was pleased to see Kimberly's bare shoulder. That was a sight he could stand waking to any time.

"Jim Morris, wake up!"

Both of them sat up, confused. Jim tore his eyes away from Kimberly's breasts and answered.

"What is it, Vicki?"

"This is Pearl."

"Oh, sorry about that." Jim belatedly remembered he was now living aboard the station. "What is it, Pearl?"

"There is an attempt being made by some humans to take Jade Samurai and return to Earth. They have possession of most of the ship. And, they have hostages."

"Hostages?" Jim was wide awake now. "Who tried to steal the ship?" Even as he asked, he knew the answer.

"Security Chief Nagami and Naga Furukawa are the ringleaders. It appears they have less than a dozen men with them."

Kimberly spoke for the first time. "Jim, you're wounded. You're not even close to one hundred percent. You can't do it all!"

Jim stopped. He knew this was hard on her, but she had to understand. When and if necessary, he did have to do it all.

She stood on the bed, stark naked, hands on hips, glaring at him. Another time and he would have appreciated the view. "Do you have a death wish or something?"

He felt his lips tighten and didn't answer.

"I don't want you to go to that ship, Jim." She sounded determined. "Let McGregor do it."

"He's got a family, now," Jim snapped.

"So do you!" She spoke quietly, but he flinched as though she had shouted.

"Kimberly, I have to." He was pleading with her now.

"No, you don't." She didn't give an inch.

Jim started trying to find his clothes. Kimberly stood there, looking furious. "Jim..." she began, in a dangerously quiet tone that sent warning lightning bolts into his brain. He ignored them and looked for his shoes.

"There is now some urgency," Pearl interrupted. "Your heir, Afsaneh Riahi has been taken prisoner."

He came to a halt at the computer's words, looking at Kimberly in dismay. Her expression changed to one of horror.

They both stood there for a moment. Jim was sick with fear and his stomach kicked in rebellion. Kimberly was the first to galvanize into action.

She began hunting clothes, throwing them on. He watched her for a moment. "What are you doing?" he asked, surprised at how mild his voice sounded. "I'm going, too." Her voice didn't leave any room for discussion, so he finished dressing.

"You know there's nothing you can do, don't you?" Jim asked as he tied his shoelaces.

"That's not the point," Kimberly said curtly. Jim realized she was furious, thankfully, not at him. "We're a family. We stick together as a family." She headed out the door and Jim rushed to catch up.

"I was wrong," she said as he matched her stride. "This is your affair. And I want you to finish it." Her voice was so cold that Jim shivered. "And them."

He thought of the young girl he'd helped raise from birth, and his voice hardened. "Whatever it takes."

"This entire cruise, first Toshida, then Nagami and Furukawa have been riding you, trying to provoke you." Kimberly was calm, but her voice was as frigid as the space outside the station. "Well, if you get the chance, give them what they want. And Jim?"

"Yes?" He'd never seen Kimberly in this state, even when she was mad at him.

"Kill them all if you have to!" Kimberly's voice shook.

"Whatever it takes," he repeated. Jim wasn't sure he liked this vengeful side of her, but she had hit his intentions right on the head.

"Do you want a raft or something, to save your strength?" Kimberly looked at him with a worried expression. He knew he looked like dog crap, huge bandage around his head, bulky padding on his left shoulder. He wasn't really feeling all that great, either. But he kept silent about it.

"No, I need to loosen up, stretch a little in case I get into anything with Furukawa," Jim flexed his arms and shoulders as he walked. "Pearl, tell us what happened."

"Nagami had several of Captain Tachibana's sailors on his payroll with Sukuru. They struck in the middle of the night shift."

Jim swore. Of course Nagami would have had men hidden in the crew to keep an eye on Hiroaki. Typical big corporation paranoia.

"Commander Asaya had the bridge and was captured. Nagami has split their forces into three groups, the bridge, engineering, and the main hatch. They caught your heir following Nagami and Furukawa. She has been taken to the bridge. When Samantha identified the situation, she informed Vicki and myself. Jade Viking was on patrol, but has since landed."

"Has anyone tried anything yet?" Jim thought about Afsaneh, and knew his question wasn't just about counterattacks or takeoffs.

"They tried to cast off, but Samantha ignored the orders. She has opened the outer hatch, admitting Sergeant McGregor and his men from the Jade Viking. They caught the guards by surprise, killed one and captured the rest with no casualties. Captain DelaRosa managed to free Asaya and get him off the bridge. The rebels on the bridge appear to have only two handguns. They also have disruptors, which are useless, and two Japanese swords, one of them Asaya's."

"Unfortunately, they have figured out that Samantha is not going to cooperate. They manually overrode the hatchs to the bridge and to engineering, locking themselves in. The group in engineering is four men with AK-47's. They are pinned down by some of McGregor's men."

"Can Samantha help subdue them, in any way?" Kimberly's voice sounded hopeful.

"The four in engineering can be gassed. It may be fatal, however. It's designed to knock Srotag or Tryr out fast, and is very powerful. The bridge cannot be gassed."

"Why not?" Jim was surprised. "It turns out we could have done that on the Jade Viking."

"This is a Tryr ship. They assume that they will control the bridge. The Ananab assume everyone, including the guards and bridge crew, will be out to get them."

"And rightfully so," Kimberly muttered under her breath.

"True," Pearl agreed.

They came to the junction to the concourse. Lasty and a number of Baerd appeared from the side corridor. He looked nervous, but fell in step with Jim and Kimberly.

"Jim Morris, we've heard about the situation on the Tr--uh, Jade Samurai." The slender alien looked uncomfortable. "Is there anything we can do?"

Jim looked over in surprise. Direct action was out of character for the Baerd. "I don't know. Is there anything you can do?"

"We aren't very good at fighting," Lasty admitted. "In fact, we don't know how. But you've changed our lives forever, and you've shown us respect." His voice grew stronger with emotion. "It's time we earned our own self-respect."

Several of the other Baerds murmured their agreement.

At that point Gudd came out of a side passage with several Hoags. They carried heavy tools, nervously shifting them from hand to hand. The leader of Jade Viking Hoag cleared his throat and hesitantly began.

"Jim Morris, I heard what Chief Lasty said, and we would like to add our support. I fear it is but rhetoric, but we want to do anything we can to help."

Kimberly made a sound and Jim looked at her in surprise. She wiped her eyes and glared at him. "Okay! And I cry in movies, too! So sue me."

Jim put a hand on her shoulder and they walked on, the entourage of Baerd and Hoag following. "Typical lawyer mentality," he kidded her, trying not to think about Afsaneh.

She drew back to slug him, but stopped herself. "I hate lawyer jokes." She didn't quite snarl. Then she turned to Gudd and gave him a genuine smile, her eyes still glistening. "Thank you, Gudd. And you too, Lasty. All of you are wonderful."

The two leaders make self deprecating remarks and most of the Baerd began to shift into the pink spectrum. Jim covered his smile with a hand, then turned his mind back to the situation at hand.

"Update, Pearl?"

"Nagami has just demanded the ship be released to his command, or he will kill all the hostages. In addition to your heir, they hold two other humans, two Baerd and two Hoag on the bridge. The group in engineering have the same number of prisoners."

Jim's mind raced. "Have you cut communication between the two groups?"

"No, that would be a function Samantha would perform. Since the group in engineering seems to be hesitant to kill anyone unnecessarily, she has allowed the link to remain active."

"Right," agreed Jim.

They turned into the passage that led to Jade Samurai's berth, and stopped dead.

Ahead of them, the hall was packed with people. Taga Motari and Kiri were standing in front. Behind them were Kabu, Omi, Jozen, Sakai,...in fact, what appeared to be the entire cast and crew from *Weeping Winds of Fury*. Yvette was there, Frederick, Jerry...everyone. There were also numerous members of both the American and Japanese crews.

Commander Asaya stood off to the side with Captains Lang and Tachibana, conferring. The young officer had swollen and cracked lips, and was having trouble speaking. They stopped at Jim's approach.

Kabu stepped in front of Jim and bowed deeply. He had a bandage similar to Jim's on his head, but had his bow and quiver in hand.

"Jim, we stand ready to do whatever you need us to." His eyes belied the calm voice. They showed a fury that could barely be contained. The rest of the film crew reflected that same emotion. Afsaneh was loved by all of them, even if she did sometimes drive them nuts.

"Thank you," Jim said simply, not trusting his voice to say more. As he turned to Captain Lang, he saw Kiri come forward and hug Kimberly. He ground his teeth together and nodded curtly to Lang.

"Captain." Then he looked at Asaya. "You okay?"

The young commander looked at him in frustrated dismay. "Mr. Morris, I apologize for failing to protect your ward. I was taken by surprise by that bastard Furukawa. They took my sword!" This last was a cry of anguish. "When Danny, ...uh, Captain DelaRosa burst into the bridge, I was unarmed, but standing near the hatch. He shot one of the mutineers, and I think the same shotgun blast may have damaged their assault rifle. Then he was pulling me out, and Nagami was firing at us with my pistol! At that point, they had Afsaneh at the far end of the room. There was nothing we could do!" He lowered his head in shame. "I'm sorry, so sorry."

Jim put a hand on the young man's shoulder. He was torn between shaking or comforting him, but chose the latter. "You did what you could." Then he was back to business.

"Captain Lang, I will negotiate with the mutineers." Jim met Lang's raised eyebrow with a shrug. He didn't expect the older man to like being told what was going to happen. "It's going to come to this at some point. Let's cut to the chase."

The two captains exchanged looks. Tachibana opened his mouth, then snapped it shut. Lang cleared his throat, sounding irritated. "You might be a little too close to the situation. Perhaps we should..."

"Captain, you know Jim is Afsaneh's best hope." Kimberly glared at Lang. "And he's too close to the 'situation' to stay out of it."

Frederick Farmer gave Jim a meaningful glance and stepped forward. "Captain, I really think you should let Jim handle this. He is the most qualified. And, if he rips their lungs out in the process..." The director shrugged expressively.

It was Captain Lang's turn to glare. "Believe me, Mr. Farmer. I have no problem with that. But, I don't want to see..." Jim recognized his cue and slipped through the crowd. As he entered the Jade Samurai, he heard the captain's frustrated voice, "Where did he go?" and his pace quickened as he moved through the corridors of the ship. This wasn't a time for a committee decision.

"Update, Sam?"

"May I assume 'Sam' is a diminutive of Samantha?" Her voice was deeper than Vicki or Pearl's.

"That's right," Jim agreed, mentally kicking himself.

"Nagami instructed his men in engineering to kill one of the hostages." Jim's head shot up in alarm. "But," she continued, "the gunmen in engineering don't want to kill anyone. They seem to be having second thoughts about the wisdom of following Nagami at all."

"Cut communication between the two groups and patch me through to engineering."

"Go ahead."

"Hello, to whoever is in charge in engineering. This is Jim Morris." He paused, listening, hoping they would answer.

"What do you want?" The voice sounded suspicious.

"I want you to consider your options." Jim said. "The ship will not obey any order you give it. If you surrender your weapons and open the hatch, no action will be taken against you. I give you my word."

"How can we be sure we can trust you?" Jim thought the man sounded hopeful.

"You don't have a lot of choices," Jim reminded him. "We can gas your compartment, you know. But we would rather you cooperated. You were just following Nagami's orders." Jim's voice was very cold and ominous, and it wasn't an act. "If anything happens to the hostages, or we have to storm your position, you'll all die."

"Let us think about it a minute." The man sounded frightened.

"Don't take too long." Jim was curt. "And we are severing contact with the bridge. You're on your own."

Jim arrived at the bridge hatch. James McGregor stood there, assault rifle looking like a little toy cradled in his thickly muscled arms. DelaRosa and two other men were there, as well.

"Hello, gentlemen." Jim nodded to them and McGregor stiffened his back.

"Sir..." he began, but Jim interrupted him.

"Save it." Jim raised a hand to stop the apology. "We'll get through this, trust me." He sighed. It couldn't be delayed any longer. "Sam, connect me with the men inside."

"Jim, maybe we should..." Danny DelaRosa looked stubborn and Jim realized the young officer wanted a piece of the men trying to steal his first command. Jim held up a hand and DelaRosa subsided.

"Nagami. This is Jim Morris. I'm outside the hatch, and I'd like to come in." Jim's jaw ached from clenching his teeth. "I'm unarmed."

"I'm sure you are." Nagami sneered. "What about all the men around you? Don't forget who we have in here. Your new ward, your best friend's daughter hasn't been hurt. Yet."

"I'm fine, Jim!" Jim sagged in relief when he heard her voice. Then he heard a slap and Afsaneh cried out.

"You will keep your mouth shut!" Jim listened to Furukawa's voice, and his head felt light with the fury coursing through his veins.

"You can't move this ship without me," Jim began, trying not to think about Afsaneh trapped in there with those... "You've probably noticed the computer has locked you out. I have the key."

"You think I'm a fool?" Nagami sneered. "You will get this pretty girl killed."

"I will order everyone away from the hatch if you'll open it. This your chance to get me where you want me." Jim held his breath, waiting.

"I think I have you where I want you," Nagami gloated. "Outside, listening in, while I hurt the one you love."

Jim found it hard to breathe now. He was careful to control his voice when he spoke. "I knew that weasel Furukawa was afraid to fight me."

"I want him." The Japanese martial artist hissed. "Let him in!"

"You idiot! He's baiting you, and you're falling for it!" There was disgust in Nagami's voice.

"It's what you want, too! Don't pretend it isn't!" Furukawa wasn't backing down.

Jim motioned Danny and his men back. They all had stubborn looks, but when he glared at them, McGregor took DelaRosa's arm and pulled him down the corridor.

"Well, cowards, the coast is clear. Open the door." Jim tried to project all the contempt he felt. It wasn't hard to do. "I promise there is no trick. Let me in and release the girl, and I'll show you how to make the computer work."

For long moments there was no sound. Then something slid sideways and the hatch slowly opened. There was a nervous looking Japanese sailor on the other side with a pistol pointed at him.

Jim walked past, ignoring him. The hatch made an ominous clanging as it closed and locked behind him.

Nagami and Furukawa stood in the middle of the bridge. The setup was similar to that of the Jade Viking, but smaller. But there was still plenty of room for a fight. Nagami had a holstered pistol, and held a katana, still sheathed. Furukawa was unarmed.

Jim ignored them both. He looked to the captain's throne where Afsaneh stood. Her face was still red on one side, and there was a trickle of blood coming from the corner of her mouth. She looked frightened, but not so much so she couldn't function. One of the rebels stood next to her, holding her arm. The one that had opened the door moved to her other side.

Jim looked at the little red stream of blood that stood out in such contrast to her light flesh. It grew in his eyes until he could see little else.

"Who?" His voice was hoarse. She looked at Furukawa and Jim spun on his heel.

"Wait!" Nagami glared at Jim and pointed the sheathed sword at him. "Show me how to release control of the computer!"

"Let the girl go, first." He knew what to expect and wasn't disappointed.

"She's not going anywhere. She's our insurance."

Jim shook his head. "This ship doesn't move until she's safe."

"We'll kill her," Nagami threatened.

"You're going to kill her anyway."

"True." The Japanese shrugged. "But there can be quite a difference in the ways she can die. Tell me how to make the computer work!"

"I think not." The time for talking was about to end. A sense of calm overtook Jim. He hadn't felt quite this way in many years, but he could remember it well. It was in his dreams, frequently.

"Maybe Naga should soften you up a little, first." Nagami's eyes narrowed. "Are you trying to stall or something?"

"No, no stalling." Jim had heard enough. "This ship isn't going anywhere. All you can do now is die." He looked at Furukawa in contempt. "Or if you get lucky, kill me, then die."

Nagami glared at him. "You said you could make the computer obey me!"

Jiim smiled, but without a trace of humor. "I lied."

Nagano turned to one of the guards holding Afsaneh. "Shoot him!"

"No! You said I could have him!" Furukawa shouted in anger. "I will kill him!"

"Not on your best day, ass-hole." Jim bared his teeth.. "Shall we dance,

Naga?"

"My pleasure." Furukawa pulled his shirt off, revealing a lithe, firmly muscled torso. He began circling Jim, moving his arms slightly, weaving them in a hypnotizing fashion.

Jim ignored the other man's maneuvering, watching Nagami move over by Afsaneh and her two guards. One of them held his pistol on the other hostages that huddled against one wall. Nagami looked furious, his frustration at the failed hijacking evident.

Jim sensed rather than saw the move by Furukawa. The Japanese feinted at his head, then went to the ground to try a sweep. Jim dived over the low kick and almost passed out from the pain when Furukawa came right back with his other foot to Jim's injured shoulder. The sweep had been a feint, also!

Jim tried to submerge the pain as he continued rolling to stay away from the other man. He didn't quite get clear in time and a foot caught him in the side. He grunted and then was on his feet, backing away.

Furukawa stood watching him, gloating. "I knew you were overrated. Maybe you could fool the others, but not me!"

As he said the last, he rapidly advanced, trying to pin Jim against one of the computer consoles. But Jim didn't give ground this time. The blows flew between them so fast that they were both acting on instincts, years of practice and competition giving them automatic blocks, kicks, and punches that the other either parried, or avoided.

Then they were separated again, circling each other, looking for an opening. The look on Furukawa's face was one of surprise. That exchange had been something neither of them had probably experienced in years. Against almost anyone else, some blows would have gotten through, and the even trade would have quickly become a barrage, overpowering in its intensity.

Jim knew he couldn't keep that kind of pace up for long. His head throbbed, and his shoulder was bleeding again. In fact, the bandage was half torn off. With one hand, Jim ripped the rest of it free and Furukawa's eyes lit up at the sight.

"It looks like the kittens really did a number on you, movie star." His laugh was vicious. "I'll bet they aren't as tough as you pretended."

Jim faked a kick but the other didn't fall for it and was ready for the real attack. Furukawa's foot slammed into the side of Jim's head, and he flew across the floor, desperately trying to recover his feet. Another kick landed against his ear and he would have passed out, but for the sharpness of the pain.

He blocked the third kick with one hand and did a sweep of his own. Furukawa gracefully dove over the foot and rolling, came to his feet across the room. He was ready for the expected follow-up, but Jim hadn't pursued. He snorted and looked at Nagami. "This, this is supposed to be a great martial artist?"

Jim paid no attention to him. He pulled the remnants of the bandages off his head. It revealed a deep gash that started over his left eye and ran to his left ear, ending with the tip of the lobe missing. Afsaneh moaned when she saw the horrific wound. It was oozing blood, as was his shoulder.

Jim threw the bloody wrappings off to the side and gave Furukawa his full attention. He made no attempt to get into a defensive stance. The Japanese took it as a sign of weakness and began to close.

"So, your specialty is hitting little girls?" Jim's voice was emotionless, a thick coating over the pain and anger he felt.

"I like hitting bad actors, too," Furukawa gloated. "And after I finish with you, I think I'll make a woman out of the little girl."

Jim ignored the taunts, and began circling to the left, his hands at his sides. The he leaped forward, kicking in a Korean Tae Kwan-do style. Furukawa correctly predicted how to block and what the followup was. Which was why Jim's unorthodox second kick caught him in the chest.

That blow would have ended the fight right then, but for the fact that Jim was unable to put much power into it. To come back with that kick, he had to do it off balance and out of position. Properly executed, in the right stance, it would have crushed every rib in its path.

The surprise was worth as much as the pain it caused as a look of startled astonishment came to Furukawa's face. Jim came right back with an unlikely, unpredictable combination of kicks and punches that had Furukawa scrambling to block.

The Japanese fighter left his right arm extended inches too far, for just an instant. Jim caught the other's wrist with his left hand and pulled, yanking Furukawa off balance. Jim twisted the limb as he pulled, spinning to the left to bring his crooked, right arm down on his opponent's exposed elbow.

Furukawa screamed in pain, all the while bringing his left hand up to counter the expected backhand to his face. His voice went up in pitch and volume when Jim's right foot tore through his right kneecap. Then, Jim's delayed backhand caught his exposed face as he stumbled, trying to keep weight off his injured right leg.

Jim casually walked around his enemy as Furukawa tried to stay upright.

His right arm hung useless, and his right knee would never function correctly again. Blood poured from his nose and he looked stunned.

Another day, place, or person, and Jim would have stopped. But this was today, on Jade Samurai, and this man threatened hit Afsaneh. He feinted with one hand and caught Furukawa's left wrist with his right hand. Jim kicked up with his right leg, and Furukawa's right elbow could now bent in any direction.

Furukawa was in shock, his eyes glazed with pain, and Jim could have safely ignored him as a potential threat. The Japanese couldn't lift either arm, and only one leg worked at all. Within moments he would be lying on the floor, unconscious.

Jim stepped in close. "For Afsaneh." He spoke so softly, no one else in the room could hear. Then he smashed Furukawa in the nose with the heel of his left hand, driving the bone and cartilage into the other's brain, killing him instantly.

Jim slowly turned to look at Nagami, who was staring at him in amazement. Anger filled the older man's face and he unsheathed his sword, the pistol at his side forgotten. Jim looked around and saw Koro Asaya's family sword in its scabbard, hanging on one arm of the captain's chair. Too far away, he knew.

Nagami began an intricate pattern with his blade, moving at a deliberate pace. He sneered at Jim as he gave orders to his men. "Kill the girl. But hurt her first. Rape her if you like."

The two men looked at each other, uncertain. One of them looked down at her and Jim could tell he would be willing.

"Afsaneh, just like our workouts. Don't hold back." Jim's voice was urgent. He spoke quickly to galvanize her into action. She snapped a hand into the face of the lecherous guard, trying to duplicate Jim's deathblow to Furukawa. She missed a direct hit, but it caused enough pain for her to pull free of his grasp.

Nagami shouted in Japanese at his men. "She's just a girl, you idiots!"

"She's not just a girl, you idiot." Jim snarled. "She's my daughter, and I've been training her since the day she could walk."

Nagami said nothing and attacked. Jim fell to the ground below the first slice, then vaulted into the air to clear the second. He rolled hard to the wall, causing the third attempt to miss also.

He came to a halt one knee down, one foot planted as Nagami swung an overhead blow designed to split Jim's skull down the middle.

Jim brought both hands up and together to catch the katana blade between his palms, the razor sharp edge inches from his face. Nagami gasped as the sword was immobilized. Jim also gasped. He'd never actually tried that before in real life. He'd done it for movies, and with practice blades that wouldn't seriously hurt him if he missed. But this...this was all too real!

He came off his bended knee with his left foot connecting with Nagami's stomach, then face, in rapid succession. The older man stumbled backward and Jim had to release the blade to avoid getting cut.

"Jim!" came a cry from Afsaneh, and Asaya's sword flew through the air. Jim caught it in full stride and, without stopping, unsheathed it. He whirled to face Nagami, who was just recovering from the blows. Jim risked a glance and saw that she was more than holding her own with one guard, and that the two crewmen had jumped the other. Satisfied, he turned back to Nagami.

"You're dead, you bastard!" Nagami was spitting, he was so furious. "I've trained on the sword for decades with masters. You've only fought with your hands and feet."

"You poor fool." Jim's tone belied the sympathy implied by the words. "My movies have never showed everything I can do." They had a furious exchange of blows and parrys, none of which connected with flesh. "I also have some small experience with the sword."

They swept by each other again. This time, Jim received a needle-sharp slice along his left side. *What was it with that side, anyway! First the shoulder, then the head wound, now this. Starting tomorrow, my training gets seriously more intense.*

They slowly circled, both of them moving their blades in a formal, stylized fashion. Jim came to a halt.

"Drop your blade and surrender, now. Or die." Jim slowed his breathing to a normal pace. He raised his blade high over his head. "Your choice."

Nagami roared his defiance and charged. Jim parried the attack, using the momentum to aid his own as he spun around. His final blow was too fast to see. More important, it was too fast for Nagami to see.

Jim lowered his blade and watched the body fall, the impact of the floor tearing free the remaining tiny strip of flesh holding Nagami's head to his body. It rolled a few feet and came to a halt against the wall.

The hatch opened with a loud wrenching sound, and McGregor fell through, crowbar in hand. Asaya, DelaRosa and a host of others poured through behind him, guns at the ready.

Jim handed the sword to Koro Asaya.

"I believe this is yours, sir" Jim staggered a little as he bowed. "Thank you for it's use, and please forgive my not asking permission first. I'm afraid it needs cleaning, now." Exhaustion rolled over Jim like a ocean wave.

Afsaneh was being violently ill into a bucket that a Hoag had somehow found in time. One of the men she had been fighting lay still on the floor, his head at a curious angle to his body. The other was unconscious, with a Baerd sitting on top of him, blushing furiously.

Jim walked over to the young girl as she finished. He pulled her close and held her, soothing and talking quietly. Later, neither of them would ever remember what he said, but it calmed them both.

He looked over her head and saw Kimberly standing close, watching. He smiled wearily, and she came and put her arms around them both.

Jim sighed. In time, they would get cleaned up and rested. Wounds would heal, both physical and emotional.

But at that moment, just the holding was enough.

CHAPTER TWENTY-EIGHT

Groundhog whistled tunelessly. After hours of perusing numerous web sites, unending data bases, and countless hidden files that were "impenetrable," little doubt remained in his mind.

No one, not even those cunning bastards at Sukuru, had the slightest clue what had happened to Jade Viking, or the thirty-five hundred people aboard. *Interesting.*

This had never happened before. Failure was not something he was familiar with. If he were capable of feelings, he might have been irritated.

Will Spencer gently cradled the phone, leaned back in his Italian leather chair and closed his eyes.

Groundhog had struck out. Oh sure, if anything new showed up, it would be pursued, but for the moment, the matter was on the back burner. Will groaned as he replayed the final words of the conversation.

"Don't worry about it, Mr. Spencer," Groundhog had reassured him. "After all, you've got insurance, don't you?"

Oh sure, I've got insurance, Will thought savagely. But it's my insurance company. I could have gotten outside insurance, if nothing else, to back up my own. In fact, Kimberly had insisted on it.

Unfortunately, Will had overridden her, behind her back. So his initial cheapness would cost him...millions. Between the physical loss of the ship, the benefits to employees, the lawsuits by the survivors of the deceased, he would be lucky to keep his doors open, much less take advantage of the lucrative deals he'd swung with Sukuru.

With a sigh, Will opened his eyes and looked at the framed portrait of

Kimberly Martin on his desk. With a sudden burst of energy, he sat up and tossed the picture in the bottom drawer of his desk.

"The only bright side of all this," Will said, as he took one last look before he closed the drawer. "Is I don't have to hear you say 'I told you so!.'"

Jim Morris whistled a tuneless melody under his breath as he toweled his hair dry. He pulled a pair of cotton mini briefs on and examined his jaw. Much as he hated to admit it, Afsaneh really did do a better job of trimming his beard than he did.

He wrapped the towel around his waist and walked out into the living room. The door to Afsaneh's bedroom was open and he called to her.

"Hey, chica. How's it going? You still here?"

"Be right out...Jim." Her muffled answer drifted out to him. He noticed the hesitation and grimaced. Yet another issue to deal with at some point.

He was standing there deliberating when she appeared in the doorway. He glanced at her, then did a quick double-take. She was wearing a black evening dress. It went almost to the floor, but had slits reaching her hips on either side. The top wasn't too low, although with her build it certainly was accented. Tiny straps were the only shoulders, and when she twirled he saw that the back neckline went below the waist. He also saw that any movement showed a lot of leg. And more.

"No." He was ready for an argument, but she was surprisingly docile.

"Okay, let me try something else."

Jim blinked. No argument? *Damn, these aliens can shapeshift and they've replaced Afsaneh!* "Where did you find that dress?"

"Kiri loaned it to me," she said as she disappeared back into her room. Jim waited for a moment, then pulled off the towel and continued drying his hair. A minute or two later, he heard her zip something and hurried to wrap the towel back around his waist.

Afsaneh popped out the door in time to see him knotting the towel. She looked at his tousled hair and raised one eyebrow, grinning.

"What you got on under that towel, huh?"

"None of your business," he replied, trying to cow her with a glare, and failing. "I've got underwear on," he admitted, a little defensively.

"You know that modesty in this family is going to become a moot point eventually, don't you?" She smirked at him. "I'm certainly not shy."

"No shit," he muttered under his breath. Then he looked at what she was wearing. It was sweater material and clung tightly down to its mid-thigh hem. It was also white and featured the fact that she was not wearing a bra or slip. "Uh uh." He shook his head. "I'm afraid I can't support that choice." She made a face at his pun and sniffed as she headed back to her room. "You'd better start getting ready, yourself," she called out as she left.

"I think I'd better get your wardrobe settled first," Jim returned. "Cut out the intricate plan and show me what you're really planning to wear."

Her head popped out, holding the sweater dress in front of her. "You figured me out, huh?"

Jim just snorted and glanced at his wrist, pointedly.

"Okay, okay. Just give me a minute." Her head ducked out of sight. Soon she came out again, and Jim whistled in genuine admiration.

She wore a light green dress that also reached down to her mid-thigh. At least there was no slit on the sides. The neckline was mildly provocative, showing some cleavage, but she wore a white waist-length jacket that tempered the effect enough to satisfy him.

"You look great," Jim admitted, groaning inside as he thought about all the boys he would be hating in the years to come. "Why didn't you start with this one?"

"I had to prepare you for it." She smiled at him. After a moment, her expression turned serious. "Can I ask you something?"

"Sure." Jim looked at her warily.

"The other day, during the fight." She stopped, her skin getting a little closer to the shade of her dress as she pictured that final scene. She took a deep breath and continued. "You said I was your daughter. What exactly did you mean by that?"

"Well." Jim said, thinking about what to tell her. "I have been training you since you could walk," he stalled.

"You know what I'm talking about." She folded her arms and waited.

"I'm not putting you off, but I need to start getting dressed." Jim glanced at his wrist again.

"You're not wearing a watch!" She protested. "Fine. You start getting dressed and we can talk. Come on." With that, she walked into Jim and Kimberly's bedroom. He sighed and followed her.

"Hakim told you about back when we met your mother, right?" She nodded. "Well, what did he tell you? And turn your back. Not facing the mirror. Come on, I need to get dressed!"

Smiling, she faced the bathroom door and answered his question. "She told me that both of you dated Mother, and then you did some traveling. And while you were gone, she and Daddy fell in love and got married. I did check the dates, and I think they got a little careless in their protection, too.

Jim hurriedly pulled on his pants. Sitting on the edge of the bed to put his socks and shoes on, he noticed that the combination of the mirrors on the bathroom door, over the sink, and the third mirror above Kimberly's make-up table could have given Afsaneh a perfect view of him dressing. That would explain that little smile earlier. He had to admit that she was right. Modesty wasn't going to last long in this family. She was waiting for him to continue, and he sighed. *This is a hell of a time to do this.*

"Well, it's true. When we first met your mother, we were both in love with her..." And, in bits and pieces, he told her the story of the weekend that changed all their lives forever. As he told her, she came over to sit next to him. When he got to the rape scene, he had to stop and give her his handkerchief. And then she sat there and quietly listened to the rest of the story, hanky in hand, occasionally dabbing at tears.

"So who really is my father?" she asked after he finished.

"We never did a paternity test," Jim admitted. "We both loved you and your mother, but he was married to her. From the moment you were born, Hakim considered you his daughter." Jim smiled to himself. "And I considered you his, and my, daughter."

He sat there, dressing forgotten. Shirt half buttoned and tie in one hand, he held both hers in his other. "If you want to know, I'm sure we can find out."

"I can do the test very simply." They both started as Pearl spoke up for the first time.

"Pearl, stop before you say another word about this subject." Jim was firm. "I do not want you to perform this test unless we specifically ask you to. This is Afsaneh's decision, and I don't want you or anyone else telling her prematurely."

"Thank you," Afsaneh said simply. "I don't know what I want. Part of me wants to know, definitively. But part of me dreads finding out that Daddy...isn't!"

Jim waited. He sympathized with her, but it had to be her choice. He would never want to hurt his old friend, or his memory, but at the same time, Jim really did love her like a daughter and considered her such.

"The one thing that really bothers me," Afsaneh admitted hesitantly. "Is that one of those rapists might be my..." She couldn't say it.

"It could only be the one of them, if any." Jim said grimly as he stood, tie in hand, and turned up his collar.

Afsaneh shuddered and watched his first attempt to do his tie. It ended up only reaching halfway to his waist, and she shook her head in resignation. "Give it to me," she said, taking the tie and looking at it skeptically. She turned him around to face her and began doing it for him.

Jim had a sudden thought. "What if we could tell if it was definitely either Hakim or myself, without revealing which? Pearl?"

"Yes, that is possible."

He looked at Afsaneh questioningly. "What about it?"

"What if it's neither of you," Afsaneh asked, a little fearfully.

"Then you have two adopted fathers that have loved you all your life, and it doesn't change a thing." Jim looked at his tie in the mirror, impressed.

She saw his gaze, and smiled, a little wistfully. "I always did Daddy's, too. Will you still love me if I'm the biological daughter of a rapist?"

He pulled her in close and hugged her hard. "Punkin, I will always love you. And I always have, and always will love you as my daughter. Pearl can store the test results in case you want to know more at a later date."

Afsaneh held his jacket for him. She smiled and he blushed as she caught him inspecting himself in the mirror.

"That's okay," she teased him. "Everyone's a little vain." Jim laughed and looked at the clock on Kimberly's side of the bed. He winced and said. "You need to get going, but you don't have to decide now."

He watched her agonize over it. "Pearl," she finally said. "Please tell me, without telling me which, if either Daddy or Jim is my biological father." She closed her eyes tightly. Jim waited, pretty sure he knew the answer..

"Yes, Afsaneh. One of them is your biological father." Pearl's answer was almost immediate.

"You did the test that fast?" Jim didn't believe it.

"No. I did the test when it became apparent it would be necessary. For your information, both of you are already late, and Yvette is looking for Afsaneh right now."

Jim looked at Afsaneh and was surprised to see tears running down her cheeks. "Thank you, Pearl." Her voice cracked a little. Jim used the hanky to wipe the tears away.

"I've got to go." She sounded hesitant. "I've always thought of Daddy as...well, as Daddy. It wouldn't be right to call you that."

"I know," Jim said, feeling selfish as he recognized his own disappointment at her words.

Afsaneh stopped at the door, and looked back at him. They stood there for a moment. Then she smiled. It was a real smile, without a tinge of sadness that he could see.

"Today is going to be fun." Her smile grew wider. "I'll see you in a little while...Father." And with that, she was gone.

"I'll see you soon," Jim whispered, surprised at how moved he was. He sat for a while, thinking.

"Jim, are you there?" Yvette's voice sounded from the outer door.

"Be right out," he called. As he stood, he considered for a moment, then shrugged. "Pearl, I noticed that Vicki, Sam, and you all call Afsaneh the 'Heir'. You would only do that for one reason, wouldn't you?"

"Yes," was the simple answer.

"And not just based on my calling her my daughter."

"That is true. Our programming dictated checking the moment we recognized the possibility."

He found he was crying and with great difficulty, recovered his composure. He stood and took a step towards the door, then stopped. "Please call her Afsaneh. If I can figure this out, so can others. Tell Vicki and Sam the same. Oh, and Pearl?"

"Yes?"

"Thank you very much."

"You're welcome, Jim Morris."

He started to the door again, but her voice stopped him.

"She really does have your eyes."

He remembered Hakim's last words, and thought about what his old friend would probably have said right about now. Something very funny, but poignant, Jim decided and smiled. Then he chuckled. He was still chuckling as he met Yvette coming in the door.

"What's so damn funny, you idiot." She had a flower in her hand. At least, Lasty had said it was a flower indigenous to his home planet. She pinned it to his lapel, then took him by the arm as she would a small child. "You've got eight minutes! Let's go!"

Kimberly stood looking at a wall. It was a blank wall, but she could see so much! Kiri stood nearby, rubbing her hands together, adjusting her hair. Tugging the slinky turquoise dress down her hips, she muttered. "I need to go on a diet."

"Not!" Janice Wooley and Kimberly both spoke in unison. Kimberly turned and laughed at her. The Japanese actress didn't have an ounce of fat anywhere on her body.

"Have you thought about after all this?" For Kimberly, it was a constant nagging in the back of her mind. "We're only sending the Jade Viking back to Earth. What will you do?"

Kiri shrugged. "I've changed my mind so many times already about this. Going home isn't going to be any picnic either. What do we do? Get dropped off on the Golden Gate Bridge and say we were kidnaped by aliens? Oh yeah, and they kept our ship."

The other two women laughed and Janice agreed. "It's going to be tough, but Yvette and I are going back. Jim wants us to take everything he and Hakim own, consolidate it, and begin creating some sort of...I don't know, front. We can't just drop this bombshell on Earth. There would be mass hysteria. Not to mention every government on the planet trying to get an edge for their own hidden agenda."

Kimberly nodded. "I know. He's been talking about it a lot. I know he's planning on staying out here to help defend this station. Plus, he's kind of a symbol, a gathering point, to stand against the Ananab."

Afsaneh rushed into the room at that point. All three women frowned at her. She smiled weakly. "My father and I were having a talk," she said.

Kimberly snorted and then stopped dead. Afsaneh smiled at her when she saw the reaction. Yvette came in and saw the young girl and sighed in relief. Kimberly shook herself and looked at Kiri. "Can you give me a moment with the brat?"

Kiri nodded. She was pretty quick and had probably caught it also. She pushed Yvette and Janice in front of her and winked at Kimberly. "We'll be outside. Take as long as you need." She grinned an infectious grin. "We won't start without you."

Kimberly nodded and looked at Afsaneh. "Are you okay?"

"I'm going to be fine." Afsaneh came and adjusted the long evening gown Kimberly wore. It was a light blue strapless, and she had never worn it before. Kimberly thought it matched her color nicely.

"You look beautiful," Afsaneh said simply.

"Thank you." Kimberly squinted at her in mocking surprise. "Is it really you, Afsaneh?"

The young girl laughed again and stepped back and gave her the old up and down routine. "You clean up pretty good, for an old lady." She turned serious for a moment. "Jim and I had a talk. He told me about when he, Daddy, and Mother met. And all the things they went through."

"He did?" Kimberly thought the timing was a little strange, but didn't say so. "Are you going to be okay?" she asked again.

"Yes, thanks." They hugged and Afsaneh clung to her a moment. "I want to call him Father, because he's going to be mine from now on, and he may have always been."

Kimberly nodded.

"You know I've always thought I could remember my mother." Afsaneh hesitated. "Some people thought it might be from pictures, but I really do think I remember her. But that was a long time ago. I don't think she would mind sharing the title. Especially with someone as nice as you."

Kimberly had trouble speaking for a moment. Then they hugged again, hard. "Whatever you want, dear."

"We've got a hot date," Afsaneh reminded her as they reluctantly pulled apart. "Mom."

Arm in arm, they left.

Lasty shifted his feet nervously. This was a story he would be telling his children, and their children, too. When he had been asked to escort guests to their seats, he had thought it a menial job, more appropriate for a Hoag. He had reluctantly agreed, more because of respect for the Jim Morris than anything else. After all, they all owed him so much.

Then he noticed the others selected. Captain DelaRosa, Commander Asaya, the brooding Human giant, McGregor, the archer Kabu, and more. It hadn't taken him long to realize what an honor he'd been afforded. He was the first Baerd to take part in a Human ceremony that went back thousands of years. In fact, according to Captain DelaRosa, he was the first nonhuman of any sort to ever take part. The captain had mentioned several exceptions, but said they hadn't been ushers. He would have to research these...what was the name? Oh yes, sheep.

He held an upper arm out to a short female as he'd been instructed. She oohed and blushed in that peculiar human fashion. It wasn't nearly as colorful as a Baerd, but after all, who would expect it to be?

As he turned to lead her to a seat, mate in tow, he saw a group of Baerd staring at him in awe.

And why not! He thought he looked very impressive. This tunic was his best. The numerous swirling shades of blue complimented his pale skin nicely, and the pink belt matched his eyes perfectly!

He saw Dutter among them and stood a little straighter. Yes, things were definitely looking good to him.

Jim was talking to Captain Tachibana, resisting the urge to look at his wrist.

The older man would take the Jade Viking back, with whoever wanted to leave. It was surprising how many wanted to stay. Captain Lang, for one, had decided to remain at Osaka.

They had been on the bridge, looking at a view of the Earth by the P'Tassum on its initial approach. Lang had sighed, and said it almost looked like a piece of jade floating in space.

How appropriate, they had chuckled.

Lang said there was no one left alive on that piece of mineral that would miss him. And, he laughed, this could be a great career move. After all, he really hadn't been ready to retire.

Frederick Farmer, now standing on Jim's other side, was evidently thinking about the same topic.

"I'll be returning to Earth," Farmer admitted. "But you never know. I might be back."

"If anybody comes back, they better bring me a few cases of wine," Jim said, looking at Tachibana pointedly. "And sake."

The Japanese captain began to say something, but then stopped as familiar music began. All three of them turned to watch Kiri walk slowly towards them. The room had been decorated for a party, and as far as Jim could tell, almost every human not on duty was here.

The Tryr and Srotag prisoners had been loaded on the smallest freighter and released with a warning not to return, so there only minimal need for security. Anyway, Pearl would warn them if there was a problem.

Kiri walked up, gave Jim a little kiss and backed up a few steps. She gave him a wink. "Now you die, round eyes," she whispered. He smiled as Taga Motari shushed her.

Then he was watching his daughter stride slowly up the center aisle that had been formed in the crowd. She looked radiant and he was proud of her. She hugged and kissed him and moved over next to Kiri.

Then they all turned to watch as Kimberly and Captain Lang appeared. It seemed to take an eternity for them to walk down that aisle, but for Jim, it was all too quick. Then they were in front of him and he distantly noticed the captain nod and the music stop.

But all he could see was Kimberly. She glowed with an inner peace and happiness that he could feel spread to include him.

The future was an unknown. One alien ship was almost certainly at Earth this very moment, and the Ananab could launch another attack any time. Somehow, without causing a panic, the Human race had to be warned and prepared to enter a new era.

But those were all worries for tomorrow. Today, all he could see was Kimberly standing before him. The smile she gave him made his knees weak.

"Well?" She cocked her head, waiting.

Jim smiled back, then broke into a grin.

"Very."

Then he took her hand and, together they turned to face Captain Tachibana.

He beamed at them and began.

"Dearly beloved..."

Made in the USA
Columbia, SC
10 October 2024

43363961R00176